THE NAKED MOON

THE NAKED MOON

HEART & HAND – BOOK THREE

NICOLE E. KELLEHER

jewel lake books

Jewell Lake Books LLC
www.jewellakebooks.com

Cover Design by Kanaxa
Mapwork by Nicole E. Kelleher

The Naked Moon, Heart & Hand: Book Three | Nicole E. Kelleher – 1st ed.
ISBN 979-8-9857041-4-3

Dedication

For my family. All my love.

The Prophecies

*Recitation to the Goddess as recited by the Fanm
to her followers in The Southron Isles*

After blood and storm
And scorched flesh and bone
Banished from her dark lands
Into the cold sea
Betrayed by love, by family
Gentle hands and grace brought breath
And yet our Goddess heals
And waits.

*Lost Translation from the Exiflos
The Mother's Library, The Fenrhi Temple, Naca'an, Nifolhad*

Duty and shield to cast out blind obeisance
Truth and healing be a warrior's protection
One saved by four
Five control the sixth
But first and last, there will be blood.

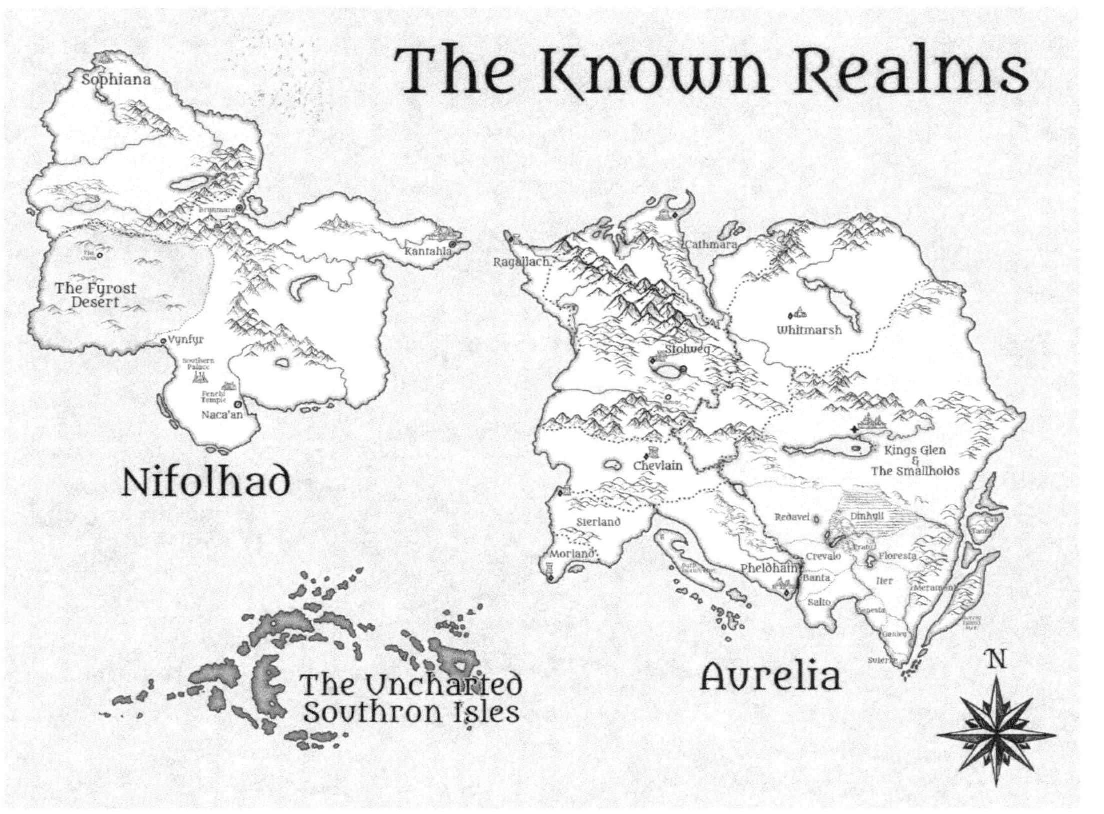

The Known Realms
Nifolhad
Sophiana
Brunmara
Kantahla
The Fyrost Desert
Vynfyr
Southern Palace
Fenrhi Temple
Naca'an
The Uncharted Southron Isles
Ragallach
Cathmara
Whitmarsh
Stolweg
Chevlain
Sierland
Morland
Redavel
Dimhyll
Crevalo
Floresta
Phelohaln
Banta
Iter
Meramene
Salto
Gensiva
Suler
Kings Glen & The Smallholds
Aurelia
N

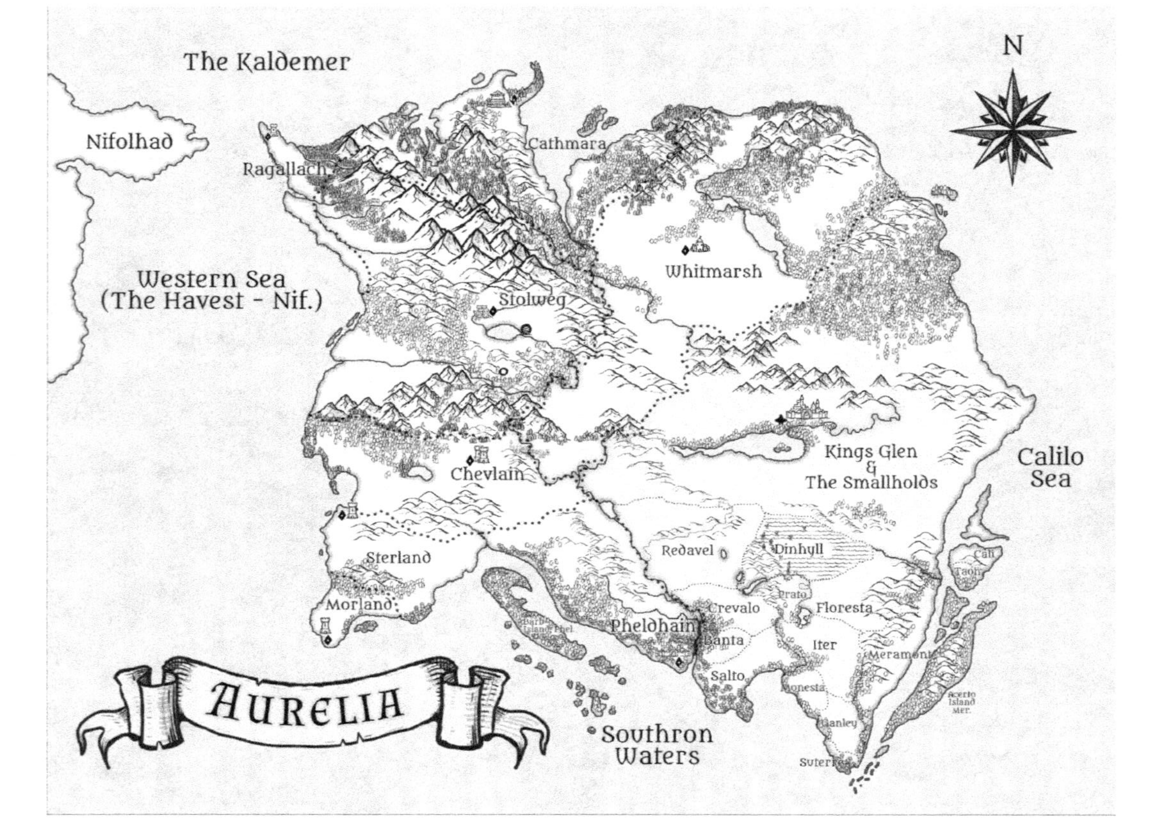
The Kaldemer
Nifolhad
Western Sea
(The Havest - Nif.)
Ragallach
Cathmara
Whitmarsh
Stolweg
Chevlain
Kings Glen
&
The Smallholds
Calilo
Sea
Sterland
Morland
Redavel
Dinhyll
Prato
Crevalo
Floresta
Pheldhain
Banta
Iter
Meramont
Salto
Sonesta
Hanley
Suter
N
Southron
Waters
AURELIA

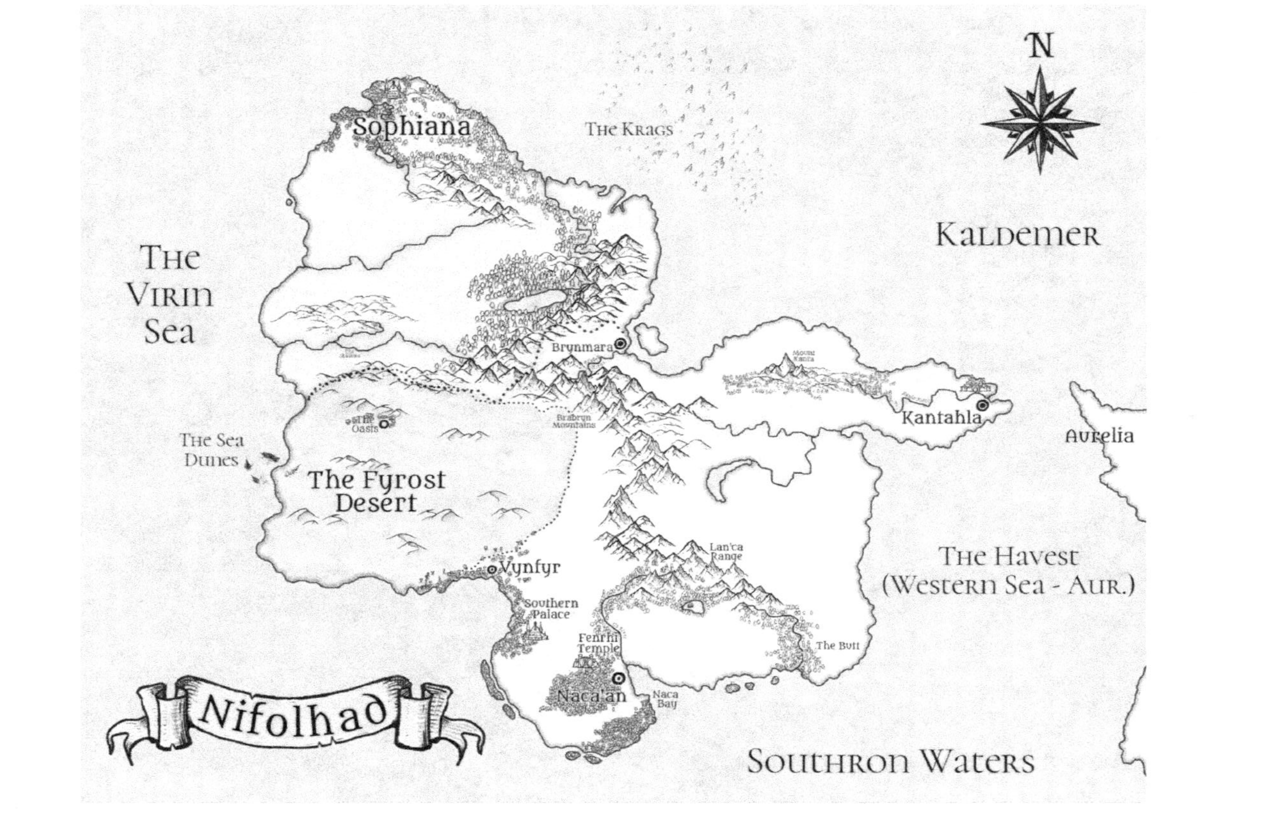

N
Sophiana
The Krags
Kaldemer
The Virin Sea
Brynmara
Mount Kaora
Kantahla
Aurelia
The Sea Dunes
The Oasis
Brabryn Mountains
The Fyrost Desert
Lan'ca Range
The Havest
(Western Sea - Aur.)
Vynfyr
Southern Palace
Fenrin Temple
The Butt
Naca'an
Naca Bay
Nifolhad
Southron Waters

Prologue

In the Twenty-ninth Year of the Great Peace betwixt the Realms
of Aurelia and Nifolhad
The Island of Bornesto, The Southron Isles

"Sold!" the innkeeper shouted above the weaving sailors and Islers. Warin flinched at the clap of the wood block on the scarred and pitted bar. If he ever got his hands on his brother...

Captain Grieg, *his* captain, tugged on the rope lashed around Warin's wrists. "Be gentle with him, Marlita. Warin is a mite more tender than his brother was. And unlike Lord Marten, this lordling is bound for the Aurelian Guard upon his return."

"Lordling?" the woman who had bid the highest declared and laughed, handing Grieg a fat purse. "He's two heads taller than you, Grieg!"

Warin's leash was passed into the woman's hands—granted, it was around his wrists and not his neck, but that didn't change the fact that she owned him, even if it was only for a night. Grieg laughed. "Still, Mar, don't ruin this one. Especially as I like him better than his brother. He has a good heart, he has. For an Aurelian, that is."

"I'll be the one to judge his heart, Grieg," she bandied, winking at Warin. "Aurelian or not." There was a good laugh over the insult, but Warin didn't miss the look that passed between his captain and the woman. Marlita pulled him through the morass of drunken sailors and bawdy women that filled the inn's taproom. Winks and nudges and catcalls were his escort through the crowd, and when someone playfully slapped his rear, it didn't sting nearly as much as the blush he knew to be staining his cheeks. Marlita tugged the rope again, dragging him out of the inn and into a narrow alleyway.

The auction was a Southron Isles rite of passage. Untried men, those of eighteen summers or more, could be taken from their homes and brought to the Isle of Bornesto, there to be auctioned off to any woman with enough coin.

His brother Marten held the record for the highest bid for three years running. Until tonight. Grieg acted as if Warin should feel proud for toppling his brother's accomplishment, when in fact, the opposite was true. Marten was known up and down the coast as a rake of the highest caliber. Wanting nothing to do with such behavior, Warin desired to find a good wife, one who could give him a large family and who would be willing to put up with his seafaring absences. Being the second son of the Lord of Pheldhain had its benefits. Though Warin had been trained in every aspect of managing the coastal Aurelian territory, he would inherit none of the responsibility. He could, if he so chose, marry for love—as long as his bride could strengthen Pheldhainian holdings. A tug on the rope reminded him of his current predicament. He could abstain, of course. Marlita would hardly be able to force him into a coupling. But then, Grieg would have to return the purse, and its coin was right now paying for a night of feasting and drinking for the entire crew. No, there would be no slipping this noose.

He vowed then and there that Marten would pay for this prank, even if it took Warin his entire life to make it happen. He loved his brother, but the humiliation of being dumped from his hammock, bound, gagged, and auctioned off could not go unanswered. Marten had probably thought he was doing him a favor, knowing Warin had not yet slept with a woman—so what that he was nearly nineteen? There was plenty of time for such activities. He'd heard about some of the more adventurous ladies at High Court in Kings Glen and was sure there'd be an opportunity for an interlude or two there. He wasn't worried that his inexperience would call him out; he'd read about and studied the subject enough to hide the fact that he was a virgin. A mutually agreed upon assignation at court would hurt no one. And when the time came to wed, he would be more than able to please a new bride.

Marlita was moving faster now, urgent to reach their destination. He would simply look upon the tawdriness of this whole affair as would a scholar. For Warin, the pursuit of knowledge was dearer than sailing the seas.

His mistress led him through a maze of connected corridors and courtyards, and past colorfully painted doors in shades of amber, aqua, and tourmaline. Marlita finally drew to a halt before a coral-hued door. Warin lifted an eyebrow, letting it draw up the corner of his mouth; it was an expression he'd perfected, one that annoyed his brother to the extreme. She smiled at him, a bit too knowingly, and he thanked his good fortune that she still had her teeth. In fact, they were straight and bright in the dusky light. She drew him through the doorway.

Her living quarters were surprisingly spacious, boasting a cooking area, a partitioned section for bathing, and of course, a large sleeping platform covered with brightly covered cushions. But it was the large opening facing the sea that drew Warin forward. The gentlest of ocean breezes ruffled the gauzy fabric hanging from the thick, wood lintel. Marlita glided across the room, tucking the sheers into ornate hooks to expose the full view of the ocean. She undid the knot binding his wrists, then left him standing alone near the opening.

Warin took in the terraced hill as it gently sloped some seventy feet down; he could pick out hundreds of abodes, similar to the one he was in, only more diminutive in size and elevation. The entire hillside curved like a crescent moon to cup the tiny cove where ships of various sizes and designs bobbed peacefully in the water. Only one more tier rose above Marlita's—she must be wealthy in her own right. Behind him, she lit several oil lamps, casting a muted glow throughout her home. When he heard murmuring, he turned from the entrancing view.

She knelt before an altar, facing a colorful mural, and was praying. As was his nature, he committed the details to memory to later add to his journal. The artwork was unlike anything he'd ever seen: an ornate depiction of a woman with multiple arms. Each hand held an object—a branch, a blade, an orb, and more, and then marked with unfamiliar runes next to each.

Marlita was getting to her feet, and Warin turned away, feeling as if he had somehow trespassed. He heard a gurgle and splash, once, then twice, and a moment later, felt a nudge against his shoulder.

He faced the woman who'd outbid her companions for the right to test and claim his manhood. "This should help you to relax." He accepted the cup, studied her eyes for any malice, and finding none, he drank it down. She poured him another. Determining age was a tricky business in the Southron Isles, and it was rumored that the women here had special balms and lotions that kept age at bay, but Warin guessed her to be around thirty years old.

"Thirty-eight," she supplied, intuiting his train of thought. "And experienced enough that if you pay attention, you might just learn something this night." Warin downed his second cup. "Easy," she soothed. "Too much of that and you'll not be able to stay awake. And trust me, you want to stay awake."

Warin choked, and Marlita smiled. "I have to know...why did you bid so high?"

"Novelty, I suppose. And you're a comely man, aren't you?" she appraised. "Grieg was wrong. It was my sister who won your brother, not I. She said that he was a selfish lover."

"Can we please not discuss my brother right now?"

And this time, Marlita did laugh, merrily. Whether it was her frankness or the drink, Warin was unable to stop from joining her. She poured him another cup, then picked up hers and tapped it against his in a toast. "Fine in form *and* a sense of humor." Before he could reply, she slipped out of her garments and stepped forward. A warm breeze, one smelling strangely of the desert, gusted into the room; the oil lanterns flickered before guttering completely. The moon had risen, and its light washed her skin in a milky-blue aura. Her curves were voluptuous, her bronze-kissed skin smooth and unblemished. Then, he saw them—the indigo designs, here and there dotted with crimson, swirling and banding around her upper arm. She stepped closer again, and tipped his cup to his lips so that he finished the sweet-and-spicy drink—he would have to describe its taste in his—

She took it from him, setting it aside, nearing him so that her peaked nipples pressed against his chest. Thoughts of his journal evaporated when he felt the pebbled points through the thin linen of his shirt; his groin tightened in anticipation. It was...not unpleasant.

She traced her fingers over his shoulders and down his arms until, taking one of his wrists, she brought his hand to her breast. He fondled her, gently at first, then with more finesse, as she moaned encouragingly. He had an overwhelming desire to taste her flawless skin, and he dipped his head to kiss her neck, her shoulder, then lower to her breast. She arched her back, and he was quick to support her. And while he feasted, he realized that she had pressed her center against his groin and, surely, she could feel his arousal. She seemed not to mind and, when he slipped his hand lower to cup the firm globe of her buttock, she moved against him, moaning her pleasure when he pressed back. She drew herself up then and ran her hand down his side and around to his front.

"Let's see what you're made of then." She slid her hand down the hard length of him. Her eyes widened and her gaze flew to his, and Warin managed a shrug. "Looks like I got more than I paid for," she purred, reminding him that he should feel ashamed, compromised, something, at having been auctioned off. But Marlita was expert in her dexterity, and the affront flew away. He wanted to do to her that which she was doing to him. So, he set himself to the task, matching her unraveling of his senses with an undoing of hers. He let her moans and pants and gasps be his guides and pleasured her as she sought to free him from his breeches. But as wickedly adept as her fingers were, they were no match for Warin's, untutored though they were. He played with her until she came apart, then supported her until she could once again stand on her own, all the while placing gentle kisses and nips along the column of her neck and the smooth curves of her breasts.

She stared up at him. "You've never...?"—He shook his head—"How then?"

"I read. Prolifically."

She devoured him with her eyes, and her hands resumed their task, but not before she stripped him of his clothes. She sought out his erection, and she pressed her nakedness against his. Before he knew what she was doing, she slid down his body to kneel before him. And when she leaned forward, applying lips and tongue and teeth, Warin knew he had not read nearly enough.

Afterward, she walked over to the table where she'd set her cup and drank from it. She looked up at him and smiled at his expression. "You weren't expecting that, were you?"

He shook his head. "No, only..."

"Yes?"

"I'm just wondering if the same will work for you."

And Marlita laughed, then drew him to her bed. "Let's find out, shall we?"

· · ·

It was late the next morning when Marlita roused herself to seek nourishment. She piled bread, pickled dove eggs, and fruit onto a large plate, hooked her finger around a jug of fresh cider, and set them quietly on the table near the bed. Warin, yet sleeping, was a tangle of lanky, muscled limbs. Dark whiskers shadowed a face carved for seduction, and long lashes dusted his high cheekbones. She sat on the edge of her bed and, careful not to wake him, placed her hand on his chest. Grieg had said that Warin possessed a good heart, and coming from her friend, such a compliment was worth investigation. She reached out with her mind, gauging the length of his life and the weight of its contribution. Their encounter had changed him: he would strive too long to find a perfect wife, missing opportunities over and again for a happy life, endlessly searching for the elusive *true love*. And then she saw his death.

"Much too young." She sighed, and he stirred and took her wrist.

"Too young for what?" he asked and grinned, mistaking her meaning. But he was too observant by half, and he sat up. "What's wrong, Lita?"

She smiled at the endearment. "Nothing, Warin. Nothing at all." Telling him his fate would lead him to ask questions that she was forbidden to answer. It broke her heart to think that someone so kind and generous would have such an abbreviated time in the world. He rose from the bed, selected one of the plums she'd set out, and ate it in a few bites.

He was a superb specimen of a man, and Marlita admired his posterior as he bent down for his breeches. He was putting his second leg in his pants when he saw her watching him, and he hopped-fell back toward the bed. He shrugged into his shirt, then grabbed for his tunic to reach for something in a hidden pocket.

"I want you to have this," he explained, extracting a small purse and pouring the contents into her palm. Six, fat pink-hued pearls glistened in the morning light. "I know I'm probably insulting you by breaking your customs, but I don't want there to be money between us."

She frowned at him.

"You're not angry, are you? It's not coral. They're conkle pearls from Pheldhain. We've trained the river minks to fish for them and—"

"They're beautiful," she finally admitted. "And I'm not angry at your gift. It's just too much. You have been so generous already. Grieg was right; you *do* have a good heart."

"Then why are you frowning?" A look had washed over his face, one of surprise that quickly transformed into panic.

Marlita laughed. "Don't worry, Warin. I haven't fallen in love with you." She closed her eyes and offered up a silent prayer to the Goddess, asking forgiveness for what she was about to do. Hers was a world where men were not to be trusted.

Loved? Yes.

Forgiven? Always.

Trusted? Never.

Their lore had taught them that even the Goddess's brother was capable of betrayal, for hadn't it been he who had banished her to the sea? Marlita was a direct descendant of the woman who had finally netted and rescued the

Goddess, pulling her from her watery crypt. And in return, the Goddess promised to make her home above the Southron Waters as long as the inhabitants of the Southron Isles worshipped her. The Goddess's gratitude still washed over them with each new sunrise. Her warmth spread over the Isles, bathing the air with the temperate climes that reached even to the southern shores of Aurelia. If she was displeased, she would send her tempests raging across the seas.

Marlita opened her eyes. "Forgive me, Goddess," she begged again, calling to her deity and falling into a trance. When she stared down at Warin, she viewed him through two pairs of eyes—hers and the Goddess's. She touched his cheek with one hand and his chest with the other. "Upon your heart, I bestow these gifts: for all your days, you shall be marked only by good fortune; you shall have adventure and pleasure; and as you gave equally to this woman, so shall all of your lovers give to you." Marlita blinked; Warin was caught up in her gaze, and so did not see the pale blue glow disappearing from her fingertips. She drew them away, and where she had pressed her hands, a faint aura remained.

"Er, thank you?"

She gazed about her room, then out onto the terrace, waiting to be struck down by some unknown force. It seemed she had not angered the Goddess after all, for the sky was blue, the sea calm, and the breeze soft. "The tide will soon be turning, and Grieg will want to make sail. Come. I'll return you to your ship." There was nothing she could do about his cursedly short life, but at least Warin would live it to the fullest.

They reached the pier where his ship bobbed to find Grieg and some of the crew ready and waiting to haze him. But one look at the mark peeking out from his open collar, and they respectfully nodded to Marlita and went about their duties.

Grieg stepped forward as she was saying goodbye. She kissed Warin, but he pulled her closer and folded her into his arms. Then, as if embarrassed, he bowed to her and climbed up to the ship's deck, where he threw himself into the work of readying the vessel to sail.

"What have you done, Marlita?" her friend demanded of her. "How is it that he bears the Goddess's mark?"

"I only wanted to give him her blessing, nothing more. She...She did it, through me. Take care of him, won't you?" she ordered. "I know he's an Aurelian, but you were right. He is different from the others. Remain loyal to him, and do not worry about crossing the Goddess. I will explain to Fanm Larenne."

"Be careful, Mar. The Fanm has always been jealous of others who are used by the Goddess." He took her hand. "I know you're forbidden to tell me what you saw, but if he matters to you, can't you pray for intervention?"

"You always knew me best, my friend. Even more than my own sister." She stared up at the ship. "For Warin, I will risk trying."

CHAPTER ONE

Pebbles

A decade later, during the reign of the Usurper Steward King Diarmait, The Principality of Sophiana, Nifolhad

Warin turned down another corridor and ran into yet another dead end. The palace in Sophiana was impossible, and he was hopelessly lost. He had refused to ask Madyan, his Umbren friend, to show him the way...again. Especially as his current destination was a rendezvous with one of the ladies he'd met at Queen Aghna and King Ranulf's wedding feast.

No, the fierce Fyrjian warrior would likely clout him with her staff rather than help him find his way to a tryst. From behind him came voices, so he backtracked and was just in time to see the heels of several servants rounding the next bend; he hastened to catch them before they, too, were swallowed in the maze. Almost upon them, he rounded another corner, and...they were nowhere to be seen. Perhaps some of the missing emissaries sent to Nifolhad by his king had perished in this labyrinth.

That was a sobering thought, for one of those lost was his cousin. While it was true that his mission had been to locate the abducted Lady Claire of Chevlain—a successful adventure in its own right—he also wanted to discover the truth behind the missing emissaries. Three Aurelian nobles sent by King Godwin to Nifolhad to treat with the Usurper King Diarmait were never seen again. There was no mystery as to the demise of the first two emissaries— tortured and killed by Diarmait. But the third, his cousin, had been sent to Sophiana, the princedom ruled by Ranulf. Warin had yet to find a single trace of his relative.

He continued on, passing several doors before turning a corner and coming face-to-face with Madyan.

"Gone astray again?" she asked, clearly bemused by his lack of directional sense.

"If I had another week here, I might be able to find my own chamber," he admitted, eliciting a rare smile from his desert warrior friend.

Madyan possessed that air of mystery that had always intrigued him, but she was better suited as a friend than a lover. She was also in the unique position of being a Fenrhi as well as a woman of the Fyrost Desert, home to the nomadic tribes in the vast wasteland that covered a large portion of Nifolhad. Even now, her Fyrjian roots eclipsed her Fenrhi responsibilities. If he had to bet on it, Warin would hazard that Madyan was part of the upper crust of whatever hierarchy the Fyrjians adhered to. And even though he had determined the best course did not include a dalliance with the woman, he wasn't so blind that he couldn't see how beautiful she was behind the habitually stoic scowl she'd adopted. Warin recognized a mask when he saw one.

"Take two lefts, then a right," she instructed. "The room you are looking for is the third door on the right."

"How do you know where I'm going?"

"Because I just witnessed a lovely noblewoman entering what looked like a storage room for linens. By herself."

Warin pulled her into a great hug, leaving her looking a little bewildered. "Thank you, my friend. We were just—"

She shook her head. "Just don't leave her with a broken heart. It would be rude."

He laughed at that. "She already knows we sail on the morning tide, so no risk—" He stopped when she held up her hand. "Right. No details. And don't worry about the voyage. I am never one to kiss and tell." Madyan actually laughed at that, and they both continued on their separate ways, albeit his gait was more purposeful.

True to Madyan's directions, he found the door, tapped lightly, and entered, only to find his assignation tapping her foot impatiently. "Apologies for my tardiness. I vow to make it up to you, and in the best way I know how."

• • •

How foolish she was acting, Princess Anwyl lamented. All because of a man. Her education, her training, the years spent honing her skills in the arts of conversation and diplomacy—all of it had flown out the window. All because of one inane foretelling. It didn't help matters that the seer was none other than Ni'Mala, the leader, or Mother, of the powerful Fenrhi Temple. Almost everyone in Nifolhad feared the Fenrhi women. But not Anwyl. She had friends there, including her cousin Radha—one of the Fenrhi Artists, the elite quartet of women who marked each member with their caste, chosen or otherwise.

Anwyl thought back to the day she had met another of the Artists, a woman named Hedra. Hedra had been an initiate then, wearing the dust-colored garments of the Earth Caste—the providers and artisans of the Fenrhi temple—as almost all new initiates did. It was the day that Hedra's caste presented itself: Sylvan—the healers of the Fenrhi. Her cousin Radha had gone to another: the Kena—the temple's truthseers and vision-seekers.

The women of the temple were supposed to be impartial, dealing their visions and cures and poisons to both sides in the ongoing fight for the crown. Anwyl's own brother Ranulf had thought to bolster his claim to the throne by marrying Princess Claire of Aurelia after it was discovered that she and her sister were direct descendants of the Nifolhadian Royal Family. Ranulf, ruler of the princedom of Sophiana, the only place in the known realms where the sacred pijala trees grew, was now instead happily reunited with and married to Aghna, the true claimant to the throne of Nifolhad. Together, they would oust the Usurper Diarmait once and for all. Civil war would inevitably ensue, and Anwyl shuddered to think of the consequences should Diarmait succeed.

During Aghna's secret exile, Princess Anwyl had witnessed the atrocities that Diarmait and his son had committed. Though she was tucked safely away in Sophiana, the rest of Nifolhad had been thrown into dark and evil times. But the people remembered Aghna's father, King Cedric, and how he had loved them, and they would love his daughter even more. Especially with Anwyl's brother by her side.

Diarmait had done what no other monarch had been able to do. He had been the instrument of terror that caused the Fenrhi to finally shed their neutrality. With a strong council guiding and checking her, the Mother would support Aghna and Ranulf. And Anwyl? She was being sent to Aurelia to secure the aid of King Godwin and Queen Juliana. Diarmait's days were numbered, as were his son's, Prince Bowen.

Anwyl had met Bowen the day she made friends with Hedra. It was the day the course of her life had changed, that pivotal moment when fate's many paths wove themselves together and made her the person she was at this very moment—Princess Anwyl of Sophiana, Keeper of the Pijalas, High Advisor to King Ranulf, Royal Historian, Sister-in-Law to High Queen Aghna, and soon-to-be Nifolhadian Ambassador to Aurelia. That momentous day, so many years ago, had put her on this road, and she often wondered what would have happened if even one of the variables had been different.

What if she hadn't destroyed the beautiful paths that Hedra had created? Anwyl could still hear the chaotic skittering of the multihued pebbles and remember the ugly delight she had felt at the destruction. It was as if the fabled Sky Goddess from the Fyrost Desert had blown the stones to all corners of Nifolhad. She had gleefully dug her heels into the ordered paths of the royal gardens and scuffed and raked her feet through the intricately designed nexus of the six differently hued pathways, imagining the stones were her nemeses. The utter discord had given her turbulent mind the release it required, and only the sound of pattering feet and the breathless pant of someone who'd been running had brought her to a halt.

Anwyl even remembered her words, spoken with such entitlement: *"There, so much prettier mixed all together, wouldn't you agree?"* And then she had stared straight into the face of Hedra, no older than she at the time. In one trembling hand, she'd gripped a tiny rake; in the other, a divided carryall, each compartment filled with varying colors of meticulously sorted gravel. The girl hadn't made so much as a peep at Anwyl; she hadn't needed to. She'd simply surveyed the carnage, then settled at the nexus of the six paths, putting to rights the ruin, one tiny pebble at a time.

Overcome with shame, Princess Anwyl had burst into tears. She lowered herself down alongside the Fenrhi initiate, scooped up a handful of the stones, and began the laborious process of sorting the different colors. It was the beginning of a friendship that lasted to this very day. And none of it would have come to pass if not for her cousin Radha's betrayal and Prince Bowen's maliciousness.

What if Bowen had never pushed her to the ground, or if Radha had come to her aid? Family was supposed to protect family, even when they disagreed. One smashed nose later, and a refusal to apologize, and Anwyl had been expelled from the royal audience hall where she was supposed to meet Princess Aghna and King Cedric. No one wanted to hear why she had struck Bowen, even ignoring her bruised and bloodied knee. No one would have understood her reaction because no one had heard what he'd whispered to her, that she was a bitch who needed the mongrel bred out of her. Radha hadn't seen him spit at her, nor had she heard him add that it was an insult to even consider her as a future bride, suggesting instead that she join the Fenrhi's Blood Caste. At the time, it hadn't mattered that Anwyl didn't know what the Blood Caste was; Bowen's tone had been explanation enough.

That day, if Anwyl hadn't destroyed the paths, she and Hedra would not have been restoring them when the new Fenrhi Mother, Ni'Mala, and her council were walking by. They would not have noticed Hedra's artistry, nor the calm way she had soothed Anwyl's wrath. Hedra would not have been marked as Sylvan, and more, as an apprentice to the Artists.

It was Ni'Mala who had set Anwyl on the course of scholarship. The Mother had charged her to study her history, and that of Aurelia's, and when Anwyl had asked why, she had replied, "I sense that you have a special capacity for knowledge, Princess. The day is coming when your brother will need your sage counsel. Learn everything you can so as to assist him in difficult times. Your gift is a rare one; use it wisely."

"What kind of gift? Like Radha's?" Anwyl had asked hopefully, for she had always felt like there would be nothing in her future except marrying for some alliance.

"Not quite. No, Princess, you yearn for more. And you have a way with people, an ability to touch their hearts and minds, effortlessly bringing them to your way of thinking, making them feel that they are worthy of more." The Mother had smiled softly after that. "Most girls your age wish to hear of love."

"All right," Anwyl had conceded after Ni'Mala waited expectantly, though she cared little about love at the time, especially since the incident with Bowen. "Will I find true love?"

Ni'Mala closed her eyes for a moment. When she opened them, they seemed to blaze golden. "For you, fate is fickle: love and hate can be so easily interchanged. I can only say that you will find what you need when you need it. Perhaps a dark-haired, blue-eyed stranger to protect you from yellow-haired princelings who push girls down in the dirt. But do not worry. You will know him when you meet him."

A thousand times, Anwyl had picked apart that encounter, and always it struck her how sad Ni'Mala had seemed when she had spoken of Anwyl's future. It wasn't until Anwyl and Ranulf had returned to Sophiana that they learned of the deaths of their mother and father. Ni'Mala had seen it and had been trying to prepare her.

She paced to the window in her chamber, unsuccessfully squashing down the anticipation fluttering in her chest at the thought of a long sea journey with the man who had recently arrived in Sophiana.

"Why now?" she demanded of her empty chamber, unable to keep the Aurelian Guard from her mind. She picked up a tiny pouch and dumped the contents into her palm: pea gravel from the path, one pebble for each of the six colors—an old gift from Hedra. "Why should I be bothered that he hardly noticed me? Or that my opinions seem to carry little weight for him?"

She squeezed the stones in her fist, resisting the urge to fling them across the chamber. "Of course he thinks I'm a ninny. I've done nothing but natter on like an untutored girl and have comported myself without a trace of the royal blood flowing through my veins." Anwyl sat at her escritoire and pushed at the gravel with her fingertip as she parsed each interaction she'd had with the Aurelian Guard named Warin. He had arrived a week past, escorting the fleeing Aghna and Claire from the edge of the Fyrost Desert to the palace.

"I must think about this problem methodically," Anwyl determined, recalling how he had smirked when she'd referred to her brother as Rani. To be fair, she *had* delivered an uninterrupted stream of nonsense as she escorted Warin, Princ—Lady Claire of Aurelia, and the Princess Aghna to their chambers in the palace. She hadn't been able to stop herself from babbling incoherently; even her brother had looked askance at her.

Anwyl rearranged the pebbles. The stones had been handled so many times that they were as shiny as polished glass. It wasn't a nervous habit that had her fussing with them. She simply liked to keep her hands busy while working out a difficult puzzle. If her pebbles were not handy, she would practice tying sailing knots. Anwyl possessed a multitude of methods to cope with frustration, little tricks to help her to remain calm and collected when faced with any troubling situation. Her current one? Impossible.

She simply lost her wits when around the insufferable man with the sable-colored locks and brilliant blue eyes. The pebbles were not helping her. Sighing, Anwyl pulled out a length of cord and, swiping the stones aside, started with simple single-rope stoppers and worked her way to hitches, then bends. The bigger the conundrum, the more intricate the knot, and much too soon, she was tying mats and creating her own patterns with her rope. She lost herself in the moment, her hands working by rote as her mind emptied itself of every thought, one after another, until only the texture of the rope, the tension of each loop, remained. Eventually, she became blessedly lost to everything except the intricate pattern and infinite symmetry of her creation. Minutes passed into an hour, and Anwyl, much less in a quandary, set the mat that she had created on her table.

Thank goodness for Mergo, the Sophianan Shipmaster. He'd taught her every sailing knot he knew, tasking her with memorizing the benefits and failings of each. He'd also trained her in the rudiments of sailing, and many pulled muscles, rope burns, and blistered hands later, she'd excelled at every task Mergo had thrown her way. And when the old sea-master finally confessed to her brother that he had naught else to teach her, that she could deftly handle any position on a ship, including command, Rani took another tack and turned over the care of the sacred pijala trees to her capable hands. She had thrown herself—heart and hand, mind and soul—into their tending, and the orchards had thrived under her watch.

Never before had the harvest of the pijala trees yielded more pihaberries. And it was this fruit that could protect the people of Nifolhad from the forced persuasion of the few rogue Kena women. Pihaberries warded the mind, lifted the heart, and strengthened the soul. It was one of the reasons that no one else could be ambassador to Aurelia, for Rani was making a great gift of saplings to King Godwin and Queen Juliana. Who else but Anwyl could tend to the difficult trees, coaxing them to grow and reproduce?

When her lady-in-waiting entered the chamber, Anwyl put her ropes away and began brushing her hair. Her longtime companion had walked over to look at the gown on the bed. "You look so beautiful in this dress, Anwyl. Shall I pack it for your journey? There's plenty of room."

"No, Bess, I don't think I'll have an occasion to wear it again for some time," she replied, stepping into her changing area—she always dressed herself, unwilling to let even her best friend see her naked. "A dress like that would never survive the rigueurs of travel." She had only worn it this afternoon in order to appear more sophisticated than she had been acting of late, but the Aurelian Guard had been nowhere to be found. He was probably with his captain, inspecting his ship, *Lita's Pearl*. Maybe she should pack the gown, perhaps wear it one day at Kings Glen. She peeked out from around the corner to tell Bess but saw that her friend had already stowed it in one of her traveling trunks. "How shall I manage without you, Bess, my dearest friend in the world?"

"I've no doubt that you'll take Aurelia by storm; the Aurelians will line up to be your friend. Mayhap the blue-eyed Lord Warin will be first to queue," she teased.

"Oh, Bess, I should never have told you what Ni'Mala predicted." As young women, she and her confidant had discussed love and marriage and the handsome men who had visited their court. Bess might not be a blood relative, but Anwyl thought of her as a sister. The three orphans, they had called themselves, for as it was with Anwyl and Rani, so too had Bess lost her parents, nobles from a minor house in the Brabryn region. Bess was now newly married, and her current state precluded her from traveling, especially on tempest-roiled seas.

Anwyl was tying the laces on her chemise, and her shirt slipped from her shoulder and exposed her collarbone as she came from the other room. Bess had laid out Anwyl's seafaring boots and tunic—no dresses or slippers would do on a ship—and *tsk*'d. "Anwyl, you have new bruises! Umbren master or not, I think I'll have a word with Venna."

In addition to her studies, taking care of the pijalas and the myriad duties at court in Sophiana, Anwyl had been tutored by the women of the Fenrhi Temple. The healers of the Sylvan Caste had taught her everything she needed to know about poisons and their antidotes. Afterward, Venna of the Umbren Caste, the protectors, had been sent to Sophiana. Anwyl had applied herself to learning all that she could about defensive arts from the truculent Fenrhi woman.

Now, she simply shrugged at Bess and covered her shoulder. "It no longer hurts, and it no longer matters, for Venna will not be joining me on this particular adventure, will she?"

"No, but I wonder if she didn't leave you with a more permanent mark." Bess stared pointedly at Anwyl's leg. "I can see you trying to come up with some fib, but we both know that you are unable to lie."

Anwyl shrugged. "Better to say nothing then."

"First, Sylvan, and now, Umbren. Don't look at me like that, Princess. You can't have a bosom friend for nearly eight years and not catch at least a glimpse of her naked."

"But you never said a word."

"Because it's your secret," Bess said matter-of-factly. "Did you join them?"

"The Fenrhi? No, and I never will. That's not my path. Hedra only wanted to honor me. And...I don't know...the markings make me feel stronger. And more confidant."

"You know I like Hedra, but the Fenrhi never do anything without some ulterior motive." Bess sighed. "You have the most beautiful skin, Princess: all honey and bronze. You and Prin—King Ranulf both. Don't forget: one day, you'll have to explain your secret to a husband."

Anwyl pretended to swoon dramatically, pressing the back of her wrist to her forehead and falling onto her bed. As she had hoped, Bess laughed.

"As if you could ever be a damsel in distress," Bess shot back. "Wait a moment. Perhaps that is what Aurelian men want. You could pretend to need saving, and handsome Lord Warin could come to your rescue." Anwyl gave her an incredulous look but saw how hard her friend was trying to not laugh. They burst out in a fit of giggling.

"You'll end up saving him, I suppose," Bess predicted. "Just as you save everyone else." Her friend reached down and rubbed her pregnant belly, her smile slipping a little when her babe shifted uncomfortably.

"Go rest for a while, Bess. I can finish here." With her friend gone, Anwyl stared at her reflection. She pulled her hair into an intricate knot, setting it with the long hairpins gifted to her by Venna. Anwyl hadn't known what to say to her longtime instructor. The only things Venna had given her over the years that she had trained Anwyl in the Umbren arts of combat and defense were contusions, sore muscles, a black eye, and the occasional bruised rib.

The corner of her lip lifted, remembering how she had tried to thank Venna for the gift. Her Umbren tutor had whipped one of the pins from Anwyl's grasp, spun her around, and then held the sharp point to the princess's neck. It took Venna a moment to realize that she should have taken both hairpins, for as she held Anwyl's life in her hands, so too did Anwyl hold hers. She had released the princess with a grunt of approval upon noting the other deadly pin hovering near her eye. It was then that Venna introduced her to Jenai, an Umbren messenger who had come to Sophiana with a message from Ni'Mala. Only, it turned out that Jenai was one of the four Fenrhi Artists.

Venna was newly gone to Naca'an and the Fenrhi Temple, and Anwyl almost missed the woman. She had never found out what had caused Venna to be so angry, but she knew to not ask. Despite Rani's attempts to shield her from the horrors happening outside the borders of Sophiana, Anwyl overheard enough that she would be forever grateful for her training. She'd noted the mark of Blood Caste on Venna's shoulder when her tunic had been tugged too hard during one of the training sessions. Four main Fenrhi castes: Earth, Sylvan, Kena, and Umbren. Two supporting castes: Blood and Ni'Mala's caste, the Mother. The Mother Caste wore the amber tones of honey, and only one woman ever belonged at a time. But Blood Caste was entirely different. Every Fenrhi woman could belong to Blood Caste, though in theory, the women who donned the red only volunteered themselves for a week of service. Fenrhi from all castes could enter the pleasure hall of the temple. In the past, it had been an honor to sacrifice your body for that week. Fenrhi women never married, so what mattered the forfeiture of a little blood for the gift of a child?

But when Diarmait had murdered his own brother and seized the throne, everything changed. He started with the systematic enslavement of the women of Nifolhad, everywhere except Sophiana and the Fenrhi Temple. While Rani's armies kept Sophiana safe, the women of the temple had been forced down a different path to secure their autonomy—using their bodies as currency.

The price had grown more and more dear as the years went by, and they found themselves unable to sate the warped appetite of Diarmait and his ilk. Ni'Mala, as Mother, had failed to protect her brethren, for she'd been rendered mute and blind to the horrors by the strongest of the Kena minds, a woman of incredible power named Rhiannon. Blood Caste's true purpose disappeared like so many of the Fenrhi who were sent to Diarmait's palace in Kantahla.

At least in Sophiana, women were treated as equals to men, but then, Sophiana had always been an enlightened princedom. And like every prince and princess of Sophiana before them, Anwyl had been expected to school herself in the art of pleasure and love. Countless books and scrolls filled a special section of the palace's library, one to which only she and Rani had access. Traditionally, her mother would have taught her, as her father would have done for Rani. But with their demise, their education became self-directed.

Those first days when, years ago, they had returned to Sophiana to discover their parents dead had been horrific. Over a thousand people, mostly the elderly and the very young, had perished during their absence, and no word had been sent to Naca'an to forewarn them. Anwyl counted her blessings every day that Lord Etain had been with them. It was thanks to his quick adjudication that her brother was proclaimed the rightful ruler of Sophiana. Doing so had protected their domain and their people from being incorporated into the holdings of High King Cedric. And later, Lord Etain's counsel had proved invaluable, helping to keep Sophiana out of the clutches of the Usurper. It was at his urging that Anwyl was tutored in history as well as the strategies of the great battles. He had taught both Anwyl and her brother not only the intricacies of negotiation, but the nuances of diplomacy as well.

Lord Etain never once looked at her as if she were an unschooled child playing grown-up. And just like that, Anwyl's mind tripped back to the Aurelian Royal Guard, Lord Warin.

Anwyl's normally disciplined mind could not fathom her yearning to throw herself at this stranger while part of her brain stood by and watched in horror the spectacle of her own creation. She screwed up her face in painful embarrassment when she remembered how Warin had made the *talk-talk-talk* gesture with his hand to the stable boy, thinking Anwyl distracted by Lady Claire.

"I only have myself to blame," she admitted aloud. For eight years, she had steeled herself against this inevitable meeting, searching the face of every man she met, waiting for the moment when she would *know*. Her heart had not made a single flutter over any of them, and she had kissed a few to make sure.

So back to her original problem—why Warin? She sat at her desk and contemplated her erratic behavior. From the moment she saw him cantering up the road with the others, she'd been acutely aware of his presence. Her insides had gone topside-over when he'd dismounted and strode forward, his long, muscular legs carrying him closer to where she stood with her brother. She'd actually pulled back and out of view just so she could study him without being noticed. "Drool over him, more like."

Even now, she shivered remembering how his voice had plucked at her heart in the most unusual and strangely exciting fashion. "He's a challenge, that is all," she averred to her reflection in her chamber's looking glass. "I am simply interested in him because he isn't interested in me. Not because of any vague foretelling of Ni'Mala's. It's probably because he's the first man in over a year that I've met with dark hair and sapphire-blue eyes that sparkle like jewels the color of the sea and—" She put a stop to that line of thinking and focused on packing her travel desk with her favorite quills, writing paper, and wax and seal. At the last moment, she scooped up the pebbles, put them in their velvet pouch, and tossed them in as well, closing the lid on the escritoire and latching it.

"I'll just have to show him," she determined. "I have an entire two-month sea voyage to convince him that I am just as mature, just as intelligent, and just as useful as Lady Claire." It hadn't gone unnoticed by her how he deferred to his friend as if she were the wisest woman in the world; she and Claire were the same age!

"I will not allow him to agitate me. He will not cause my heart to flutter and my tongue to wag. And when he can't help but fall in love with me, I'll give him the same look that he has given me—as if he is a child to be patted on the head and indulged, but not taken seriously. Only then will we be on equal footing."

. . .

The Watchtower on Barb Island, Pheldhain, Aurelia

"First our nephew, then Warin. And now Marten," Lady Téana worried. "Will we lose more of our sons to the sea?"

Lord Marin drew his wife to his side and kissed the top of her head. "We don't know that we have lost them, at least where Marten and Warin are concerned," he assured her, though his heart, too, recognized the possibility. "We raised two very resourceful men. I have hope yet that our boys will return." He didn't need to add that Warin lived a charmed life, getting out of dangerous situations again and again. No, Lord Marin was not worried about his younger son. But such was not the case with Marten.

Together, he and his wife watched as the ship carrying their niece, Lady Murel, to Cathmara, where she would press her suit for Lord Trian. The ship would skirt the western coast of Aurelia, stopping in Ragallach to refit and to deliver a letter to Lords Tomas and Ailwen. Its contents were brief. A simple request to the trustworthy Aurelian Guards assigned to manage the coastal territory: deliver the enclosed missive to Warin should he make port in Ragallach. Their son had sailed off to Nifolhad nearly a year past—and without a royal warrant or so much as a fare-thee-well to his mother—to find and liberate the Chevlain woman, Lady Claire.

"When Warin returns," Lord Marin said to his wife, "with or without Lady Claire, he'll most likely make port in Ragallach, and his friends will give him my letter. And if he has found Lady Claire, he'll sail directly to Cathmara to give her time to claim Trian's hand in marriage. Our niece, Lady Murel, will be there to convey my message in person."

"Is that why you were so keen on her vying for Trian's hand? So that she could be there to deliver a message?" She looked up into his eyes with a wry expression, one that their sons had inherited.

"Murel needs a husband. I doubt Lady Claire is still alive. And Trian is an excellent match; he has much influence at court, and another union with the Cathmarans will only strengthen our house. Besides, I want Warin to return here with all haste, especially if I am to throttle him for making you worry."

His words had the desired effect: Lady Téana laughed, something she'd been doing less of late due to the recklessness of her sons. "Come," she said, taking his hand and drawing him toward the ship that would ferry them to the mainland, "it's time to go home. The fates of our sons are in their own hands now. Pray we taught them well."

The Chute

The Cliffs of Ragallach, Aurelia

Warin left Captain Grieg at the wheel and worked his way to the bow to stand next to Lady Claire. The waters below heaved the ship upward, then dropped in increasingly precipitous plunges. Claire gripped the rail and acknowledged him with a curt nod before turning to study the tempest chasing them down. Tempests, he amended. Along with the violently piling storm clouds barreling toward them from the northwest, a maelstrom of Nifolhadian ships were closing in on *Lita's Pearl*, bent on her capture and destruction. From the blinking of lanterns as the sea dipped and swelled, Warin estimated that there were at least four vessels, but the distance and the night conspired to nullify any certainty.

The ships bore down on *Lita's Pearl*, driving her inexorably into the deadly cliffs of Ragallach. She was unable to sail onward, for if she moved any closer to the cliffs without seeing the marker, her hull would be rent by shivving rocks. Those stony blades could peel a ship's hull from its ribs faster than Warin could remove a lady's stays. He turned back to gauge the growing storm, made impossibly darker than any night by the bolts of lightning fissuring the sky. He caught Claire's eye. She, at least, was calm, and he took heart. Claire had seen for him a different future, and he trusted that they would survive this night. He searched the ship for Princess Anwyl and found her leaning forward over the bowsprit. He would have yelled a caution but knew enough about her now to know that she would not heed him. He should throw her over his shoulder and into the hold, but Madyan would likely flay him if he tried.

The ship lurched in the growing waves, and he nearly risked Madyan's ire, but then he saw that the princess had a rope wrapped around one of her wrists. Like Captain Grieg, she cared nothing for the ships riding down on them and never once took her strafing gaze from the cliffs. A concussive crack split the sky, and the first drops of rain hammered against the wood planking of the deck.

To make port in Ragallach, vessels were forced to seek entrance into the Chute—a narrow fjord in an impenetrable face of rock. Hundreds of feet, the cliffs rose, sheer and uninterrupted for leagues down the coast of western Aurelia. The Chute was only wide enough for one ship to slip through at a time. Watchers manned the cliffs both day and night, waiting to signal any and all friendly ships. From the sea, the jagged opening in the cliff face was impossible to discover, for the fjord angled sharply as it cut through the land. Only seasoned pilots attempted entrance on this western port; all others sailed north to Cathmara, then traveled overland, backtracking to Ragallach.

Fist-sized splatters of rain smacked the deck with such force that they threw droplets back up into the air, making the world look as if it had been upended. A terrific explosion of lightning arced across the sky, momentarily blinding him. His vision returned in a blink, and his eyes fixed on the princess he'd sworn to protect. She leaned impossibly forward, against the rail, ignoring the wind driving her soaking tendrils of hair to whip across her face. She tensed and gripped the rail tighter, bracing herself for the first storm-crested wave that would hurl them closer to the cliffs.

"There!" she shouted over the deafening noise. "Ten degrees to the south!"

Warin searched the towering cliffs of Ragallach, straining to see that which she claimed to have spied—the signal light, the all-important guide to safe harbor on this treacherous coast. The barrelman manning the raven's nest shouted to the captain, confirming her sighting a moment later. But Grieg had already acted upon the princess's word; he trusted her like she was part of the crew. Warin had yet to decide if she merited his own trust as well.

The ship lurched as the captain pulled at the wheel. The princess twisted around, pushing back the wet locks plastered to her face, and finally looked behind them. A great swell of water lifted the ship up and forward. They rode it down and with terrifying speed, just making the Chute and missing the jagged wall by the skin of their sails. To either side of them, the waves crashed against the cliffs, shooting enormous plumes of spray into the storm-wracked sky. Grieg expertly steered their vessel down the giant crest of water. Princess Anwyl's keen eyesight had given them the extra seconds they'd needed to survive.

Warin shuttered his praise. For though her face seemed carved of stone, the wildness in her eyes betrayed her turmoil, and he turned to see what held her enthralled. The Nifolhadian ships were not nearly as nimble as *Lita's Pearl*, nor were their captains as proficient as Grieg. The vessels, helpless in the raging sea, hurtled forward. Over the keening wind, Warin imagined he could hear the sailors' screams. A section of mast and sails came caroming around the corner of the cliff-face, only to be sucked under as another tempest-raised wave broke. Pushed through the funnel by the wind and rain, Warin's ship was soon distanced far from the raging storm. As the swell evened out, it carried *Lita's Pearl* gently forward. She navigated another turn, and the howling of the wind and the crashing of the waves were mere whispers and low rumbles. Only then did Princess Anwyl turn away from the carnage. Her expression was outwardly calm, but in her eyes, Warin beheld grief, and he was reminded that the dying sailors were her countrymen.

$$\cdots$$

One Week Later

High in the tower, Anwyl stared out of the narrow slit in the wall. The calm sea sparkled in the noonday sun, hiding under its beautiful surface her deadly shoals and rocks. Once the storm had passed, Lords Tomas and Ailwen, both of them Aurelian Guards and tasked with the keeping of the fortress and forts of Ragallach, had sent every available boat to search the waters for survivors. There hadn't been any. The flotsam that had been pushed into the chute was the only evidence that Diarmait's ships had even crossed the Havest—or Western Sea, as the Aurelians called it. It'd been Warin who'd corrected her, as if she were a student requiring schooling. She sighed. At least he had acknowledged her loss that night, somehow seeing the regret and pain she'd tried to hide—he led the search.

Things had not gone as planned on the crossing. She had thought it the perfect opportunity to convince herself that Warin was not the man of whom Ni'Mala had spoken. She had made it her goal to get to know him better, if only to prove herself right, but he'd never stood still long enough for them to have a conversation. Claire, sensing her frustration, had sought her out when Anwyl had taken refuge in the hold with the horses. As talented as any of the Kena women, Claire had offered to look into Anwyl's future, but Anwyl had declined, explaining that what she knew of her fate so far was already too great a burden.

Claire had smiled and agreed it was the wisest course of action but left her offer open in case Anwyl changed her mind.

And now, Claire was gone to secure her betrothal with the Guard Trian, taking Madyan—Anwyl's only link to Nifolhad—with her. Daisy, her newly hired maid, entered the chamber and set a tray on the nearby table. The young woman had finally gotten over her initial nerves at being around Anwyl, and she now offered her usual bright smile.

Anwyl had expected some reticence from the people when she'd first arrived, but the animosity and distrust toward her and Madyan had been palpable. Then Claire had explained how the Ragallachan people had lived in fear of their lord, the now-deceased Lord Roger, and had blamed his Nifolhadian blood for their oppression. Their hatred was justified, and she worked doubly hard to earn their trust, all the while detesting the fact that she was forced to lie to them. Anwyl had not traveled so far from home to simply plant trees and act as an ambassadress; she was here for a much more dangerous reason. But Rani and Aghna had counseled her to remain silent regarding her ulterior mission. She wasn't about to damage the relationship of goodwill she had been building over the last week.

"Pardon, my princess," Daisy said, interrupting her thoughts, "but Lord Tomas awaits without, seeking to join you for your breakfast."

Daisy was the daughter of a lesser noble in Ragallach. Her family had been visiting the castle and had departed several days before *Lita's Pearl* had arrived. Upon hearing the news, she had ridden back to the stronghold to offer herself as a lady's maid to Anwyl. Her performance was just passable, but her cheerful attitude more than made up for any missteps. She was a bright girl and a quick learner. Anwyl nodded to her, and Daisy bade Tomas enter.

"Good morning, Princess," he greeted. "I thought we could breakfast together before I escort you to the orchards." Anwyl gazed at the tray of food and saw that the kitchen had provided extra, something Tomas must have requested in advance. She smiled at the handsome and dashing young guard. Young? The cherubic nobleman was probably a year or two older than her. Still, she liked Tomas. At least he didn't treat her like a child. She had thought perhaps to use him to make Warin jealous, but immediately denied the very idea. She was a princess, after all, and Tomas had welcomed her and supported her when she had suggested that it would be more efficacious to transplant two of the pijala trees before continuing to court, instead of having to return here to install them months later.

Warin had wanted to leave with all the pijala trees; he was eager to be off, Anwyl realized, having been gone from Aurelia for so long. She had assured him that planting two saplings each in Ragallach, Stolweg, and Whitmarsh would in no way delay their journey. Indeed, she had posited, lightening their load would only induce the draft horses to improve their gait. Even Ailwen supported the idea, citing that the sooner the trees were planted, the better chance they would have. Warin had grudgingly conceded, and Anwyl hadn't seen him since.

She and Tomas enjoyed a light meal of berries, fresh bread, and a soft cheese made of sheep's milk. Ragallach had the finest sheep in all of Aurelia, and their wool was a sought-after commodity in all the known realms. The shepherd's wife had gifted her one of the finest woolen cloaks that Anwyl had ever beheld, stating that she would be happy for it when they crossed the northern range, even in high summer.

"Shall we go?" Tomas asked, offering her his arm and escorting her from the keep.

Warin was waiting in the courtyard, talking to a buxom woman, laughing at something she had said. The way the woman jutted her hip and looked up at him through lowered lashes set Anwyl on edge. She averted her gaze and smoothed her features before Warin noticed her. He gave the woman a short bow, then joined her and Tomas. Tomas covered her hand with his, and she realized that she'd been holding his forearm in a death grip. She relaxed her fingers underneath his warm and steady hand, grateful for his silent support.

They made their way to the orchards, where a sturdy-looking woman waited.

Tomas greeted her first. "We were supposed to meet the Orchard Master this morning," he said, looking hopefully at the tenders standing near the cart. "Jillen, I believe."

The woman raised her eyebrow but chuckled good-naturedly. "There's no Jillen here. I'm Jilleann, the Orchard Mistress."

Anwyl smiled at Jilleann and introduced herself as they walked to a section of the orchard that was protected from the constant winds that streamed over the cliffs and across the fields of the long and narrow territory. The two pijala trees were waiting, snug in their protective crates.

"How came you to be the orchard mistress?"

"My family has been tending these orchards for longer than we can remember," she began. "Both my father and my husband shared the duties, but that was before they passed on. Let me think…it'll be five years this winter."

"I'm so sorry. That must have been difficult for you, losing both your father and husband."

The woman nodded. "Those were darker days. But my mother is still alive, and I have my daughter—she's eight now. I would've moved, but with Lord Roger dead and gone, my daughter is safe. Tending the orchards is in my blood, so with no one else taking up the responsibility, I continued my family's work. I don't think anyone here ever thought to deny me. And, well, the orchards help to feed the people, and despite the harsh clime, we've been successful with some of the hardier fruit trees."

"I hope you are teaching your daughter to follow in your footsteps."

"I've already started," she said with a wink.

With the men trailing some ways behind, Anwyl grew increasingly optimistic. The section of orchard closest to the edge of the cliff was nearly the same terrain as where the pijalas grew in Sophiana. She bade Jilleann instruct her tenders to bring the two saplings closer. Anwyl took a shovel from one of the workers and, along with the orchard mistress, broke ground for the saplings.

"Wouldn't it be better to plant the trees where they will be more sheltered?" Tomas asked, taking up a pickax to help break up the hard earth. Warin stepped in to take her shovel.

"That's all right. I can manage," she told him. "I helped crate most of these trees and that involved digging them up first."

"Please, Princess," he offered, holding out his hand. She gave him the tool, heartened somewhat that he wanted to help her, at least until he added, "'twould not do if you injured yourself before our journey to Kings Glen has even begun. I swore to your brother to see you safely there."

"I daresay, Warin, I know how to use a shovel, but you go right ahead. I'll see to uncrating the trees. With a pry bar…and a mallet." She faux-gasped, unable to curb her exasperation. She grabbed the tools and headed to the dray carrying the saplings. She didn't know why it bothered her that he thought she couldn't manage, but it did. She'd planted, transplanted, hauled, trimmed, grafted, nurtured, and netted more saplings than even the orchard master in Sophiana. But if Warin was so set on digging the hole for her, let him. She made short work of the crates, and the tenders helped her to slide the two trees into place. Anwyl eyed Jilleann's hole and nodded, then studied Warin's work.

"Deep enough?" he asked, jumping into the hole to demonstrate its depth. There was nothing in his tone bespeaking his usual annoyance, and Anwyl nodded and held out her hand to help him out. She braced her legs as he came up and pulled. But his foot caught on the pry bar she had set on the ground, and he stumbled, catching himself on the back of the mud-caked dray.

"Oh, Warin, I'm sorry." She tried to brush some of the larger clots off his shirt. Her hand froze when her palm brushed over the spot above his heart. She pressed against his muscled chest and wondered at the intense heat centered in that one spot. His heartbeat remained steady, while hers pounded wildly in her chest.

He took her hand, gently lifting it away. "You're only rubbing it in," he said quietly before letting her go. When she looked up at his face, she expected to see annoyance, but his expression revealed nothing. He ran his fingers over his forehead and through his hair, leaving a trail of smudged dirt. She gave him her kerchief and was about to explain why, but he had already turned away.

"Serves him right," Tomas whispered, a playful smile on his lips.

"Why would you say that?"

"Because, last night, he and—" he stopped mid-explanation, looking embarrassed.

Without a doubt, Tomas had been about to mention the woman in the courtyard. Anwyl focused on the task at hand instead, and soon, both saplings were planted. The earth was tamped down, and rings of soil built up around the slender trunks. A small herd of sheep trotted through the orchard, nibbling at the grasses underneath the fruit trees. "This is perfect," Anwyl exclaimed.

"How so?" Tomas asked.

"The sheep and goats in Sophiana often mow the grasses growing in the pijala orchard. You need not worry about them damaging the trunks: the bark is bitter and makes them sick, so they avoid it."

"Thank you, Princess," Jilleann said, curtsying. "I promise to write to you at court with accounts of the trees' progress."

On their way back to the castle, they walked past fieldworkers, sheep tenders, and the many soldiers stationed in the austere territory. To a one, they smiled at her and called out greetings.

"I must say, Princess," Tomas began. "You have a way with people. It took nearly a year for the Ragallachans to warm up to Ailwen and me. Why, I didn't even realize the orchard master was a mistress. I wouldn't be surprised if they miss you when you leave."

"They're a proud people, and I don't blame them for their initial cold welcome after all they must've endured under Lord Roger. Especially if he was half as cruel as his brother, Prince Bowen." Anwyl paused, turning to take her leave when the arms master approached with two quarterstaffs.

"Princess Anwyl," he greeted, sweeping a deep and elegant bow to her. "I wanted to thank you for the Nifolhadian stave you gave me. Your countrywoman, Lady Madyan, said that you might appreciate a stout rod. So, I have here two of Ragallach's finest for you."

"They're beautiful, Girard. Thank you." She studied the hawthorn staffs, hefting one, then the other, giving each a deft twirl before deciding on the plainer of the two. "The balance is remarkable. You are very kind."

"'Tis a pleasure, my princess," Girard gushed, earning him an exasperated look from Warin.

"Princess Anwyl," Tomas asked excitedly, "do you...are you...? I did not realize that you were skilled at quarterstaffs."

"I am sure that I am not as skilled as you, Tomas. Lady Claire told me of your prowess. I wonder, would you care to exercise with me? With Madyan gone, I am lacking a partner."

"It would be my honor, Princess."

"I don't think that's a good—" Warin started.

"Oh, thank you, Tomas. It has been months since I've had any real practice. The ship was too confining a space. Girard, can we borrow the other stave?" He beamed at her and tossed the quarterstaff to Tomas. "Why are you scowling like that, Warin? Do you wish to fight me instead?"

"No, Princess," he rushed to say. "I just think it unwise to—"

"Will you excuse us for a moment, Tomas?" She waited until Tomas and Girard were out of earshot. Perhaps it had happened when he didn't trust her to dig a hole, but Anwyl was growing tired of his overbearing attitude, and a bit of her usual fire kindled along her spine. "Warin, if we are going to be traveling together, then you'll have to accept that I am as adept with a quarterstaff as I am with a shovel. Stop worrying so much about my welfare."

"I don't want you to injure yourself," he tried to explain.

"I grew up with the most protective brother in the whole of the known realms. But even Rani would not question my judgment when it comes to the things in which he knows me to be proficient—activities like sailing, digging holes, and even quarterstaffs. I will be fine," she insisted. "And I promise to go easy on Tomas."

He opened his mouth to respond, then sealed his lips together in a disapproving line. After a curt nod, he excused himself and stalked into the castle.

. . .

Warin had been about to forbid her to fight, and without good reason. What was Tomas thinking? Princess Anwyl was not a warrior like Lady Anna of Stolweg, nor even had the skill anywhere near to that of Anna's sister, Lady Claire of Chevlain. He had no clue why the idea should irk him so. In fact, he'd been out of sorts ever since they had landed in Ragallach.

If he were honest with himself, he had woken too early and on the wrong side of the bed. The woman he'd planned on entertaining throughout the night was, when he finally roused himself from slumber, quite put out with him. He'd apparently imbibed too much and had passed out sprawled across her sleeping pallet, causing her to have to sleep elsewhere. She returned early, and with breakfast, for which he was grateful, but she had made a point of banging and clanging every object in her room to wake him.

Warin couldn't remember a time when he'd left a woman unsatisfied. Drink had never been an issue, and he had tried to recall how much he'd consumed. The memory was a blur. It had taken the entire morning to convince himself that it was a onetime aberration, and he chalked it up to his months at sea and the stress of protecting the princess. Not that he was blaming her for his earlier incapacity...well, maybe a little. But his practical side made him re-examine his brusqueness toward her. He was tired, pure and simple.

He was on his way to his chamber when Ailwen hurried past him. "You're headed in the wrong direction, Warin, if you want to see if the princess has any skill at quarterstaffs, that is."

"I do not." The memory of her hand above his heart came back to him, and how she seemed unable to move. Even now, he could feel the heat of her palm on his chest.

"I would think you would like to see some of the Nifolhadian form," his friend went on. "She mentioned that she had some training from those Fenrhi women."

"I doubt that she knows more than the basics. Tomas is bound to be disappointed."

"Hmm." Ailwen studied his feet for a moment, then looked up at Warin. "For a princess of Nifolhad, she's not exactly what I thought she'd be."

"What is that supposed to mean?"

"Oh, I don't know. She's just...more than I imagined."

Before Warin could respond, Ailwen turned and left him standing alone in the corridor. He went to his chamber to think. An ache had crept up his neck and had a viselike grip on his skull. He rubbed his temples.

So, the princess had Fenrhi training. Her cousin Radha was of the Kena cast, a seer. Perhaps the talent ran in the family. Warin didn't relish the idea of escorting someone with the insights of a Kena all the way to Kings Glen. "Hypocrite," he said to himself. "Lady Claire is gifted, and I trust her implicitly. Why not the princess? Both she and her brother claimed to know nothing of my cousin's whereabouts." He ran his hand through his hair. "How, then, did Anwyl know her way about *Lita's Pearl* if she had never seen a Pheldhainian ship?"

He entered his chamber and stopped. Something was off. He studied his belongings, and everything seemed to be in place. But he couldn't shake the feeling that someone had been in his room. Probably just a servant tidying up, he told himself. A tickle of a memory gnawed at his brain. An argument. Two women. Then, nothing.

"Gah, I feel old." He stood before the small reflecting glass that he used when he shaved his whiskers and noticed that his face was smeared with mud. No one had thought to tell him. That wasn't quite the truth, he realized, looking at the wadded-up scrap of cloth in his hand. The princess *had* pressed a kerchief to him.

CHAPTER THREE

A Shift in the Wind

Steward King Diarmait's Palace, Kantahla, Nifolhad

Prince Bowen sat on the edge of his bed and ran his hands over his scruffy jaw. Normally, he kept his face meticulously shaved whenever in Kantahla—his father had insisted upon it in the past, and as Bowen grew older, it became too tedious to argue. The blankets rustled behind him, and he took in an eyeful of the blond woman still sleeping. She would have an interesting time explaining to her husband why the delicate skin on her neck was chafed. As if sensing his examination, she shifted under the blanket, exposing one very long and beautiful leg. The bruises on her knees from the time she'd spent on all fours the previous evening had not yet purpled. Bowen drew back the cover to expose her hip and buttock, wanting to see the marks his fingers had left on her when he'd held her, gripped tight, as he rode her.

Hell, his own knees would be as bruised as hers, and he chuckled and brought the palm of his hand down in a swift slap on her buttock. She woke with a start. The wariness in her eyes as she realized where she was and with whom was unmistakable, though she managed to quickly mask it. Bowen prided himself on being unpredictable with his mistresses, and she had no doubt heard the rumors about his darker activities. "Time to wake," he said, in a good mood for once, and traced his fingers up her leg to her hip, where he caressed her bruised skin. She smiled and rolled onto her back, slightly spreading her legs in invitation, though the blanket kept her demurely covered.

"I like how you look with a beard," she murmured.

"I'm sure. But tell me, how will you explain the whisker burns to your husband?"

"Phelan won't even notice. He hasn't touched me in over a year. I don't think he can—how should I put this?—perform anymore."

This was Lord Phelan's fifth wife, and the most adventurous of them all—Bowen should know, for he'd also bedded the first four. He drew the blanket away to expose her completely. "Then perhaps you would like some more." Instead of nuzzling her neck, he buried his face between her legs. She shrieked as his rough stubble scraped ruthlessly across the tender skin of her inner thigh, and he lifted his head to gaze up at her.

"Don't stop, my prince!" she begged.

Number Five—he didn't actually know her name as she had only ever been introduced as Phelan's wife—always appreciated a little pain with her pleasure. And Bowen was only too happy to give her an ample dose of both. It was the least he could do after her performance last night.

• • •

It was well past noon when Bowen finally made it to his father's chambers. Steward King Diarmait's trusted advisor, Lord Phelan, gave him an annoyed glance as he entered, either for being late, for the self-satisfied smirk on his face, or for arriving unshaven. Bowen cared not a whit, for his heart was dancing a merry jig: Lord Phelan looked horrible. The long hours fretting over when Diarmait would turn on him were taking a physical toll on the man. The delight Bowen felt in the turn-about circumstances was almost as good as bedding Number Five.

Hell, who was he trying to convince? It was infinitely better. For years, Lord Phelan had undermined his efforts to impress his father, causing endless notes of discord in an already tenuous relationship. Phelan cast him a beseeching look. No, Bowen would not say one single word in Phelan's defense. Let the man grovel; it would do him good. All his expert advice had handed Nifolhad on a silver platter to Aghna and Ranulf.

Of course, Phelan was only partially to blame. Bowen's father carried most of the load, even committing fratricide in his failed attempt to rule over the whole of Nifolhad. As plans went, Diarmait's had had merit, at least in the beginning. With his brother King Cedric dead, Diarmait was supposed to have forced his niece, Princess Aghna, to wed Bowen. Bowen would've been declared king, and a new ruling line would have emerged. But Diarmait grew too greedy, no doubt after listening to Phelan as he fed Diarmait's hubris. New plots and schemes were hatched. The worst of them, assassinate Aghna—that turned out well; she was now queen.

Along with the news of her marriage, word had come that it'd been Lord Warin of Pheldhain's ship that had taken Bowen's schemed-for replacement bride back to Aurelia, and with the upstart Princess Anwyl from Sophiana as well. He rubbed the bridge of his nose out of habit—long since healed from when it had been broken. It rankled him still that there was a permanent bump on one side.

"Still bothers you, doesn't it?" Phelan asked, a malicious gleam in his eye.

"No, I'm just worn out after last night's activities. You wouldn't understand, of course." He stood, then reached down to adjust himself in his breeches. "Fifth time's the charm, or so I hear." Phelan nearly turned purple. Served him right. Bowen had spent years overcoming that humiliating day. And then Phelan would make some comment, reminding his father and anyone else within earshot how Princess Anwyl had knocked him flat.

But enough. Bowen had no time for arguing. Thanks to his father's boundless rapacity, everything was now in ruins. His best course of action would be to play the dutiful son—secretly enjoying his father's downfall—while coming out of this futile civil war with his head still attached to his neck and his vast holdings in Kantahla intact. For now, he could do naught but wait.

A small part of him acknowledged that he should feel something for his father, pity even, but he didn't. He wasn't physically able; Diarmait had beaten any empathy out of him when he was a child. His father had expelled Bowen's mother from Nifolhad by casting her adrift and alone on the sea. But fate had taken at least one murder out of his father's hands when Lady Ulicia had managed to survive. A perfect storm, one that was unseasonably strong, had pushed her small craft across the Havest back into the embrace of her parents in Ragallach. If he were a believer in the ancient gods and goddesses, he might even think it had been divine intervention that had saved his mother. But he wasn't a believer, not in anyone but himself. He was cold and calculating, and without a single remorseful bone in his body.

Well, there was one thing for which he was sorry—Roger. He blamed his father for the loss of his younger brother. Bowen had only ever seen Roger as a rival, a tool his father used to torment him. If only he had embraced him, perhaps the two of them would have been able to stand up to Diarmait.

"No matter now," Bowen said to himself.

"What was that?" Diarmait asked from his bed.

"Nothing, Father. I was just thinking about Roger."

"Roger? He betrayed me. Worthless failure. All of this is his fault. If Roger had been able to control his wife, he wouldn't be dead. Have—" his father stopped speaking midsentence and stared at Bowen's whisker-shadowed face, frowning as if he couldn't remember what he'd been about to say. Bowen held his gaze, waiting, and eventually Diarmait went off on another tangent, this time directing his rant toward Phelan.

His father's behavior was becoming increasingly erratic. Perhaps if they had heeded Bowen's counsel, they would not be facing a losing war against Queen Aghna and King Ranulf. He bit back the taste of bile at the thought of acknowledging her ascension as Queen of Nifolhad.

So immense was his father's arrogance that he'd spread his forces too thin while Prince—King—Ranulf bolstered his own defenses. The great Steward King Diarmait, with his blood-fisted grip on Nifolhad, had watched in abject confusion as his hold on everything south of the Lan'cá Mountain Range slipped through his fingers. Half of his army had been called back to defend Kantahla's border at the Goremi River; the other half was fighting Ranulf's army. Once held in check at the border of Sophiana, the support for Aghna and Ranulf had swelled in the Brabryn region, and combined with Ranulf's army, their followers had pressed forward to the Brabry River and laid siege to the city of Brynmara.

At least, that was how Diarmait and Phelan perceived things. To Bowen, the story was quite different. Diarmait's army occupied Brynmara, and Ranulf's men were trying to liberate it and its populace—the city's inhabitants were actively working against the soldiers stationed there. With the supply lines cut off from without and their stores stolen or sabotaged from within, it would be less than a year, months perhaps, and his father's forces there would be forced to capitulate.

Before the city was besieged, Bowen had argued for withdrawing from Brynmara and making a stand closer to Mount Kanta and the surrounding foothills. Their supply lines could've remained intact, both there and where part of the army was holding the line at the Goremi River. Diarmait had dismissed the notion and had accused Bowen of cowardice. He preferred listening to the sycophantic murmurings of his council, with Lord Phelan being the biggest lickspittle of them all. Bowen couldn't completely blame the man; the Steward King had accused nearly every person in his court of treachery. More than one noble had been tortured and put to death based on nothing more than unsubstantiated rumor and paranoia. Bowen went to great pains to protect and insulate those nobles he knew were loyal to him. They'd long since been sent from Kantahla and out of Diarmait's reach and were acknowledging, with Bowen's sanction, Queen Aghna as the rightful regent.

"I demand the death of every Fenrhi in Nifolhad," Diarmait sputtered suddenly, shifting to an entirely new topic. "They'll be hiding, but their markings will give them away. A door-to-door search and inspection of every woman, beginning here in Kantahla." Lord Phelan cast a nervous glance at Bowen as Diarmait raged about conspiracies and assassinations. The harangue was feebly delivered; Diarmait, though he would never admit it, was not the same man as he once had been. "Any one of them could be a Fenrhi witch." He tried to get out of the bed that had become his throne, but Bowen was on hand to mollify him. His father lay back, refusing to accept his defeat. Once extraordinarily handsome and robust, Diarmait had become a husk of a man. His moods swung from manic protestations to sullen doldrums.

Phelan was too busy wallowing in his own fears to be of any use—he'd backed the wrong horse. Across Nifolhad, people were celebrating the ascension of Queen Aghna and her marriage to King Ranulf. Diarmait's control of Naca'an had dissipated in less than four cycles of the moon. His control of the Fenrhi likewise evaporated. Nobles in the south were disavowing themselves of their connection to him, even those linked to Diarmait's house by marriage and blood. They preferred taking their chances with Aghna's beneficence. What could a ruler expect when the majority of his army had been threatened and coerced into following him? And the nobles? The more one paid for loyalty, the thinner its fiber, until all that remained were cobwebs.

Bowen still marveled at how swiftly the transfer of power to Aghna had gone. Initially, she and Ranulf hadn't sent a single soldier to Naca'an, nor to any other region of the realm, save the Brabry River. It had been the Fenrhi who had orchestrated the uprising in the south, and they did so with very little bloodshed. The Mother, no longer under the control of Bowen's half-sister, Rhiannon, was smart enough to know that she needed to reorganize her brood. Diarmait had been shocked to find that the women of the temple he'd thought under his thumb had, in fact, secretly established themselves in every town, village, and city south of the Goremi River.

The Fenrhi web was of the finest filigree; not even the Mother had known it existed. For years, the women had been passing messages, watching and spying, and most of all, waiting for a shift in the wind. And when the weather changed, they emerged like rain clouds over an arid desert. The people of

Nifolhad soaked up their care as if they'd been dying of thirst. It was almost as if the women had known that a rightful heir existed and had prepared and planned for her return and ascension.

Bowen had ferreted out the truth. During those first few months, when all was chaos in the realm, he had interrogated the last of the Fenrhi women still imprisoned in Diarmait's palace. All but one of them claimed ignorance of the secret network of women. It'd been one of the Sylvan who had finally succumbed to Bowen's torturer. The story she was forced into telling explained, once and for all, the link that Lady Claire had to Nifolhad and her possible claim to the throne through her direct lineage to the exiled Prince Aghnar of so many generations past.

Bowen studied his father's haggard face. Those still loyal to him prescribed his condition to his dashed dream of becoming the legitimate king. But here, too, Bowen knew the truth. Diarmait had been tainted by none other than the Fenrhi women he had so oft abused and discarded. Over time, tiny slips of poison had been given to his father: in a drink or bite of food, from a kiss or a caress of fingers. Doses so minute they went undetected but, with each exposure, compounded in his organs. His father could languish for years, or he might perish before the leaves began to bud in the spring. And though Lord Phelan was only beginning to show the signs, he, too, would suffer an early death. Bowen had to admire the Fenrhi—their patience, their persistence, and their commitment to their cause.

As for himself, Bowen wasn't worried. Only once had he partaken of the services offered by the Blood Caste. And though he'd been involved in numerous interrogations by torture, every physical act had been completed by one of his men. He had never deigned to sully himself by touching his victims. He kept his mind firmly fixed on his own future, accepting the inevitable—one day soon, he would be forced to bow down before Aghna and Ranulf. When the time came, he would do so willingly, prostrating himself before all, if only to make sure he came out of this mess with his head intact.

His old plans for revenge against the Chevlain women who had murdered his brother would be set aside. He would paint himself as Diarmait's pawn and accept whatever censure was handed to him—the epitome of contriteness, the perfect example of a steward prince. And as he learned from the Fenrhi, he would be patient and wait. Being the son of a prolific lecher had one advantage—Bowen had over a dozen half-siblings and more nephews and nieces than he could count. Rhiannon was not his only relative in the Fenrhi's sacred temple. His father, the Fenrhi, and even King Godwin of Aurelia, who he once thought to depose, were completely blind to how far Bowen's reach spanned over the realms. Diarmait had paid little mind to his bastard offspring, allowing Bowen to scoop them up in a net like so many little fish. They were loyal only to Bowen.

When his father began to snore, Bowen rose from his seat near the bed. "Go get some rest, Phelan," he recommended. "You're starting to look as tired as my father." A satisfied warmth spread through him when he saw the panicked darting of Phelan's eyes as he digested the import of Bowen's observation.

"Yes, of course, my Prince," the man blustered, then scurried from the chamber. Bowen headed to his father's council room. He needed a quiet place to think and to plan. He would survive the coming storm; he might even prosper from it. Gazing down at the charts strewn over the table before him, he spotted the map of Aurelia, and an idea wormed its way into his brain. In Aurelia, his future resided—his birthright and a possible bride.

• • •

The Royal Palace of Queen Aghna, Naca'an, Nifolhad

"We could always call her back," Ranulf suggested as Aghna finished sealing the diplomatic pouch they were sending to King Godwin and Queen Juliana in Aurelia. She'd had the same idea, many times. But Madyan deserved some time away from Nifolhad. Her desert friend had sacrificed too much already, including her family, and even her blood.

"Not yet, Rani. The day will come soon enough when Madyan will have to return. The Fyrjians, those who remain, will need her."

"Those who remain," he said wonderingly. "We've no idea how many people there are in the Fyrost. Hundreds, possibly thousands."

"Then it is doubly good that Madyan is my friend." Ranulf had fallen silent. "What is it, my love?"

"I was surprised that they were so organized. All this time, they have been gathering their people, fighting Diarmait's reign in quiet ways, taking out his supply lines, even thwarting his messengers who dared to cross the Fyrost. I wonder, did Madyan know?"—Aghna quirked her eyebrow—"Of course she did. She'll need a title when she returns. What was it that the Fyrjian emissary called her?"

"Malikáfyr." Aghna was thoughtful for a moment. "It's as good a title as any, and one Madyan deserves. Fire Queen. She's the last direct heir to her line, Rani, the last noble princess of the Fyrost, those believed to be the first people of Nifolhad. Madyan and her family were always protecting me, long before I fled to the Fenrhi Temple."

He nodded. "I remember her father well, but it was her mother who made a bigger impression. She was formidable. At the time, I did not realize who it was that I sent to warn you."

Her husband and king bent down to kiss her head. Years ago, when Aghna had been held prisoner by Diarmait, Ranulf had hired a Fyrjian family to smuggle a message to her. He had read the message aloud to them, making sure they knew the import of what they carried. He never received a reply. Then news of Aghna's death reached him, and for three years, he mourned the loss of his betrothed until that day when she'd miraculously arrived in Sophiana, all due to the efforts of Madyan.

"She never talked about her family to me, not really," Aghna explained. "I only guessed at her noble lineage. I'm honored that she told me about her parents the night before she sailed to Aurelia. She said that her people would come to visit us one day and that we could trust them."

"And will we?"

"I trust Madyan, and that is enough."

• • •

The Fenrhi Temple, near Naca'an, Nifolhad

"And how is your cousin, Princess Anwyl?" Ni'Mala, Mother of the Fenrhi, asked.

Radha was always wary of the Mother when she inquired after her family. Though Ni'Mala was making an honest effort at becoming a better leader for the Fenrhi, Radha was a long way from trusting her. This wasn't the first time Ni'Mala had expressed an interest in Anwyl. Better for her to know that Anwyl was no longer within her reach. "She is well, Mother. Taking Aurelia by storm, no doubt."

"She's already in Aurelia?"

Already? Two of the other Fenrhi Artists, Gudrun of Earth Caste and Jenai of Umbren, looked on with little interest. But in Hedra's eyes, there was a flash of warning. "Yes. Queen Aghna has asked her to be Nifolhad's ambassador to Aurelia." Of the pijala trees, she said nothing. "It is kind of you to ask after her."

Ni'Mala laughed. "Oh, Radha, you always did see plots where there are none. I have always liked Princess Anwyl. She was a special girl when first I met her; she has grown into an extraordinary woman."

Radha acknowledged Anwyl's intelligence and sage counsel to Ranulf. But extraordinary?

"Sometimes when we are close to a person, we cannot see them for who they truly are," the Mother said wisely. "Is that not correct, Hedra?"

"I—"

Ni'Mala lifted her hand in a placating gesture. "I realize there is still mistrust between us. After everything I allowed to happen here, I will have to work hard to prove myself to you."

"But much of the blame rests with Rhiannon," Gudrun, the oldest of the Artists, allowed.

"Thank you for that, Gudrun, but ultimately, I was responsible. I realize you wanted someone else in my place, and it means much that you now allow me to retain my position as Mother. And with the assistance of this council, I intend to work diligently to reunite our castes, for that is my purpose, is it not?" She rose from the cushions. "I would not have been marked with the honeycomb otherwise. So, in the spirit of our new beginning, I will tell you all about a little-known prophecy." She retrieved a scroll and carefully unrolled the parchment.

Gudrun stared down at the markings. "It's beautiful," she said wistfully.

"Yes, the artisans of old were divinely gifted."

Radha and the other women gathered around the table. At first, the designs appeared to be the usual Fenrhi exiflos, the six-petaled depiction of the Fenrhi Tenets. Each caste was represented by its ancient symbol, but upon closer examination, instead of the tenets, different symbols replaced the usual writings.

Beside her, Gudrun gasped. "If you translated this, then you knew all along what Princess Claire represented. Why did you never say anything?"

"Do not forget," Radha reminded, "though they are true princesses of Nifolhad, the Chevlain sisters prefer to be called ladies."

"Ladies or princesses, it matters little," Ni'mala added. "Rhiannon's power is great. I worry that we will not be equipped for her return. And her influence over me was such that all matters other than her own agenda were cast aside to be forgotten. A good thing, too, for she never knew of the existence of these scrolls."

The women of the Fenrhi council nodded their agreement.

"I was prevented from completing my translations because I was compelled to do other things. It was only after my mind had cleared that I remembered studying these with my predecessor. They were hidden away, and Rhiannon never knew."

"This exiflos prophecies the incarnation of a great leader, one who embodies the six tenets," Radha translated reverently. "Prin—Lady Claire."

"Not just one leader," Ni'Mala pointed out. "One leader with four captains."

"Only four?" Radha asked.

"Yes, strange, isn't it? Some of the translations indicate that six will be involved in the prophecy. But then others clearly point to only five saving us from some great evil; perhaps we are not yet finished with Diarmait." She pointed to one of the petals. "I believe Princess Claire to be the embodiment of harmony, the Mother's Caste. But like the Mothers of old, she is imbued with the best of all the tenets. And her sister, Princess Aubrianne, had she come to us, would have surely been marked for Umbren with elements of Earth, and even Sylvan. And Princess Anwyl..."

"Anwyl?" Radha challenged. "Not my cousin. Why, she's just a—"

"Sylvan master," Hedra revealed, surprising everyone except the Mother, Radha noted.

"As well as Umbren," Jenai added, giving Hedra a shrewd look. "Venna came to me after you asked her to train the princess."

"I'm astonished that you are ignorant of this, Radha. And of her primary calling," the Mother teased. "Kena."

"Kena?" Radha nearly sputtered the word. She did not like the direction in which this conversation was headed. "Princess Anwyl has never displayed any proclivity as a seer."

"Must I remind you of the core principle of the Kena?" Ni'Mala calmly asked.

"Enlightenment, but—"

"Have you ever met anyone with Anwyl's commitment to knowledge? Or the ease with which she understands any task thrown her way? You and King

Ranulf sent her to Aurelia to act as Nifolhad's ambassadress. Your cousin possesses the gift of pushing, but not in the way Rhiannon manipulated the talent. Princess Anwyl's is the purest form of encouragement. Her skills in diplomacy and negotiation are a natural extension of her heart. If she requested it of me, I would happily have you mark her with indigo."

"She would never wish it," Radha insisted.

"And why not? She has already been marked with the green of the Sylvan caste—yes, I knew, Hedra," Ni'Mala admitted.

"And Umbren, too," Jenai proudly revealed.

"You marked my cousin without consulting me? Does Rani know? I mean, King Ranulf. Is he aware that you turned his sister into a Fenrhi?"

"Radha," Ni'Mala soothed. "She is *not* Fenrhi. Like the Princesses Claire and Aubrianne, she is...more."

CHAPTER FOUR

Marked

Stolweg Castle

The antithesis of Anwyl's wishes persisted. She had done everything in her power to impress Warin, from helping the sailors on their perilous sea-crossing to her expert care of the pijala trees as they'd traveled from Ragallach to Stolweg. For goodness' sake, she'd dived into the Stolweg River a few days ago, all in an effort to stop one of the wagons from sliding down an embankment after one of the draft horses spooked. Anwyl would not suffer losing a single sapling. Besides, there hadn't been rain in over a week, so the river was slow-moving at best.

She was a mature, intelligent, and useful woman, not the naïve girl Warin held her to be. He needn't have bothered jumping into the river to pull her out, for she was an excellent swimmer, a fact that the Lady of Stolweg, Claire's sister, had pointed out when she saw that Anwyl was making it to the bank on her own.

Meeting Claire's sister sopping wet from the Stolweg had not been ideal, but Anwyl soon found that Lady Anna was a kindred spirit. She was a self-sufficient woman, leading an active life, training her Chevlain steeds, managing an efficient keep, and practicing her archery, all the while taking care of little Celeste and carrying a babe in her belly. Had she not been so far along with child, she would have been practicing with her sword, knives, and quarterstaff as well. The Lady of Stolweg was such an accomplished châtelaine that Anwyl had asked her what would be left for her husband to do when he returned from the northern territory of Cathmara.

Anna had assured her that there were many men in Aurelia who believed in the women they loved, even if they required a little schooling in the subject. Warin had piped in, averring that he and the men from Pheldhain were such men, and Anna had laughed and laughed, leaving him with a perplexed expression.

That first afternoon in Stolweg, Anwyl had explained to Lady Anna why she was a rightful Princess of Nifolhad, that generations past, her line was seeded by the far-removed uncle of Queen Aghna. Because of the direct matriarchal lineage from the exiled Prince Aghnar, Anna and Claire were true princesses of the highest royal house in Nifolhad. Anna's young daughter Celeste had clapped joyfully upon being told that she was a princess as well. After word had spread through Stolweg, the blacksmith had fashioned a thin circlet of bronze for the young child to wear as a crown.

Anwyl closed her travel desk. She had just written a letter to her brother and finished sealing it with a glob of wax. She stood to shake out her skirts, for her assignation with little Princess Celeste was upon her. No sooner did she have the thought than there was a light rap on the door. "Come in." The chamber door opened, and Anna's maid, Grainne, entered, holding Celeste's hand. "Good evening, Little Princess," Anwyl said brightly, picking up Celeste and swinging her in a circle.

"Are you ready, Princess?" Grainne asked. Then, seeing that Anwyl's traveling clothes were still rumpled where she had left them on a chair, she stepped over to shake out the cloak and hang it on a hook. "Where's that girl of yours, the one from Ragallach? Daisy, isn't it?"

Daisy chose that moment to fly into the room. She looked Anwyl up and down, seeing that she had tended to herself, and her shoulders slumped. "Oh, my princess, I'm so sorry. I got lost on my way to the kitchen, then lost again on my way back here. There are so many stairs, and the upper corridors all look the same."

"No harm done," Anwyl soothed but saw Grainne roll her eyes. "We'll arrange for another tour of the castle tomorrow. You needn't wait up for me." The poor girl looked panicked. "Your room is just next to mine, to the right."

Daisy curtsied and started toward the door, but Grainne blocked her. "Shouldn't you put away your mistress's things first?" she tutored, though it was kindly done. The girl nodded, and Grainne led the way from the chamber, escorting Anwyl to the banquet hall.

Anwyl took Celeste's hand in hers and smiled down at the toddler. "I can't wait to taste Doreen's specialty." It had been Claire, while a-sea, who had lauded Doreen's cooking, saying that which she missed most were Doreen's coveted meat pasties. Warin and Pieter had vehemently concurred. When the castle's cook had asked if there was anything special that Anwyl would like for her first evening in Stolweg, she knew just what to request.

It was to be an intimate banquet, one of celebration, for she and Warin had given Anna the news that her sister, Claire, had safely returned to the shores of Aurelia and was now making her way to Cathmara to claim and hopefully wed Trian.

During their meal, Anwyl began explaining the importance of not just the pijala trees, but the cache of pihaberries she was to distribute throughout the realm. "The pijala fruit is sacred; it infuses the mind with clarity. It's much more than a symbolic gesture from Queen Aghna and King Ranulf; it will ensure that both Aurelians and Nifolhadajans remain free-thinking."

She and Warin then spent the evening explaining the Fenrhi Temple and its caste system. They started with the Kena Caste and how the pihaberries protected a person's mind from the rarest of Kena talents—the ability to control a weaker person's actions.

"Did my sister spend time with these Kena women?" Anna asked Warin, interrupting him midsentence.

"She did, Anna. But Claire was much stronger than they expected. She, uh..."

Anwyl was surprised at Warin's lack of words and took Anna's hand in hers. "Your sister is very powerful, but she has a good heart. With a little help, she was able to see through their manipulations. My cousin Radha is Kena, and one of the Artists. She—"

"Artists?"

Lady Anna's patience was growing thin, but Anwyl kept her voice calm and explained. "The Artists—one each from Kena, Earth, Umbren, and Sylvan— help to determine where Fenrhi initiates are placed and how they are marked."

"What do you mean *marked*? What exactly did they do to Claire?"

Anwyl watched as the fierce warrior in Lady Anna of Stolweg surfaced. Having also lost her parents, it was a sentiment Anwyl could appreciate—she had felt the same protective urges for her brother.

"As we've finished eating," Warin interrupted, "why don't you and I and the princess go to your library? We can talk there, in private."

"Warin..." Anna growled.

"Please," he begged of her and got up from the table.

Anwyl rose as well. "One of the many things that impressed me about Claire is that she is a very private person. She would not want to be the object of gossip. The Fenrhi are complicated. Warin is right. We should retire to a location that is more private."

Anna stood, then stalked out of the hall. Anwyl made to follow her, but Warin held her arm. "I know the way. Best let Anna alone for a few minutes. She's very protective of Claire."

"I can understand that."

"Perhaps. But she's lost Claire twice now. You see, when Prince Bowen destroyed Chevlain and slaughtered her parents, Anna spent months thinking Claire had been murdered as well. Claire's and Anna's lives were just beginning to settle when Claire was abducted by Diarmait's men. It took every fiber of will she possessed to remain in Aurelia while I went off to search Nifolhad. Only the thought of leaving Celeste prevented her from joining me."

"I understand. Thank you."

"No thanks necessary. I only want you to know that you are not the focus of her anger."

He'd never talked to her like this before—as an equal. "Will you help me to explain the changes in Claire? I mean, I can tell Anna about the Fenrhi and the castes and everything else, but you knew Claire before."

"Of course." He led the way to where Anna was waiting. She poured wine for all of them, and they sat down to what promised to be a long night of explanations.

Warin explained how the Fenrhi were a group of women who lived in a great complex on the outskirts of Naca'an. He told her about Madyan and how she had helped Claire to reach the sanctuary of the temple after she had escaped the ship that had transported her away from Aurelia. Then, Anwyl described the temple and the six different castes—the four main groups: Umbren, the protector caste; Sylvan, the healers; Kena, with their special powers of sight and foretelling; and finally, Earth, and their commitment to service and duty. She finished by telling Anna about Blood Caste and how Claire used her brief time there to escape the temple with Queen Aghna and Madyan.

"You've yet to tell me how this relates to Claire being marked," Lady Anna reminded.

"The final caste is comprised of one person: the Fenrhi Mother. Each caste is designated by a color, and when an initiate's caste is chosen, a permanent design is applied to her skin."

"And to which caste does Claire belong?"

Anwyl looked at Warin for a moment. "There's no easy way to say this, so I'll just come right out with it. Claire was marked for all six." Anna jumped up, nearly spilling her wine, and began pacing, but Anwyl knew the only way forward was to tell her everything. "Some of the Fenrhi wanted her to replace Ni'Mala, the current Mother," Anwyl calmly continued. "My cousin wanted her to be queen. Even my brother thought to wed her for her bloodline. But Claire helped save Aghna, and the rightful queen was reunited with Rani.

"Your sister is a very powerful woman, Anna. The markings will help her to focus her strengths. I promise you," Anwyl continued, "when you see her—"

"What? I won't notice them?"

"No, you'll notice, but..." Anwyl struggled with her explanation.

"It doesn't matter," Warin helped. "Anna, they are a part of her, as if the designs were meant to be there all along." Anwyl nodded her thanks. It was exactly the right thing to say.

"Claire always hid her gifts. Now everyone will know. How was she marked and where?"

Warin led Anna back to her seat. "She's beautiful, Anna. She's the same Claire, and more. And she no longer hides her gifts. Staying with the Fenrhi, being marked, her abduction...everything that happened to her made her stronger."

Anna settled back in her chair, smoothing her hands protectively over her growing belly.

"Warin, might Anna and I have a few moments alone? There are private matters about the Fenrhi that, as a woman, I can better explain. Please." She could see his reluctance to leave, but he did. When the door closed, Anwyl pulled her chair so that she sat knee to knee with Anna.

"What was done to Claire, without her consent, was wrong," Anwyl conceded. "My cousin and the other Artists...they lost their senses in their zeal to oust the Fenrhi Mother. But your sister has come to embrace the markings. And from what she shared with me before we parted in Ragallach, she has accepted her gifts and, if she does not win Trian's heart, she will be all right. You and your sister come from a very resilient and noble line."

"What do the markings look like?"

"I can show you, but I must have your word to keep this between us." When Anna nodded, Anwyl drew up her skirt, letting the folds settle high on her lap, baring her thighs.

"Oh, but they're beautiful," Anna breathed. "Are you Fenrhi?"

"No, but I was trained by both a Sylvan and an Umbren master. The Artists honored me by giving me these marks."

"Green for Sylvan and black for Umbren?" Anna guessed.

"Your sister has these colors, as well as indigo for Kena, dusty gray for Earth, and crimson for Blood. And underneath it all is the amber color of the honeycomb, signifying Mother. Her face is unmarked, and when we parted ways, her hair had grown to just below her ears." Anwyl pushed at the fabric in her lap, letting her skirt fall to the floor.

"If Queen Aghna had not returned when she did, my cousin would have done anything to secure Claire's hand for my brother. The people of Sophiana were, for the most part, protected from Diarmait. But the rest of Nifolhad…you must understand how horrible it was. Entire families disappeared, at least until the Fenrhi reopened the doors to Blood Caste for Diarmait and his men. Doing so took the pressure off the populace, but it also caused a schism within the Fenrhi ranks. Half of the Kena Caste have since quitted the temple. We don't know what happened to their leader, Rhiannon. And she is as powerful as your sister."

"And this is why the pijala trees are so important?"

Anwyl nodded. "Rhiannon sought to use Claire, to control her. My cousin believes she was *damaged* before she joined the Fenrhi, back when, as a child, she lived in Diarmait's palace. It's no excuse for what they did, but the Artists believed that if Claire had simply been marked for Kena, Rhiannon might have been able to control her. She never can now."

"Your mission—planting the trees and distributing the pihaberries—it's very important, isn't it?"

"More than you could ever know," Anwyl said quietly. Of the other reason for her being in Aurelia, she spoke not. It was why she hadn't allowed Claire to read her. She was making friends here: Anna, Claire, Tomas, and Ailwen. Even Warin, to some negligible extent. Her guilt at withholding vital information from them was a small burden, one she would carry until her brother advised her otherwise, or until she found proof of their suspicions. And once he did, she would speak to King Godwin and Queen Juliana before she told anyone else, for one could never really tell who had been influenced by a Kena. Not unless they were powerful enough, like Lady Claire.

• • •

Warin knew exactly what would lighten his mood as he strode toward one of the outlying farmhouses set well outside the curtain wall. The occupant, Derri, was a lovely, bright woman, one with whom he had dallied in the past. Her delicious stew, oven-warm bread, and intelligent discourse were exactly what he required. And if they fell into her bed afterward, all the better. He never visited a woman with the expectation of a tumble, but happily, that is where they usually ended.

Derri's husband had died years ago; her children were all grown and married with sons and daughters of their own. And Derri, because she was an efficient tenant and enjoyed her farming life, had stayed in her home and worked her parcel instead of moving in with one of her children. She and Warin had met at one of the many festivals Anna and Lark held at the keep. And though their first night together had been one steeped in wine, they woke the next morning, neither embarrassed. Derri was unapologetically open about her needs, and Warin saw to it that he never left her unsatisfied.

She had also made it clear from the beginning that she wanted nothing more from him than an occasional tip—as she liked to call it—if the timing worked and if they were both in the mood. A woman had needs, after all, and she did not wish to be involved with a local man because it would lead to unwanted expectations.

And now, once again, Warin stood before her door, hand poised to knock on the thick wood planking. It had been over a year since he'd visited, and although he knew they were more friends than lovers, he hesitated. She might have met someone. He frowned at that line of thought; he'd never second-guessed himself before.

"Is that you, Warin?" a familiar voice asked from behind him. Warin turned to find Derri coming up the path. "I'm pleased to see you returned safe and sound. Come here, so I can make sure you are whole." She pulled him into a fierce hug, then held him at arm's length to take his measure. "Something's troubling you, my friend."

Before he could deny it, Derri took his arm and led him inside. "Are you hungry?" She was already spooning stew into a large bowl. "Just make yourself useful and cut that loaf for me." He did and then slathered the crusty brown bread with butter. They ate their meal quietly, neither feeling the need to fill the room with conversation. When the last drop of his second helping was sopped up, they cleared the table, then went to sit by the hearth. Warin added more wood to the fire, while Derri opened a jug of cider and poured two large mugs. "Still haven't found what you've been searching for, have you?"

Leave it to Derri to get to the crux of his problem. He shook his head.

"Did you find Lady Claire?"

"I did. She's making her way to Trian as we speak."

She took his hand in hers. "So, you've been off on your adventure for over a year and haven't found true love. Did you think to locate it on your ship? Or in Nifolhad?" He knew she didn't expect an answer. "When are you leaving for court?"

"Before the week is through, I expect." He explained his current circumstances and his mission to deliver Princess Anwyl to Kings Glen. Surprisingly, Derri wanted to hear all about his charge, and he spared no detail from his description, from her well-meaning meddling to her insistence that everything be done exactly as she prescribed. "Lady Anna is inviting everyone to the castle for an impromptu celebration in the princess's honor. I'll introduce you, if you like."

"I should enjoy that very much."

He spent the rest of the evening regaling her with tales of his time in Nifolhad, from the finding of Claire in the midst of a fight with Diarmait's soldiers, to the reunion of Queen Aghna and King Ranulf. They sat quietly together after that, enjoying the fire and drinking their cider.

Warin hadn't realized how tired he was until he woke the next morning, slumped in the comfortable chair near the dying embers in the hearth. Derri had covered him with a blanket. As quietly as possible, he stoked the charred wood, adding more fuel until a merry fire burned. The store of firewood was nearly empty, so he slipped outside to restock her supply. And when he saw that hardly any remained that was split, he grabbed the ax. It was short work, and in no time, Derri had an ample reserve, one that would last a few days until her sons could replenish the pile.

Grabbing an armful, he strode back to the rear door of her cottage; she stood there, smiling at him. "I've breakfast inside. Did you sleep well?"

Warin fully expected to have a kink in his neck, but when he twisted his head and hunched his shoulders, he found that he was surprisingly limber. Hard work did much to relieve a man's aches. "Aye, Derri," he said, following his friend inside.

"You know that you will always be welcome in my home, Warin," she said later as they breakfasted on eggs and ham. "Always." And just like that, the terms of their friendship had changed. Their relationship as lovers had run its course and would only serve as an impediment to each of them finding something permanent. It had taken the year-long separation to make them see it.

"I expect you to dance with me this evening," Derri ordered as she saw him to the door. "After you introduce me to this princess of yours, that is." Warin was about to correct her; Anwyl was not *his* princess. But she stood on her toes, kissed his cheek, and then pushed him out the door.

He walked down the path leading to the lane that would take him back to the keep, the sensation of her hands pushing him out her door fresh in his mind. He came to an abrupt halt, standing all by himself on the lane. A memory, Anwyl's cousin Radha, someone else, and being pushed into a corridor with a single question hanging in the air—*You're sure he won't remember?* And as fast as the memory had flitted through his thoughts, it was gone. Warin frowned. Had the other person been the princess?

"What am I not supposed to remember?" he asked himself, earning an odd look from a passerby. And more importantly, why had the pihaberries he'd been consuming not protected his mind?

CHAPTER FIVE

Partners

"We'd best head down now, Princess. Doreen keeps a tight schedule. I'm still amazed that she's going to tell you the secret to making her pasties. How did you convince her to teach you?"

Anwyl smiled and winked at Grainne. "My secret weapon did all of the negotiating."

"Carry horsy?" Celeste asked hopefully.

Anwyl nodded and knelt down, and the toddler climbed, with Grainne's assistance, onto Anwyl's back. Thus secured, Anwyl stood and followed Grainne out of the room and down the corridor to the stairs that would bring them closest to the kitchen.

Earlier in the morning, Anwyl had met again with Anna, this time to give over both Stolweg and Chevlain's supply of pihaberries. They decided the best place to secure them would be in Doreen's larder. Under the cook's directions, the crates were placed in the cool, underground room. She and the cook spent a good hour going over different ways the berries could be incorporated into their meals. Returning to the kitchen, they had been greeted by Celeste. She had run in to show off her new crown. Doreen asked if she wanted a sweet, but she replied quite seriously that princesses only ate pasties. And that was how Anwyl had been invited to learn the secrets of Doreen's specialty—Celeste had asked the implacable cook to teach them, and Doreen couldn't refuse.

"Right on time, Princess," Doreen welcomed when they entered the vast kitchen. "There's an apron behind you. One for Celeste too." The little girl stayed interested for all of five minutes before Grainne took her over to a bench where they played with bits of dough, forming numbers and counting them. Soon Doreen and Anwyl fell into a companionable conversation interspersed with instructions regarding the finer points of her recipe.

They were taking the third batch from the hearth when Warin and Tomas stepped into the kitchen. Doreen moved to block Warin from reaching for the cooling pasties, waving him away with a large wooden spoon. "You just wait until later," she warned the guard, then turned to Anwyl. "I swear, the man can smell them from a hundred leagues away and comes running just when I take them from the oven. He eats them in two bites!"

"I've a year of missing your cooking to make up for," Warin pleaded from where he loitered near the entrance. "You make the best pasties in both realms—they're irresistible."

"That won't work with me, m'lord. Now off with you. We've more work to do."

Tomas laughed and slapped Warin on the back. "He bet me that he could charm at least three from you."

"Can I try one?" Celeste asked sweetly.

"Of course! You and Princess Anwyl are my official testers." Doreen turned back to Warin when he audibly scoffed. "Don't you scowl at Princess Anwyl as if she's stealing from you. She's spent all day with me, making the dough and the filler, and baking what will be your dinner...*if* you start behaving better."

"You taught *her* your secret recipe?" he asked aghast.

"M'lord!" Grainne admonished from across the room. Celeste was glaring at him. But Anwyl laughed, slipping several piping hot pasties into her apron pocket and winking at Tomas. He grinned and pushed Warin from the kitchen and out into the courtyard while Doreen sliced one of the steaming pasties into pieces for Celeste.

"I'll be right back, Doreen," Anwyl said. "I need to—"

"Don't think I didn't notice what you put in your apron." But she was smiling. "Go ahead now. They're best when they're hot."

"Thank you!" Anwyl exclaimed and kissed a surprised Doreen on her cheek before racing out of the kitchen and into the courtyard. She handed a pasty to Tomas first, whose thanks were profuse, then one to Warin. He took it, grudgingly, and she nibbled at the third.

"My word, Warin! You could at least thank the princess. She's risking Doreen's wrath after all."

"It's all right, Tomas," Anwyl soothed, chewing thoughtfully. "He's only upset that Doreen shared her recipe with me. Perhaps if you start being nicer, Warin, I'll make a batch just for you one day." She flashed a disarming smile at him as she turned to go back to Doreen's kitchen, happy for once how the afternoon had gone and not wanting Warin's bad humor to ruin her day.

"Thank you, Princess."

She stopped and turned back to him. He had said it quietly, and though it was sincere, Anwyl got the impression that Warin did not wish to be obliged to her. "It was nothing. Truly."

...

Warin rubbed the back of his head where Tomas had cuffed him.

"What is wrong with you, Warin? She was only trying to be nice. In fact, I think she might have actually flirted with you. Although I cannot fathom why, considering how you behave around her."

"Flirting? I think not, Tomas."

"Well, she didn't offer to bake pasties for me, did she? And we're friends."

Warin stared down at what remained of the still-warm pasty, somehow no longer wanting so badly to eat it. "I'm just tired," he claimed, as they walked back to the keep. If he were honest with himself, it wasn't because the princess had given it to him—he wasn't a petty man. His earlier good mood was gone, and the more he strived to identify the reason, the darker his thoughts turned. He'd been made to forget something by Radha, or the other woman who'd been in Ranulf's study. Ranulf's study! Warin finally remembered where he had been, but the revelation only led to another question with no answer. He would bet a bag of pearls that it had to do with the princess and something she didn't want him to know. He just had no proof.

In the space of returning to the keep and eating the cooling pasty, his mood had changed to downright sullen. Worse, he'd just been extremely rude to the princess. It wasn't her fault that Doreen was taken with her. He forced himself to take a bite of the meat pie she'd pilfered for him. Being responsible for a person's safety and not trusting them set his teeth on edge. And he wanted to trust Princess Anwyl, didn't he? Everyone else seemed to, even Claire and Anna.

Warin choked. Could his—dare he consider it?—angst stem from conflicted emotions where the princess was concerned? Tomas started slapping him on the back. Hard. "I'm fine, Tomas!"

"You were turning blue...well, not blue exactly. Teal perhaps. Seemed a good reason as any to hit you again. Damn!" Tomas swore. "I nearly forgot! This came for you after you departed Ragallach." He handed over a neatly folded packet, and Warin recognized the wax seal of his family's crest—a lunastra flower surrounded by three swimming river minks. The divot mark from the Pheldhainian pearl set in his father's signet ring never looked so ominous.

"I couldn't find you last night," Tomas explained. "It's the reason I came looking for you."

Warin took the packet. He should have written to his parents already, at least to let them know he was safely returned. "If you'll excuse me, Tomas, I need to read this. I'll see you later tonight at the celebration."

"Take a nap first," his friend cockily suggested. When Warin didn't respond with a clever barb, Tomas grabbed his arm. "You really are in the doldrums. You know, the celebration tonight might just be the thing to, er, elevate your mood. Maybe you need a night with a good woman."

He gave Tomas a rueful grin. He'd tried that already, though he wouldn't admit it to his friend. Tomas was right; he had to break out of this slump. Perhaps it was as simple as finding a change of company. Granted, he wasn't the same man he was a year ago. The game of hearts he played with the ladies at court no longer held the same allure. Warin took a deep breath, forcing the tension from his brow and the tightness from his jaw.

"Get some sleep, old man," Tomas japed, hitting Warin where it hurt him most.

"Only children need naps, Tomas," he called over his shoulder, determined to feel better. "I suggest you go find your bed."

"That's more like it," Tomas called after him as he left him behind.

Once in the privacy of his room, he opened the letter from his parents and read.

Warin,

I'll not start this letter by railing against you for your reckless adventuring. For if you are reading these words, then my prayers and those of your mother have been answered. I understand why you felt it necessary to try to save the Chevlain girl. We hope that you were successful in your quest.

Here in Pheldhain, there is unsettling news. A strange ship has been hounding the coastal smallholds. Our friends from the Southron Isles assumed it was one of our new vessels from Marach. When several ships from the Southron Isles were attacked, our old allies withdrew from us. You know full-well how sailors embellish their tales, and stories of this fantastical vessel abound.

Your brother, Marten, took up residence in the fort on Barb Island where he would be ready to give chase should this ghost ship appear in our waters. He did not have to wait long. The guards in Sea Tower reported that one of our ships

With expectations for your safe return to Pheldhain,
Lord Marin

Warin pulled a sheet of paper from his writing desk and shot his quill with ink. He wrote to his parents, assuring them of his good health and success in his mission, and briefing them on his current and unavoidable responsibility. When finished, he strode off to secure an able-bodied messenger. If only his father had given a description of the ship, he might be able to ascertain whether or not it was part of Diarmait's fleet.

Warin paused. Could he ask the princess what she thought? She'd spent considerable time on Nifolhadian ships. "Not quite yet," he said to himself before resuming his search for a messenger. No sense involving an outsider in his family's woes. That's when he saw the princess's maid scurrying toward him in the hallway.

"Are you lost, Daisy?" he asked kindly, not wishing to alarm the already skittish girl.

"No, m'lord," she replied and nervously dropped to a curtsy. She clutched a messenger packet to her chest as if worried he might attack her. Warin eased back a step, giving her some breathing room.

"Say, if you are giving that pouch to Grainne for the messenger, can you add this?"

"Of course, m'lord. Right away." She tentatively held out one hand, and without making any sudden motions, he placed it in her fingers. After thanking the strange girl, he returned to his chamber.

• • •

Outside, the festive courtyard was decorated with autumn foliage and strung with lanterns. Anwyl followed Grainne and Anna to the banquet tables where

Doreen was finishing putting the final touches on the food—an array of cold meats and cheeses with breads and fruit piled high on serving platters. The pasties they had made earlier had been set on trays in the center of the table. Another table held a cask of cider, and wine was on hand as well.

"Good evening, m'ladies," Warin greeted as he and Tomas approached—at least his mood seemed improved, Anwyl thought with relief. Before she could respond, a large group arrived, and soon the courtyard was filled with people laughing and eating.

"Derri, so good to see you!" Anna exclaimed and then bussed the newly arrived woman's cheek with a kiss. "How is your elbow?" She turned to Anwyl. "Derri had a run-in with a goat."

Warin frowned. "You should have told me. I would've chopped more firewood for you this morning."

It took every ounce of willpower Anwyl possessed to keep her face pleasant and composed.

"My arm is as right as rain." To prove her point, she playfully elbowed him in the ribs, then gave him an expectant look.

"Ah, yes, I promised, didn't I? Princess Anwyl"—he made a flourish with his hand—"allow me to introduce you to a good friend of mine. This is Derri."

"It's an honor to meet you, Princess," she greeted with a curtsy.

"Thank you," Anwyl somehow managed. "It's lovely to make your acquaintance."

Warin stepped back. "Well, ladies, if you'll excuse me for a moment, I think I'll find out why the musicians aren't playing."

"Remember, you promised to dance with me!" Derri called after him, then turned back to Anwyl. "I've never before met royalty, Princess. When Warin said he would introduce me to you, I was so excited."

"It's why I am here…to meet new people. And to give Nifolhad a face." Anwyl's smile was too broad; and she knew she was speaking too fast. She took the woman's arm in hers, though it was the very last thing she wanted to do, and led her to where Grainne and Doreen were making final adjustments to the tables. "You must be hungry. We made pasties."

As Derri pulled ahead to greet the others, Anwyl seized the chance to study her. Derri was a lovely enough woman but much older than Warin. No wonder Warin viewed her as a child.

Derri began helping Doreen and Grainne when more trays, these filled with sweets, arrived. Anna came over to stand next to her.

"Are you all right, Anwyl?"

"What? Oh, yes, of course."

"Come, I'll pour you some cider." The musicians struck the first chords of a lively tune, and Anwyl watched as everyone stood around looking at each other. She realized that they were waiting for her to begin the first dance, and because Lord Larkin was away...

"Princess, would you do me the honor?" Warin asked.

Anwyl nearly choked; she put her hand in his, and he drew her to the center of the courtyard. He was a superb dancer, and he expertly spun her in perfect time to the beat. Tomas then asked Anna to dance, and soon, others joined in. When the song ended, Warin stepped back and bowed before her. As he straightened, he hesitated, staring into her eyes, and for the life of her, Anwyl could not guess what thoughts were going through his mind. Another song commenced, and he escorted her back to the others. Tomas was first to beg the second dance.

For the remainder of the evening, she danced with many partners, but not one compared to that first dance with Warin. She could still feel the heat on her waist where his hand had rested. Not even the fact that she saw him dancing with Derri, and more than once, could dim her good spirits as the evening wound down and the guests began to depart for home. Soon the only people remaining were Anna, Warin, Tomas, Grainne, and Derri. The five of them sat down for one last cup of cider. Anwyl nibbled on one of the remaining tarts.

"It's been a lovely evening, Anna. The people of Stolweg are very kind."

"I'm so happy you enjoyed it." She smothered a yawn with the back of her hand. "I'd completely forgotten about Lark not being here to offer you the first dance. Thank you for stepping in, Warin. You saved us all from an awkward situation."

"Always happy to do my part when duty calls, you know that. Especially when there's a damsel in distress."

Anwyl added her laughter to the chorus of chuckles from the group, each completely oblivious to the fact that she had died inside, just a little, after his pronouncement. He hadn't asked her because he'd wanted to; he'd asked her because it'd been his duty.

"And speaking of damsels, I think it's time that I escorted Derri home. Stay here, my dear friend, and I'll saddle a horse."

Anna roped in Tomas to stack some of the benches on the tables, and Anwyl found herself standing alone with Derri.

"It was such a nice evening, Princess."

Anwyl nodded, and an uncomfortable silence stretched.

"Warin mentioned that he'll be escorting you to Whitmarsh soon. I've visited a cousin who lives there. And you'll enjoy meeting Lady Elnoura and Lord Baldric. They are fine people."

For once, Anwyl didn't know what to say. She felt that ridiculous smile spreading across her face and was helpless to stop it.

Derri looked wistfully around the courtyard. "Life at Stolweg was much different before Lady Anna and Lord Larkin. Lord Roger, Lady Anna's first husband, was an evil man; my husband died protecting me from his men. As for Warin, he's a good man. And he's only a *friend*."

Before Anwyl could deny Derri's implication, Warin returned leading a sedate palfrey.

"Ready?" he asked, lifting Derri into the saddle when she nodded.

"After all the dancing, a good night's sleep is what I'm looking forward to," Derri proclaimed. "And the faster you get me home, the faster you'll be able to return to your own quarters." Warin swung up into the saddle behind her with a confused expression, and Anwyl could swear that Derri gave her a meaningful look. Oh dear, was she that transparent?

"Princess, can I escort you back to your room?" Tomas offered.

Anwyl was suddenly tired—tired of chasing Warin, tired of trying to impress him, tired of pasting a smile on her face while inside her heart was breaking. And most of all, she was tired of forgetting her promise to herself whenever he offered her a kind word: that she had sworn to determine her own fate. Nodding, she took Tomas's arm.

"Good night, Anwyl," Anna offered, then put a motherly hand to Anwyl's forehead as if she were fevered. "Oh, I'm sorry. Habit. It's only that you look a little peaked."

"Just weary," Anwyl said. "I'll see you in the morning. Thank you again, Anna." Tomas led her away, and she barely remembered walking, but suddenly found herself before her door.

"Are you sure you're feeling all right?" he asked.

She nodded and thanked him, then slipped into the blessed privacy of her chamber.

With Daisy already retired to her own room, Anwyl sat near her hearth and pulled off her shoes. She barely had enough energy to take off her gown. The brisk autumn air filled the chamber, so she tiptoed quickly across the cold floor.

"Ouch!" Her bare foot had come down on something small and hard. She bent down to pick up the offending object and was surprised to find a small green pebble. "How…" It was one of her six—it must've fallen from her writing desk, though how it came out of its pouch, she could not fathom. She set it on the table to put away in the morning, then slid underneath her blankets. As she stared at the ceiling, the way it felt to be held in Warin's arms came unwelcome to her mind. She refused to cry. She vowed to do nothing that wasn't becoming of a princess of Sophiana. In two days, they would leave Stolweg, making their way to Whitmarsh, then Kings Glen. She had a mission, and failure was not an option.

Trials

As if someone had doused the only lantern illuminating a dark, starless night, the sun was likewise blotted out. Anwyl gauged the approaching storm, wondering when Warin and Tomas would return. They had started early that morning, crossing into the valleys and farmlands of Whitmarsh. Verdant copses dotted the fertile countryside, and the plethora of game animals under the shaded trees made no attempt at concealment as they rode by. Tomas had suggested they stop midafternoon so that he and Warin could try for a deer. Anwyl offered to see to the setting up of their camp and the organization of the horses and wagons. The men hired as drivers in Ragallach were efficient and hardworking. Of course, Warin had insisted on supervising until most of the work had been completed, and so he and Tomas started late.

Far off, thunder rumbled, deep and low. A wild gust of wind had the tent flaps whipping in the deepening gloom, and she raced to secure them. The gale ripped at the branches of the trees, rending the ochre- and rust-colored leaves from their limbs.

"Where are they?" she muttered as a more substantial rumble rattled the vale. The tempest twisted around the nearby trees, setting even the largest limbs to creak and groan in protest. When she heard a terrified whinny, Anwyl peered into the unnatural dark.

One of the wagon drivers was attempting to calm the draft horses but was blind to the peril of Anwyl's mare and Warin's and Tomas's steeds. Brave horses that they were, she could see they were becoming increasingly agitated, secured as they were to a lone oak tree about a hundred paces from the tents.

Boom! Anwyl actually ducked at the thunderclap. Two of the drivers ran from their shared tent, and Anwyl directed them to see to the wagon teams. She raced to the oak tree, reaching it just as the skies opened, pounding her head and back with what felt like fist-sized raindrops. She would have to be fast, for with the thunder, lightning was guaranteed, and the oak was the last place to which the horses should be secured.

She managed to unhitch her mare, made it halfway to where the wagons had been parked, when one of the drivers raced to her, taking her dainty mount's lead. She turned and ran back to the oak to retrieve the destriers. Tomas's horse was closest, and she'd begun loosening the already sodden slipknots when another volley of thunder rolled above her, deafening even the sound of the rain and making the muddy quagmire around her tremble.

"What are you doing?" Warin shouted, his voice barely audible over the raging storm. "Get back to the tent! I'll get the horses."

"Where's Tomas?" she yelled.

"Helping the drivers. Go! I have this!"

"There's not enough time!" Above them, the sky was roiling. "See to your horse." She ignored Warin and focused on the knot. It finally gave, and she took the lead and a handful of the steed's mane and swung up onto the stallion's back to ride toward the tents. She risked a glance at Warin; he had just freed his horse. The loudest thunderclap she'd ever heard cracked across the sky, and his horse bolted to catch Tomas's. Warin managed to maintain his footing and raced from under the oak. Tomas ran forward, snatching the lead of Warin's horse as Anwyl slid from his. She peered back into the gloom just as Warin's foot caught a tree root, sending him sprawling into the mud. She started toward him but was thrown back by a percussive force and a blinding lightning strike. She watched in horror as nature ripped apart the oak tree; Warin's prone body jumped straight up several feet before slamming back into the sodden earth. Ozone and smoke filled the air and wind-fanned flames engulfed the oak. There was a great rending of wood as an enormous branch ripped away from the trunk. And Warin, in the midst of struggling to his feet, was struck down once more.

She ran forward. The heaviest section had missed him, but he was pinned in a cage of lesser branches, flames moving aggressively toward him. Tomas and one of the drivers arrived, and together they shifted the heavy branch, allowing Anwyl to pull him free. He immediately rolled to his back to put out the flames on his tunic, then crab-walked backward while Anwyl grabbed him under his arms and tugged. A safe distance from the wrecked tree, Anwyl fell back, landing on her rear in the muck with a great splash. Warin scooted the rest of the way next to her, dazed and staring at what was left of the tree.

Then, as quickly as it had struck, the storm dissipated, moving south and away from them. The winds eased, and the sluicing rain lightened to a soft mist. To the west, the setting sun broke through the clouds in a spectacular show of light and color. The driver stumbled away to help the others, and Tomas dropped down next to Warin, his eyes as wide as saucers. Warin managed to sit up. Anwyl stared at them both, her expression no doubt as shocked as theirs. Warin's mouth opened, then closed, then opened again. After the howling of the tempest, her ears rang with the quiet around them. It was then that she noticed Warin's hair. As each strand dried, it sprang to attention. Anwyl did the only sensible thing she could after the insanity of the storm—she burst out laughing. Tomas, noticing as well, joined her. He reached out and waved his palm over her head, and Anwyl felt a tingling sensation.

"You, too, Princess," Tomas informed her. And they burst out laughing again.

"You could've been killed!" Warin shouted.

"Why are you yelling?"

"What?"

"Why are you yelling?" she asked louder.

He shook his head. "What?" he shouted again, touching his ears and coming away with bits of leaves, turf, and mud.

"Oh dear," Anwyl said solemnly, handing him a soaking handkerchief. She did her best to suppress a giggle; Tomas was not so circumspect and hooted with laughter.

Warin glared at him, dragging himself to his feet and pulling Anwyl from the ground as well. He set his hands on her shoulders, and her blood seemed to sizzle at his touch. "Don't *ever* act so recklessly again," he scolded. "You are more important than our horses." Then he lumbered away.

She swung around to argue. "Don't you—"

He stopped and grabbed her by her arms, pulling her closer as if he wanted to hold her against him, but reversed himself to push her at arm's length, as if he could not bear to have her so near. She felt scalded as his gaze ripped over her, no doubt assessing her for injury. And like the abrupt end of the storm, he set her away from him and stalked off, lurching in the direction of the wagons. Anwyl turned to see Tomas's reaction, but he had missed the exchange; instead, he stood staring at the burning tree as if it held the secrets of the world.

Anwyl gazed wonderingly after Warin and realized that no matter how much she tried to slip fate's noose, her heart still hammered in her chest when he was near. Love. Hate. Admiration. Disdain. For all the affection she held for him, she was miserable for it. His opinion of her had not changed one whit since the day he'd met her. And though they had months to travel still, it likely never would.

At least Tomas was a good companion. He'd kissed her once, true. And it had been pleasant; but the embrace had been nothing compared to the promised passion of Warin's lips. She had set Tomas straight, and he'd apologized, all without a single dint to his pride. In fact, if anything, he'd become a better friend, as if putting the awkward moment behind them allowed him to be himself around her. Gone were the silly compliments that would have most women fawning over him. Their conversations now were about their mutual interests—hunting, horses, and the art of quarterstaffs.

She had marveled at how the two guards, completely opposite in looks and charm, managed to have every female they met falling over themselves to capture their attention. Warin, with his dark hair, olive complexion, and suave manners; and the younger Tomas, a bright, fresh, and fair man, full of youthful charm. She would miss Tomas, for after Whitmarsh, she and Warin would continue to Kings Glen, and Tomas would return to Ragallach. Anwyl went back to her tent, her mood dampened by more than the weather.

• • •

The familiar and enticing aroma of bacon and the comforting noise of a busy inn roused Warin the next morning. Not for the last time, he was grateful that Princess Anwyl was an excellent horsewoman, and after the excitement of the storm, they'd started early the next day, making good time, and coming upon the Crossroads Inn earlier than he'd thought possible. Fortune had been with them, and some of the best rooms were available at the normally full hostelry. They agreed to a two-night stay to recuperate and dry out.

The last couple of weeks, the princess had grown more and more subdued, at least around him. With others, she was her usual bright and chirpy self. Warin wasn't sure why this bothered him, but it did. He dressed quickly and made his way to the common room where the princess and Tomas were already breakfasting.

"...if you really don't mind," Tomas was saying. "Good morning, Warin," he added, glancing at Warin's head and darting his eyes quickly away.

Warin's normally smooth, wavy locks were singed, and chunks stood out in frizzled clumps. He'd tried everything to calm the strands—washing his hair with soap, applying various oils, then washing it again when he couldn't stop sneezing from the oil. Nothing worked. He ran his fingers through his hair. Static pops winked on and off.

"Cider vinegar," the princess said.

"Pardon?"

The princess stopped the young serving girl who'd been sashaying by, trying, and failing, to capture the attention of the two men.

"How may I help you, Princess?" she asked brightly.

"I'm in need of another cup of vinegar," the princess replied.

"Oh, yes, of course," the girl said, examining Warin's hair, then hurrying off.

"Comb the vinegar through your hair," she explained to Warin. "Then leave it in for twenty or so minutes. It removes the static every time."

Warin eyed her hair. Her dark, wavy locks were smooth and shone beautifully in the morning light. He sat down and dug into the plate of cheese, bread, and bacon that had been set before him. The serving girl soon returned, leaving a cruet on the table. When Warin lifted the stopper, the pungent scent of vinegar replaced the delicious scent of his meal.

"Wrap your head in a cloth too. And cover your eyes so the fumes don't irritate them." She smiled at what must have been an incredulous look on his face. "Trust me; it'll work."

"You've been hit by lightning before, then?" he teased, unable to stop himself from flirting with her. He'd almost kissed her the day of the storm, so relieved was he that she was uninjured, and had vowed to better control his impulses. Her eyes widened, just a fraction, and then she laughed. And this time, it wasn't at his expense. It felt nice. Too nice.

"I'm happy to report that yesterday was my first lightning strike." She pointed to the cruet. "It's extremely cold on the Kaldemer Sea in the winter," she explained. "And dry. You've no idea the havoc it plays with a woman's hair"—she gazed at his energized mop—"well, perhaps you do." She leaned forward as if conspiring with Warin and Tomas. "I'll let you in on another secret—apple vinegar is also the best remedy for an inconvenient encounter with a striper."

"What's a striper?"

"Surely Aurelia has this animal," she exclaimed. "Small, black fur, with a white stripe from nose-tip to tail. Very smelly when threatened, but otherwise harmless."

Tomas burst out laughing. "We call them skunks here."

"Skunks," Anwyl repeated. "Yes, I like the sound of that. Anyway, cider vinegar works best if ever you find yourself on the receiving end of a...*skunk*."

Warin watched her as her face bunched up, indicating a bad odor when she said the word. It was charming. Perhaps the lightning bolt had fried more than just his hair. He held up his hands in surrender. "No, please don't tell us you—"

"All right, I won't tell you." But she held up three fingers and winked at him. And it was that action, the perfectly timed wink, that removed the blinders from Warin's eyes. Young silly girls did not wink at mature men; grown women did. A thousand possibilities raced through his head. He hadn't wanted to be attracted to her before because he thought her too innocent. Perhaps even too young. But now... No, it was impossible; any dalliance with the princess could prove disastrous to the peace between the realms.

"Are you sure you're well?" Princess Anwyl touched his hand, drawing his attention back to the moment. Her fingers were warm and soft against his skin, and he slowly drew his hand away. She frowned at him, curling her fingers closed and drawing them back to her side of the table.

"I am. Fine. I mean, I'm fine." She didn't look convinced. Neither did Tomas, for that matter. "Really. Probably just need to eat."

"If you're sure..." He nodded, and she rose from the table. Tomas stood next, and Warin looked from him to her as she took the young guard's arm. "I was going to ask if you wanted to join us," she started. "We're heading to the field behind the inn to practice quarterstaffs. The Fenrhi incorporate acrobatics into their practice, so I thought I would show Tomas some of the maneuvers."

"I'm afraid that I'm past the age of flying through the air," Warin grumbled, and the princess frowned. "Besides, I have a date with this cruet of vinegar." He said it lightly, wanting to erase the crease between her brows and wondering why that suddenly mattered to him. It was ridiculous, he knew, for he would have liked to see some of the Fenrhi-style fighting. He pointed to his half-eaten breakfast. "There are other tasks demanding my attention this morning."

"Try to get some rest afterward," she counseled, giving him an odd expression that he couldn't decipher. "You don't look yourself. I'll come to check on you when we're finished."

He watched his friend and the princess exit the inn. "Get some rest?" he said to himself. "I'm not an old man in need of a nap." But hadn't he just said the very same?

"What was that, m'lord?" asked the girl clearing away the empty plates.

"Nothing," he grumbled again. He stared at the door through which Tomas and the princess had passed. Seeing them on such friendly terms gnawed at his gut, as did the way Tomas's hand rested on her back.

He grabbed the remaining chunk of bread and cheese, picked up the cruet, and returned to his room. He would not *allow* himself to become involved with the princess. First, he'd sworn to protect her and see her safely to Kings Glen. Second, she was so much younger than he—a small part of his brain reminded him she was the same age as Lady Claire, a woman he once thought to wed. Third, a dalliance with Princess Anwyl might alleviate his boredom, but it would not see him closer to his goal: a woman he could love, one with a title and land in Aurelia; not some wandering expatriate from Nifolhad. And if those were not reason enough, the king and queen would never countenance such behavior on his part. He may have gotten away with the affairs and flirtations with some of the queen's ladies, but with a princess of the royal house of Nifolhad? Not for all the pearls in Pheldhain.

He didn't even like her, not really. "That rings false," he warned himself as he entered his room. Somehow, she had done the unthinkable—she'd grown on him. Well, it would be better for them both if he kept his distance. He would have to guard against flirting. Her wide-eyed expression when he'd almost kissed her after the storm came to mind. "Oh, hell, I'm not even sure if I trust her." The times that he had mentioned his missing cousin, she had claimed ignorance of having met him, then quickly changed the subject.

Adding to his mistrust of the princess was that he *knew* something had happened to him in Sophiana. That little forgotten moment teased his memories again. He shook his head; still nothing.

Warin poured the contents of the cruet into a mug and dipped his comb into it. The amber colored vinegar splashed, the morning light sparkling off the flowing liquid—*"Here, try this. It's even better than Nifolhad's best mead. Trust me, you'll love it."*

"What the hell!" Warin cursed. "What am I not recalling?" He focused on the words and the voice. It was familiar, and female. Was it the princess? Her cousin Radha? Queen Aghna? Or someone else?

The memory was as fleeting as a woman's skirts swishing from a room. No, he could not treat with the princess. An affair with her was not only unwise, it was the last thing he needed. Even if she'd looked so sweet, winking at him when she told him about the skunks. He set the vinegar down and faced the small looking glass before him. "Princess Anwyl is naught but a duty. Her safe delivery to Kings Glen is my only concern. I will not achieve my heart's desire with her." He repeated this several times aloud, trying his best to convince himself.

CHAPTER SEVEN

Insights

Castle Whitmarsh

Lady Kathryn of Morland continued to struggle with a difficult translation when her maid, Petra, joined her in Castle Whitmarsh's library. They had recently departed Kings Glen, stopping to visit her friends, Lady Elnoura and Lord Baldric, before continuing home to Morland. Kathryn set down her quill—Petra would not wait on pretense and would immediately launch into the reason for her interruption. She'd been with Lady Kathryn for years and knew best how to judge her mistress's mood.

"Begging your pardon, m'lady, but the Lady of Whitmarsh sent me. Warin of Pheldhain has arrived. And he's returned with a princess from Nifolhad. They are being greeted by Lady Elnoura and Lord Baldric and will then be brought to meet you in a few minutes." She paused to catch her breath, looking over her shoulder and then whispering, "If I may add..."

"Always, Petra."

"The princess appears...discomfited, m'lady. I can't put my finger on it, but something weighs heavily upon her."

Petra was more than a simple lady's maid-cum-companion. She was also a good friend, and Lady Kathryn had come to rely on her astute observations. She had a way about her, or rather, an old way. Too few people of Petra's ilk and talents remained in Aurelia, and if Petra said that there was something amiss with the princess, then something was amiss.

Lady Kathryn stood and smoothed her skirts when she heard voices in the hallway outside of the library. Just how long had she been working? She caught Petra looking at the unsightly creases on her gown with a wry expression.

"It'll be a couple of hours, m'lady, until a room can be made up for the princess and her maid." Then her friend swept open the door to reveal Lady Elnoura and a striking, dark-haired woman with the greenest eyes Kathryn had ever beheld. Even as weary as the princess appeared, she was exquisite. Warin, one of her son's closest friends, followed on their heels.

"Kathryn, I just knew you would still be working," Elnoura started. "We've a special visitor—Princess Anwyl of Sophiana." Kathryn stepped forward, and Noura made the introductions. Warin, ever the gallant, bowed low and then kissed her cheeks four times in the preferred greeting of the southern territories.

"Good afternoon, Lady Kathryn. You look as lovely as ever."

"Warin," she greeted, then turned to regard the young woman standing next to him. "Princess Anwyl, this is an unexpected and most pleasant surprise."

"I thought that the princess could rest here—the library really is the most comfortable room in the castle—while I see to accommodations for her, and Warin," Elnoura explained.

"I just can't imagine what happened to the messenger, Lady Elnoura," the princess fretted. "We sent a letter weeks ago to announce our impending arrival."

The Lady of Whitmarsh Castle waved her hand in the air. "I need no letter to welcome you to my home, Princess. Just a little time to make sure your room will be comfortable. And please, everyone calls me Noura."

The princess nodded, and when Noura departed, Lady Kathryn drew her deeper into the cozy room. She glanced back at Warin. "Warin, I am sure you would like to converse with Lord Baldric..."—He nodded as Petra shooed him from the library—"There's a good man."

As soon as he departed, the happy mask the princess had affixed to her features slipped.

"M'lady, if you'll excuse me," Petra said, giving her an I-told-you-so expression. "Princess, I will see that your maid is given quarters near yours."

"Her name is Daisy," the princess informed them. "Poor thing; I think she's homesick. Could you please make sure that her room is made up before mine?"

Petra nodded, then closed the door behind her. When Kathryn turned back to regard the princess, her serene façade was back in place. If it hadn't been for Petra's forewarning, Kathryn might have missed the momentary flagging of composure.

A wistful sigh whispered past the princess's lips as she neared one book-lined wall. "This room reminds me of home."

It was said so sadly that Lady Kathryn swept over to her and pulled her into her arms. Almost at once, the princess's staunch reserve collapsed, and she dropped her head and wept. "There, there, Princess. It can't be as bad as all that." She held the young woman, gently patting her on the back.

Princess Anwyl drew herself away and wiped her tears from her cheeks. "I'm so sorry, Lady Kathryn. I'm just weary of everything going wrong. Another lost message; one more hiccup in a very long line of mishaps. Lady Anna did not receive my letter either. I just hope the king and queen have received word from my brother and sister-in-law. My mare threw a shoe—twice. Somehow, the roof of my tent was torn when it was packed. Then—"

"Come, Princess. Let's sit by the fire; Petra is bringing refreshments, and I promise that your chamber will be ready soon. We'll have a bath sent up, and you'll be able to take a good long soak to chase the cold from your bones and wash away your worries along with the road's dust." She helped her young guest remove her traveling cloak. "This is damp; was it raining?" When the princess all but collapsed onto the couch, Lady Kathryn covered her lap with a blanket to ward off a chill. She handed her a goblet of the wine that she had been warming near the hearth, and the princess gratefully accepted it.

"It was sunny when we left the Crossroads Inn. By afternoon, there was a steady drizzle, one that lasted all night and into the next day. It rained the entire journey, only letting up early this morning. It was almost as if the clouds were tethered to the wagons. I don't mind rain, but this, it was oppressive. Tomas said he'd never seen it so dreary, and that he might as well have stayed in Ragallach. Then Daisy fell ill. Again. She really tried her best to be helpful, but she was near feverish. Warin used a tarp and my quarterstaffs to construct a lean-to in one of the wagons to help her stay dry. Poor girl. And then there was the problem with my tent." Anwyl took a sip of wine. "Oh dear, my apologies, Lady Kathryn. I shouldn't be bothering you with this."

"Don't worry about that, Princess. Tell me, what happened to your tent?"

"We didn't notice the tear in the roof until it was too late. Just my luck that my traveling trunk was underneath the hole; and open. Most of my clothes are damp." She gave Kathryn a beseeching look. "Oh, please don't bother Warin with that last bit. His mood hasn't been the same since he was struck by lightning and then set on fire by the tree that fell on him. And he had his hands full with so many other misfortunes, I didn't have the heart to tell him about my things. He would have insisted that we switch pavilions."

Lightning! That was a story Kathryn definitely needed to hear once the princess was rested. "No wonder you're upset."

The princess remained quiet, transfixed by the flames in the hearth, but her eyes shone with unshed tears. Lady Kathryn knelt before her and lifted her feet onto the couch before tucking the blanket around her. She took the goblet from her and set it on the side table, then placed a plump cushion next to her. "You just rest here, and I'll see what is keeping Petra."

The princess nodded and rested her cheek on her arm. By the time Kathryn made it to the door, she heard Anwyl's delicate snore. After her nap, she and Noura could give their lovely guest some much needed pampering. For now, Lady Kathryn had an assignation with a certain Royal Guard. Warin had caused more than his fair share of broken hearts, and she was sure there was more to Princess Anwyl's melancholy.

Petra slipped into the library just as Kathryn was leaving. "A messenger arrived," she whispered, handing over a packet emblazoned with the royal seal. "And I could not locate the girl, Daisy, though Lord Warin seemed unworried. He said that she was forever getting lost. Lord Baldric has the guards searching for her."

Kathryn opened the packet and immediately recognized her half-sister's script. She read the letter addressed to her, glanced at the princess, and then penned a quick response to the queen. "For the messenger," she told Petra, slipping her reply into the royal pouch and handing it to her maid. "Feed him, tell him he has two hours to rest, and give him a fresh mount. He must return to Kings Glen with all due haste."

. . .

"There's nothing to tell," Warin pleaded. "We finished planting the pijala trees in Ragallach and Stolweg, then traveled by the King's Road. I am quite looking forward to the end of this little assignment."

That Warin was not telling her everything was obvious. Kathryn narrowed her eyes, surprised that he could not see that which was so plain. Well, she wouldn't be the one to betray the princess's feelings.

"It looks like you will get your heart's desire, Warin."

"What do you mean?"

"I just received word from the queen that you and Princess Anwyl are to journey as expeditiously as possible to Kings Glen. An escort will be here in three days to take over responsibility for the saplings."

He sat up at that, looking suddenly brighter. Then he frowned. "The princess will not wish to be separated from her precious trees. Did the queen state her reasons?"

She did, but Lady Kathryn was not about to divulge the information to Warin, not when it concerned the princess personally. "There are matters of state to which Princess Anwyl must attend," she answered vaguely. "You'll have a week of rest here, then you must ride for Kings Glen."

"Does Princess Anwyl know?"

"Not yet. I have a letter from Queen Juliana for her; and one from her brother. When she is finished resting, she can read them."

An hour later, Lady Kathryn quietly slipped into the library. She had spoken with Noura, and they agreed that Kathryn would take the lead with the princess's care. Petra, too, would help, for word had come from the guards that Daisy had ridden off. She'd told the guards that she missed her family and would make her way back to Ragallach. Baldric had already sent men to track her down and, if they could not convince her to return, at least provide an escort to see her safely home. It was strange. Princess Anwyl had been genuinely concerned for the girl's welfare, and Daisy had not even left a note to say goodbye. She would not bother the princess with the news until she had a good night's sleep. Besides, perhaps Baldric's men could convince the girl to remain, at least until Kings Glen.

Lady Kathryn crossed the room to sit at Noura's desk. Princess Anwyl was just stirring, and when her eyes opened fully, she looked about her in clear distress over having fallen asleep as she had. "Do not fret, Princess. You've had a trying journey and deserved some rest."

"Please call me Anwyl," she begged, rising to wander around the library before making her way to Noura's desk and sitting across from Lady Kathryn.

"Only if you call me Kathryn."

"Agreed. I pray you'll forget my breach of etiquette earlier. I don't know what came over me. I haven't cried like that since, well, it's been years."

"That's too bad. I've always found that an occasional good cry can relieve so much. If only men would do it, perhaps they wouldn't be so battle-ready all the time." Kathryn handed the princess the letter from the queen. "These arrived for you while you were sleeping. The first is from the queen and king, no doubt welcoming you to Aurelia. The other is from someone dearer to your heart."

Anwyl broke the royal seal and began reading the first letter, then nodded. "I suppose if it's imperative to reach Kings Glen..." she said unhappily, clearly not liking the idea of leaving the trees behind. She eagerly opened the second letter. "It's from my brother." Her face grew more and more serious as she read. She finished, and then clasped it to her breast.

"I hope it isn't bad news."

"No, just troubling." Her gaze drifted over the papers spread out on the table where Kathryn sat, and she pointed to the piece of ancient text over which Kathryn had been toiling. "Where did you get that?"

"This? It's from Queen Juliana. I've been trying to decipher it." She moved it so that Anwyl could better study the parchment. "Some of the markings match those found on the henges here in Aurelia. I'm afraid its meaning has eluded my best efforts."

Anwyl rotated the paper forty-five degrees. "You've been looking at it sideways. Even if you knew what the markings represented, translating a coherent message would've been impossible from that angle."

Lady Kathryn's eyes widened as she looked back and forth between the text and her notes. "But how do you know this?"

"I wouldn't be much of a scholar if I didn't. I've studied those markings all my life, though I am amazed that you have a piece of the Six Tenets of the Fenrhi here, or rather one of the many copies that have been made over the centuries. This one looks very old; it could be a first transcription from one of the original exiflos."

Kathryn gave her an encouraging nod to expound.

Anwyl picked up a piece of blank paper and drew a hexagon. She next drew spokes from the center to each corner, dividing the shape into six equal wedges. "Do you see how the parchment tapers toward the top? The piece that you have would fit here." She expertly drew the fragment's shape onto her sketch, then elucidated more. "Each section represents one of the castes. The top of each page would have a hole in it, and all six pages would be set on a central peg so that they could be fanned out when on display. The petals are later furled for storage. What you have here is a tiny piece of one of the castes' petals, its rules, or laws."

"The Tenets of the Fenrhi. Tell me, are they a secret sect of women?"

"Not quite a sect, and secretive in their ways, but not secret."

"The Fenrhi," Kathryn repeated wonderingly. "So that is what they are called. We know so little of the history of Nifolhad. And always in the old scrolls, there are hints of a group of women. And a temple. Would you be willing to tell me about them?"

"I would be honored to share what I know," the princess said, then began making notes on the paper where she had drawn the exiflos. Petra and Noura slipped into the library, followed by Warin.

"I ran into these lovely women in the corridor and came to offer my arm to—" He looked over her shoulder just as Anwyl lifted her head to see who had interrupted them. Kathryn noted with interest that her earlier enthusiasm was instantly shuttered upon seeing Warin. "—You both," he finished.

"Thank you, Warin. But as you can see, the princess and I are in the middle of a complex explanation of a difficult translation. I must beg of you to forego our company this eve. We are on the cusp of a great discovery."

"Of course, though I would be happy to assist."

"Quite unnecessary. You see, it's a Fenrhi document, and Anwyl is apt to be more proficient than you in this. Noura, come take a look!" Kathryn felt only a little bad about dismissing her son's friend, and so added, "Thank you for your offer, Warin."

She noted that when he smiled, it did not quite reach his eyes. Bowing, he went to the door. "M'ladies, Princess, I bid you good evening then."

"Good night, Warin," the princess said distractedly, glancing up at him with a brief smile, and then digging back into her work.

Kathryn instructed Petra to bring their meal to the library. Both Petra and Warin departed, and Kathryn hurried back to her desk where Noura was looking at the document with interest. Anwyl had not been idle during the interruption. "If you have some shears, I could show you how the exiflos works."

"I do. But first, allow me to show you to your chamber where you can bathe and change into something more comfortable than your damp traveling clothes. We can meet back here in an hour."

"I will only need half that time!" Anwyl promised, her energy returned.

"Excellent."

Hours later, the three women still had their heads together as Anwyl made a simple wheel, or flower, of the Six Tenets. She instructed them on the basics of four of the six castes, writing on each of the petals:

Earth: duty and sacrifice – the artisans serve in Earth Caste
Sylvan: empathy and intuition – the healers
Umbren: protectiveness and honor – the shield maidens
Kena: enlightenment and truth – the seekers of truth and knowledge
Blood: passion, love, birth, and death – all can serve
The Mother: unity, clarity, and harmony – there is only ever one

"There would be layers of petals, you see, and multiple exiflos, each devoted to a single topic, defining how each caste would relate to the topic and to each other." She drew the Fenrhi symbols unique to each caste. Lady Kathryn studied the fragment of Fenrhi text, looking back and forth between it and the symbols Anwyl had drawn.

"This bit is from Sylvan," she declared.

"Yes!" Anwyl exclaimed. "You already see the similarities."

"But what does it mean?"

The princess frowned.

"What is it, Anwyl?"

"First, you must understand, the castes were formed to serve each of the other castes, with the Mother serving all. For Umbren, training in defensive arts as well as stealth and, well, killing. The Sylvan aid their sisters with healing. In order to cure, they must first understand the poison."

"And be able to replicate it," Kathryn guessed.

"More than that, I'm afraid. When necessary, the Sylvan provide poison to the Umbren Caste."

"Indeed."

"Fenrhi writing is highly nuanced and subtle. It is often meant to mislead. This is a small piece of a single petal from a single layer of an exiflos on a certain type of poison and its cure. Without the entire petal, nay, the entire layer, it would be impossible to replicate the recipe."

"How do you come to know so much about them?"

"My cousin Radha is one of The Artists, and belongs to Kena, though she can only read impressions of what will be. It was her artistic talents that ensured her an important position within the temple." Of course, Kathryn and Noura needed to hear all about The Artists, which then led them to discuss the Kena and how they had tried to take over the other Fenrhi Castes.

A knock on the door interrupted them, and Noura had to excuse herself.

"Princess Claire could tell you more about the Kena."

"Princess? You mean Lady Claire of Chevlain? What has she to do with these Kena?"

"Oh, dear. I may have misspoken. Her story is not mine to tell. I'm sorry."

Kathryn put her hand over Anwyl's. "Claire is my son's sister-in-law. She and I have grown close over the years. I have long suspected that she had some special talents, similar to Petra's. But I understand your hesitance. Why don't you just tell me what you know of the Kena?"

Princess Anwyl nodded. "To be honest, I know the least about Kena Caste, and even then, it would take weeks to impart everything." She paused. "You asked earlier if I had received bad news from my brother. He wrote to tell me that the Fenrhi Mother, Ni'Mala, has had a vision regarding my future. The current Fenrhi Mother's beginnings were simple, but she displayed the much-revered talent of foretelling not just another's fate, but the possibilities that might unfold if they were to take different actions. She saw that if I were to return to Nifolhad, it could cost me my life. For the foreseeable future, Aurelia will be my home and the success of the pijala trees will remain my mission."

"Why are these trees so important?" Kathryn then asked.

"They produce a very special fruit called the pihaberry." The princess pulled a small bag from inside her tunic, opened it, and spilled a few dried berries onto the desk.

"I've heard of these," Lady Kathryn exclaimed, "from the captains who sometimes make port in Morland."

"Try one," Princess Anwyl recommended and smiled at Kathryn's astonished expression as she chewed the sweet fruit. "Delicious, aren't they? They also clear the mind and can even prevent the manipulation of one's thoughts and actions."

Kathryn felt the effects immediately. "Manipulation by the Kena, you mean?"

The princess nodded. "Those of royal blood should be immune. For others, the pihaberries are an effective defense. It is our hope that we can find a suitable clime here in Aurelia, a place where the trees can flourish, making the seeds available to all. A gesture of goodwill," Princess Anwyl reiterated. "The wholesome benefits of the fruit are multifold, and the medicinal uses are too numerous to count. As for the Kena, I have seen how they are able to manipulate those with weaker minds—my brother and I made sure the fruit was available to everyone in Sophiana; it is part of the reason Diarmait's spies were unable to infiltrate our borders.

"As Aghna and Rani liberate more and more of Nifolhad, they intend to give the fruit to all of their subjects. Unfortunately, Sophiana is the only place where the trees thrive. Diarmait has tried, unsuccessfully, to locate and destroy our orchards. If we can find a suitable clime in Aurelia for the trees, we will never have to worry about their extinction. Unfortunately, saying that the propagation of the pijala tree is challenging is an understatement."

Kathryn nodded. Her already sharp mind was now honed to a keen edge, and she noted how deftly Princess Anwyl had sidestepped her question about the Kena. She would learn Petra's take on the young woman before forming her own opinion.

"Lady Kathryn, there is more that I wish I could tell you," the princess added as if reading her mind, "but I have been instructed to speak with your queen and king first. I will make sure that your sapling pairs are separated from the wagons, as well as a supply of pihaberries to take with you when you leave for Morland."

"Thank you, Princess," Kathryn said, liking her more for her forthrightness. "I would like to join you tomorrow when you transplant the trees here."

"I'll be honest. I know they will grow and bear some fruit, but I think Whitmarsh is too tame a territory for their liking."

"Then they should do well in Morland; we've still a bit of wild in our land."

• • •

Less than a week later, Kathryn found herself missing Anwyl. The young woman had insinuated herself into her heart almost as much as her daughter-in-law, Anna. Queen Juliana must be made aware of the princess's unhappiness, which, as far as Kathryn could determine, was due to an acute lack of close friends with whom to confide. She pulled out a sheet of paper to write to her sister. The day before, another messenger had arrived from Kings Glen, bearing a copy of an ancient Aurelian text, one that had ties, strangely enough, to the Southron Isles. The messenger was waiting now for Kathryn's reply and, with a fleet mount, would make it to Kings Glen before Anwyl and Warin. It was time for Kathryn to return to Morland and to her own library, where she could reexamine her collection. Thanks to the princess, she could study her scrolls with fresh insight.

My dearest sister, Juliana,

I only knew the young woman for a week and already I feel the absence of Princess Anwyl in my heart. She has the capacity to make the dreariest of days bright, and I will miss her keen intellect. You may be assured that she is more than a courtly princess from Sophiana, even if Warin presents her otherwise. She is a trained scholar, one of the highest caliber, especially for one so young. She has the rare ability to see nuances and subtleties in even the most arcane text. It is almost as if she draws from the minds of the ancient writers their original intents and thoughts. More, she sees scholarship not as many do—a thing to be coveted and held close as a secret—but as a gift to share, as if by doing so, she is helping to enlighten our world. She is, in a word, remarkable.

But the princess is also homesick, sister. Keeping her occupied with the translations did much to alleviate her unhappiness. Imagine how pleased she would be if she had access to your library. She expressed an interest in learning about the Southron Isles, for it is one area where she feels she lacks instruction. Of course, materials regarding these mysterious lands are nearly as impossible to procure as the information regarding a secret temple of women in Nifolhad— they are called the Fenrhi, by the way, and the princess has promised to tell you all about them. Queen Aghna and Prince Ranulf gave us a valuable jewel when they sent Anwyl to our shores.

I hesitate before divulging the following to you. But I, like you, cannot resist the chance to play matchmaker. I fear that Anwyl will need more than your library to ensure her happiness. For months, she has subsisted with the company of Warin. And while I believe that he has been nothing but respectful to her, a friendship did not form between the two. This, I am sure, will surprise you, considering how comfortable Warin is around women, especially those with keen minds. They have so many common interests: sailing and scholarship being the greatest. In fact, I would hazard that neither knows of the other's interest in the latter.

To this end, I suggest that we recruit Ladies Caroline and Beth's assistance in making sure that the princess has confidants at court. Lady Murel is the same age as Anwyl, and I have written to her uncle, Lord Marin of Pheldhain, requesting that she be sent to Kings Glen. If she were to travel by one of Lord Ronan's new ships, she could arrive near the same time as the princess. Both new to court, I am sure a bond would form between the two women. I have, dear sister, acted on your behalf in this matter, as I know that you would see the wisdom in doing the same.

In an unrelated matter, both the Princess and Warin have expressed concern over the delivery of messages between the territories. Letters sent by them to give advance notice of their arrival never made it to their destinations. Of course, these letters were not sent by Royal Messenger. I am sure it is nothing, but it is better to err on the side of caution. To that end, I will send one of my men to accompany your messenger, who is right now waiting for this reply.

Pray, give my best to my brother-in-law and king and my nephews, the princes, and their families.

Your loving sister,
Kathryn

Post Scriptum: The princess made mention of certain visions regarding her future. She was loath to discuss them, so I did not press her. But there is something about the princess's presence here in Aurelia that may warrant another look at the translations we've made thus far concerning the prophecy we've unearthed.

Lady Kathryn dusted, then folded the paper, and placed her seal upon it. There was a tapping at her door, and she looked up. "Perfect timing, Petra," she greeted as her maid brought in her meal. "Please locate Farnum and tell him to pack a change of clothes and some supplies. I want him to ride with the messenger to Kings Glen." Petra nodded, but Lady Kathryn was already pulling out some of the translations that she and the queen had yet to finish. Petra had said something to her, so she stopped and looked up. "What was that?"

"Don't forget to eat, m'lady," her friend ordered, smiling. Petra knew her well indeed.

Masquerade

Early Spring, Kings Glen, Aurelia

"Please do not tarry, Princess," Lady Caroline counseled, as if she knew that was Anwyl's exact intent. "The musicians will soon recommence. I promise you, the evening will grow more diverting now that everyone has had the chance to rest and take refreshment. Certainly, the dancing will be less regimented." Lady Caroline checked her reflection and adjusted her mask one last time. Lady Shan had gone on ahead with Murel and several others who had finished their toilette in the lounge reserved for the queen's ladies.

"I'll be along presently," Anwyl stalled.

"I'll give you five minutes. Any longer, and I'm coming back to find you. No sneaking off to the library," her friend observed too shrewdly.

Anwyl's eyes widened; that had been her plan all along. "I promise," she said, though she knew her heart wasn't in it. Lady Caroline, mollified, swept from the room.

Alone, and at peace from all the chattering, Anwyl cursed in the most un-princess-like fashion. Nearly every night boasted some event or another, and the endless evenings were taking a toll on her patience. Thankfully, this would be the last for some months. Spring had come early to Kings Glen, and the crated pijalas had begun to bud; they needed to be put into the ground. In two days' time, she would travel through the Aurelian Smallholds, delivering a pair of saplings to those chosen by the king and queen. The royal orchard master would see that other saplings were delivered to Cathmara in the north, and Pheldhain, Sterland, and Chevlain to the southwest. "Bother," Anwyl groused; Warin had been assigned to accompany her. At least Tomas would be with them on the journey, though they would part ways once they reached Floresta where his family held title. Anwyl longed to visit Claire and Madyan at Chevlain, for she had made no progress on her mission and needed their counsel. Months ago, she had written to Rani to ask his advice and had yet to receive a reply. A visit to Chevlain and to the two people in Aurelia who would most understand her predicament would alleviate her guilt for not being honest with her new friends, but it was not to be.

As for Warin, she hadn't seen much of him since coming to Kings Glen. Perhaps he wasn't her dark haired, blue-eyed stranger after all; the tug on her heart belied that thought.

Anwyl studied her reflection in the looking glass and pinched her cheeks to pinken them, remembering too late that she needn't have bothered, for she would be covered by her mask before rejoining the festivities. It had been Lady Murel's idea, dressing in the garb of the Fenrhi women.

Stories of Princess Claire's exploits in Nifolhad had circulated throughout the realm. And with the tales, some taller than others, the women of the Fenrhi Castes had taken on an air of fantastical mystery. Only three people in the realm were well-enough versed on the true history of the women across the sea, and two of them were enviously tucked away at Chevlain. No matter how factual Anwyl's descriptions of the castes had been, the nobles would embellish her accounts to the point of ridiculousness.

Her friends at court—Ladies Caroline, Beth, Murel, and Shan—had seized upon the idea of dressing in the traditional costume of the Umbren. Anwyl smiled. Lady Caroline had taken Shan and Murel—both ingénues to the games and intrigues found at any royal court—under her wing and had enlisted Anwyl's help in steering the two awestruck women down a respectable path, one that veered away from a few of the more intent-on-seducing-the-maidens lords and guards. It mattered not that Princess Anwyl was younger than both Shan and Murel; she possessed, according to Lady Caroline, the unimpeachable demeanor and comportment of royalty. She need only lead by example. If only Lady Caroline knew how often Anwyl was tempted to run off to find some secluded pond or lake where she could strip off her trappings and swim under the wan light of the moon, unmolested by probing and curious stares.

She reached for her mask but found it missing. All five women, fast friends now, had dressed in the dark tunics and leggings of the Umbren—daring indeed for women to dress so in Aurelia; few could get away with it. And though Anwyl's was the only authentic costume, they each had sashes about their waists and the high leather Fenrhi boots encasing their legs and feet, declaring their femininity to lord and Royal Guard alike. Each wore a cape and hood to hide their hair and shadow their features, thus making them indistinguishable from one another. Fantastic designs had been painted on their hands and exposed wrists to mimic the markings of the Fenrhi Castes. And finally, they disguised their faces with dominoes—one each of Sylvan green, Kena blue, Earth gray, Umbren black, and the soft-honey color of the Fenrhi Mother.

Anwyl's mask was the dusty gray of Earth Caste. "There you are!" she exclaimed upon espying it on a nearby bench. She set it in place, pulled up her hood, and gave herself one last cursory examination. She turned her head to see better in the light of the lamps set near the looking glass; the molded silk was the color of honey. Lady Beth had taken the wrong mask.

"No matter. I'll find her, and we'll make the switch." Such was her plan when she departed the well-appointed room to rejoin her friends.

She could hear the musicians pluck up a new tune, one with a lively beat, and by the time she made it to the entrance of the Royal Hall, the dance was in full swing. She saw her four friends whirl past in a blur and was content to stand on the edge and enjoy the scene. Suddenly, the delicate hairs on her nape lifted. She knew without turning that it was Warin who had come up behind her. Anwyl wanted to say something to him, if only to prove to herself that she had control of her faculties, but her words stuck in her throat like thick porridge.

"Lady Beth," he greeted, his tone pitched deeper than usual as his gaze slid to the amber-hued mask. The seductive timbre of his voice vibrated through Anwyl's core, causing her to shiver. Who was she trying to fool? She would always be fascinated by Warin, even now, after her friends—thankfully oblivious to Anwyl's infatuation with the guard—had chronicled his past flirtations, though they both ruefully admitted that it had been some time since he'd indulged in their feminine wiles.

Anwyl's heart nearly stopped when his hand slipped under her cape to run his fingers up and down her back. Her posture softened toward him, and she couldn't help herself and sighed, her exhalation a clear announcement of her desire for more. Warin stilled, then slid his arm possessively around her waist, pulling her closer. Anwyl knew she should stop him, had been about to protest, but he pulled her from the Royal Hall, down the corridor and deeper into the castle. He didn't stop until he came to a dimly illuminated passageway—Anwyl recognized it as the one leading to the library.

"It's been a long time since we dallied," he said, drawing her into her favorite place in the whole of Kings Glen. "I had not thought that you had any interest in rekindling what we once shared."

Their hurried departure from the hall had left Anwyl breathless, and she searched her brain for a polite way to point out his error in identification. But he was holding her by her waist, his arm and hand warm and heavy against her, and she could think of nothing to protest. The room was lit only by the dying embers in the hearth, and when he turned her to face him, Anwyl was rendered mute by the deep blue of his gaze. Her own features were made indistinct by her hood and domino, and she doubted that even the slightest hint of her bright green eyes was visible. His smile dripped with sin, and he pulled her closer to him, so close her body was molded to his muscled torso.

In Sophiana, Anwyl had been courted by several young lords of Nifolhad, had even kissed a few, but they were mere acorns to Warin's full-grown oak. The wild bird that had replaced her heart ricocheted in her chest, seeking escape. Any thought of revealing herself evaporated when he leaned forward to press a kiss to her lips.

And heaven help her, she kissed him back. Willingly. Wickedly. Of course, Warin would never see her as anything but an addlebrained princess, so she was determined to take advantage of this one chance. She'd long pined for such a moment, to know what it would be to kiss him instead of always wondering if her dreams were simply foolish fantasies, built up into fairy-tale proportions. Besides, he would never know it was she who he kissed, so what harm?

Their embrace intensified, and he drew her tighter to him, seemingly as lost as she. He caressed the sensitive skin on her neck, massaging her nape and behind her ear with his thumb. Anwyl responded by deepening the kiss, daring his tongue to play court with hers. She thought the action impossible yet managed to press her length even closer to his long body, drawing forth a satisfied snarl from him. Her hands came free of her cape, and she dragged them up and over the hard planes of his chest. He nipped at her lips, her chin, the edge of her jaw, and she gasped, unable to stop herself. She could feel his heart, where her hand rested over it, pounding inside his chest. When he cradled her breast through her tunic, she moaned and drew his face back to hers with an urgency that demanded all his attention. He shifted their bodies so that she was pinned against a wall of books, and Anwyl's mask nearly slipped free from its securing ribbons. She barely managed to catch it and turned her head, panting from their exertions.

"Lady Beth?" he whispered, sounding lost, and it was a cold and hard reminder to Anwyl that Warin would never willingly kiss her. His passion would always be reserved for other women. "Beth," he whispered again. "I don't—"

She was wrong to have fooled him, and she placed her fingertips to his lips to stop him from saying more. She couldn't survive hearing his words of endearment and passion meant for another. She shook her head, and he took her fingers in his hand and pressed kisses to their tips.

"Beth," he insisted in a hushed voice, "I didn't expect—" They froze at the sound of approaching voices, and he pulled her to a shadowed alcove in the bookcases. "Stay here," he ordered softly. "I'll not let anyone discover you." He lifted her knuckles to his lips and brushed a kiss against them, then strode to the door.

The voices grew more distinct, and Anwyl recognized one as belonging to the odious Lord Herlewin's mother, Lady Eunice. No amount of refusal by Warin would deter Lady Eunice once she caught scent of a scandal. If she were discovered here, alone with Warin, then Lady Beth's reputation would be forever tarnished. Worse, the queen might force a marriage! Anwyl could never do that to her friend.

For months, the princess had spent the better part of her days exploring the Royal Library; she knew the room as well as the king and queen did. While Warin held the door nearly closed with his boot, she lit one of the oil lamps, turning the flame to the lowest level. Silently, she felt her way across the far wall, searching. When she found the tome she sought, she tipped it forward; the entire shelf shifted back. Anwyl pushed it, opening the gap just enough to slip away. Warin was busy blocking Lady Eunice from entering, and so hopefully did not notice her egress. Using the secret passage she'd discovered months before, she hied back to the Royal Hall unobserved. She located Lady Beth and gestured desperately to her friend.

"My dear Princess, why are you wearing my domino? Good gracious! I took yours by mistake, didn't I? No wonder Lord Herlewin was so intent on dancing with me." Anwyl pulled her friend away and out of earshot of the revelers. "Why are you carrying that lamp?" Beth must have finally noted her distress, and asked, "Anwyl, what happened? Are you all right?"

"Yes." She hastily handed the lamp to a passing servant. "I'll tell you, but you must promise to never tell another soul that our costumes were confused."

"Of course, on my honor," Lady Beth vowed. "Now tell me, what is amiss?"

"Well, just as Lord Herlewin mistook you for me, so, too, did I inadvertently confound Warin."

"Oh dear. I may have let my identity slip when we danced earlier. But Warin and I are friends, Princess. Why should that be a problem?" Anwyl pulled her masque away and traded with Lady Beth. She was blushing, and she was sure her lips were red and swollen. She quickly put her own domino back in place. As Lady Beth did the same, Anwyl was inexplicably compelled to look toward the Royal Hall's entrance. Warin had arrived, and as if drawn by the same unseen force, he homed in on her. Even from across the room, she saw the uncertain cock of his head before his gaze turned from her and fell full-bore on Lady Beth.

"Good gracious," Lady Beth observed when she noticed his determined gaze as he began the arduous trek of weaving his way through the revelers to reach them. "Tell me what happened. Quickly!"

"He thought I was you."

"Is that all?" She sounded relieved. "It's been years since he and I…"

"We kissed," Anwyl rushed to admit, "in the library. And he… We… It was…"

"Good gracious," Lady Beth pronounced again.

"Stop saying that! What am I going to do?"

"Leave Warin to me. I can handle him. Now hurry away…you won't want to be here when he reaches this alcove. He's smarter than any man I know and will sense that you are exercised."

"He can never know it was me, Beth," Princess Anwyl entreated, and her friend drew an X across her heart.

"Did you at least enjoy it?" Anwyl felt her face and neck flush red, and Lady Beth hid a smile behind her hand. "Good graci—sorry."

Nothing good about it, Anwyl thought angrily as she skated past Beth and then slipped away from the revelers into a corridor meant for servants. Her anger at herself was only eclipsed by the ire she felt toward Warin. She'd spent the last year tamping down her feelings for him until they were less than dust. Then the oaf of a man swept in and stirred them up. And she just *had* to know what it would be like to kiss him, didn't she? She made it to her chamber, relieved that her maid was absent, and tore off her domino and threw back her hood. The imprints of his lips on hers and his hands on her body still burned. She was cursed to live the rest of her life knowing that which was possible but would never be. She could almost hate him for it.

When he'd finally rid himself of the cloying Lady Eunice and her friends, Warin had wheeled around to resume his conversation with Lady Beth. His smug satisfaction at having thwarted the indomitable Eunice had been quickly squashed upon finding that there was no damsel in the library to protect. The fact that Lady Beth couldn't have flown out of the high window did nothing to refute the fact that she had disappeared. Warin was abashed to discover that he was not cognizant of every secret passage, secluded alcove, and hidden niche in and around the castle. He'd had to thrice search the shelves before locating the book that was askew. He wondered when and with whom Lady Beth had discovered its existence, for though she was an intelligent woman, she was not known for her scholarly pursuits.

His thoughts returned to the incendiary kiss. He'd never felt the like, not with any woman, and certainly never before with Lady Beth. Certainly, he'd enjoyed the time he spent with the women at court and around the realm, but never had he lost control of himself as he had this evening. And over a simple kiss, no less! If Lady Beth had not had the wherewithal to turn away from him, he might've taken her there, pressed against the books that he so loved, with no concern for the fact that there would be no escaping—at least, he hadn't thought there was—notice of any daring to trespass into the Royal Library. Only Lady Eunice's cackling laughter had saved them from being caught.

Warin growled as his route to Lady Beth was impeded again and again by the dancing revelers. He couldn't account for what had happened and was almost sure that Lady Beth had been as shaken as he by the unexpected flare of passion between them. Losing his head over a woman, one he'd trifled with before, *and* a good friend, was not only inexplicable, it was unacceptable. If he didn't kiss her again, and soon, he wouldn't be able to prove to himself that it had been a fluke. A result of the masquerade, perhaps.

The constant shifting of dance partners had thrown him off his direct course, and he frowned, pausing to reestablish his bearings. And like an osprey sensing its prey beneath the waves, his gaze pierced through the visual assault of vibrant costumes swirling and weaving before him to the alcove where Lady Beth waited. He made straight for his target.

"Warin," Lady Beth greeted, calm and collected and in complete opposition to his own comportment. "About what happened in the library..."

CHAPTER NINE

The Sea Hare

Kantahla, Nifolhad

"We got a right good price for that wool, Cappy," Dugan congratulated, his voice pitched low. "More'n enough to buy the silks and sail home with a tidy profit."

"That we did," Captain Juna agreed, resisting the urge to pat the fat coinpurses he'd strung around his middle and under his tunic. Trading had improved since the new queen and king had risen in Nifolhad, but not in Kantahla. There were cutthroats lurking around every corner, and he regretted sending three of his men ahead to buy the silks, thus splitting his forces.

The other captains from the Southron Isles refused to barter in Kantahla, preferring the safer ports of Naca'an, Anvyr, and Sophiana. But rumors were that the sanctions on Kantahla, both from Queen Aghna of Nifolhad and King Godwin of Aurelia, were taking their toll on the seat of the Steward King. If *The Sea Hare* hadn't been so damaged by that freak storm, he would never have risked making port here. He needed coin, and a goodly amount, and the merchants in Kantahla had paid premiums for his goods.

Ahead, the alley narrowed.

"Stay alert," he cautioned. Dugan, his first mate, and a sailor named Crespin loosened the ties on their scabbards.

No sooner had he made the pronouncement than three burly men ranged out across the alleyway. "Three more farther back," Dugan hissed, drawing his sword. The captain was confident that he and his men could handle these ruffians; they didn't appear to be trained in swordplay.

"Now, now," the lead thug began, his voice muffled by the rag that covered his lower face. "No need for weapons. Just hand over your purse, nice-like, an' we'll be letting you on your way with nary a tickle."

The captain drew his sword in answer, and the attack was on. Their fairest chance would be to break through the forward obstacle, then race back to the ship. Only seconds remained before the aft attackers reached them. Juna was first to charge the would-be thieves, sword drawn. His men followed. But he'd made a fatal error—the ruffians had more than rudimentary training.

While the captain and Crespin took on the forward threat, Dugan turned to intercept the fastest of the three running toward them from the rear. Juna wounded one adversary and turned to take on another when Crespin was dealt a deadly blow. Dugan, after wounding his man came to stand back-to-back with his captain. "They mean to kill us, Cappy."

"Aye, but not before we do some serious damage." He thrust his blade into the gut of one of the attackers. At the same time, Dugan was struck and fell to the cobbled ground. The captain dragged him against the wall and stood facing his assailants.

"Five men against one? Where's the game in that?" The questions had been asked by a plainly dressed man who had happened upon the scene.

"It's none of your concern," the lead thug snarled. "Best be gone, or you'll end up skewered."

The man touched his finger to his cap, then proceeded on his way. Cowardly bastard, Juna thought, and raised his sword against the five advancing men. If he was lucky, he could kill one of them before they took his life. The sound of a sword slithering from leather gave his heart small hope as the lone man turned back and attacked with great vengeance. The battle was swift, and the gang's leader was knocked to the ground. Juna used the distraction to take out one of the others, while, with the grace of a master swordsman, the newcomer pivoted and knocked down another. The only man left uninjured looked at his bleeding friend, dragged him to his feet, and together, they hightailed it up the alley.

"My gratitude," Juna panted. The man nodded while the captain helped Dugan to his feet. "I'm Captain Juna. That's Dugan, my first mate."

"I go by Dorn." He peered down the alley. "They'll be back with reinforcements," he warned. "You'll need to make it back to your ship if you want to live."

"I won't leave Crespin's body here," Juna stated, giving his arm to Dugan as he struggled to his feet. "Can you make it, man?" Dugan's leg was bleeding from a gash that ran up his thigh.

"Let me," Dorn offered, taking Dugan's weight. "You can carry your man."

Juna nodded, then hefted Crespin over his shoulder. "Why are you helping us?"

Dorn shrugged. "I've history with those brutes. Besides, I didn't like the odds. They could have simply injured you and your men to relieve you of your purses." He supported Dugan as they trotted down the alley in the direction of the ship.

"But you've marked yourself by helping us. There won't be a Kantahlan shipman left who won't know that you've come to the aid of Southron Isles smugglers. Might be you should join our crew."

"I'm a docker by trade, not a sailor."

"We're sailing to Naca Bay. I hear there's better-paying work there. If you can haul a line, you're welcome on my ship, and it'll earn you your passage to a better port."

Dorn rubbed his chin and looked back down the alley. "Naca Bay, then," he said. "But we'd better hurry."

They stopped talking and picked up the pace, making it to the ship before their attackers returned. His other men had just returned with the silks. With a few commands, they slipped from port, riding the outgoing tide. Captain Juna surveyed *The Sea Hare* as sails were hoisted, catching sight of Dorn. He was a tall, strong man, and he threw his muscles into the work and his voice into the song. For a docker, he knew his way around a ship.

• • •

The Island of Zilaren, the Southron Isles

"I do not appreciate being pulled into the affairs of the landers," Fanm Larenne intoned, pinning both Captain Grieg and Marlita with a hard stare. They kept their eyes downcast. "You may leave, Marlita. And thank your sister for intervening on your behalf. If not for her, you would have paid more than the mark for disturbing the Goddess in the petty affairs of an Aurelian. I would have thought that you learned your lesson years ago the first time you interfered with that man's fate."

The woman who reigned over the Southron Isles stared down at Grieg as Marlita hastened from the room, and the weight of her gaze was a physical force that sent him supplicating to his knees. It was at his behest that Marlita had asked a boon from the Goddess, something that should only be accomplished through the Fanm, if one dared to ask.

"I have always liked you, Grieg," Fanm Larenne intoned, and he worried that this private audience meant his end. "You have walked the right side of the line, never taking a misstep that would make me question your loyalties. Years and years, your family has served the Lords Pheldhain, watching and training their children, all without meddling in their affairs. Why now? What is so important about this son of Pheldhain that you would risk your own fate and that of Marlita's?" She glided closer to him, and Grieg shrunk, waiting for the final blow. Instead, she touched his shoulder and bade him rise.

"Tell me what is so important about this Warin of Pheldhain that you would gamble with not only your life, but those of your crew as well."

"He is different, my fanm," Grieg averred.

"So are all Aurelians and Nifolhadajans. That is not reason enough. I will give you one more chance to answer my question."

"Years ago, Marlita told me what was to become of him."

"Yes, I remember. A man destined to search for love, then die an early death upon its discovery. She should not have tampered with his threads."

Grieg nodded. "She only wanted him to have a full life, at least for the years that remained to him. She gave him confidence; that is all. She did not change his fate."

"Confidence is a greater gift than you know, Captain Grieg." She paced back to her throne and sat back upon it to stare down at him. "And I know that she gave him more than that. But you, you have yet to give me a good reason for your betrayal of our ways, and I—"

"Pardon, Fanm Larenne." He knew it was a risk to interrupt her, but he needed to tell her the rest if he was to come out of this audience alive. "Pray, let me continue. If you do not deem my reason worthy, then I will take my own life and bother you no more." She narrowed her eyes, but her silence was acquiescence enough. "It is true; I have grown to love Warin like a son. He honors our ways, despite being an Aurelian."

The fanm required good reason to petition the Goddess, but he had to be careful about how much he revealed. If she were to discover that Marlita had shared with him the one thing Fanm Larenne feared, she could and would obliterate every person in Marlita's circle—in other words, lay waste to the entire islet of Zilaren. A carrot, hidden in a herring, was what he needed here, and he prayed he knew how much bait to dangle before her.

"It was during our mission in Nifolhad. A woman approached me. She said that she was a seer and needed to tell me of a prophecy regarding a princess and a dark-haired stranger, and the great love that was destined to grow between them. Love, my fanm," he said, drawing out the word, "Is that not worth any risk? Can—"

"A seer?" she asked, leaning forward.

Thank the Goddess, Grieg thought, she took the bait. "Yes, my fanm. While in Nifolhad, we discovered a group of women who call themselves the Fenrhi. Their hierarchy is very similar to that of the Isles, except they live without men." It was a risk giving her so much information, but he needed her distracted from wanting to punish Marlita while remaining open to helping Warin. Fanm Larenne had grown increasingly paranoid over the years, and she turned to stare out her window at the moonless night. He could hear the waves breaking below and wondered if his bones would soon join them. He liked to think that his life would end a-sea, not dashed upon the rocky beach. And certainly not by his own hand, for he would honor his promise if she so commanded. He would do that and more to protect Marlita. The Fanm was quiet for a long time, staring as if entranced, and he realized that she was communing with the Goddess. She leaned back, then refocused her gaze on him.

"The Goddess does not like being tricked, Grieg. Nor do I. She assisted Marlita once before with Warin of Pheldhain. She will not lift the curse, but she is willing to bargain for his life.

"The Goddess will demand a harsh price. If a life is not paid before Warin's time is through, then he and the princess will be forfeit. It is you who must decide who to sacrifice. And it must be someone he loves. Now go, Grieg, before I lose patience with you. Go and console Marlita. Her willfulness came at great cost: she wears the blood mark now. That was her payment to the Goddess. No higher price exists."

Grieg nodded, then made his way as quickly as possible to find Marlita. She was home, and she ran to him when he entered. "You survived," she said. "But the cost?"

"I had to tell her about the Fenrhi. And the princess." She sat heavily at her table. "But I did not tell her about the Aurelian sisters, especially about the younger one."

"Then there is still hope," Marlita prophesied.

CHAPTER TEN

Witnesses

Nine months later, Kings Glen

"It is unpardonable that you left her alone with him," Lady Shan from Scúr rebuked.

Once Warin decided that he could no longer involve himself in the princess's affairs, he'd excised himself from her life. He'd spent months escorting her through the smallholds, planting the pijala trees, and trying to keep his distance. Her always cheerful outlook had the effect of luring him, and any other red-blooded man in the vicinity, closer. He had hated being deliberately aloof, but it was for the best. No sense in allowing the princess to become enamored with him, or he with her, if nothing could come of it. She was a princess of Nifolhad; he was a landless lord of Aurelia, a second-born son.

Besides, he had bigger worries. The latest communication from his father told him that Marten was still missing. Warin's captain had been ordered to take *Lita's Pearl* and search for news of his brother, both in the Southron Isles and Nifolhad. Captain Grieg was an adept pilot with an able crew, and Warin had trusted his ship to the man's care for years. Warin had read between the lines of his father's letter—they wanted him home. With luck, King Godwin would soon give him leave.

Being away from court would afford him a modicum of much-needed distance from the princess. He might seem impervious to her charms on the outside, but on the inside, he wanted nothing more than to wrap her up in his arms and kiss her until her toes curled. Thrown together all those months had been torture, but he'd managed it, by heavens! Whenever he found himself returning a flirtatious mot, he reminded himself that she was an impediment to his goal of finding a wife, family, and home.

When his friends grew suspicious of his cool mien where the princess was concerned, for Warin's repartee with the ladies was renown, he decided that a more drastic measure was required—one that would take their scrutiny off him and transfer it directly on the princess. If he had to be cruel to be kind, then he would do it, even though it went against his grain.

During their travels together, the princess had gone on being her oblivious cheerful self, drawing him in, needing to be rescued from her little misadventures with every turn of the road. Warin still felt a pang of guilt for what he'd done in the stable, knowing she had been in one of the stalls and would hear his conversation with Tomas, a conversation that would guarantee that she would desire no more to be in his company. Later, Tomas had confronted him, demanding to know why he disliked her so much. And thusly called out for his actions, Warin surprised himself by admitting to his friend that he didn't entirely trust her. Tomas had nearly punched him for the affront against the princess's honor—everyone *always* took her side—and had stalked away. They had avoided one another for the rest of the day, and Tomas departed for Floresta before the sun rose. As for the princess, she'd kept to her room that evening. Except for the little hiccup in their travel plans the next day—Warin forced himself to not think about the consequences had he not arrived at the inn in time—he'd been satisfied with the turn of events.

"—wise in the ways of courtly games, but—"

Warin was paying little heed to Lady Shan. With a practiced expression of someone who'd spent years amidst the intrigues at court, he gazed at the lovely woman before him, hiding his exasperation as he strained, even now, to not turn toward the person he had convinced himself to think of as his nemesis. Several months had passed since their return, and she was ever persistent in his thoughts. He wondered if she'd bewitched him somehow. Perhaps used some Sylvan love potion that her Fenrhi cousin gave her. Fenrhi potion...there was more to that line of thinking, but, as always, the threads unraveled.

Warin's ability to avoid the princess was almost as good as his success in finding love. If only that follow-up embrace with Lady Beth had yielded more than a pleasant warmth in his gut. The passion of the kiss in the library had ruined him, for he was determined to find a woman who could deliver the same. Damn. He was staring at the princess again and so forced himself to instead reflect upon the transformation of Lady Shan from Scúr.

Lady Caroline had outdone herself with her two protégés, Warin's own cousin Murel and the lovely Cathmaran maid before him.

"He's not to be trusted," Lady Shan continued. "Why, just last week, he made the most inappropriate..."

Warin tried to let the words flow over him and out of his retention. It was no longer his concern, he reasoned, almost convincing himself. But if surreptitiously observing Princess Anwyl at court these months had taught him anything, it was that she was a proficient at handling lords and royal guards alike. Focus, he silently scolded himself, and turned to admire the way Lady Shan's tight bodice and low neckline pushed up her breasts like two ripe peaches. And as she became more animated in her discourse, the globes flushed the color of the same said fruit. Sadly, he wasn't interested in Lady Shan either.

"Lady Caroline agrees, but has yet been unable to intercede," Lady Shan went on without pause, oblivious, or perhaps not, to Warin's admiration. "She's been so occupied of late and hasn't had a chance. I shouldn't want to bother the queen, but I worry for Princess Anwyl. She's twenty years of age, true, and more intelligent than most of us here, but she's *book* smart. She's been protected from the worst that court has to offer. The way she talks about her brother, he must have sheltered her from the ugliness of men like—"

Warin smiled pleasantly as she went on, unable to completely divest himself of the conversation, one-sided though it was. He had firsthand knowledge of exactly how sheltered the princess was. She was naïve, headstrong, and willful. Intelligent? Probably. Book smart? He'd never seen her crack a tome, though she had been granted access to the library. Warin realized that he was coming close to thinking well of her and mentally turned from going down that road. Instead, he reminded himself that the princess always followed her own prerogative, to hell with the consequences. She'd put herself into a dozen or more dangerous situations, always assuming that he would be at her side to bail her out. And rescue her he had, over and over again as they traveled throughout Aurelia delivering the precious pijala trees. And though he would never own up to it, it had been exhilarating—like riding out a tempest in the Southron Waters. He never knew what would happen next when in her company.

"Just look, will you?" Lady Shan begged. "She disguises it well, but she's miserable."

He gazed across the Royal Hall to where Princess Anwyl stood her own against the attentions of the obnoxious Herlewin. Her outward expression was serene, but underneath, he sensed tension, as if she was stretched and at risk of snapping. Indeed, she did appear miserable, and it came to him suddenly that it wasn't Princess Anwyl's fault that love eluded him, and his actions that day in the stable had probably hurt her more than he wanted to admit. With the epiphany, the guilt of what he'd done crashed down on him. She'd been a happy, if not exuberant, young woman, full of hope and optimism for the important task which had been set upon her by Queen Aghna and King Ranulf. And as each week of their return journey ticked away like the trees she'd transplanted one by one, her once unrestrained joy disappeared until there was little left of the girl he'd met in Sophiana. How could he have thought it necessary to hurt her?

"Because you weren't man enough to avoid her on your own, you needed her to avoid you," Warin groused under his breath. He was the cause of Anwyl's unhappiness, not Herlewin.

"Warin, please pay attention," Lady Shan demanded. "I'm trying to tell you something important."

He was barely cognizant of what she was saying as he realized that he himself hadn't been happy either. He missed his friends—Lark and Anna, and Trian and Claire. He'd erroneously believed that returning to court would provide him with at least some entertainment, especially with the queen's ladies—Lady Caroline, in particular. But she was always otherwise occupied.

And he was bored. Finding love wouldn't be enough for him. If saving the princess's hide over and again was any indication, he craved adventure as much as he wanted someone with whom to share it.

He nodded pleasantly as Lady Shan continued her litany of complaints against Herlewin. Inwardly, Warin groaned. There was nothing he could do to reverse the damage he'd done. And if he could not, he could at least help the princess extricate herself from the greasy lordling—lord, Warin corrected himself, remembering Lord Fordwin of Dinhyll, Herlewin's father, had recently died. He gazed across the Royal Hall to find Princess Anwyl gone. Lord Herlewin was lumbering toward his mother, Lady Eunice—her husband's demise had caused her normally pinched expression to tighten to near-cracking. She somehow managed a brittle smile as her son approached, but it did nothing to hide her cold and calculating expression.

"—Caroline warned me, of course," Shan was saying. "Especially to steer clear of the mother, Lady Eunice. I think that Princess Anwyl—"

"Why Lady Eunice?" Warin interrupted, suddenly alert.

"Haven't you been listening, Warin?" Lady Shan chastised. "With Lord Fordwin dead, Lady Eunice has lost much of her standing at court. She wants her son settled. And when I say settled, I mean married to someone rich, influential, and above the normal rank and file of the nobility at court. Herlewin gave me only a cursory show of interest, discovered I was from Scúr with no direct link to Lord and Lady Cathmar, and was quite literally shooed away by his mother. Lady Caroline later overheard her talking to Herlewin about taking care not to ensnare the wrong bird. Really, Warin," she added, sounding much aggrieved, "why do you think I've been begging you to intercede on Princess Anwyl's behalf?"

"My error, Lady Shan," he replied regretfully. "I'll not allow myself to be so distracted when in attendance with you again." Warin watched as Lord Herlewin made his way determinedly from the Royal Hall. "As always, you are a delight, but if I am to follow your instructions, I must take my leave." He bowed, then headed toward Lady Eunice.

Before he could reach her, she turned and began to follow in her son's tracks, taking with her two of the older dames at Kings Glen. Warin had already guessed her design—the princess and the lordling would be found in compromising circumstances by two of the most respected fixtures at court. Anwyl would be forced to accept Herlewin's suit to save herself from disgrace. Foiling Herlewin's scheme depended on Warin finding her first and with witnesses of his own. He drew closer to the three women.

"They say the pijala trees planted in the pampered orchards here at high court and elsewhere are suffering but are thriving in the most inclement locations."

"Then surely Dinhyll should have been gifted with saplings," one of the matrons tossed out while the other gave an unladylike *hoot*.

"Surely," Lady Eunice agreed, ignoring the barb about her smallhold's lack of pastoral beauty and continuing her falsely happy chatter. "I've heard they are even bearing fruit in Ragallach and in the Cathmaran Mountains. It seems to be not a question of climate, but one of terrain. Still, the specimens here are interesting to behold and..."

The orchards, of course. No other reason existed that would compel the princess to hie off alone solely on the word of Herlewin. Warin veered off to take a less cultured, but altogether much more direct route. Turning a corner, he stumbled upon none other than Lady Caroline and, surprisingly, the gruff Lord Cordhin from Cathmara.

"Oh my," Lady Caroline pouted. "We've been discovered."

"Never mind that," Warin exclaimed. "I'm in need of your assistance."

"You look like you're bent on rescuing a damsel in distress," Lady Caroline teased, then widened her eyes at his grim expression. "Princess Anwyl and Lord Herlewin, I presume. Lady Eunice is simply awful. The only reason anyone put up with her was because Lord Fordwin was such a fine man and so loyal to the king. Where can we find them?"

"The orchards," Warin grumbled, and they all doubled their pace. The saplings had been planted in the center of a secluded and walled garden, the perfect place to set a trap. They managed to reach the entrance's archway well before Lady Eunice, but what they beheld upon entering the garden was so unexpected that no one could speak.

Lord Herlewin was prostrate on the lawn and unmoving. Anwyl stood above him with a wooden stake in hand, lifted high to wallop him again should he rise. She saw Lady Caroline first, and relief flooded her features. "The rear entrance," Lady Caroline urged, grabbing Cordhin and Warin and racing across the green space. "Come, Anwyl, they are almost upon us!" Just outside the garden wall, she stopped them all and held her finger to her lips. Moments later, they heard Lady Eunice's shriek.

"We must go," Anwyl whispered.

"No, we must be seen," Lady Caroline countered. "And all of us together."

"Trust her," Warin entreated, placing her hand on his arm. "Just follow Caroline's lead."

Anwyl gazed up at him with a curious glint in her eye, then shuttered her expressive features. But she didn't pull away and managed to follow calmly behind her friends.

"Princess," he whispered, gesturing to her other hand. She frowned, then saw that she still gripped the garden stake. She tossed the slender baton under a convenient boxwood. Ahead, Lady Caroline gasped prettily. "Ready?" Warin asked. The princess nodded, and they were in the thick of it.

Lady Eunice was helping a now conscious Herlewin to sit. The two other ladies *tsk*'d and fretted. Lady Caroline and Cordhin offered various suggestions and remedies but did nothing to help the man from the ground. Lady Eunice cast an accusing glare at Anwyl while the matrons were being distracted by Lady Caroline.

"You little..." Lady Eunice seethed. "How dare you strike my son? You'll pay!"

Beside him, Anwyl seemed to shrink. It was so unlike her nature, that he wouldn't have believed it possible if he hadn't been there to witness it. He wrangled control of the situation from the spiteful Eunice before it devolved into something that Anwyl's reputation could not survive. "M'lady," Warin began. "What are you going on about? The princess has been in my company and that of Lady Caroline and Lord Cordhin this last hour. Surely you don't think to blame the ambassador of Nifolhad, a princess of the Royal House, and the protected and honored guest of King Godwin and Queen Juliana, for your son's misfortune? It is clear to all who have just arrived that Herlewin must have tripped on a root and knocked his head."

"Twice?" she screeched.

"Come now, Lady Eunice, you are overwrought."

Lady Eunice hissed at him—hissed!—then struggled to assist her son from the ground. Whether his head was still addled, or he had a sudden stroke of sagacity, Herlewin kept his mouth clamped shut, for had he spoken one untoward word against the princess, Warin would've made sure that more than his head was rattled. Cordhin finally helped the heavyset man to his feet. Holding his temple, Herlewin was dragged away from the orchard by his spitting-mad mother. Lady Caroline winked at Anwyl, and then she and Cordhin escorted the older women away.

There hadn't been time before to ask, so Warin turned to see if the princess was all right. He saw that her gown was torn, and he was near overcome with rage. The only thing that stopped him from going after Herlewin was that he didn't want to leave the princess alone. "Did he hurt you?" he demanded. He looked to the sky to calm himself, letting his breath leak slowly through his clenched teeth. Then, he cradled the princess's hands in his. "Are you hurt, Princess?" he asked more gently, searching her face.

She threw her chin up and glared at him, trying to extricate herself from his grasp. He tightened his fingers, not wanting her to slip away. But she yanked free, teetering backward and dodging him as if his touch had burned her.

"You've never cared before," she accused. "What matter is it to you now?"

"Princess—"

"Your duty to my welfare ended with the planting of the last pijala tree," she said, throwing his own words from the stable back in his face before spinning on her heel and leaving him only with his own anger for company.

"Perhaps I did my job a little too well," he said to no one. He'd never intended that she should hate him.

* * *

Anwyl stormed away. "Don't you dare cry," she ordered herself, then swiped at the tears that defied her command. "You hurt that disgusting excuse for a man more than he hurt you." She said all of this to herself as she marched back to the castle, trying to convince her heart that she wasn't crying because of Warin, but because she'd been tricked by Lord Herlewin and his mother. Little did Herlewin know that even if he had managed to compromise her honor, Anwyl's brother would never allow her to marry such an undignified cur. More likely, Lord Herlewin would have found himself skewered by Rani's sword. Duels had been banned in Aurelia, but she was a Princess of Nifolhad, and allowances would certainly be made.

It had been seeing Warin again and having him pretend that her well-being mattered to him that had broken the dam of her emotions. And then he'd touched her, asked if she'd been hurt by Herlewin, and that one horrific moment from the past bubbled to the surface.

Anwyl made it inside the castle and past the Royal Hall without encountering a soul; Warin had not followed her. That he had witnessed her embarrassment at being outmaneuvered and then accosted by Herlewin was bad enough. But whenever her eyes fell upon the man that fate had dictated she would love, she remembered the day she discovered Warin's disdain for her. It was the same day that all her future hopes had been destroyed.

They had just finished planting the last pijala sapling and were on their return trip to Kings Glen. Stopping at an inn, they discovered none other than Tomas—he was on his way to visit his family in Floresta. It had been months since Anwyl had practiced quarterstaffs, and after getting settled in their rooms, she and Tomas agreed to spar. Anwyl rushed to change into her Umbren garb, then left the inn to meet him outside of the stable. He was not waiting for her when she arrived, so she decided to check on her mare. With a curry comb in hand, Anwyl stepped into the horse's stall. That was when she heard voices—Warin and Tomas had entered.

"...and little has changed in Kings Glen, my friend," Tomas had been saying. "At least when it comes to the queen's ladies, though Lady Caroline has been scarce. Your cousin Murel was a refreshing addition when she last visited."

"What about Murel?" Warin had demanded, his tone serious.

"No, no. Not like that. She and Lady Shan are as thick as thieves. No one would dare...er, and not because of you, either..." Tomas had stopped his bungled denial and narrowed his eyes. "Don't tell me that you hold your niece to a higher standard than your own. Where is your sense of fair play and the progressiveness for which all Pheldhainians are celebrated?"

Warin had chuckled. "Overruled by the oath I made to my uncle, I'm afraid. Don't worry, Tomas. I trust you. And you are right. As much as it pains me to say it, Murel has the right to make her own decisions."

"Try to sound like you mean that if you ever repeat it to Murel. Now tell me, how have you fared with the princess these last months?"

"You've no idea. I will not be happy until I am back at court and done with this mission."

"You make it sound like she's a terrible companion," Tomas said. "The princess I traveled with is a lovely woman, vibrant and intelligent and—"

"I'm a Royal Guard, not a nursemaid. It's been torture having to constantly watch her so that she doesn't land in some misfortune or another. And the incessant chattering. She acts as if she is the foremost expert on every subject. I long for a conversation with a grown woman. The first thing I'm going to do after I hand over *the Princess* to the king and queen is find Lady..."

Anwyl hadn't heard the rest as they left the stable; she hadn't needed to. She reached out for the wall, dropping the curry comb to clunk against the wood planks of the stall. Even now, her throat clenched, remembering how her tortured gulps did nothing to fill her lungs. She had fallen for a man who despised her. Worse even. He had no respect for her whatsoever.

When she had finally emerged from the stall, her breath and her emotions under control, Tomas was standing in the middle of the stable. "I heard something drop," he'd explained, looking everywhere but at her. "I came back to...I'm so sorry, Princess. He didn't mean it. I don't know why he...Warin can be..."

"I'm fine. Just...don't tell him that I heard." Then, like a cloudburst, her tears had broken free.

"You have my word." Tomas had pulled her into his arms to comfort her while she sobbed. "And more so the fool is Warin that he can't see that you love him." With those words hanging in the air, she had fled back to the inn and to the sanctuary of her room.

Overnight, her heartache transmuted into anger, so that by morning, she had lost all the sound judgment she'd spent her life cultivating. When Warin was late to rising, and then had leisurely strolled into the stables to check that the wagons were ready, her ire spiked. He had wished her good morning, smiling as if he meant it, but she knew it for the lie it was. When he declared that he wanted to eat breakfast before departing—she had been sitting in her saddle for a quarter hour already—Anwyl had told him plainly that he could catch up to her on the road. He chuckled as if she jested and walked away to disappear inside the inn. Anwyl had ridden off without him, ordering the wagon drivers to follow behind.

Now that she was returned to court, she was finally able to contemplate the consequences of that impetuous decision. She'd never in her life done anything so counter to her good sense—well, there was that time when she punched Prince Bowen and broke his nose. But what stung Anwyl's pride now was not that Warin didn't like her, but that she had proved him correct—she *was* a silly damsel in need of rescuing. That day, she'd vowed to never again allow a man to affect her behavior to such an extent. She might be cursed to love Warin, but that didn't mean that she had to like him. Right at this very moment, she yearned for the solitude of her chamber where she could pick up one of her ropes, tying up each angry thought into the intricate knots. She tried to determine the fastest and shortest route, weighing them against the more circuitous paths where she could avoid running into castle inhabitants.

Her fingernails dug into her palms—it was futile. Warin would always believe that it was his *duty* to protect her honor. She hated that word as much as she hated the feel of Herlewin's hideous lips.

She was not Warin's responsibility. In the garden, he had taken her arm, pretended that he cared and tossed her back into the miasma of her shattered heart and storming emotions. She could still feel the heat of his fingers, and she flushed at the sensations his touch had provoked. And just like that, the memory of the masquerade and their illicit embrace surfaced.

"Damn him!" she yelled, startling one of the palace servants. Wonderful, now she had dishonored Nifolhad, for news of her outburst would spread throughout the castle. It was more than she could take, and her tears finally broke free. Oh, how she despised the man she couldn't help loving.

Hearing voices and not wanting to be seen in distress, she ducked into the closest room at hand. She closed the door, her back against it, and found herself in the Royal Library, one of the few places in Kings Glen where she felt completely at home. Here, she found peace with her truest friends—the scrolls, and tomes, and journals shelved therein.

CHAPTER ELEVEN

The Library

If she closed her eyes and stopped her ears, Anwyl could almost believe that she was home in Sophiana in the vast palace library, surrounded by ancient scrolls and tomes, stacks of paper, meticulously kept journals, even pots of differently hued ink, each identifiable by their unique aromas. Their library was the finest in all Nifolhad—Anwyl could only imagine what Diarmait had done with such a treasure; he was not a ruler who valued education and enlightenment.

She pulled in a deep breath through her nose, taking in the comforting smells of ink, oiled-leather binding, parchment and dust, until the odors permeated her senses, erasing her worries and fears. These were the fragrances that were heaven to Anwyl. They never failed to soothe the tempests of her thoughts, centering her as she lost herself in the discovery of unknown geography, histories of long-ago battles, and songs and poems from generations past.

She made her way to her favorite high-backed couch, pleased to see that the tome she'd been reading—*A History of the Southern Territories*—was waiting for her return. She hefted the massive book onto her lap and opened it up to the spot where she'd left off. Her tears dried up after ten minutes, her trembling hands stilled after fifteen. Her troubles took flight with each passing hour—Herlewin's scheme, her homesickness, Warin and her broken heart. Even when someone entered, she kept her head lowered, absorbed by what she was reading. It must have been a servant, for when she took a moment to stretch, she noticed that someone had kindly placed a carafe of wine and a tray of cold meats with bread, fruit, and cheese on her side table. She poured herself a goblet and sipped and nibbled her way through the history of Morland.

Anwyl loved history best, and Aurelia's was so different from Nifolhad's. Her country's past was riddled with myth and superstition, its ruling families purported to have descended from goddesses and gods alike. Aurelia's past was spattered with a myriad of royal houses, each with minor kings. It had been the Great War that had united all of Aurelia under one high ruler.

Anwyl poured herself another glass of wine, kicked off her shoes, and tucked her feet under her legs. She soon finished reading about Morland and moved on to Sterland, all the while taking copious notes on the passages she deemed needed further research, had incomplete information, or were marred by errors. Eventually, she nodded off, her hands still holding open the tome resting in her lap.

. . .

Queen Juliana had heard all about the attempt to inveigle the princess into marrying Herlewin. Such behavior would not do, and Lady Eunice would be held accountable. Lord Herlewin and his mother had been quietly given their marching orders. They would be gone from court by the end of the next day. Let them stew in their soggy little smallhold. Princess Anwyl was too important an asset to the peace between Aurelia and Nifolhad to have her be the victim of such an affront. Besides, Aurelia had laws against such behavior.

She smiled, thinking of Anwyl sitting by herself in the library. Juliana had known exactly where to find her and then had gone there to make sure that she was unhurt. But the young woman looked perfectly content, sitting alone, studying a book bigger than her waist. So, she had left her in peace, ordering refreshments to be quietly delivered to her favorite guest.

The queen loved having the princess at court. A mother of two princes, Juliana had quickly grown to think of Anwyl as a daughter. They shared the same love of history and, together, they'd tackled the translations of many an old scroll. Anwyl would ofttimes decipher some rune in a way that Juliana had never imagined. She'd given orders that the corner couch, the one facing away from the door, was for Anwyl's sole use. Any books or papers left behind on the table were not to be disturbed. Fresh quills were set out after each day of use, and the ink reservoirs kept full. There were very few in the realm granted admittance to the Royal Library; one had to earn the right. Currently at court, save the queen, king and Anwyl, the only other true scholar of history was Warin.

As Queen Juliana returned to the library, the most recent letter from Queen Aghna weighed heavily on her mind. Aghna and Ranulf had decided that in the best interests of the new peace between the realms, Anwyl should be married to an Aurelian nobleman, preferably one with title and land, though this was not a hard-and-fast requirement. A union between a noble of Aurelia and a royal daughter of Nifolhad would both strengthen the ties between the two realms and secure a safe and progressive place for Ranulf's sister to live. She would continue as the Nifolhadian ambassador and would oversee the ever-important tending of the pijala trees.

In the last letter, Aghna had written that her cousin, Prince Bowen, had attempted a reconciliation, claiming that he'd been forced by his father into committing the terrible deeds for which she knew him responsible. Aghna did not trust her cousin, and with good reason. She expressed King Ranulf's worry that Anwyl would be targeted by their enemies. They were wise enough to not believe every sycophant that knelt before them and proclaimed their fealty. Nifolhad's recovery from the dark years imposed upon it by Diarmait would be a long one.

Juliana gazed at the envelope in her hands. It was a letter for the princess from her brother. The queen had no reservations that the princess would dutifully, if not proudly, do as instructed.

Deeming it time to check on her charge again, Queen Juliana entered the library. Anwyl was napping, the tome teetering precariously on her knees. She lifted it gently away and set it on the table. With the weight gone from her lap, Anwyl shifted on the couch, then blinked open her eyes. Seeing the queen, she made to rise, but Juliana forestalled her and sat next to the young woman.

"I've received another letter from Nifolhad," she told Anwyl. The mere mention of her home had the young woman's face brightening. She'd arrived over a year past, an effervescent addition to their shores. Reports came in from around the realm, praising her kindness and the thoughtful advice that she had provided during the months she had toured the country with Warin. Then, Warin had written to *warn* of their return. His words, usually so elegantly glib, had been almost terse. When the two had finally returned, the young, idealistic woman was gone, as was her optimistic outlook on life. To be sure, she was as kind and thoughtful as ever, just guarded. She had become a serious woman, one no longer inclined to flirtations and games. Queen Juliana oft wondered what had happened. Warin, when asked, only provided vague answers to why their accident-riddled journey had gone awry.

"Are they well?" Anwyl asked. "What news is there?"

"They are," Juliana replied, smiling. "Kantahla is under siege, and Bowen has been ordered to appear before them in Naca'an. It is time for him to answer for his crimes. I'll let you read about it for yourself, but first, there's a letter for you from your brother." Anwyl's face brightened more as Queen Juliana placed the folded sheet in her hand. She started to break the seal, then paused.

"Ah," the princess stated, understanding coming into her eyes. "My next assignment, I assume." She broke the seal, then read the letter aloud.

"My dearest sister Anwyl,

I am so proud of everything you've done. Queen Juliana has written to say that you are equipping yourself as only a most seasoned diplomat could. I never doubted your success. She has said that you are a welcome addition at court, and she has grown to love you like a daughter."

Anwyl paused here, and Queen Juliana patted her knee.

"I think you must already know what we need you to do, for us, for Nifolhad, and for yourself. But I wanted to be the one to tell you—it is time that you married, and it must be to a noble from Aurelia.

I could list the many ways that this would help Nifolhad, but you have always been an intelligent woman, and I won't insult you by pointing out the obvious. What you do not know is that every day, Aghna and I hear of plots and schemes. Some against our family; some against the Aurelian Royal House; and yes, even against you.

Moreover, noble houses throughout Nifolhad, houses that happily linked themselves to Diarmait, are clamoring to unite with us. You, my dear sister, are at the center of this maelstrom—Radha predicted this would happen, and thus we sent you to foreign shores to distance you from any threats to steal your hand. I do not trust any man here well enough to deem them deserving of you.

I mentioned plots; we've heard dozens. From kidnapping to ransom to forced marriage. Every single one makes me afraid for your safety. As much as we miss you and need your sage counsel, we cannot yet allow you to return to Nifolhad. You must stay in Aurelia, where you are safe. There is no better protection than a marriage to one of the nobles there—once wed, you can no longer be used as a pawn.

I wish to impress upon you that the choice of husband is yours. I hope and pray that you find a man you are able to love and respect. One who will hold you dear and in the same high esteem as we do. Once married, you will be able to safely visit us—in Naca'an, or perhaps even in Sophiana. When you do, you'll come not only as my sister, but also as an aunt, and this is the happiest news of all, for Aghna is with child.

With great affection and respect, your brother,
Rani

Post Scriptum: Princess Claire once mentioned a certain list of eligible bachelors. If one exists, it might assist you in making your decision.

Queen Juliana took her hand. "Rarely does one with royal blood have a choice in who they wed. Your brother gave you that, at least."

She nodded, then looked up. "Claire told me about the list. She said that it was created for Anna by the king and had Stolweg's security in mind, and that it was used again for Claire with an eye for Chevlain's future lord."

"Ah, the infamous list," Juliana said. "If I tell you a great secret, will you promise to keep it?" Anwyl nodded. "The list never existed."

"But Claire and Trian? Oh, I see. An incentive."

"And Lady Aubrianne and Lord Larkin," the queen went on. "You see, they required more of a nudge than a royal decree to push them down the right path. They needed competition, even if it was imaginary. I never dreamt that I would ever have to compose an actual list, but I suppose that I will have to for you." Queen Juliana leaned back and regarded the young woman next to her. "People underestimate you, Princess. Not your brother or Aghna, nor I or King Godwin, but the other nobles in this realm...they do not truly see you. Woe to your future husband if he does not recognize your worth."

"Yes, but I have no idea where to start my search," Anwyl admitted. "I don't even know who I can trust."

"I heard about Herlewin and his mother. Lady Caroline said that you handled yourself admirably, but she was worried that the situation had shaken you."

"I'm afraid Lord Herlewin is the one who is rattled. I...I struck him on the head with a stake."

"Was it he who tore your gown?"

"My gown?" She looked at her dress and frowned at the ripped seam on her side. "I hadn't noticed. I was too busy—" She stopped suddenly, looking quite ill.

"Deep breaths," Queen Juliana prescribed, "and perhaps a sip of wine."

Anwyl did as instructed, then continued. "Herlewin told me that he'd heard one of the pijala trees had contracted fire blight. I had to go and check for myself; one mustn't allow such a disease to go untreated. But it was a lie, of course, a way to catch me unawares. He grabbed me from behind. Before I knew what was happening, he...his mouth...my lips." Her face was a mask of disgust. "He held me, trapped against him. The stake was near at hand, and I, well, I whacked him, and as hard as I could. Twice." She gazed down at her hands, embarrassed.

"He deserved much worse," Juliana insisted. "And you need not worry about Herlewin. Though he has a rather impressive goose egg on his temple, the physicians assured me that there would be no lasting damage. He is even fit enough to travel."

"Travel?"

"Yes, my dear," Queen Juliana explained. "It is time for him and Lady Eunice to return to Dinhyll Castle. Between you and me and King Godwin, I have expelled them from court. They leave tomorrow morning; you'll not have to see them again." The queen smiled, seeing some small relief on Anwyl's face. "As for finding a husband, I think we should keep it a secret that you are looking. You've spent time with the nobility residing here. Is there any man who interests you?"

Anwyl shook her head much too quickly.

"You're sure?" Juliana pressed. "You looked like you were thinking of someone specific."

"No. I mean, yes. Once, I thought...but no. Not anymore."

"All right, then," the queen said. "Why don't you retire for the evening? Tomorrow, I'll send the seamstress to you, and we'll have your gown mended. In the meantime, I'll speak with the king, and we will find a solution to how best to go about your search."

"Thank you," the princess replied.

"It's my pleasure, dear."

"No, not just for helping me. You know that I lost my mother and father when I was young. Rani and I raised each other. I could always count on him, and now you too. You've been so kind, and it means more than I can say." Then she leaned forward and kissed the queen's cheek before standing to leave.

"I've grown very fond of you as well," the queen replied, her eyes glistening.

A servant entered and held the door for the princess. Queen Juliana waited until she was gone, then beckoned the servant forward. "Please find Lord Warin; I require his immediate presence."

CHAPTER TWELVE

Common History

"What have you done now?" Lady Caroline demanded.

She was a woman accustomed to being in-the-know, but Warin had no answer to give. While he was respected at court, it wasn't often that he was summoned to a private audience with Queen Juliana. "I've no idea," he answered honestly. Three years ago, the summons could have been for any of a multitude of infractions, usually all having to do with the queen's ladies. But Warin had tempered his amorous ways. "I'd give odds that Lady Eunice is involved."

"I wouldn't if I were you. Haven't you heard? She and Herlewin have been banished from Kings Glen."

"No," Warin faux-gasped.

"Yes," Lady Caroline conspired. "Now go. You mustn't keep the queen waiting, especially in her current mood."

Warin swallowed, then bowed to his good friend of many years. His long strides ate up the distance to the library. He paused outside its entrance, exhaled, then stepped inside and drew in a deep breath. He loved this room. Very few of his peers knew of his bookishness, even less so of his ardent study of the great histories of Aurelia and Nifolhad. Queen Juliana was one such person. She had recognized a fellow scholar in him when he'd first joined the Royal Guard and had given him access to the library and all its contents. She was presently perched behind her desk, and she looked up as he neared.

"I'm almost finished here," she told him, indicating the letter she was writing. "Why don't you sit over there? You can join me in a moment." Warin sat on the couch to wait and saw that there was a carafe of wine and two glasses. "Help yourself," the queen added. "And if you'll pour one for me as well..." She went back to her writing.

Warin did so, and then frowned at the book that had been left open on the table. It was the history of the southern territories and one of his favorites.

Who would be so careless as to not return the tome to its rightful home on the shelf? He picked it up to put it away.

"Please do leave that there," Queen Juliana called from across the room.

He wondered who would be interested in the rather dry historical reference book. When he set it down on the table, a thin sheaf of papers slipped to the floor. Someone had been taking detailed notes. He picked up the scattered pages and started reading, curious to know the person's opinion. The script was neat and precise, the penned thoughts insightful. The reader had made a list of discrepancies that appeared in the lineage of Morland's noble family—the family whence his good friend Lark had come. Warin knew of the errors in the text, but the unknown historian had gone a step further. He had researched the mistakes, drawing from other sources in the library, confirming and refuting the claims made in the great book. It was a very thorough cataloguing.

There were three notations with question marks noted on the paper—quill and ink sat conveniently on the table, all but begging Warin to assist. In his long and elegant script, he quickly provided answers to two of the queries. For the third, he consulted an older, pre-Great War history on the smallholds that he recalled contained a reference to the third Liege of Morland. He flipped through the pages and was about to make note of the source when the queen beckoned him. He slipped a page marker into the book, then set it next to the great tome.

Carrying the goblets of wine, he sat across from his queen. She took a sip after he handed her the cup, watching him over the rim as if taking his measure anew. Warin took a deep draught from his goblet to squash his growing anxiety. Experience had taught him to never trifle with the queen; one had to be especially alert when conversing lest they might miss vital and oft-disguised subtext. Most people would leave her presence and then later wonder why she had used a certain word or phrase. Only the quick-of-mind had the wherewithal to parry words with her. From her expression, Warin deemed this to be such an occasion, and he mentally opened his mind to more than her words.

"I have a job for you, Warin," she started simply enough.

"Impossible, my queen. For there is nothing you could ask that I would consider work," he replied, using courtly words to better gauge her disposition.

"Hmm. Perhaps." She smiled, seeing straight through his flattery. "It may interest you to know that Lady Noura of Whitmarsh once told me of the role you played in the union of Lady Aubrianne and my nephew, Larkin. I don't think that I've ever thanked you for your intercession." He nodded but dared not verbally acknowledge his involvement—Warin wanted no one to realize that he was a romantic at heart. "Did you know that one of the court minstrels has written a song about you?"

"I have heard a rumor to that effect, although I was assured that my name is not mentioned directly."

"No," the queen confirmed, "you are not called out as the matchmaker, but the verses are supplementing your already—robust?—reputation." Warin inclined his head but did not interrupt. "You also affected the reunion between Lady Claire and Trian. You, my dear man, are a romantic."

"Or perhaps I am removing my competition," he quipped, but inwardly groaned that his queen gauged him so easily. He never saw the sense of allowing others to know his true desires; he'd be hounded by every eligible noble daughter in Aurelia. Lady Claire, gifted with sight, had told him that love would find him, but he had never had the chance to ask her who his heart's mate would be. Of late, he was certain that he would not find her here at court. He seemed forever doomed to be the groomsman. "I would do anything to be of service to my friends," he averred.

"Yes, even risking your king's wrath by gallivanting off to Nifolhad to rescue Lady Claire last year."

Warin knew to remain silent on the subject. He had escaped royal censure only because he'd been successful in bringing Claire back to Aurelia after she'd been abducted. Still, he was man enough to stand by his decision. "An attack upon those we love is an attack upon our house."

"Ah, yes, the Pheldhainian motto. You fisher minks are a fiercely loyal group," she said, referencing his family's crest.

The queen was looking much too satisfied, and Warin changed the subject to what he hoped would be safer territory. "You mentioned a task, my queen."

"Yes, a delicate one." She indicated the folded letter on her desk. Even with the wax broken, Warin could see that it bore the royal seal of Queen Aghna. "Go ahead," she offered.

Intrigued, he read the letter quickly, and when he looked up, the queen's expression remained pleasant. Could it be that she wanted him to marry Princess Anwyl? Panic blossomed in his chest at the thought. He knew he was somewhere near the top of the king's list of marriageable nobles, but wed the princess? Queen Juliana was studying him, no doubt amused that he failed to mask his emotions from her discerning gaze. He quickly shuttered his feelings, though it was too little, and too late.

"Princess Anwyl accepts this new responsibility, but she has confessed to feeling no attachment to any one man in particular. Her brother is adamant that she be allowed to choose her groom. Which leads me to your role in her betrothal." Warin swallowed and forced himself to remain outwardly calm under the queen's gaze. "Under the guise of tending to the new pijala orchards, you are to once more escort Princess Anwyl throughout the realm, the unspoken goal being an introduction to certain eligible noblemen.

"Anwyl," the queen continued, quite possibly cognizant of Warin's emotional and unexplainable inner turmoil, though he hoped the opposite, "has become like a daughter to me, Warin. You have proven yourself to be an excellent judge of character when it comes to matchmaking, and in your hands, I know that the princess will be spared from odious men of the mien of Lord Herlewin."

She continued on, mentioning the notorious list, the route they would travel through the realm, the various candidates. All the while, Warin's emotions were at war. He was both relieved that she hadn't asked him to marry the princess and disappointed by the same measure. It defied reasoning. He tried to focus on her words, on the subtle indicators that would give him clues to any ulterior motives, but he could not fully concentrate. Part of him welcomed the opportunity to make amends with the princess. And part of him wanted to hie to the coast, find the fastest ship, and escape to the Southron Isles. Months on the road with Princess Anwyl? He wasn't sure if he could survive her again. He shook his head to clear his warring thoughts.

"No?" the queen asked, misinterpreting his gesture.

"No," Warin answered immediately. "I mean, yes, of course I will."

"Why, Warin, I don't think that I have ever seen you flustered. Is there something about the princess that you are not telling me?"

The queen was too astute for him to prevaricate. "Princess Anwyl may not want me as her escort."

"Why ever not? Did something happen between you?"

"No, my queen," Warin assured. "However, she was quite upset with me when we last spoke." He went on to explain the princess's reaction to him in the orchard.

The queen narrowed her eyes at him. "She used those words—*your duty to her welfare* ended with your mission?"

Warin suddenly felt as if someone had punched him in his stomach, though he was careful not to reveal this to Queen Juliana. She simply stared at him, waiting, and he realized that he had no choice but to confess what he'd done.

"I only meant to teach her a lesson," he began. The queen leaned back in her chair and crossed her arms. "I had best explain from the beginning."

Warin gave an account of all the predicaments Anwyl had gotten into and how he was the one usually covered in muck, or struck by lightning, or—he stopped when he realized how much of a grouser he sounded.

"This lesson..."

He was doomed. He knew it. The queen knew it. There was nothing for it but to go on, apologize, and hope that he wouldn't lose her respect when he was done. "All of that rescuing," he began. "I found myself growing..."

"...*fond of* Princess Anwyl?"

"More like *attracted to*. I worried that..."

"...it would be inappropriate?"

"And unwise. I was, er, concerned that the princess might have similar inclinations."

Except for one brow, precariously arched high on her forehead and seemingly rising higher and higher, the queen's face was made of stone.

"I made sure that she overheard me complaining about the journey and, well, about her. I wanted to spare her any heartache she might get from falling in love with me." Perfect. He sounded exceedingly full of himself when he put it that way, and he felt the noose tighten.

"Warin, how could you?"

There would be no turning back now, and he leveled his gaze at the queen. "I know how ridiculous I sound, but during the mission, she never missed an opportunity to make light of the many dangerous situations we encountered, situations that many times she instigated. Her naïveté, her lack of mature judgment...I was worried that her heart would be broken."

"So, your solution was to break it yourself." He remained silent, intuiting that his queen did not expect a reply. "Is that all?"

He slumped. He would not lie to his queen; there was no honor in it. "That night at the inn, Tomas and I may have imbibed too much. I woke up late."

"Yes, yes. We all know that you are not a morning person. Pray, continue."

"I went to the stable, and there she was, waiting, everything packed and ready to go. Even my horse was saddled. Princess Anwyl didn't so much as glance my way. She just drummed her fingers on the pommel of her saddle. I don't know what came over me, but I, well, perhaps I was ashamed of what I'd done. Not ready to face her, I told her that I wanted to eat breakfast first. I left the stable and went to do just that, taking my time. An hour later, in a better mood and with an apology in mind, I returned to find her already gone. The wagons too.

"They had less than an hour's lead, so I set off at a canter and soon came upon the wagons." He paused, sat straighter, determined to look Queen Juliana in the eye while he told her the worst. "Princess Anwyl was not with them. She had galloped off on Corroba, saying she wanted to stretch her mare's legs, and that she would wait for them at the next inn."

"Warin!"

"She was only on her own for fifteen minutes, twenty at most. I found her at The Breakneck Tavern." The establishment had been named for the gallows which had once been erected there and was now a notorious stopping place for men of a certain ilk.

"The Breakneck!"

"Nothing happened to her, I swear. I stepped in, and when the men saw me, they immediately backed off."

"How many?"

He swallowed. "Three."

"One of them being the tavern owner?"

"No, he was only watching." Before she could say anything, he added, "He's gone now; I made sure of it. His daughter runs the place; she's changed the name to The Jolly Stewpot. It's quite homey now."

Queen Juliana held up her hand. "Tell me exactly what happened."

"She was sitting at a table, preparing to eat," he began. "If it's any consolation, I don't think they stood a chance against her. She'd armed herself with a fork and—" He stopped again.

The queen's lips were set in a thin line, and her nostrils were flared. "And just what lesson did you *think* you were teaching her?"

"I really couldn't say, looking back on it now."

"Warin!"

He lifted his hands. "I'm not making light of it, I swear. I never let on that I was there. I didn't want her to think that I had rescued her yet again. I was trying to put some distance between us."

"And you wonder at her reaction after being accosted by Herlewin."

"Please try to understand, my queen. She traipsed around this realm as if she were protected by an entire army, all without a care for what could go wrong, and I—" Warin hung his head, stabbing his fingers through his hair. "No wonder she is so angry with me. I failed her."

"Consider this as well, Warin. For months, while she, in your words, *traipsed around this realm as if she were protected by an entire army,* she was always aware that you were there, ready to help her if she needed it. The princess trusted you. Implicitly. She believed in you. No wonder she was so changed upon her return."

Warin hadn't thought that the queen could say anything that would make him feel worse about his behavior than he already did. "I never meant to go so far."

She continued to stare at him, her expression unreadable.

"So, you see," he went on, "Princess Anwyl will most likely want a different escort." The queen remained silent. "Of course, I will do as you request. I was only concerned for the princess—"

Queen Juliana raised her hand to stop him. "And nothing else happened?" she asked, her voice giving no clue as to the direction of her query.

"No, my queen, nothing that I recall." Now was not the time to mention that he did not fully trust the princess; it would only cause more questions, some that might bring to light the difficulties his family was having.

"Then I see no reason why you cannot escort her again," she declared. "Consider this your one opportunity to atone for your mistakes. That will be all, Warin."

He stood and bowed. "As you command, my queen." At the door, he hesitated, and she peered up at him from where she sat with her correspondence.

"Yes?" she asked.

"I won't fail you this time; I won't fail the princess."

"I know."

Warin looked around the library that he was so fond of, hoping that he hadn't lost the queen's regard. His gaze fell upon the stack of books. As he hadn't departed, the queen gazed expectantly at him.

"I was wondering...who is reading that history?" he asked, indicating the heavy tome.

The queen waved her hand dismissively. "Just another scholar; no one you need concern yourself over."

"I only thought to offer my assistance in their research."

"That is kind of you," she replied noncommittally. "Good night, Warin."

"Good night, my queen," he said soberly, and then left her to her writing.

. . .

After he closed the library door, Queen Juliana stood and paced. She believed Warin had told her the truth, at least the truth as he knew it. Her womanly insight told her a different story. Anwyl was an intelligent woman, Warin's belief in her naïveté aside. Could it be that she had fallen for the greatest rake in the kingdom?

And what about Warin? The queen had purposely phrased her request to make him believe that she was asking him to marry Anwyl. He'd dallied one too many times with her ladies for her to ignore such a spectacular opportunity to cause him discomfort. But he'd nearly fidgeted right off his chair. Then, when she didn't name him, he had looked almost dejected.

The queen walked to the table where Anwyl had been working. Her neat, concise script juxtaposed against Warin's long, elegant hand—so different on the surface, yet exactly the same in the quality of content. It was time to pen an *actual* list of suitors for Anwyl. Charming, handsome, intelligent nobles all. Warin thought the princess an innocent; it was time to allow the perception of other men to open Warin's mind to the truth.

She sat down and put quill to parchment. Finished, she folded and unfolded the paper numerous times, even staining it with tea to age it. She gazed across the library to where her two favorite historians' handwriting was married in ink. Then she looked at her list again. It would need to be written in another hand, one that the princess would eventually come to recognize. It had been a long time since the queen had directed the matchmaking at court. Knowing her quarry to be quite intelligent, she would have to be especially subtle in her maneuvering.

CHAPTER THIRTEEN

Letters, Lists, and Lies

The Royal Library, Kings Glen, Aurelia

Warin watched as Queen Juliana drew a sheet of worn paper from her desk, upon which twenty or so names had been inked: *The List.* She spread it out between them so that he could see each name. There was Larkin's, near the top, with a line drawn through it. Warin's name was first, and he couldn't help feeling some pride that he was so esteemed. At the bottom, Trian's, likewise crossed out. Warin raised his eyebrow.

"Due to Cathmaran betrothal customs, Trian's name was not on the original register and only added at the request of his aunt, Lady Cafellia," the queen supplied. "But it matters not, for there is absolutely no weight given to the placement of a name."

The queen dipped her quill to her inkpot, then set it above the paper, poised to add or strike out a name at her whim. "Let's clean this up a bit, shall we? First," she said, crossing off six names in short order, "the noblemen who have wed."

"Lord Savaric is recently betrothed," Warin added, and the queen struck his name.

"And let us not forget Lord Herlewin." She eliminated his name with a decisive stroke. "A good start, but we need to whittle this down more.

The queen was ruthless. Starting at the bottom of the page, her quill disqualified noble after noble. When she paused near the top of the list, his chest tightened. The quill's nib hovered while she stared at the paper, then she slashed his name from contention. "As you mentioned before, the princess cares little for your company."

Those had not been his exact words, and he bit his tongue to stop from pointing it out. The queen was studying the list with a pensive expression. "I wonder…"

"My queen?" Warin asked.

"Princess Anwyl never mentioned a name, but I did get the sense that there was someone who once caught her interest. When I asked her"—Warin held his breath—"she said no. Ladies talk, Warin, and princesses are no exception. They are only more circumspect with their confidants. What was it that I heard?" She drummed her fingers. "A kiss, perhaps. Did you notice if she formed an attachment with anyone when you traveled together?"

The very last thing Warin wanted was to add another name to the list but doing so was the surest way to keep Queen Juliana off his scent. "She was equally friendly with all, my queen," he finally replied, not at all pleased with the direction the conversation had taken. "But...I suppose she and Tomas got on well enough." It fairly killed him to say it.

"Indeed. Thank you, Warin," Queen Juliana exclaimed, drawing out a new sheet of paper and handing it to him with the quill. "Please start a new list; I will dictate the names. First: Tomas." She consulted the original paper, then read off those who were not felled by her stroke. "Lords Wymark and Ernald." She paused between each to give him time to write. "Then Galerin. Tanfiel. Corclain. Jusper. Brontson. And Umfrey."

Warin snorted.

"And what is the matter with Lord Umfrey?"

"My pardon, but he is nearly fifty."

"I see your point," she conceded. "No to Umfrey. Then we must not add Lord Hamond for the same reason. That leaves me with only Lord Ronan to add." Warin hesitated, then added the last. "Is there something wrong with Lord Ronan?"

"No, my queen," Warin quickly replied. His hesitation was only due to his knowledge that Ronan was a well-known rake in the smallholds. Not much else was known about him because he tended to eschew court and its political games. "He is as suitable as the rest."

"Hmm. Perhaps, even more. He's a handsome man. Smart, rich, and has title to the largest and most profitable smallhold in the realm. Perhaps your hesitation was due to his family's purchase of ships from Cathmar."

Nothing in Aurelia escaped the attention of the king and queen. "It would take many ships and many more years before they could even dream of matching my father's fleet. Besides, his trade is local while my family prefers...diversification." Everyone knew Warin's family's wealth, while founded in shipping and legitimate trade, was rumored to have been greatly bolstered by smuggling. The queen's half-smile told him he'd amused her.

"How would you like me to proceed?" he asked. "Does the princess know of the list?"

"She does. I'll make a copy, and you must hold on to this one."

Warin slid the paper across the desk, then stood and paced. He remembered the history book that had been left across the room and made his way there. An open note rested atop the pile of books and papers, and he picked it up.

To the considerate scholar who assisted me in my research,

Thank you. I had almost given up on the missing information, and the journal that you so thoughtfully bookmarked allowed me to finish my study of the history of Morland. I have now moved on to Pheldhain—I admit to saving this for last as this territory holds great interest for me. It is the only territory in Aurelia with connections to the mysterious Southron Isles.

The lack of information on that island realm, one that has withstood being conquered by both Aurelia and Nifolhad, is, in of itself, most intriguing. I am eager to divine its noble lineage and write about its unique and exotic culture, proving that its influence is more far-reaching than any suspect. I have my theories and hope to see them proved. And as Pheldhain seems to have the closest ties to the Southron Isles, I am looking for illumination in their history.

With much appreciation,
A Fellow Historian

Warin knew more about the history and culture of Pheldhain than any other person in the realm. It was his home, after all, and he had explored every inch of it. His knowledge of the Southron Isles was better than most, but barely nicked the surface of the mystery enshrouding the region. He quickly penned a reply offering his assistance, then returned to the queen when she called to him that she had finished.

"Here it is," she stated, restoring the list to his care. "Remember, the pijala trees are your outward mission, *not* the finding of a groom for the princess. I'm afraid if the truth were revealed, she would never again find peace."

"Ernald of Redavel first then, while we visit the pijalas planted in the Smallholds."

"You needn't go to Whitmarsh, Chevlain, or Stolweg. But if you are inclined to do so, you could winter with your family in Pheldhain. I don't need to mention that it will give the princess more time to get to know your nephew, Tanfiel. I'm sure she would love to meet your parents and also experience the unique clime of your home."

"Cousin," Warin corrected.

"Pardon?"

"Tanfiel, my queen, is my cousin.

"Oh, I only assumed…you're so much older than he. Which reminds me…what news of your older brother?"

Older than Tanfiel? Only by six years! Stay focused, he berated himself, the queen was asking about Marten. Warin's family had put it out that his brother's ship had sailed to Naca'an to resume trade with Nifolhad, and that it was an extended journey. The excuse grew thinner with the passing of each month and his continued absence. "If I know my brother, he and his crew are lounging in some tavern in Naca'an." He said it lightly; the queen and king did not need to know how worried his parents were.

She studied him for a moment, then gave him a noncommittal nod. "Too bad for Princess Anwyl that your brother is already betrothed." Warin choked. He couldn't help it. The queen raised an imperious eyebrow at him. "You have two more weeks to prepare for the journey."

"We could depart earlier," Warin offered, clearing his throat. "If the princess wishes it, that is."

"Anwyl is already making preparations, but I have a surprise for her." She leveled him with a serious gaze as she spoke. "Coming to Aurelia has not been easy for Anwyl. She brought no one from Sophiana with her, not even a lady's maid to tend to her needs. And the one from Ragallach deserted her. You do realize that very few noblewomen would attempt traveling without at least one trusted servant in attendance. Yet, she had done so with you, and without complaint. And here at court, with not a single person with whom she shares a common background…I can only imagine how lonely she must feel."

Warin had to admit that he hadn't really given it much thought. The pressure on the princess to constantly represent Nifolhad in a positive light must have been extraordinary. Yet everywhere they'd visited, her engaging conversation had thawed more than one prejudiced heart. Warin suddenly realized that her know-all-about-everything attitude was, in fact, owing to her passion and dedication to the success of the pijala orchards and her sense of duty to portray Nifolhad as an ally to Aurelia. There were a few at court who outwardly welcomed the princess but, behind her back, cut her to pieces. She could not have failed to notice those hidden looks and quiet murmurs. Princess Anwyl was turning out to be of sturdier stock than he believed. Perhaps she had more in common with the Chevlain sisters, Ladies Anna and Claire, than he had credited.

"She must be homesick. I hadn't—"

"Of course you hadn't considered it," the queen interrupted. "Why would you empathize with someone who you think of only in terms of a person you must protect? This is why I have asked Claire's companion, Lady Madyan, to journey to Kings Glen and accompany you both on your trek through Aurelia. I believe her to be a resilient sort and not in need of any protection for her own person."

"An accurate description," Warin agreed. "Madyan is quite skilled in defense. She will most certainly help in that regard should any situation necessitate it. I'm curious though. She and I are acquainted, and she never before mentioned that she was of noble blood."

"Was her bearing ever anything but noble?"

"If anything, she is one of the most regal women I know."

"Then why would she mention it?" Queen Juliana leaned back and studied him. "Warin, you still have much to learn about women. In regard to Madyan, Queen Aghna wrote of her extraordinary heritage. Her Fyrjian title does not exactly translate to queen, but it's close. For simplicity's sake, the king and I have settled on *lady*."

"Then I look forward to seeing her again and having my Fyrjian friend tell me her history."

"As long as you remember that I want this to be a surprise for the princess." She turned to look over at the table where Warin had been. "I see that you found the note that was left for you. My friend was quite grateful for your assistance."

"I am at his disposal should he need me."

"Difficult, now that you will be traveling." She tapped her fingers on her desk again as she regarded him. "I wish to follow Anwyl's progress in the coming months, and she and I will exchange letters through royal messenger. Should my friend require your help, I will include any requests in the correspondence packet to the princess, and you may respond using the same."

"Thank you, my queen," Warin stated, wondering why the queen was keeping the man's identity secret. "His observations are astute. I look forward to helping where I can."

Queen Juliana's lips twitched, but she stood, and Warin's audience was finished. He took his leave, fortunate to have escaped the Royal Library without revealing too much about his brother.

"Oh, and Warin," the queen called out, "when you do see your parents, give them my best. We realize that re-establishing trading ties with Nifolhad is a lengthy process, and we appreciate your family's assistance, especially considering how Murel's brother was lost." She paused, studying him, but Warin only nodded, not giving any indication that he suspected his cousin's disappearance might have ties to Sophiana.

"And now your brother," she continued. "Marten has been gone too many months. Lady Téana must be sick with worry over him. Has Captain Grieg uncovered any clues as to his whereabouts?"—Only his years at court saved him from revealing his shock that news of his captain searching for Marten had made it to the queen's ears. And if the queen knew, then so did the king. "No? Then let us hope that *Lita's Pearl* returns and brings your brother and his crew safely back to Pheldhain." She held his gaze for the longest moment, then turned from him to study some letter on her desk.

"My queen," he said, then bowed his way out of the library, a great welling of unease filling his chest. There was more to that last bit of conversation than appeared on the surface. Had she been trying to warn him or was she simply reminding him that the reach of Kings Glen spanned the entire realm?

He needed to get word to his parents, but the message had to be secure. Who could he trust? "Murel." Warin changed direction and went in search of his cousin.

• • •

Three days had passed since Queen Juliana had informed Anwyl that it would be Warin escorting her throughout the realm. The irony of it all was not lost on her. Thus far, she'd managed to avoid him, and would continue to do so until their departure. As she entered the library, she resolved to not allow his presence to affect her search for a husband. "At least I have time to bolster my defenses."

When Anwyl reached her work area, she saw that a note had been left for her. The queen had only told her the person who had helped her was a fellow historian. Anwyl had drawn the conclusion that it was a man, for his script, although elegant, was bold, and his writing lacked the flourishes of most feminine minds. She opened the note with great anticipation as it was her most honest interaction with anyone at court.

Dear Fellow Historian,

It was my pleasure to assist you with your research. It is not often that I find another as dedicated as I to the understanding and interpretation of the past. I believe that it is to the past where we should look for inspiration as to what the future will provide.

And as one with an extensive knowledge of all things Pheldhainian, I can only laud your sensible decision to keep the study of this intriguing territory for last. More, I have visited one of the Southron Isles and might be able to provide you with some insight as to their culture.

Many in the realm, save the Cathmarans, would be shocked to discover that the women of the Southron Isles determine their own fates with respect to marriage. Though, to be more accurate, it is not so much as a marital rite as it is mate selection. For in the Isles, marriage is not a custom to which they adhere. Of course, I write from the perspective of an observer and historian. And if in this I can be of assistance to you, please ask.

Sincerely,
One More Aurelian Scholar

"Extraordinary," she exclaimed, setting his note aside to dive into the history of Pheldhain. An hour stretched into two, and she discovered that she had amassed a number of questions left unanswered by the text she was reading. She hesitated, then drew a sheet of paper from her sheaf and set her quill to the page.

Dear A.S. (Aurelian Scholar)

I am just two hours into my study of Pheldhain and find myself with more questions than answers. My study of the region is such that I am attempting to find some commonality between Aurelia and the people of the Southron Isles. Moreover, I am determined to find proof for my theory as to why the Southron Isles remain so isolated. There are almost no written accounts or histories of this region. This lack of information is no doubt due to the secretive nature of its inhabitants. But I believe there to be another reason, one that I do not wish to reveal until I have more evidence.

Those closest to me would warn you that I love a good mystery and can be quite tenacious in my pursuit. If you are honest in your offer to assist me with my research, please take a look at the assembled questions that I have written out thus far.

In hopes of receiving your insightful reply,
F.H. (A Fellow Historian)

Post Scriptum: Your account of the matriarchal structure of mate selection in the Southron Isles was fascinating; it reminds me of another region that I once studied and reinforces my theory.

Anwyl reviewed that which she'd written, then attached her questions regarding Pheldhain to her note, setting the two sheets of paper on top of the book she'd been reading. She stood, smoothed out her dress, and went in search of the queen.

CHAPTER FOURTEEN

Reunion

Princess Anwyl, perched upon her ornate seat, felt as though she were on display before all and sundry. Beside her, the queen and king spoke with their favorites at court. Anwyl's upcoming journey across Aurelia, ostensibly to inspect the pijala saplings, would begin the next day. Today, though, she had to endure yet another reception held in her honor. As she gazed across the room, her eyes unfailingly fell on Warin. He glanced up at her and nodded, but then returned to his conversation with Lady Caroline, Lord Cordhin, and Lady Beth. He hadn't tried to approach her again after that embarrassing incident in the orchard, but neither had he been avoiding her, as was his habit. In fact, he'd seemed sincere when he told her about visiting Pheldhain and his surety that his parents would enjoy making her acquaintance. Still, Anwyl was not willing to drop the carefully constructed guard around her heart.

The weeks had flown by, leaving her little time to frequent the library. A.S., as she'd nicknamed the man who'd signed his message *Aurelian Scholar*, had only jotted down his thoughts in regard to her latest research notes and a brief explanation that he was unable to write at length, promising to do so at a later date. Anwyl, though she knew not why, maintained her anonymity by signing with *F.H.—Fellow Historian*. From the way he had written to her, she was positive that he believed her to be a man.

The exchange allowed her to be herself without the trappings of her title, and she was looking forward to continued letters ferried to her by the queen's messengers. Anwyl stifled a sigh, mentally wiped her face clear of the expression that, to anyone who truly knew her, would proclaim that she wished to be anywhere else but here, exposed. She felt the queen's eyes on her and straightened her already poised posture.

"You look like you would rather be in the library, my dear," Queen Juliana whispered, then patted her hand.

"Am I so easy to read?"

"Only to me. But you mustn't leave just yet, not when we've gone through such great lengths to arrange a surprise for you." She smiled at Anwyl before nodding toward the massive doors to the hall. With a flourish, the posted doormen pulled them open.

A hush fell through the room, only to be broken by Warin's pleased exclamation. "Trian! Claire!"

"Go ahead, Princess," King Godwin encouraged, leaning forward and smiling kindly at her. Anwyl skipped down the steps to the main floor. The crowd parted as she rushed to greet her friend. Almost two years had passed without the Lord and Lady of Chevlain presenting themselves to the king and queen. They'd been given this boon after everything they had both sacrificed for the realm. Claire's once-shorn scalp was now covered by a beautiful cascade of gleaming brown hair. Though she wore it free of plaits, she had pulled it away from her face, proudly revealing the permanent markings that the Fenrhi women in Nifolhad had inked upon her. Her arms, likewise marked, were bare up to her elbows, and every guest in the hall craned their neck to see that which had only been a rumor.

Except for Warin's warm greeting and the ensuing backslapping as he and Trian embraced, no other noise could be heard. Anwyl worried for Claire; she herself had been the object of whispers and speculation and knew just how badly the hushed voices could hurt. The whispering had grown loud enough to be deemed a breach of etiquette. Claire appeared nonplussed, and she ignored everyone around her, save Warin. When she finally saw Anwyl, her smile was so warm and genuine that Anwyl almost burst into tears. For once, she didn't care what anyone thought, and ran to her friend. Their combined laughter echoed through the hall.

"Princess Anwyl," Claire greeted. "And your majesties." She curtsied to the king and queen and then gave them a wink that left Anwyl wondering. Then, Trian stepped aside to reveal another figure, this one garbed in the Fenrhi tradition of Umbren Caste.

"Madyan!" Anwyl exclaimed. No wonder people had been whispering; there was a Fenrhi warrior in their midst. Anwyl and Madyan had become fast friends while they had sailed together from Nifolhad to Aurelia, only to have to part ways in Ragallach. Anwyl turned to the king and queen and nodded her thanks, then she took Claire's and Madyan's hands and pulled them both to her.

"Oh, but you are here, and I must away tomorrow. Would that you had arrived sooner."

"But I am coming with you, Princess," Madyan revealed. "At least for part of the journey."

"Truly?"

"Yes," she promised. "It's been too long since I wandered, and I find myself craving an adventure before I return to Nifolhad."

"You are going home?" Anwyl asked, trying and failing to hide the longing in her voice.

Madyan nodded solemnly. "My desert beckons."

A trumpet sounded to signal the banquet. As a group, they entered the dining hall and climbed the dais, and Anwyl was so happy at that very moment that she forgot every veiled whisper and assumptive glance ever cast her way.

She was behind her friends, and when someone took her elbow to help her up the steps, she glanced up and right into Warin's smiling eyes. They were the same deep-ocean blue that they had always been, and Anwyl forced herself to look away. "What?" she said, for when Warin smiled, it was never for her, but at her.

"It's nice to see you happy," he said.

"And why shouldn't I be happy, Warin?" she asked, pausing one step higher than he to level her gaze at him. "I am among friends again."

"Princess—" he started, but she didn't want to hear, and stepped away from him lest he ruin her elevated mood. Thinking too much about Warin made her angry, and that made her sad, and then angry all over again.

. . .

It was a bright and clear morning. Summer temperatures clung stubbornly to the early autumn month, and Warin sat on his Chevlain steed, Konjimar, and perused the entourage of riders and wagons behind him. Anwyl and Madyan took turns hugging Claire goodbye, having already taken their leave of the queen and king. There was a wagon full of the gear they would need once autumn wrested control from the summer and the air cooled, and, he noted wryly, several quarterstaffs and bows, all of Nifolhadian manufacture. A second wagon had been laden with gifts from the king and queen and items from various nobles at court to be given to their families throughout the realm. Anwyl was astride Corroba, her Fyrost Desert mare.

"Good journey to you, my friend," Trian stated. "When this little tour is complete, find time to come by Chevlain if you can."

"I would love to," Warin replied.

"Sage travels, Warin," Claire offered with a smile.

"Don't you mean *safe* travels?" Warin asked, but she only smiled. He wanted to hear her reply, but the princess had started off, conversing quietly with Madyan as they rode through the gates.

"You'd best not be left behind," Trian said glibly. "They might get it into their heads that they don't need you."

"With the arsenal Madyan loaded into the wagon, they probably don't," Warin replied with a chuckle. He signaled the wagon drivers to start and then wheeled Konjimar around to trot after the two women.

• • •

Trian watched the procession leave the castle grounds, losing view of them when they passed through the outer gates. "Are you going to tell me what is bothering you, my love?" he asked.

"I'm not sure, and that is my quandary," Claire replied. "Still, I would speak with the king and queen. My dreams have been disquieting of late."

"About Warin? Or is it Anwyl?"

"Neither, at least not directly." When she frowned, Trian kissed her forehead. He started to step away, and she tugged at the threaded strands of hair he'd taken to wearing again. Only, these new strands departed from his Cathmaran heritage in that they included the same rainbow of colors inked on his wife's skin—blue, amber, moss, dust, coal and blood red. She gave him such a kiss that he wondered if they couldn't put off the audience with the king and queen. "Come on," Claire teased. "The sooner we get this over with…" Trian needed no further encouragement, and they went to find their majesties.

On the way, a page met them to inform them that the king and queen were expecting them in the Royal Library. They were escorted there, announced, and waved to a comfortable-looking banquette set near the hearth. "Thank you for arriving so quickly," Queen Juliana started.

"We were already on our way to find you, my queen," Trian replied. "Claire has…" He paused, not quite sure how to proceed. "Claire has worrisome information that she must impart to you. You may have heard rumors that she can see—"

"Yes, yes," King Godwin interrupted. "Anwyl told us about the Fenrhi and their caste system: healers and defenders, and those called to duty and service, as well as the caste which—how did she explain it?"

"Seeks enlightenment," the queen supplied.

"That's it," the king said. "We also understand that these traits are considered great gifts in Nifolhad, and that you, Lady Claire, are endowed with certain abilities." Claire nodded and held out her arm to the king so that he and the queen could examine her markings. He frowned, reached out to touch her skin, then stopped. Trian worried suddenly for Claire. If King Godwin decided that she was to be feared...

The king cleared his throat. "Lady Claire," he began, "you and your sister, in the name of duty, have sacrificed more than any family in the realm. Thanks to Queen Aghna and Princess Anwyl, we know about the castes and about the plot to make you the Mother of the Fenrhi and eventual Queen of Nifolhad. She also shared with us your sacrifices in ensuring that she and King Ranulf rose as the rightful leaders. More, you have affected the return to health of one of my most trusted guards, Lord Trian, and have given Chevlain a loyal and noble family from which your line will continue. Juliana and I shall be forever indebted to you and your sister. Your mother and father would be very proud of you."

The queen leaned forward. "Your markings...are they runes of some sort? Do they have a purpose?"

Claire lifted the straight veil of her hair away so the queen could better see her neck. "No, they are not runes, my queen. Simple designs to help me to focus on what needs to be accomplished."

"Nothing simple about them," the king corrected. "They are beautiful. Is it true? Are you able to foretell? Or do you need to cast stones as Trian's aunt does?" Claire smiled, but Trian was surprised that the king knew of his Aunt Cafellia's abilities.

"Nay, sire, I need no stones. Visions come to me when I look for them." Of her other abilities, she said naught. She would be forthcoming if asked a direct question, Trian knew, but she would offer nothing freely.

"This is the reason Trian and I sought you out," Claire continued. "Sometimes, my sight is clear, as it once was with Warin and Anwyl. Other times, what I see is confusing. It is from these jumbled visions that I am forewarned. One in particular, having to do with Prince Bowen, has me concerned."

"What have you seen?" Queen Juliana asked.

"He was on a ship," Claire replied, "anchored off our shores. Everything I sense tells me that he wishes to do harm here." The king and queen regarded one another. "That he *will* do harm."

"'Tis strange indeed, then," the queen observed. "For just last week, we heard from Queen Aghna that Bowen is currently a...*guest* in one of the towers in Sophiana. They have yet to decide his fate but assured me that his incarceration is indefinite."

"Aghna's letter suggested that Prince Bowen thinks to make a claim for Ragallach," the king explained. "He is the blood heir of Lady Ulicia, daughter of Lord Stephan and Lady Ascilia of Ragallach. Ever since his brother's demise, the territory has been without lord or lady. Tomas and Ailwen have been keeping the fortress for us until we can find a suitable and permanent leader. As there is no one else left who carries Lord Stephan's blood in their veins; Prince Bowen is the rightful heir."

Beside him, Claire became quite still. "But you will not allow this," Trian stated calmly.

"We will not," King Godwin vowed. "We will never forget that he murdered your parents, Claire."

"Aghna and Ranulf rejected his request to return here, then threw him in a tower." The queen took Claire's hand. "They would never subject you to that. Besides, Prince Bowen is also responsible for a multitude of deaths and crimes in Nifolhad; he will face justice there. However, if somehow he manages to pursue his claim and comes to Aurelia, we will grant his request."

"I see. For if he takes Ragallach as his own, he becomes your subject," Claire surmised.

"And subject to your laws," Trian finished. "His prior actions in Aurelia can then be deemed traitorous, and you can order his death."

"Precisely. But we will write to Aghna and Ranulf and so confirm that he is still captive. And to give them warning that he may try to escape. If he ever returns to our shores, he needs only step on Aurelian soil, and he is ours. On a ship, we can do naught but watch and wait to see what he will do." The king rose from his seat, drawing Trian away as well. "Come, I believe our wives have more to discuss."

"My queen," Trian said and bowed. "Wife," he added to Claire, kissing her cheek and whispering, "I will see you soon."

•••

"Years ago, when you spent time here as one of my ladies," Queen Juliana began, "I realized there was something special about you. Though you conversed with all and participated in every aspect at court, you kept a part of yourself separate. I understand now. And I think that your gifts are much greater than you let on." Lady Claire remained quiet, offering nothing. Juliana didn't mind; the daughters of Chevlain had proved their loyalty many times over.

"I saw and approved of your growing friendship with Warin, but I could never quite picture you together, and I worried that the two of you might be so caught up in your sense of duty that you would make an unwise union."

"I knew early on that Warin and I were not intended to be together," Claire said. "He was always destined for another."

Juliana smiled at that pronouncement. "When I first heard news of you and Trian, I admit to being surprised. Seeing you together, however, I am supremely happy for you both."

"I think, my queen, that I am not here to talk about me or my husband."

"No," Juliana agreed. "You mentioned a vision regarding Warin and the princess. Were they *together?*"

"I once told Warin that he would find someone he could love and that he would fight against the truth of it. Then I met Anwyl." She smiled wistfully. "It was a foregone conclusion that they were meant for one another."

"Yet?" Queen Juliana prompted.

"As I mentioned, I am able to have visions, when I so choose, about anyone. I can control them now, of course, but when I was younger..."

"Your fainting spells," the queen surmised.

"Yes."

"And what do you know of Warin and Anwyl?"

"I know that Warin loves her, though he is still too stubborn to admit it and recognize that his frustration is not caused by being near her, but from being apart. And Anwyl, in a way, she has always known. You see, Ni'Mala, the Fenrhi Mother, once foretold that the princess would fall in love with a stranger from a faraway land, one matching Warin's description. And that prediction...well, you know Anwyl. She's a scholar; it's in her nature to fight against the idea that her fate is predetermined. Besides, I think she has given up on him returning her feelings. Things would have been much easier for her had Ni'Mala never made her prediction."

Claire frowned, and Juliana waited. "My queen, the visions about them needing each other are strong, but they are also confusing. And I've been so preoccupied with Bowen. When I do center my thoughts on Anwyl, I see that she will marry, but not Warin. And I sense tragedy for him. Then, in the next moment, I believe that Anwyl and Warin will unite. More, I have seen both Warin's death *and* his future with Anwyl. Two very disparate outcomes: tragedy versus happiness."

Queen Juliana sank back into her chair. "I see. Was it this way with you and Trian?"

"No, thank the heavens. I have never been able to divine my own future. I am...immune to reading Trian's. A gift, really. If I may ask, how came you to sense the attraction between Warin and the princess?"

"Observation," Juliana replied and wondered at the soft smile that played on Lady Claire's lips. She told Claire about Anwyl's loneliness, about her correspondence with Warin, though they knew not to whom they wrote. She related to Claire the details of Queen Aghna's decision that Anwyl marry an Aurelian noble, about the list of suitable husbands in Warin's possession, and Anwyl's acceptance of her fate. "I have tasked Warin with finding her a groom, hoping he will see her through other men's eyes. Mayhap his own will open."

• • •

Leagues away in a dilapidated and forgotten keep

"You'll do as I tell you," the brute threatened, "or your brother'll pay dearly for your disobedience!" He squeezed Winn's wrist even tighter to drive home his point. Only nine years old, with almost as many years teaching him the harsh reality of life, and Winn was able to control his agony as the bones in his wrist ground against each other. Any tighter, and they would surely snap.

"Yes, yes! Just stop hurting him," Lou cried, pounding ineffectually at Winn's tormentor. "I'll do whatever you say!"

Winn didn't think he could withstand the pain much longer. Harsk's crushing grip lessened, and Winn steeled himself for what was coming. Their guardian was cruel beyond words; he gave a vicious twist, and Winn felt one of his bones crack. He waited until the man left his room before he allowed himself to choke on the gasp that he'd held back.

"I'm so sorry, Winn," Lou cried. "This is my fault; I should've agreed with him right away. I just don't want to leave you here alone."

"You have to do as he says," Winn commanded. The keep's housekeeper entered the room, medicaments and bandages at the ready. All the servants were aware of the abuse Winn and Lou's guardian doled out, but they could do naught to stop it. They suffered from the same cruelty, sometimes worse. "Now go pack your things. It'll be harder for the both of us if you tarry." The housekeeper tutted at them as she examined his wrist before splinting his arm; Lou nodded and hastened away.

"Your father would be proud of you, Master Winn, the way you take care of Lou, what with you being the younger of his children. Proud, I say, and your mother too."

"If Lou is safe somewhere else," Winn admitted, "I'll be better able to avoid Harsk, won't I?" He winced when he tried moving his fingers.

"'Tis a small break and will mend quickly," the old housekeeper promised.

"It always does," he replied, thinking of the day when he would be grown up enough to defend himself. "It always does."

CHAPTER FIFTEEN

Redavel Castle

The Smallholds, Aurelia

News of their travels had spread throughout the Smallholds, and no one seemed to think it strange that a Nifolhadian princess was touring Aurelia for the sole purpose of looking at trees. What did surprise Warin was the overwhelming welcome displayed each time she arrived at a place she'd once before visited. Her recollection of names and faces was extraordinary, and where he once thought her to be a flit-about, he now saw her as a diplomat of the highest rank.

Warin nudged his horse closer to her and Madyan so that he could better hear their conversation. Madyan was telling Anwyl that the two pijala trees planted in Chevlain were doing well, and he was curious as to why Anwyl seemed dissatisfied with the account.

"One pijala tree can produce enough fruit for a keep or castle and its household," the princess explained. "An orchard can produce enough for an entire territory. It is not enough that the trees flourish. The seeds must be given the chance to naturally produce new trees."

"Can't they take cuttings?" Warin asked.

The princess appeared surprised by his interest, and after a moment, she responded. "Grafting only produced stunted trees with negligible yields; the pihaberries themselves—impotent. Propagating with seeds is also untenable."

"But there *are* orchards," Madyan pointed out.

"By chance. You see, sometimes we find pijala seedlings miles away from the main orchard. When we find these shoots, we transfer them to our orchards, though a few have been left to grow on their own in the wild. Finding and protecting these stray trees is a challenge."

"Can't you simply leave some of the fruit on the trees and let nature take its course?" Warin asked.

She shook her head. "There is no rhyme or reason that our master gardeners have discovered. Allowing the fruit to ripen and drop is no guarantee that a seedling will take root. We've had seasons where not a single new tree has developed. Pijalas are temperamental."

"We're coming up on Redavel; how fares their progress?" Madyan asked.

"It remains an orchard of two trees." She sighed. "The orchard master has nearly given up hope. Though their pijalas have taken root and produce fruit, they have had no new saplings. Unfortunately, I still receive letters detailing methods of taking cuttings and trying to sow the seeds in various types of soil, this despite me reiterating that these methods have already been tried and have failed. The orchard masters of Aurelia are a stubborn group."

Madyan snorted.

Warin looked ahead. The verdant green valley of Redavel was the least likely place that the pijala trees would flourish. It was as nearly a bad location as the walled garden in Kings Glen. But the royal edict had been clear. Harvest the pihaberries, then focus on producing additional trees. King Godwin wanted pijala orchards throughout the realm. If the seeds were abundant, they could be given freely to his people. He did not want the fruit to take on the sacred role that it had in Nifolhad.

They remained quiet for the rest of the afternoon, and when they emerged from the forest through which they rode, they were met by their first welcoming party.

Lord Haden of Redavel had ridden out to greet the princess. The seat of his smallhold, still a half-day's ride from their location, was home to his son, Lord Ernald, one of the noblemen deemed fit enough to be a possible husband for Anwyl. Neither he nor the princess had met the lordling, for Ernald did not frequent court. Looking at him now, riding behind his father, Warin could immediately exclude him from the list of potential grooms. He was all of nineteen years and was a rail of a young man, barely managing to control his old palfrey. Moreover, it was clear that he was not interested in Princess Anwyl; his manners toward her bordered on rude. Lord Haden muttered something into his son's ear, and he finally deigned to half-bow in his saddle in acknowledgement.

Lord Haden wanted to immediately visit the pijala orchard, and as it was on their way, the princess agreed. She positioned herself so that she rode next to Ernald, leaving Warin to ride ahead with his father. They had ridden nearly an hour, and Warin—growing fatigued of listening to Lord Haden lament the deplorable condition of his pijala trees while ignoring his counter-attempts to reassure the Lord of Redavel that King Godwin knew it to be a difficult task—turned in his seat to check on the princess and the lordling. He expected her to be in a snit at the man's ill manners. Much to his astonishment, the two were deep in conversation. Princess Anwyl was smiling and nodding, and Ernald's expression held not a trace of his former hauteur. Warin managed to catch Madyan's eye, and she shrugged at him as if nothing were more natural.

It wasn't until after they had examined the saplings—the princess exclaiming the excellent care of the young trees—and reached the castle, that Warin had a chance to ask the princess how she had won him over.

"What do you mean?" she asked, then pressed her lips together in a taut line as she dismounted. Her foot came down upon a loose cobble, and she gave a delicate yelp. As she continued on her way, Warin was first to notice the strain in her expression, but it was Madyan who called their party to a halt, recommending that she be carried. A great fuss was made, despite the princess insisting that she was fine. Lord Haden was too old to carry her and Ernald simply lacked the strength, so Warin stepped forward and, before she could protest, scooped her into his arms.

She weighed little-to-nothing and was frowning up at him. "What?" Warin asked. "Walking will only make it worse."

"*Hmpf*," was her only rejoinder, but her pained expression lessened somewhat.

And Warin, desperate to make peace with his charge, slowed his pace, falling behind the others. "Tell me, what did you say to the young lordling to make him so attentive to your every word?" he asked, hoping to start a polite conversation.

"Why is it that when you say *lordling*, it sounds like an insult? Ernald is a nobleman, learned and talented in what he has chosen as his vocation. Think you less of him because he prefers to stick his nose in a book and not some—" She stopped herself and slanted a look at him. "He and I have common interests," she stated, more self-possessed. "You know the ulterior motive for this journey as well as I. Would you have me look only at a man's physicality to determine his worth? I am not so shallow as to believe that only a handsome rake is deserving of my attention."

Warin couldn't credit how she managed it, cradled in his arms as she was, but she lifted her nose haughtily and looked forward. Somehow, he sensed that she was as angry with herself as she was with him. "I did not mean to insult—

" he started. "You are right, and I apologize. I forget that this must be difficult for you, and distracting comments will not assist you in making your decision." Before he could say more, they reached the entrance to the castle, and single file, they were ushered to their rooms. Princess Anwyl thanked their hosts outside of her quarters, begging the afternoon for her ankle to recover. They bowed to her, promising to send refreshments and hot water in which to bathe.

Madyan entered their quarters, dropping their saddlebags on the smaller of the two beds in the room. Warin gently set the princess on the other platform and then pulled over a chair to examine her ankle. "Madyan can help me," Princess Anwyl insisted, grimacing in pain when he lifted her heel to elevate her leg on a cushion.

"It looks like Warin has the right of it, Princess," Madyan stated, peering over Warin's shoulder. "You'll have to remove her boot. I'll go to the kitchen and see if there are ingredients for a poultice."

"King's clover will help with the swelling if they have any," Warin said. "And check to see if they have meadowsweet for the pain. She can drink it with some tea."

"*She* is right here," Princess Anwyl intoned.

"Perhaps some lavender for your sour moods as well," Madyan suggested, staring at them. Princess Anwyl threw her hands in the air and flopped back into the cushions behind her.

"*Moods?*" Warin demanded.

"Yes. I'm talking to you both," Madyan lectured. "I don't know what has happened between you, but I'm tired of it. I've spent the last month tiptoeing around you both, never able to relax. If you think I want to spend the next season riding beside the two of you, trying to get you to say one kind word to the other, you've another think coming!" She spun on her heel and stormed away.

After staring at the door for what must've been two minutes, Warin turned to regard Princess Anwyl. She was looking at the ceiling, her eyes wide and shining. The last thing he wanted to do was to say something that would make her unshed tears spill, so he turned his attention to her ankle. "I'll be as gentle as I can," he soothed. "Thankfully, you wear Nifolhadian boots that lace up." He gently prized the leather knot of her bootstrings apart, then slowly pulled the laces through each eyelet, allowing the leather to loosen to its farthest extent. When he was done, he braced one hand over her ankle to steady it while cupping the heel of her boot with the other. "This is going to hurt," he warned. She nodded and put her arm over her eyes. "Princess?"

"Just do it quickly," she said, still hiding her face from him.

He held her ankle immobile, then drew the heel of her boot up and away. The hiss of air through her teeth was the only indication of the pain she felt. He rolled down her stocking, supporting her ankle as he drew it away. Her foot was soft and delicate, he noted with a bemused smile.

"What is so funny?" she asked. He hadn't realized that she had moved her arm and was watching him.

"Not funny," he replied. "You have a very pretty foot. I was just thinking that it could belong to a princess."

"I *am* a princess."

"I know," Warin said. "Now, let's take a look at what you've done." She propped herself up on her elbows to assess the damage. Free of the constraining leather of her boot, her ankle began to swell, and she winced when he set it back on the cushion. "I'm sorry," he said without looking at her.

"It's all right; it only hurts a little."

"No," he said, lifting his gaze to hers. "I'm sorry." He didn't know if she realized that he was apologizing for all he'd done and said to hurt her, but he needed to say it.

She stared at him as if trying to discern his intent, then heaved a great sigh. "All right," she replied, then gestured to her ankle.

"If you stay off it, we should be able to depart as scheduled. But we can extend our stay if you think you need more time with Lord Ernald."

"You managed to keep the derision out of your voice that time," she noted, then winced when he probed her ankle with his fingers. "Why don't you like him?"

"Not broken," he said, more to himself than her. "It's not that I dislike him. I just don't want you to waste your time. You deserve a better husband than he would make."

"Ah," she said. "I wondered that the queen put him on the list."

"She probably doesn't know; I doubt that anyone at court does. How did you discover his secret?"

"That he prefers the company of men?"

Warin nodded.

"He spoke overmuch about their keep's minstrel. Contrary to the Aurelian belief that Nifolhad is a realm of repressed individuals, there are pockets of progressive thought, especially in Sophiana. Ernald would not have to hide what I imagine is considered weak by some in Aurelia."

"Certainly not by any in Pheldhain," Warin assured, then looked toward the door when he heard noises in the corridor. "Must be the servants with refreshments, Princess." She frowned at him. "What is it?"

"Nothing."

"Come now, I thought that perhaps we could start fresh. Tell me what I said to make you frown."

"You call me *Princess* the same way you called Ernald *lordling.*"

He was poised to deny it, but she was right. "I see."

"Please, just call me Anwyl."

Madyan entered with a string of servants carrying refreshments, bandages, various herbs and tonics, and steaming bath water.

"Lord Haden had planned a banquet in your honor," said one woman, who had introduced herself as the castle's housekeeper. "He wishes to know if, due to your injury, you will be unable to attend, and if unable, be made aware that he will postpone the festivities until you are recovered."

Warin did not want to extend their visit to Redavel longer than was necessary, and he didn't think that the princess wanted to stay either. She nodded to him, trusting him to speak on her behalf. "Please tell Lord Haden that Princess Anwyl thanks him for his hospitality and that she will attend the banquet as planned." The servant nodded, then herded the others from the room.

Madyan leaned over to look at her friend's ankle, now swollen and discolored, then carefully rubbed some balm on it. After sliding an oilcloth underneath, she draped cold wet towels over the princess's injury. "How do you plan on getting to the dining hall, Princess?"

"The same way she got here," Warin replied. "Now, if you'll excuse me, I'll settle my things in my room and tidy myself before the celebration. Madyan," he said, nodding to her as he walked toward the door. "Prin—Anwyl," he added and bowed. Her eyes, for so long emotionless when she gazed upon him, warmed a little as he closed the door.

Once in his room, he sat on the bed. As he shrugged out of his tunic and shirt, he detected a delicate spicy-citrus scent from when he'd carried the princess. It was an exotic blend, one he'd not smelled before on any of the other ladies at court, and it suited Anwyl perfectly. Still, it seemed familiar to him, though he couldn't recall whence came the odor. There was a knock at his door.

"Enter," he called, donning his spare shirt.

"Pardon, m'lord," the servant standing in the hall started. "The laundress would like to know if you need anything cleaned." Warin handed over his shirt and a few other items. "And the tunic, m'lord?"

He thought about the scent still clinging to the fabric. "No, it's fine. It only needs a good brushing," he stated. The servant retreated, closing the door behind him.

. . .

On Board *The Sea Hare*, North of Naca Bay, Nifolhad

Captain Juna choked on the very air he was desperately trying to draw into his lungs. They were two days shy of Naca Bay, and he'd finally succumbed to the debilitating sickness that had swept through *The Sea Hare*. He and what remained of his crew had somehow managed to find a cove in which to anchor, incapable as they were of sailing the ship a moment longer. Dugan had reported that at least a third of his men had died. Then Dugan himself had perished.

Juna had attempted to leave his bed more than once. When he last woke, he lay sprawled across the floor with a gash on his forehead. He had barely managed to make it back to his hammock. It'd been hours since he'd heard anything other than the lapping of water against the hull and the cry of seagulls. Gone were the moans and retching noises from his crew. For all he knew, he was the last man alive on *The Sea Hare*. He slid back into an unnatural unconsciousness, where nightmarish creatures clawed and snapped at him.

"Captain," a weak voice called. "Captain Juna. Do you live?" Juna struggled unsuccessfully to lever open his eyelids. Someone forced his clenched jaw apart, and he tasted a bitter liquid. He coughed and sputtered. "You must try to swallow, Captain. Here, just a little more. I sent for help, and the Fenrhi answered our plea. The Sylvan healers made this, and they sent someone to nurse what's left of the crew." Juna swallowed a small amount. "That's it, Captain. A little more."

A cool, soothing hand brushed his forehead. Through the slit of his eyelids, he saw a woman robed in soft blue. Beside her, looking as awful as Juna felt, was Dorn. The woman drew back, and Juna's gaze was drawn to the beautiful lines and patterns trailing over her hand and wrist, all in indigo. "You've saved me twice now, Dorn," he croaked, then succumbed to another fit of choking.

"Be still, Captain Juna," the woman spoke.

"My men?"

"I will see to those still breathing. For now, you must sleep and heal. You want to sleep, don't you?"

Dorn and the woman exchanged glances, but before he could ponder its import, his mind slipped into a numbing slumber.

• • •

"You are sure that you can trust the rest of these men?" she asked when she and Dorn departed the captain's cabin.

"Those who were stronger in mind were doubly dosed, making recovery from the poison impossible. Any that you are unable to control will find themselves relapsing."

"I assure you, Captain Juna will be no problem. You saw how easily he fell asleep. He'll *want* to follow my—your—every instruction. But when I'm done, I must return to the temple or my absence will be noted."

"I think not. I've decided that you will stay with me."

"I can be of more service to you in the temple. I can—" She stopped midsentence and ducked her chin submissively. "As you say."

"I'll need you to start with the crew right away. Cull the ones whose minds might be too strong. For the remainder, they are to implicitly follow the orders of their captain."

"And Captain Juna?"

"He will attend to mine, of course. Tomorrow, we sail for Naca Bay to retrieve Odo and bolster this crew with loyal men." The Fenrhi woman paled at the mention of Odo. "Do not worry, Vala. I'll keep him leashed. As long as you remain useful, you need not fear my dog. Now go to work."

"Right away, my—"

"Dorn," he reminded. Vala nodded, then went to administer to the rest of the crew, whether playing angel or demon, only time would tell. Dorn returned to Captain Juna's cabin. It was never too early to start sowing the seeds that they would need to take on more crew and that Dorn knew exactly where to find trustworthy men.

CHAPTER SIXTEEN

Mulberry Wine

"What do you mean *she's gone*?" Warin demanded.

"That she is not to be found," Madyan repeated impatiently. "She wanted to rest her ankle and so retired to our room. I was in and out all morning arranging for our departure and, as she had drifted off to sleep, I tried not to disturb her. When I returned to wake her, it wasn't the princess in her bed."

"Who was in her bed?" he shouted.

"Not who, *what*—bed cushions to make it look like she was under the blankets."

"Madyan," he started soberly.

"Absolutely not! She would never leave without informing us."

"She's done it before," he said flatly, not wanting to believe she could do so again.

"Without telling you first?"

Warin thought about that fateful morning that she had departed without him. She *had* told him that she intended to leave; he'd ignored her. "No," he admitted, scanning the courtyard.

With winter only months away, the servants were in the process of cleaning the castle's rugs and tapestries. The beaters were swinging away; dust billowed into the air in great gray clouds. Lord Haden approached at a fast clip.

"We've searched the grounds," he stated. "There's no sign of her. Ernald is heading up the castle search."

"When was the last time anyone actually saw her?" Warin demanded, still watching the rug beaters.

"A little over two hours ago," Madyan replied. "She was sleeping, and I pulled the blankets up to cover her before leaving the chamber."

Warin watched as two men carried a rather large, rolled tapestry to the beaters. To a person, every face was covered with a kerchief or cloth to protect them from the dust. Two more servants exited the castle. Instead of taking their rug to the beaters, they turned the corner and disappeared from view. "Where are they going?"

"To the river," Lord Haden explained. "Rugs that are overly soiled are scrubbed in the shallows."

Ernald exited the castle and, espying their group, hastened in their direction. Before Warin could ask, he shook his head. "Royals and rugs, such a worrisome start to the day."

The men who had carried the rug from view had returned, faces still covered, and re-entered the castle. "What did you just say?" Warin demanded.

"He said, 'royals and rugs,'" Madyan provided.

"Just so," Ernald confirmed. "We seem to be missing a tapestry. The servants went to retrieve it, and it was already gone. Probably in the pile waiting to be beaten. I just thought it odd because it was from the chamber next to where you stayed with the princess."

Madyan turned to Warin, seemingly gleaning his suspicion. "Penetrating the castle today would be a simple affair...with the cloths covering their faces. But who? And where have they taken her?"

Warin's gaze fell to the east. Neighboring Dinhyll lay that way, the smallhold to which Lord Herlewin and his mother had been banished. But if he were wrong...

"Lord Haden," he began. "Has anyone from the other smallholds visited you of late?"

Lord Haden shook his head, but then Ernald interjected, "Yes. Remember, Father? Several days ago, two men arrived, claiming that their wagon had a broken axle. The smithy repaired some metal ring, and Cook fed them while they waited."

"Did they say where they were headed?"

"No," Lord Haden answered. "Just that they were in a hurry to deliver their wine."

"They were headed to Dinhyll," Ernald stated definitively. "It was mulberry wine, they said. Terrible stuff, if you ask me, but it's Lady Eunice's favorite."

He was about to say more but was stopped when Warin reached out and pulled him into a great hug, then slapped his back with a newfound appreciation for the lordling. "Ernald," he stated, pulling away and climbing onto Konjimar's back, "I could just kiss you." He spurred his great steed and galloped toward Dinhyll. Behind him, he heard Madyan on her mare. He slowed only enough so that her desert horse could catch up to his great Chevlain destrier.

"I've sent the wagons on," she called to him, tossing him a bag of provisions, which he hooked over the pommel of his saddle. "We can rejoin with them once we retrieve Princess Anwyl."

Warin nodded and urged his mount faster. Madyan's mare kept apace as they crossed the shallow river marking the border between smallholds. Dinhyll was a land of hills and rises, one that would eventually give way to a hummock-pocked marshy lowland. The castle itself sat upon the highest elevation in the region, a lone butte surrounded by watery fields of rice and water chestnuts—the only two crops that flourished in the area.

Fortunately, the trail made by the wagon was easy to follow; it cut across the stubbly fall grasses in two parallel lines, as if a giant had dragged two young tree trunks over the bumps and pimples of the terrain. The wagon's drivers, no doubt, had thought to angle their route southeast to reach the king's road that cut through the central smallhold of Prato. Once upon the great route, their escape into Dinhyll would be fleet, for the raised road was flat and wide, and always in good repair. He and Madyan needed to catch the men before they left the hilly area through which they now galloped.

For over an hour they raced, up one rise and down another, on and on, slowing only when they came to one of the many low ridges spattering the region. When Warin deemed that they were nearly upon the abductors, he and Madyan dismounted and crept forward. They peered over the ridge. In the distance, a wagon was lumbering up a great hill.

"We'll wait until they go over. They haven't spared their horses and will be easy to catch on the next rise," he predicted. Madyan nodded. They rested their mounts while the wagon was pulled to the top of the hill.

As it disappeared, they remounted. Madyan's nimble horse was faster than Warin's at picking her way down the slope, but his steed's lengthy strides ate up the gap when they climbed. Both riders reached the crest at the same time. Ahead of them, only a third of the way up the next rise, the wagon trudged onward. Two men sat in the driver's seat, and when they realized that they were being pursued, they urged their team faster. It was of no use, for Warin and Madyan fell quickly upon them, forcing them to stop.

"What ho?" the burlier of the two yelled at Warin. "Are ye bandits? We carry naught but mulberry wine."

And indeed, it looked as if there were only barrels in the wagon. Madyan dismounted and was inspecting the cargo. "We've guessed wrong."

But Warin knew a thing or two about hidden goods. He drew his sword and cut the straps holding the barrels in place. Gravity and the incline of the hill lent a hand, and each keg slid off the wagon, all tumbling end over end before rolling to the bottom of the hill. In the center of the wagon bed, three kegs stubbornly refused to budge. "Lift them up," he ordered, pointing his sword at the drivers. When they hesitated, Madyan gave them each a clout in quick succession with her quarterstaff.

Thus encouraged, they climbed over their seat to the back of the wagon and hauled the nearest barrel away. The other two lifted as well, having been secured to the first, revealing that four or five staves had been removed to create a secret compartment. They hefted the partial barrels over the side of the wagon, revealing a rolled tapestry.

"If she was not still wrapped in that rug, you'd be dead where you stand," Warin swore. "Now, carry her down. And gently. Any scratch or bruise returns to you tenfold."

The men lifted the rug, then lowered it carefully to the ground. Madyan used her staff to push them away from where they hovered over their prey while Warin unrolled the tapestry to reveal Princess Anwyl, still asleep with not even an eyelash bent.

The relief Warin felt at seeing her safe was physical. He glowered at the wagon drivers. "You are lucky men today," Warin growled. "For if we'd found her in any other state—"

Madyan hissed. "This merits more than a warning. This is an insult to the Royal House of Nifolhad." She turned on the men. "You'd best tell us your intent."

"'Twas Lady Eunice who ordered it," the burly man cried. "We was to give her some special tea, so she'd sleep, then bring her quick-like to Dinhyll Castle."

"Why?" Warin demanded.

"For her wedding, I s'pose," the other driver exclaimed.

"To Herlewin?"

"Must be, though he's been away from the castle for a few weeks."

Madyan turned to Warin. "I would be within my rights killing these two, wouldn't I?"

"Yes. It's King's Law," he provided. The two men paled as Madyan argued in favor of their immediate execution.

"Please, m'lord," the younger driver cried. "I've a wee'un on the way. We was only followin' orders."

"Lady Eunice won't learn a lesson if we kill them, Madyan. The snake will just grow another head," he said, referencing an old Nifolhadian myth. He wasn't sure, but he thought he saw her lip twitch.

She twirled her staff menacingly before the two men. "Have you heard the rumors about the Fenrhi women?" They nodded again, their eyes widening. "I'm from the Umbren Caste, and if you ever speak of this day, I will know. From the shadows, I'll come for you. You will never see me. You will never hear me. Quieter than the shifting sands of the Fyrost, I am. I will know if you talk and will exact revenge for what you have done this day. Not just on you and the Lady of Dinhyll, but on your families as well."

Warin grabbed the bedroll from his horse, then transferred Anwyl to it. "Roll up that rug and return it to Lord Haden. If you do this right away, I'll write out a warrant to him to not charge you with thievery." The men nodded and soon had the tapestry back in the wagon.

"Now, go, before I change my mind!" Warin ordered, and the men struggled to turn the groaning wagon on the hill. "When you return home, be sure to tell your lady that if she should ever raise a hand toward Princess Anwyl again, even to wave at her, I will see to it that she and her son lose Dinhyll and be banished to The Skells. And tell Lady Eunice that she should expect sanctions from Kings Glen as well."

The man driving the wagon slapped the reins to the team's hindquarters. They lurched forward too quickly, and he nearly fell back into the empty wagon. But the yoked horses dug in, and their gait evened out as they pulled a much-unburdened load back the way they'd come. Warin stared at them until they disappeared over the apex, then sat down next to the princess, cradling her in his arms. Madyan tipped a barrel on end and perched herself impatiently upon it. She stood again, and paced, then resumed her seat to stare after the tracks left by the wagon. Warin was about to ask her what was troubling her when Princess Anwyl began to stir. Madyan dropped down next to her, but the sleeping woman resumed the delicate purr that vibrated against Warin's chest.

"The thing about snakes," Madyan groused, "is that you must make plenty of noise to deter them from striking." She picked up her quarterstaff and stood.

"And carry a big stick," Warin added.

"Precisely," the Umbren woman stated. She walked over to her mare and mounted the now rested beast. She gazed east, toward Dinhyll. "The acts of this viper merit more than a royal sanction. Don't worry, I only plan on poking at the nest."

"Don't get caught," he cautioned her with a grin.

Madyan snorted and then kicked her mare into a canter and was gone.

It took another hour before Anwyl began to wake in earnest. When she finally blinked at him, he smiled and smoothed her hair from her forehead. "Good day to you, Princess."

Her brilliant green eyes stared up into his, and she sighed. "So blue, deep like the sea. Would that I were a drop…" Her eyelids drifted shut, and she was asleep again. For a half an hour, Warin stared down at her, trying to parse out her unfinished statement. Her face, usually so animated, held him captive with its serene beauty. Her dark hair was undone, and thick shiny waves of it fell about her shoulders, a mantle of silky mink. He couldn't stop himself from running his fingers over her fine tresses. He reached to do so again, and she stirred.

"Where am I?" she asked groggily, seeing the hills around her and the abandoned barrels.

"Dinhyll. But you are safe. I'll tell you all about it on the way to Floresta."

"There's but one horse," she noted.

"My Konji can carry us both," Warin assured her.

"All right," she agreed with no resistance, then yawned prettily. "Who is Konji?"

"Konjimar—Konji, for short—is my stallion."

She gazed about again. "Where is Madyan?"

"She's gone to exact payment."

"Payment for what?"

"For the honor of your company, I suppose."

• • •

"You're sure that she'll be all right?" Anwyl pestered Warin again.

"She'll be fine," Warin assured her, surprisingly, without the note of annoyance that had always graced his tone before. "I worry more for Lady Eunice and Lord Herlewin." His horse sidestepped one of the many whistle-pig burrows they'd come across, and his arm tightened around her waist. To take her mind away from his proximity, Anwyl stared ahead. It had been a long time since she had imagined them riding off together into the sunset.

But here she was, and she gave a little snort at the irony. "Pardon," she said after hiding the noise in a quick fit of coughing. She gazed west and sighed. The sun was well into its descent, burning a spectacular path in fiery oranges and blazing magentas.

"Are you tired?" Warin asked, and his words rumbled from his chest, through the layers of clothing, and straight into her back.

"No," she replied a little too breathlessly. She sat straighter, hoping to create a bit of space between them. It was no use, for even though Konji's gait was smooth, each step had some part of her rubbing against Warin. His arms created a relaxed circle around her as he held the reins, his muscular thighs bracketed hers, and when he spoke, his breath puffed against her cheek. The quieter she remained, so, too, did he. She yawned again, then surrendered to circumstance and leaned back against him. If only she weren't so bored.

On the fourth morning of their ride, she woke on her own and to the sound of birdsong. Warin had his back to her and was saddling Konji. Anwyl sat up and rolled their blankets. Still seated on the ground, she used her uninjured foot to push dirt over the dying embers of their campfire.

"Good morning," Warin greeted, sitting beside her and handing her a chunk of cheese and an apple. "This is the last of our provisions, but we'll have a roof over our heads and a hearty meal before the sun sets."

"I think that we'll rest a few days at the inn," he said, studying her swollen ankle and gently probing the area while she finished eating. "Riding every day hasn't helped." He stood, then bent to lift her and carry her to a copse where she could complete her necessaries. She hadn't even had to ask him. And when she finished, she hopped on one leg to the edge of the trees. Warin rushed to scoop her up and carry her to his destrier.

She wasn't as tired as before, but still found herself bored by the interminable farmlands. Then, far off in the distance, she thought she could make out a line etched across the horizon. "Is that the High Way?" she asked excitedly, for the scenery would soon be changing.

"*Mmm-hmm*," came Warin's reply, a small noise that vibrated through her bones. "It'll be some time until we reach it; the farmlands make it appear closer than it is."

They continued to ride, but the thin line stayed frustratingly out of reach. After the interminable mounds that made up Dinhyll, Anwyl had hoped for a more diverse landscape when they had crossed into Crevalo. Yes, the hills had smoothed out, giving way to low, rolling plains, with an occasional shallow stream to ford. But the fields were brown, having been recently mowed, and windrow after windrow of drying hay passed by in monotonous succession. The effect was dizzying, and she closed her eyes.

"If you are feeling unwell, we could stop and rest."

"Good gravy, no!" she begged.

He laughed. "Are you up for a canter?"

"Oh, please, let's do. I am so bored; I feel as if I've been given another sleeping tonic." She reached out for the saddle's pommel but found she needn't have bothered. Warin leaned forward, pressing his chest to her back, and passed some silent signal to Konji. He held the reins in one hand and then snaked his arm around her waist to support her. The stallion transitioned directly into a smooth canter.

"All right?"

"Faster, please," she replied, and he chuckled.

The burst of speed as the destrier shifted into a gallop was exhilarating. And instead of holding the pommel, Anwyl latched onto Warin's arm. They raced over the fields, startling birds from their hidden ground nests, and when they came upon a brook, Warin slowed enough to take its measure, then let Konji go. His horse didn't hesitate and leapt over with ease. Anwyl's heart beat in time with each pounding hoof-fall. In very little time, they reached the raised road.

The late hour of the day saw little traffic on the High Way, and what passersby there were, streaked by them in a blur. Konjimar maintained the canter, only slowing to a walk when Warin reined back to let him rest. When they reached the stable yard of the Whistlepig Inn, they were greeted by the men driving their wagon. A rider had joined them, and from his livery, he looked to be a royal messenger.

Warin hopped down, then reached up to lift her to the ground. She was unsteady at first, her muscles still recovering their workings. Forgetting her ankle, she took a step toward the inn and winced as pain stabbed up her leg. Warin saw and would've scooped her up and into his arms if she hadn't forestalled him. "If I could just hold your arm for support..." With his assistance, she was just able to limp into the inn. Warin secured their accommodations, helped her to her room and, after seeing that her fire was lit, a bath was ordered, and a meal was on its way, went to find the Royal Messenger to retrieve their correspondence.

He had so efficiently seen to her needs that she hadn't even a chance to properly thank him. She sat on her bed and thought about the past week. Had she really been rolled up in a rug? She still couldn't believe it possible that Lady Eunice would make such a desperate attempt to force her into a marriage with her son. Clearly, her boat was missing a few oars.

There was a knock at her door, and she bade the person enter. Porters carried in a soaking basin, then buckets of steaming water. One of the wagon drivers brought in her traveling trunk, and another servant brought in a folding screen. A young girl stood outside the door, and Anwyl thought she heard Warin's voice. The girl passed within, cleared the room of everyone, and bolted the latch. She turned, holding soft bath linens and a leather satchel.

"Good day to you, your highness," she said while dipping to a curtsy. "The innkeeper has asked me to attend to you. I have bath salts and soaps and, as you can see, sheets for drying. And the Royal Guardsman, he gave me this pouch to give to you. May I help you to disrobe?"

Anwyl stood and removed her thick cloak, and the girl's eyes widened at the Fenrhi garments that she wore. Her tunic with its long panels and the linen chemise underneath were not too out-of-the-ordinary, but Anwyl suspected that the intricately embroidered sash seemed especially exotic, as were the soft woolen breeches tucked into her high boots—at least one high boot, the one she'd been missing since Redavel was now resting on top of her trunk.

"Your clothes are so beautiful," the girl said wistfully, then shook out her own full skirts. "How much easier it must be to do what needs to be done in breeches. I am forever getting caught up by my hem." She blushed. "My pardon, your majesty."

"It's quite all right... What's your name?"

"Lucilla, your highness." She curtsied again, and quite elegantly too.

Anwyl placed her age around fourteen years. She had an oval face, a tentative smile, and pretty blue eyes that were large and bright and just a touch sad. Her hair was blond and was gathered into two neat braids that ran down her back. Her bearing was proud, her speech cultured, as if she'd benefitted from tutoring. Even her nose, delicate and pointed at the tip, seemed at odds with her station. She must have trained with a noble family, perhaps as a companion to some noble daughter. "Can you help me to the basin?"

The girl was deft in her duties. "Have you always been a maid, Lucilla?" Anwyl asked, curious about the girl.

"No, m'lady, not until last year." Anwyl lifted an eyebrow expectantly, and Lucilla smiled. "It's a long story, Princess," she said.

"I seem to have nothing but time this evening," Anwyl prompted, taking care to keep the marks on her legs hidden under the hem of her chemise. "If you don't mind the telling of it."

"I lived with my grandmother, and when she fell ill and passed away, I came here in hopes of finding honest work. Before she succumbed to her illness, she and I took in sewing. I embroidered the dresses of many of the noblewomen in the smallholds."

"Oh," Anwyl said, hoping the disappointment she felt at hearing such a simple tale was not evident.

Lucilla supported her and eased her into the bath. "It's not as exciting a story as my grandmother's. Would you like to hear it?" she held out like a carrot, and Anwyl nodded.

"She was the daughter of a minor lord and lady whose lands had been incorporated into one of the other smallholds. She and her family were allowed to hold the family keep, live and earn off the surrounding land, but had to pledge their able-bodied men to their new lord. In return, the new lord of the smallhold would assist with maintaining the keep during the leaner years. My grandmother watched as her older sisters were married to various minor lords and second and third sons of other noble families, all of which lived afar. Both of her parents died before she was betrothed, so no dowry had been settled upon her. The lord of the smallhold was kind and stepped in, offering a small amount. He even arranged for her to marry one of his cousins. They lived happily in her family's keep, producing one child, my mother. Then, when my grandmother was widowed, a new lord was assigned to the keep. She had a few jewels left from her husband, a ring that had belonged to her mother, and some coin. The money went toward my mother's dowry. My grandmother was given a room at the keep, and in exchange, she took in work suitable to her one skill— needlecraft."

"But what about your mother?" Anwyl asked, sinking a little deeper into the hot bath and noticing for the first time how horrible her hair smelled—a cross between moldering mulberries and a dust-encrusted tapestry. Warin had never even sniffed his nose at her, tucked as she'd been directly under his chin. Not once. Anwyl smiled at the thought. Oh, how his eyes must have watered.

"She married and lived with my father's family," Lucilla continued. "He was a kind man, I was told, and offered my grandmother a place in their home, but she refused, saying that they were newly wed and expecting a child. I was born soon after." She paused and looked down. "Some years later, my mother and father were struck down by a fever that swept through the region. I was spared." Lucilla took a steadying breath, then applied herself to washing Anwyl's hair. "I was found a day later by the blacksmith's wife. She knew where to find my grandmother."

"I'm sorry," Anwyl said. "I lost my parents when I was young, but I have some memories of them."

"Thank you," Lucilla said. "Most people assume it was easier because of my age."

"It's never easy," Anwyl stated gently, squeezing the girl's hand. "At least you had your grandmother, as I had my older brother."

Anwyl leaned back against the basin and closed her eyes while Lucilla gently combed the snarls from her hair. "So, you are, in fact, Lady Lucilla," Anwyl pronounced as soon as the thought occurred to her.

"I've only ever known a life serving others, Princess," Lucilla admitted, handing Anwyl a cloth to cover her face while she rinsed the soap from her hair. "But my grandmother made sure to raise me as she had been raised. Attending to you is how we attended to each other."

"Who was it who took your family's keep?"

"It was Lord Fordwyn of Dinhyll, though my grandmother insisted that it was his wife, Lady Eunice. She wanted my grandmother's keep for her nephew." Lucilla stood up and added more hot water to the bath. "I'll see to setting out your clothes now."

Anwyl closed her eyes again, savoring the steamy water while Lucilla went to the other side of the screen to lay out fresh garments. Lady Eunice was despicable, Anwyl determined, and she would find a way to help her noble maid reclaim her birthright.

The girl returned to the bath and helped Anwyl out, bringing a chair so that Anwyl could sit and change into clean, dry clothes. "The guard gave me some liniment for your ankle and said that he would have your supper sent up." She helped Anwyl into bed, propping her leg on a pillow and fluffing the cushions behind her back. After pulling a warm blanket over her, she set the leather satchel next to where Anwyl rested. "I'll have the porters remove the bath water and wait while they do it. Would you like some wine or tea, Princess?"

"Wine would be lovely," Anwyl replied, liking the girl. "As long as it isn't mulberry."

"I don't think so," she replied, sniffing the carafe. After the bath was cleared from her room and Lucilla had departed, Anwyl sipped her wine and opened the pouch. There were two packets, and she broke the seal on the thickest. Inside were letters from her brother and Aghna, giving her the latest on their progress in Nifolhad. The report was both heartening and worrisome. Rani and Aghna reigned unchallenged, and Brynmara had finally been liberated. Hundreds of people had been imprisoned deep in the fortress's dungeons over the years, and it was a miracle that there were still survivors. The Sylvan had their hands full treating the former captives, and Ni'mala had sent a few Kena there to help those whose minds had been damaged. For all the hopeful reports, there were pockets within the realm that were still caught in the web of terror and suspicion. Fear of retribution held sway, especially near the stronghold of Kantahla, where Diarmait was under siege. As for Prince Bowen, despite swearing his allegiance to Queen Aghna and King Ranulf, he was still being held captive in Sophiana. As to how he would be made to pay for the atrocities ascribed to him, only time would tell.

Aghna had written that she hoped Anwyl's quest was going well and wished to hear every detail. She also made note of a gift that was included with her letter. Anwyl dumped the rest of the pouch's contents in her lap. A longish, flat box with a note attached by a ribbon tumbled out, along with a smaller pouch. First the note, Anwyl decided prudently. In Aghna's elegant hand, she read the following:

Rani and I felt that, as our ambassador, it was necessary to bestow upon you the credentials of the position. In honor of the new era of peace and prosperity in Nifolhad, we found it essential to redesign the royal seal.

Anwyl looked at the box with its inlay of mother-of-pearl and silver hardware, and found within it a beautiful writing tool carved of rosewood and fitted with a writing nib wrought from gold. There were replacement tips, ink, a blotter and several sticks of sealing wax. She picked up the writing tool from its nest and recognized well the instrument, for it was an invention of Rani's. Instead of a goose quill, the implement—carved of wood from the pijala tree— was thicker and shaped to sit easily in the hand. Its center was hollowed out and fit with a fine crystal vial, which acted as a reservoir for ink. Rani had toyed with the invention for years, knowing Anwyl's love of history and scholarship, and the princess smiled, thinking of her ink-stained hands from his many trials and failures. A tear slid down her cheek; her brother had finally perfected his invention.

Next, Anwyl plucked up the smaller parcel—a silk pouch—and drew on the string cinching it closed. She gasped. It was a signet ring, one especially sized for her. The royal seal in miniature had been etched upon the face of the ring, and emeralds stood sentinel around the crown, along with six other stones, evenly spaced apart and each a different color. She slipped the ring onto her finger and wiped her cheeks, then emptied the other correspondence pouch into her lap.

There was a letter from Queen Juliana, and she broke the seal and read. The note was brief—an asking after her search, a little gossip from court, and the usual well-wishings. It was the post scriptum that excited Anwyl, for it relayed that the other parcel was from the man with whom Anwyl had been corresponding. She tore it open to discover a small book. It didn't appear to be old and was devoid of title. Anwyl opened the leather binding to find a handwritten chronicle of Pheldhain's history. The script was long and elegant, and she recognized it at once as belonging to *A.S.* She turned a page and a slip of paper slid out.

Dear F.H.,

I quite enjoyed reading your queries. Your insightful questions have caused me to reassess my own knowledge of the area. I believe you to be on an interesting quest and think your theory that the cultural differences of Pheldhain have some other source than its clime is correct. Other areas in the realm have their share of balmy seasons, lush vegetation, and mild winters, yet subscribe to the customs and characteristics of the rest of the realm. The Smallholds of Banta and Salto are perfect examples.

Though it was difficult for me, I have decided to part with one of my most treasured possessions. It is a journal of observations regarding all things Pheldhain. In it, you will find most of the answers to your questions. You may also be interested in the maps that I have copied into the back.

One would expect the southern regions to be as warm and balmy as Pheldhain. Yet, this is not the case. There is a particular sea current which sweeps up from the southeast to the channel between the coast of Pheldhain and Barb Island. This current originates in the Virin Sea, where the desert winds come off the Fyrost, then washes down and around the port city of Naca'an in

Anwyl pulled out a blank sheet of paper and immediately penned a reply to thank him. When she finished, she folded the letter, dropped a fat dollop of sealing wax on the envelope, then pressed her thumb into it. She couldn't use her seal if she wanted to maintain her anonymity. A soft knock interrupted her thoughts, and expecting Lucilla with her meal, Anwyl put the journal and the rest of her belongings back into the satchel and set it aside. "Enter, please."

But it wasn't the young girl who entered. "How are you faring?" Warin asked, setting the supper tray next to her bed. He pulled up a chair and then poured her a goblet of wine. "I thought you might like some company."

"I was catching up on some correspondence but welcome the interruption." There was an awkward moment where they smiled politely at one another. "Please, pour yourself a cup. Have you eaten?" she asked.

"Not yet," he admitted, taking her up on her offer of the wine. "I thought you might be bored up here by yourself. You mentioned your correspondence. The messenger will stay with us through tomorrow evening, so if you have letters to write, he'll be able to take them back to Kings Glen. Say," he said, leaning closer and taking her hand. "That's a lovely ring. I haven't seen you wear it before."

"Rani and Aghna sent it to me," she explained, as he turned her hand toward the lamp so that he could better see it.

"They've changed the Nifolhad Royal Seal. The work is extraordinary. Look how detailed," he pointed out. "And in such a small area. Let me think, yes, I see now, the honeybee of the Royal House, but see here"—he pointed to the face—"the pijala tree has been added, encircling and protecting the bee."

"The tree is the symbol of my house. Aghna and Rani have truly combined them. The stones are significant as well," she started. "They symbolize—I'm sorry, this must be boring for you." Anwyl knew well and good that Warin quickly tired of her company when she expounded on some topic; his initial interest had caused her to drop her guard.

"Not at all," he replied, and Anwyl could almost believe him. "I'm not letting go of your hand until you tell me. How will you be able to eat?"

Anwyl couldn't help but giggle. She leaned forward to study the stones. Most of the jewels were emeralds, but there were six others, and she named them, "Let's see...peridot, smoke diamond, blue sapphire, onyx, amber citrine, and ruby. Each color represents the—"

"The Fenrhi Castes, of course!" Warin exclaimed, and Anwyl could no longer doubt his interest. "And the emeralds?"

"I'm not sure," she admitted.

He resumed his examination of her ring. Anwyl held her breath, realizing how close they were. Their heads were nearly touching. She bit her lip and leaned back. When she did, he gazed into her face, his eyes wandering to her hair, her eyes, everywhere.

"The emeralds are for you," he finally said.

"Me?"

"They are the exact color of your eyes. Didn't you realize?"

She shook her head and then bit her lip again. It was almost as if there was something in the space between them, connecting them. She took a shaky breath, and his gaze dropped to her mouth, and he leaned a fraction closer. Anwyl held herself completely still. And then he looked back up at her with his deep-blue eyes and blinked. He opened his mouth to say something, but a soft rap at the door interrupted him. Lucilla entered. What had he been on the verge of saying? Anwyl would never know, for he pulled back, his smooth countenance back in place.

Lucilla curtsied and waited expectantly.

"Ah, yes," Warin said. "Lucilla has a proposition. It's completely up to you, but for what it's worth, I think it's a good idea. I'll let her explain." He got up and crossed the room to leave. "I'll see you in the morning, Prin— Anwyl."

He closed the door before Anwyl could say anything, and after a moment of perplexity, she turned to smile at Lucilla. "Yes," she said before Lucilla could speak. "I would love it if you joined us as my lady's maid."

The Islet

Dorn surveyed his ignoble fleet. Captain Juna was, thanks to Vala, completely under his thrall and was now in command of *The Sea Hare*.

Odo, Dorn's right-hand man, commanded their newest acquisition, a Pheldhainian vessel christened *The Salt Wife*. Its previous crew, all save the captain, had been killed off by a plague similar to the one that had devastated Juna's crew. The difference was in its administering. Odo had dosed the water supply with too much of the poison, and the results had the unfortunate side effect of driving the men insane. The captain had to be bound and gagged and had been administered to by Vala. Though his bouts of lunacy were diminishing, he was still unable to remember his name, to say nothing about providing them with information on House Pheldhain. If not for Odo's overreaching, the man might have some valuable intelligence to impart.

That was the trouble with Odo. Unless kept on a tight leash, he ran to extremes. Dorn's orders had been explicit—capture the captain and his first mate, then hold the crew until Vala could evaluate their susceptibility to her Kena charms. Odo claimed that it was the fault of the Sylvan poison, that it had worked too quickly. Before he and his men could intervene, *The Salt Wife*'s crew ran wild, screaming that the vessel was on fire. They threw themselves overboard and into the churning sea. Odo's men threw lines to the drowning men, but the sailors had done nothing to save themselves. What Odo hadn't admitted was that he had doused the ropes with oil and lit them on fire to further torment the dying sailors. Dorn had spies everywhere, even among his own men. The only thing that had saved Odo from his wrath was that he had somehow succeeded in bringing both ships to port.

Dorn's own ship, *Reacher*, was by far the best in his ragtag fleet. She was so superior in her lines and tack that he'd had to take great pains to make her appear as desperate as the other two. From a distance, *Reacher* seemed as haggard as her sisters.

Here in his private cove, he drilled his three crews to exhaustion. If he'd had his way, there would not be a single man among them who was not from Nifolhad. But it had been Vala who had pointed out the benefits of keeping Captain Juna alive. If Dorn wanted to keep up the façade that they were Southron Isles smugglers, then Juna and his brethren would lend them credence. Already, Vala's forethought had proved invaluable. Captain Juna had led them to this uninhabited islet, one unused by other smugglers due to the curse that was believed to hang over it. These men from the Southron Isles were a superstitious lot, but Vala's influence was strong enough to overpower their fears. Dorn now had a base of operations whence his ships could slip in and out unnoticed.

The sound of chopping and sawing drew his attention to the fact that both Vala and Odo were late. Vala was never late, and that could only mean one thing—Odo had gotten her alone.

He stormed from his hut, and the men erecting the shelters for the crews gave him a wide berth. Their nervous glances into the dark roots and trunks of the islet's forest were all the directions he required. He only hoped he was not too late. Just as he was about to duck into the shaded canopy, Odo came sprawling out. He was about to head back in when he caught sight of Dorn. It was the contrite expression on the pockmarked, beady-eyed face that forestalled Dorn's anger. Worn by such a brutal man, the expression was comical. A moment later, Juna emerged from the palm fronds, Vala following close behind. She looked shaken, but none too worse for it, and Dorn breathed a sigh of relief. Losing Vala at this point in his plans would be catastrophic. And killing Odo by way of punishment was not a thought he relished. Dorn had known Odo his entire life; he was the one man Dorn could trust not to turn on him. As loyal a dog as any man could hope to own.

Juna nodded to him, then made his way back to the others, throwing in his muscles to lift a freshly hewn beam into place for the long hut that would serve to shelter the sailors. Odo followed him, deciding his best chances lay in making himself scarce.

"I warned you about going off alone, Vala," Dorn accused, advancing on her.

"But you've made no accommodations for me," she snapped. "What am I to do? Squat down near the firepit to complete my toilet? Wash in full view of every man here?"

The men were watching, so Dorn slapped her, not too hard, but with enough force to remind her who was in charge. She held her burning cheek, and he followed her gaze to Captain Juna. "You can keep him, Vala," Dorn allowed. "If you think he can protect you from Odo, he is yours to use. Just make sure they don't kill each other."

"I meant no disrespect, my...Captain Dorn."

"I'm not a monster, Vala. I can be quite reasonable. You should have brought your concerns to me before they became a problem. For the time being, you will lodge with me. When you need to tend to yourself, have Juna bring water to you and stand guard. Just be careful that you don't play with his heart; a man who thinks he's in love may act counter to your desires."

They walked toward his hut, and Dorn motioned to Odo to join them. When all three were gathered, he pinned Odo with his glare. "Don't think that just because we have known each other since our nurses wiped our asses, I won't hesitate to put you down like a cur who has bitten the hand of his master. You will not touch Vala." Odo was a little too quick to nod his agreement. "You will not harass her in any way, shape, or form. And you will not attempt to get even with Juna. Do you understand me?" Odo grumbled an unintelligible reply. "DO YOU?"

"Aye."

"You'd better. There's too much at stake here for you to ruin it because you can't keep your cock in your breeches. Now, is *The Salt Wife* ready?" Odo nodded. "*The Sea Hare* needs more repairs, so our next raid will be small. We'll go after a coastal fishing vessel—little risk of retaliation.

"Vala, you will stay here and see that the barracks are completed," he commanded. "Make sure that Juna and his crew are ready for our next run."

"They'll be ready, Captain Dorn. I have them well in hand."

"That's what Juna said," Odo joked, snickering at his own wit.

"Enough! Remember yourself, Odo. Vala is more than a Kena seer; she is my cousin, and you will respect her." He turned to Vala. "Any progress with our other captain?"

"His periods of calm grow longer with each day, but any type of flame will ignite his ravings. He is strangely resistant to my questions and cannot remember his name or his relations. With more time, I could—"

"You've had him long enough. It is time to see if Rowly can tease his identity from him." She blanched at the mention of the torturer's name. "I'll not let him inflict any mortal damage, Vala. We may still have use for this Pheldhainian captain. Tend to his wounds afterward. That will be all," Dorn commanded, and she bowed and backed her way out of his hut.

•••

Vala returned to her tent to gather her meager possessions. She had done everything her cousin had demanded of her. The newest crew would follow Juna's orders, and Juna would obey Dorn. But only so long as Vala's will demanded it. Dorn could kill on a whim, and she had to have a contingency plan. He had no idea how strong she was becoming. There was something about this southern realm that amplified her abilities.

She smiled; Dorn believed that Odo was beyond her reach. And he was, almost, thanks to the pihaberries. He would never follow her commands, but she could influence him, in little ways. Like earlier in the woods, when she'd planted the thought that he should take his time undressing. The stalling tactic had given Juna enough time to come to her aid. Suggest something innocuous, and he would comply. Over time, she would whittle down his credibility with Dorn. She'd already started when they had boarded *The Salt Wife*, pushing him to extreme actions when they had come across the ship. Only Dorn hadn't punished Odo, as she'd anticipated.

As for their captive, foretelling was not one of her Kena powers. Despite this, she knew fate had greater plans for the Pheldhainian; she sensed it in a way that reached to her soul.

•••

The Royal Palace in Naca'an, Nifolhad

Queen Aghna lounged on the most comfortable couch in the palace and draped her hands protectively over her growing belly. Her feet were propped up on Rani's lap, and his dexterous fingers danced over her soles, massaging the ache out of them.

"What else did Bowen say?" she asked him, for her husband and king had just returned from Sophiana.

"He chose his words with care, claiming that he couldn't recall attacking you as he'd imbibed too much."

"Surely you don't believe—"

"Not for a moment. He's as evil as his father. Perhaps even more."

"What did Radha and her truthseer think?"

"That nothing he said was a lie, but there is definitely something wrong. When charged with the crimes attributed to him, there was truth in his words when he ascribed the responsibility to Diarmait and his other offspring. The truthseer could not refute it."

"So, we keep him locked up."

"There's more," he said, "regarding my sister. The Mother has taken an interest in her. She was marked. And like you and Claire, she is tied to the castes, but not to the Fenrhi."

"Umbren?" Aghna guessed, knowing that she had had an Umbren trainer.

"And Sylvan. And possibly more. The only explanation Ni'Mala gave to Radha was that Anwyl is something more than she appears." Rani gave her a smile, one that, if she were standing, would have melted her knees. "I wasn't surprised, my love. I would hazard that she has a bit of Kena in her, but not like Radha." He kissed his wife's wrist, then her fingers. "So, tell me, to whom should we write first? Ni'mala?"

Aghna laughed. "You know me so well, dearest. Yes, our master puppeteer owes us a better explanation. And then we'll send word to Queen Juliana and King Godwin. It is time to apprise them of the fact that we think their kingdom has been infiltrated by rogue Kena, though we know not their purpose."

"And Anwyl," Rani added. "She must be told that the king and queen know and that she can now openly discuss her other purpose for being in Aurelia." He helped her to her feet and to her writing desk. "I'll call the messenger while you get started; he can leave on the next ship."

Rani leaned down to kiss her, then strode across the room. At the door, he stopped and turned, and Aghna looked up at him. "I believe that the king and queen shall dine privately this eve," he suggested, giving her a searing look that reminded her how much she had missed him the last few months. She blushed even before he could give her the smile that always touched her heart, and then he left her to the letter writing.

CHAPTER EIGHTEEN

Not a Pimple

Anwyl pressed her seal to the letter she'd written to Aghna and Rani. The melted wax congealed and left the mark of her signet behind. Outside, the sun had nearly risen, and there was little time remaining before the queen's messenger would depart. She unfolded the letter directed to *A.S.* and read it one last time.

Dear A.S.,

First, thank you for the loan of your most treasured journal. I am sure it will provide much respite during the difficult journey that I have sworn to undertake. I enjoyed reading the passage that you marked. That you could look upon your seduction with such objectivity and then later write about it reveals much maturity and scholarship in one who, at the time, was so young. While it's true that I have never heard of this custom whereby a man's "maidenhood" is auctioned off to the highest bidding woman, I am aware that other cultures are not as regimented in the rites of courtship as those which exist in Aurelia. Did you know that there is one territory where prospective brides must meet three challenges and prove their worth to the groom's family? I find the many constructs created for marriage intriguing, especially when simple handfasting is so convenient.

For my own part, I am happy to write that the circumstances of which I previously complained have much improved, thanks in part to an amicable understanding newly grown between myself and the object of my distress—a friendly truce where I once thought none could exist.

Finally, I must apologize for the brevity of this note. I promise to finish reading your journal forthwith and with great pleasure, and to expound upon my observations in subsequent correspondences.

Your friend in history,

F.H.

Post Scriptum: I must confess that I find myself anticipating the arrival of the Royal Messenger and our continued collaboration.

She folded the letter and stuffed it into the packet intended for the queen just as someone tapped on her door. Lucilla arrived to help her to dress, bringing with her a sturdy cane.

"Lucilla, I've been thinking...are you sure you have no other family?"

She turned away, but in a soft voice, she replied, "I must, but I have no means to contact them."

"When this journey is over, I'll help you track them down. If you want me to, that is," she added. "And I will write to Queen Juliana about your predicament."

"Oh, no! I mean, please do not bother the queen." She looked positively terrified.

"As you wish, but she is very kind. Just let me know if you change your mind."

Lucilla nodded.

"Now, take these," Princess Anwyl stated, holding out a pair of Fenrhi leggings to the girl. "They are too long for you, but as you're handy with a needle and thread, you'll soon have them fitted. We'll pick up some fabric at the next market, and you can make whatever you need to supplement your wardrobe. You'll need at least two gowns if you are to attend to me."

Lucilla's eyes glistened.

"Lucilla," Anwyl gently asked, "what is the matter?"

"I...I haven't been around kind people for a very long time."

Anwyl gave the young woman a hug, patting her back. "You deserve goodness, Lucilla. And as for Lady Eunice, well, she is quite out of favor. I do not think that she will be suffered to wield such power again." Then Princess Anwyl regaled Lucilla with the tale of her abduction, and the girl gasped and sighed in all the proper places.

"How romantic! Imagine being rescued by a Royal Guard!"

The porters arrived to carry Anwyl's trunk to the wagon, preventing Anwyl from correcting her. Romantic? She hobbled her way out of the inn and into the courtyard. Warin saw her and led her horse to where she waited, then lifted her up onto her saddle. "I see that the swelling went down enough for you to wear your boot."

"Thanks to the liniment you sent," she replied, her spirits elevated for the first time in months. "As long as I don't put all of my weight upon it, I should be fine." She brandished her new cane at him like a sword, and he pretended to parry. Almost immediately after, that same awkwardness between them descended.

After patting her mare's neck, he climbed up onto Konjimar's back, signaling the party forward. He and Anwyl rode ahead of the main group. "I wonder," Warin mused, "if Lucilla's family's home wasn't called Nocanyella Keep. I recall hearing that Lady Eunice had ensconced one of her worthless relatives there. It's a small fortress, and very old. A noble family held the lands surrounding it for generations, at least until the amalgamation of the territories."

Anwyl giggled. "In old Nifolhadian, *no'cayéllah* means *not a pimple*."

"An apt description. You see, the central region of Dinhyll is made up of round, uncultivable mounds, like a bad case of gooseflesh. The eastern half is mostly fen, swamp, and water-farms."

"And Not-a-Pimple Keep?"

He grinned. "Nocanyella is located in the westernmost region of Dinhyll, situated in fertile basin land near the great bend of the Saltana River. Let me think...yes, I remember. Nocanyella should have gone to the Smallhold of Crevalo, but the Lord of Dinhyll pledged more men to the king. Many regions profited in The Great War, some more than others."

"And Lucilla's family paid the price." She was surprised by Warin's familiarity with such a minor detail of the Great War. And as they rode, she began to realize that he was quite knowledgeable in not only Aurelia's past, but in Nifolhad's as well.

As the days passed, they rode on in companionable silence, traveling the High Way. Anwyl's newfound ease around him allowed her to let go some of her insecurities, and she no longer felt the need to fill in the gaps in their discourse with a running commentary. Moreover, she hadn't wanted to tie knots in weeks.

Her girlish nervousness over the idea that they were destined to be together had been supplanted by the beginnings of a friendship, one based on civil discourse and reasonable argument. And she was finally able to study him without that first-impression infatuation. He was much the same as the other

Royal Guards. Tall, muscular, and confident. She deemed him the same age as his friends, though younger than her brother, Rani. His sable-colored hair was cut longer than what was fashionable and fell back from his forehead in soft waves. He must have unwittingly trained it that way, she mused, as he frequently ran his hand through his hair when tasked with something difficult. Most times, he pulled his locks back and tied them with a leather cord at his nape, revealing a strong jaw and proud profile.

Few noblemen in Nifolhad wore beards, preferring to remain clean-shaven, like her brother. When she'd first arrived in Aurelia, Anwyl had spent months studying the myriad shapes, lengths, and styles worn by the Royal Guard and nobles. Unlike Trian's full beard, Warin's beard was clipped short and left most of his face uncovered. When they were at court, his facial hair had always fascinated her. Constantly changing, she saw no rhyme or reason to how he decided upon a style: beard or mustache, or beard *and* mustache, full, thin, and even—this was her favorite—a shadow of whiskers, as if he were too busy to shave, though the look was much too neat to not be intentional.

Months had passed at court before she finally identified the pattern: he followed no trend; he set it. And when other lords and guards echoed his style, he changed his appearance. Warin wore his facial hair like a fashion accessory.

For a man so tall and well-built, he was unusually catlike. Whether riding a horse, dancing, or strolling through one of the orchards, he moved with a grace of which even she was envious—not that she was awkward by any definition of the word. Warin just had that natural ease of movement that women found attractive. Dividing his time between land and sea had most likely been the cause.

Anwyl was fully aware, and slightly relieved, that her examination of him was so dispassionate. Gone were the days when her heart trembled at the thought of them together; so, too, was she finished with being angry with him. She wasn't even vexed with herself anymore for her foolishness. Such sentiments had claimed too much of her time already. She only felt relief at having finally escaped the fate—curse, rather—that Ni'Mala had set upon her. At least that was what she'd convinced herself to believe. Right. And if she reminded herself every day, it might eventually become true.

"How did you pronounce it? Nocanyella, I mean," he asked, drawing her from her musings and back to the conversation they'd had several days past.

"We stress the third syllable, and there's no second *"n"* sound," Anwyl answered, then said the word aloud, "No'cayéllah."

He repeated it perfectly. "I find the subtle language differences between our realms intriguing."

"How so?" she asked, wondering that he'd given any time to dwell on the subject.

"Our respective kingdoms speak the same language, 'tis true, but there are so many variations. Have you noticed that many of the place names in Aurelia, at least in the south, are similar to words found near Naca'an?" He spoke the city's name in the Nifolhadian way, shortening the second syllable to a simple hard *c* sound and elongating the *a*s into one syllable."

"Your accent is very good," Anwyl complimented.

"So is yours," he noted. "It is only when you speak of home that it is discernible. Madyan's is much more pronounced."

"Those from the Fyrost desert have their own language. Being nomadic, they have a mastery of all the dialects in Nifolhad. When Madyan speaks, her words are measured and seem to flow with their own rhythm." He nodded but was looking to the north. "Should we be worried that she has yet to return?" Anwyl asked.

"Not yet, I think." But he looked uneasy, and Anwyl followed his gaze. "Tell me what you know of her history," he asked.

"Do you know the story of how Queen Aghna came to be with the Fenrhi, that it was Madyan who kept her safe for over three years in the temple when all of Nifolhad thought her dead?"

"Claire related some of the details, yes. I would venture that she protected Queen Aghna just as we Royal Guards are sworn to protect our king and queen."

She nodded. "What few people know is that Madyan's blood is as noble as yours and mine," Anwyl revealed. "Perhaps more."

"Queen Juliana mentioned that, but I have not yet had the chance to ask Madyan herself."

"How much do you know of the Fyrost Desert?"

"Captain Grieg told me of the legend of the Sky Goddess, how she was betrayed by a man and then destroyed him, his people and their lands, only to be thrown into the Virin Sea to perish, so great was her grief. He claimed that it was her rage that created the rest of Nifolhad, leaving the Fyrost Desert as a warning to the peoples who survived to not trifle with powers beyond their ken."

"That's about the gist of it. But myth aside, the desert tribes of the Fyrost were the first people to populate our realm. They were the first builders, and the first to keep written records, though most are only runes etched in stone and worn away. Madyan can trace her lineage farther than even Aghna, Claire, and Anna can, back to that once-great civilization. The desert tribes were the first to read the stars, traverse the dunes, and even sail the seas."

And so Anwyl continued giving Warin a brief history lesson of the ancient Fyrjian race, and Warin listened avidly to all that she said. Experience had taught her that her stories and tutelage only irritated him. This day though, when she finished one topic, he would circle back to a point she mentioned but did not expound upon, drawing from her even more.

"I did not realize that you were so versed in the stories of the past," Warin admitted, when they finally stopped to make their camp. "Thank you for sharing what you know."

"I should be thanking you," she replied, looking off to the northwest. "You kept me from worrying about Madyan."

"If she doesn't rejoin us by tomorrow evening, we'll detour to Prato. We'll even go to Dinhyll, if necessary. But for today, this is a good place to make camp. There are some woods over that ridge, and I would like to hunt for fresh game for dinner."

"I would like to come along, that is, if you don't mind. Madyan gave me a sling when we departed Kings Glen, and I would love to practice some more."

"Your ankle won't bother you?"

"If it does, I'll ride back to camp."

He nodded, then gave instructions to the drivers to set up the pavilions and make a shelter with tarps for the horses. "It looks like we'll get rain tonight, and I would prefer to not be struck by lightning again." They cantered up the hill, pulling up after they crested the rise; below, sat a shallow, wooded valley. After continuing down the slope, he dismounted and then helped her to the ground.

Anwyl reminded herself that she should not read anything into the way his hands lingered, just a tad too long, on her waist. Or that he seemed, for that brief moment, to have not breathed until she stepped away. Nor should she believe that, when he asked after her ankle as she turned and removed her sling from her saddlebag, his voice sounded a little thick. No, she assured herself, none of those things had happened, and it was foolish to have imagined them.

They stepped into the cool shadows of the trees, both silently creeping along, senses attuned to the slightest rustle of grass or flutter of wing. He was taking it slow, she realized, thoughtful of her injury. Just upon the edge of a clearing, they both stopped, having heard the harsh double *chirr-chirr* of a pheasant. Warin nocked an arrow, and Anwyl readied her sling. From the cover of the trees, they located the nye of pheasants pecking away like pullets in the late-afternoon sun. They each took two before the rest caught on that their flock was in peril. Warin shot down another as it lifted from the ground into flight. When they returned, they had dinner and breakfast, and the camp was set and ready. With Lucilla's help, the birds were quickly dressed and spitted.

• • •

Madyan rode into camp, pleased to see that the tents had been erected. It had been threatening rain for hours. The thick mist that had risen to overtake the High Way lent a chilling bite to the air, and if not for her mare neighing when she sensed the other horses, she might have ridden past the camp. Ahead, tarps had been strung up and staked between some slender trees to shelter the horses, and she secured her mare, rubbing her down and covering her with a fresh blanket. One of the wagon drivers heard the noise and came out to assist her. Her mare wasted no time tucking into its feed and water.

Madyan ducked from under the tarp and made the quick dash to the princess's pavilion. There was a rush of air that whipped around her and a growing roar, and the sky let loose a torrential downpour just as she stepped into the shelter. Princess Anwyl looked up and, with the help of a sturdy cane, hurried to help her. "Thank goodness you are returned. Come, you need to warm yourself by the fire. Supper is almost ready." Madyan let herself be stripped from her damp cloak, then led to a basin with warm water to wash her face and hands.

"How many did you get?" Madyan asked, spying the spitted pheasants. A girl wearing some of the Princess's older garments stepped forward to claim her wet cloak, and Madyan noted the third sleeping pallet in the tent.

"Just two, and with the sling," she said. "But Warin took three with his bow. We found their nests and set snares. The silly birds came back after only ten minutes, and now we have seven in total, plus eggs for breakfast."

Madyan gave her an arched look when the blond girl stepped away.

"Oh, I nearly forgot. Madyan, this is Lady Lucilla. She'll be joining us as my lady-in-waiting." The girl returned with a warm cloth and handed it to Madyan.

"I'm very pleased to meet you," Lucilla exclaimed, and curtsied. "The princess has told me all about your desert and how belonging to the Umbren Caste is similar to the Royal Guard in Aurelia, except that you are women."

"That part is true," Madyan admitted, "except that the Royal Guard is composed of men from noble families, whereas the Fenrhi castes accept both high- and lowborn. I myself make no claim to—"

"Your blood is likely more noble than mine," Anwyl interrupted.

"The desert tribes have never sought…" she trailed off when the wind picked up and the canvas walls of the tent suddenly whipped outward and then bowed in with a great sucking *whoosh*. They all turned to the entrance in time to see Warin duck in. The princess hobbled over to him with another cloth and took his wet cloak.

"Madyan, safely returned!" He strode to her and gave her a bear of a hug. "Not that we were worried. Did Anwyl tell you how many pheasant we got?"

Madyan refrained from raising her eyebrows. Lucilla led her behind a screen where she could strip out of her damp outer-clothes. When they returned, Warin was sniffing the air with a decidedly rapt expression.

"I have to say, if our supper tastes as good as it smells, Lucilla, I might just steal you from the princess so that you can cook for me."

"My grandmother made sure I was trained in the rudiments," Lucilla replied, raising her voice as the downpour outside surged. "But I didn't cook tonight."

"Then who? Anwyl?" She nodded at him, looking quite pleased with herself. "Since when is cooking required tutoring for a princess?"

"In Sophiana, I was taught many things: hunting, fishing, sailing—"

"Don't remind me," Warin interrupted, recalling the terrifying moments when she swung in the rigging of his ship.

She rolled her eyes at him. "But the Fenrhi taught me the rudiments of healing, cooking, and self-defense. Of course"—she paused for effect—"none of that works when someone slips a sleeping draught into your tea, rolls you up in a rug, then absconds with you under the very noses of your friends." She raised her eyebrows at them, waiting, and then laughed. "Goodness, you two, I was only joking. You rescued me before any harm was done. Come, sit down and eat. We have bread and fruit from the last village. And please, Warin, tell me you found the wine and didn't get doused for nothing."

Warin pulled not one, but two bottles of wine from the bag he'd slung over his shoulder. His cocky grin had even Madyan's heart melting.

THE NAKED MOON ❧ 169

"Madyan, are you all right?" the princess demanded upon seeing her expression. "Sit. You must be exhausted." Warin grabbed the cups, then poured Madyan some wine while Lucilla made her a plate of roasted pheasant, bread, and sliced fruit.

"I'm fine, just tired," Madyan replied. The four of them sat down to their meal.

"If you are up to it," Anwyl said, "I think we would all love to hear your tale." Warin handed a cup to the princess, and she, in turn, handed him a plate of food. They were finally getting on together, and quite happily, Madyan noted.

"What's wrong, Madyan? You're making a face."

"I leave for a couple of weeks, and you become fast friends? I know I ordered you to settle your differences, but I never thought you could do it so quickly." The princess opened her mouth, but no words came out. Madyan turned to Warin, and he shrugged. "So, what happened?"

"Nothing," the princess stated.

"I saw the error of my ways," Warin explained at the same time.

Madyan stared at him, waiting for him to continue. "It was a long ride..." he began but didn't expound.

"Well, good," Madyan said, noticing that the tempest outside was ebbing. She took a bite of the roasted pheasant to the music of plinking rainwater and crickets starting their night song. The silence in the tent that followed was not nearly as uncomfortable as it had been, and when they finished the meal, Lucilla insisted that Madyan rest while she cleaned.

"Pray, tell us what happened in Dinhyll," the princess asked.

Madyan swallowed her last bite, took a sip of wine, and started her tale. "You should have told me there was a moat, Warin."

"Why? Did you have to swim?"

"No, fortunately. It was night when I arrived, but a group of riders were returning—Lord Herlewin, I think—and the sentries were about to raise the bridge. I slid down the bank and underneath. It's a very poor design. Anyone can hold on to the bottom of the bridge, and when it's raised, up you go, right to the top of the wall."

"And once you were inside?"

"I left a few hints that they'd been visited by an Umbren. Little messages, one each for Lady Eunice and for Lord Herlewin, though due to his long absence from the castle, I do not believe he was involved in the abduction. And so that they understood their predicament, I used their stationery and seals. I drank from their cups, ate from their plates—all explained in my notes—and left the evidence for them to find when they woke in the morning." She smiled, thinking about the panicked flurry when the Lord of Dinhyll and his mother woke to find letters pinned to their nightgowns. "I made sure that the wagon drivers would find reminders of their tenuous positions as well. Subtle messages that will be delivered to them by their children."

Warin lifted his cup to toast her. "Remind me to never cross a Fyrjian."

When he offered to pour a second serving, she declined. Instead, she sat on her pallet and began to remove her boots, watching her princess with interest. She hadn't seen Anwyl this animated since sailing to Aurelia on the smuggler's ship.

Warin motioned to the princess's cup, and she nodded. "Unless you want to go to sleep, Madyan."

"Don't worry about me. I can sleep through anything, if tired enough." She relaxed on her pallet, facing the opposite direction. Eyes closed, she let the ensuing conversation lull her to sleep.

"You were telling me that your father had written to you about the pijala trees and that they were doing poorly..."

"Well, yes. They were worse off than those in Redavel," Warin answered, and Madyan heard the trickling of wine being poured. They lowered their voices when she pulled her blanket over her shoulder, and before she drifted off to sleep, she heard a little more of the discourse on the saplings.

"I'm afraid that the trees may require a rougher clime—"

Madyan heard naught else until she woke the next morning to the smell of sizzling eggs and bacon.

CHAPTER NINETEEN

Meramont

Warin eyed Lord Ronan with his usual insouciance. They had joined the Royal Guard the same year, but Ronan had had to take up the duties of Lord of Meramont when his older brother died. During their initiation years, he and Ronan had looked up to Larkin, and had tried to emulate his success with the queen's ladies. It seemed that they were equally matched, being cut from the same cloth and sharing the same passions—their love of the sea and of women. A camaraderie had existed between them but not the close friendships Warin had attained with Lark and Trian. He and Ronan were just too alike, even down to their hair color and blue eyes.

Ronan was tall, well-built, and possessed of that windblown quality that the women at court found intriguing. And, as he did so now, he always appeared to be gazing off into the distance, even if he was two feet away and looking right at you. Warin knew the look. He wore it more and more of late, as if he were a-sea and searching for the next horizon. Come to think on it, Madyan, though her waves were made of sand, carried the same expression in her eyes. Wanderlust, his father had called it.

Warin had just introduced Madyan to Ronan, and the man had been exceedingly polite to the Fyrjian woman in her Umbren garb. But his eyes were currently assessing Princess Anwyl. The princess, he had to credit, took it in stride. If she was aware that Ronan was ranked first on the queen's list of eligible grooms, she didn't reveal it and blatantly took their host's measure. Ronan, Warin sensed, found her scrutiny amusing. He offered Anwyl his arm and led her into the hall, where a feast in Anwyl's honor had been set.

Something was off, and try as he might, Warin could not put his finger on it. Not until Madyan took his arm and drew him into the hall. Her action reminded him at once of his lack of graciousness, and, as he assembled his wits and his courtly mien, he realized that the princess was prepossessed of the same adroitness that the most successful women at court employed. When had she learned how to lower her eyes before looking up at a man, or to subtly sway her hips, lengthening her stride to match her escort's, all the while appearing as if she were in no hurry and simply gliding along? And with the assistance of her cane! He grumbled.

"What's wrong?" Madyan whispered.

Warin had forgotten—again—his manners. "Nothing, m'lady," he replied smoothly.

"Then why on earth are you glowering? Does Lord Ronan pose some threat?"

"No more a threat than I," Warin responded glibly, regretting his words immediately. What was wrong with him? "Lord Ronan is a gentleman. He will do nothing that the princess does not wish."

"Then I'd best be on my guard."

"What does that mean?" he asked, but Madyan had stepped away. Warin stared after her, feeling for the first time in his life out of his depth. Princess Anwyl was frowning at him. Ronan, too, was staring, one eyebrow lifted in amusement. Madyan waited patiently by her chair and made a face at him. Once Anwyl was seated, the others in the hall followed suit. There were perhaps thirty guests, mainly relatives of Ronan's, and a few nobles from the surrounding regions.

Meramont was comprised of fertile land in the southeast corner of the Aurelian Smallholds and included the long barrier island of Acerto. In addition to protecting Meramont's white sand beaches, the island boasted some of the finest fishing in the realm. Its inlets were too many to count and acted as safe havens for Meramont's fishermen, both in the lee of the sound and the treacherous reefs facing the Calilo Sea. More and more, the goods produced in the Smallholds were carted to Meramont where they would then be shipped by sea north to Kings Glen and up and around the northern reaches of Aurelia, arriving three times faster than if they were forced to traverse the broad overland stretch of highlands to reach court. Rather than cutting into Pheldhain's profits, it freed his family to focus on the more lucrative trade with Nifolhad and the Southron Isles.

"Warin?" Madyan whispered, elbowing him in the ribs. "Where are you?"

He realized then that he had stopped following the conversation. Everyone was staring. Madyan's hand flicked out as if reaching for her wine, and unseen by anyone else, she snapped her utensil at her neighbor's goblet. It tipped over, spilling wine that drained immediately into the man's lap, causing him to jump from his seat to mitigate the damage. In the ensuing havoc, Madyan leaned forward and whispered, "Lord Ronan invited you to join him and the princess on a tour of his newest ship, followed by an overnight excursion to Acerto Island."

"Thank you," he whispered back. Only the princess had not been distracted by Madyan's feint, though he couldn't interpret the look she gave him. The servants sopped up the spill, poured another goblet of wine for Ronan's relative, and Warin composed himself to answer.

"I offered to—" Ronan began again.

"I would be delighted to see your ship," Warin replied smoothly. "You must forgive my lack of attention. I was wondering after a missing member of our party. Where is Lady Lucilla?"

"She was not feeling well," Anwyl replied from the other end of the table.

"I'll have something sent to her quarters," Ronan offered, then nodded to one of the servants. "Perhaps tomorrow she will be more herself and will join us on our voyage. Do you enjoy sailing, Princess?"

Conversation around him resumed, so Warin could not hear Anwyl's reply, but her enthusiasm over what Ronan was describing was revealing enough. "Is Lucilla truly not feeling well?" Warin asked Madyan.

"She's fine. It's nothing that a few gowns for events such as these won't cure. But the princess is wise enough to know that the girl, no matter what her grandmother taught her, will need to grow accustomed to her position. Princess Anwyl is patient and kindhearted and will see Lucilla's birthright restored."

"But you're thinking…"

Madyan nodded. "Lucilla, for all her kindness, resembles a frightened rabbit. I don't know what scared her so badly, but I've talked to the princess. We're going to start training her to defend herself."

"That's a good idea," Warin agreed. "Maybe I could—"

Across the room, Anwyl laughed at something Ronan had said. In fact, she was hanging on his every word. But then, Warin got the sense that the reverse was also true. He gritted his teeth and somehow made it through the rest of the meal, course after course of every delicacy Meramont could offer.

● ● ●

Anwyl had been very much aware of Warin's discomfiture all throughout the banquet. What she could not fathom was why, with such engaging conversation around them, he was acting so mercurial. Worrying about his every mood was giving her a headache. If only she could beg off the rest of the festivities and retire to her room to reread *A.S.*'s journal.

"What are you thinking about, Princess?" Ronan asked. He had organized musicians after their meal, expecting that she and her party would enjoy a dance, but had not known about her twisted ankle. Ronan had insisted on sitting with her while she watched the revolutions of the dancers. Each time Warin swept by, she felt his eyes upon her.

"That you are a generous host," she replied. He raised an eyebrow at her, and she relented. "Oh, all right," she admitted. "If you must know, I was thinking about a book."

"And this book makes you frown?"

"Not the book. The fact that there never seems to be time to read it. This celebration is lovely, and I don't mean to take away from everything you've done, it's just that—"

"Sometimes you would rather be reading," he finished. "I have an excellent library here. It would be my pleasure to show it to you."

The princess was well-aware that if a nobleman offered to show a woman his library, nine times out of ten, he had more on his mind than books. But Anwyl was under orders to find a husband. Ernald of Redavel was not suitable; perhaps Ronan of Meramont was. Afterall, he had the requisite dark hair and blue eyes.

Who was she trying to convince? His appearance hadn't caused anything like the commotion in her heart the first time she saw Warin. Still, if she was to discover which way he leaned, she would need a few moments alone with him. Anwyl managed to catch Madyan's attention, and her friend swept closer and joined them. "Madyan, as I cannot yet dance, Ronan has offered to show me his library."

"That's very kind of you, Ronan," Madyan said flatly.

Before Madyan insisted on joining them, Anwyl added, "Why don't you finish your dance? Then you can meet us there."

Madyan narrowed her eyes. "As you say, Princess. I'll join you soon."

Ronan held out his arm, and Anwyl graciously took it. He led her out of the hall and down a long corridor. He paused at the last door on the left and pressed the latch, but the door didn't budge. "I forgot," he said ruefully, removing her hand from his arm. "The catch has been sticking lately." He shouldered it open, then escorted her into the library and closed the door behind them. "The mechanism works perfectly from the inside," he explained, then demonstrated by opening and closing the door again.

He was making her feel at ease, and Anwyl smiled at him before turning to peruse the titles lining his shelves.

"You are welcome to use my library for as long as you are in Meramont," he offered, coming to stand next to her as she slid a random book off the shelf. "That's a very boring study of the positive effects of poultry droppings versus horse manure," he provided, taking the book from her hands and setting it aside. "There are much more interesting things in this library than books, Princess."

"Oh?" This was one dance that would not trouble her ankle, and she artfully took a step away from him. What distance she put between them disappeared as he stepped closer. They were standing nearly toe-to-toe.

"Tell me," he drawled. "Why did you wish me to bring you here, alone?"

"I wanted to see if your collection was all that you claimed it to be," she flirted, running her fingertips over the spines of the books, recalling how to lower her voice to make it sound husky. As a princess of Sophiana, she either had to play this game expertly, or she shouldn't be playing at all.

He lifted his hand and shook his head. She allowed him to trace the outline of her mouth, his fingertip coming to rest on her lower lip, tugging it down. An involuntary gasp escaped her, and her eyes flicked to his, then to his mouth and the half smile he wore.

. . .

Finally, the music ended. The rotation had taken him to the far side of the room, and the dispersing dancers impeded his view of Anwyl. He made his way to where she had been sitting with Ronan just as Madyan did, but she was gone. Madyan did not look the least bit worried, and he took her arm and led her out to the hall. "He's taken her heaven knows where and—"

"It's all right, Warin. They only just departed."

"You let her go alone?"

"Princess Anwyl is well able to take care of herself. They've only gone to the library."

Conjured images of groping hands and trussed skirts and heated embraces in dark alcoves and, damn it, especially libraries played out in Warin's mind. The urgency to find her was overwhelming, and he took a step sideways to get around Madyan. She moved to block him. "Madyan," he growled.

"I'll go," she ordered. "I don't know what has gotten into you this evening, but you'll make a mess of things if you go in this state."

"Fine," he conceded. "But only if you go this instant, and I will be right behind you."

Madyan knew the way and quickly led him to the library. In fact, Warin thought, as he trailed after her, she had probably already explored the castle entire and had every room cataloged in her head. They reached the door, and she frowned. "It's locked."

• • •

Ronan's finger slid from her lips to caress her cheek before tilting her face to his. He lowered his head, his eyes heavy-lidded, and his lips met hers. He kissed her then, lightly at first, then with more enthusiasm. Anwyl kissed him back. When his tongue reached out to trace the slit between her lips, she parted them. He was very good, expert, in fact, and she gave herself up to the embrace, considering and weighing each exquisite sensation. From the stroking of his tongue against hers to the rasping of his whiskers against her skin, he excelled in this art. But it wasn't enough, she thought dispassionately. No kiss other than Warin's had ever awakened the fire in her. Damn him! His was the kiss against which she would be cursed to measure all others. Ronan, as skilled as he was, could never come close to making her feel what she had experienced the night of the masquerade.

He eased back from the embrace, quirked an eyebrow. "Too bad," he murmured when she smiled an apology up at him. Across the library, a rap of knuckles came through the door.

"That will be Madyan," Anwyl predicted. Hammering followed, and a muffled voice could be heard shouting from the other side of the door. A voice that was definitely male.

"At least tell me you weren't using me to make him jealous," Ronan begged, drawing away from her.

"No, I wouldn't do—" She stopped herself.

"It's all right," he assured her, striding across the library to open the door. "Just make sure you use this moment to its full potential."

"What do you mean?" she asked.

He chuckled. "I'm only telling you this because I really like you, Princess—Warin is as besotted with you as you are with him."

Before she could assemble a denial, he pulled open the door, apologizing for the faulty hardware. Warin nearly fell in. Upon seeing that she was safe, he turned on Ronan. But Ronan had already made his exit, taking Madyan with him and closing the door on the way out.

Anwyl stared at Warin's broad shoulders, drawn up and tight as if ready to do battle. He turned slowly to face her, his face a mask once more, but the white-knuckled fist at his side belied his calm. Ronan was wrong; Warin still thought of her as a child. "Did he injure you?" he asked, and her treacherous eyes shone with unshed tears.

She turned away from him and reached up for a book. "What an awful thing to say about our host. I'm perfectly well," she intoned with as much hauteur as she could muster. "You needn't concern yourself..." Gently, he rested his hand on her shoulder; she hadn't even heard him step near. He turned her to face him, and she held the book to her chest like a shield. He was about to say something to her but stopped himself.

Then he stared at the soft skin around her mouth; surely it was still reddened from Ronan's beard. Her lips, too, felt swollen. "Did he do this?" Warin demanded, caressing her cheek with his knuckle.

"It's not what you think."

"He'll pay for it, I swear."

"You'll swear to no such thing! He didn't hurt me. We kissed, Warin. Nothing more. You needn't concern yourself with—"

"You kissed? The both of you? You said *we*."

She nodded, gazing anywhere but at the heat blazing from his eyes. And she gripped the book a little tighter to her bosom as if to shield herself from his inanity. Of course, the subject of the tome just had to be about animal excrement.

"Of all the stupid... Don't you realize... Anwyl, you must stop putting yourself into these situations. If I hadn't—"

"Be quiet!" And for once, he left off chastising her as if she were a child and not a grown woman. "Have you forgotten who I am and where my duty lies?" His eyes narrowed, and she stepped nearer to him. "Whether I wish it or not, I must marry someone from this realm. Can there not be attraction? Passion, even?

"I came to this library to be kissed," she professed. "Just as I came to the smallholds to find a husband." She could see the heat growing in Warin's eyes, but she held her ground.

"And?" he demanded quietly, leaning forward just as Ronan had done before he had kissed her. She tried searching his eyes, but he lowered his lids to stare at her lips. Ronan had said Warin was besotted with her. Was there some truth to it? She bit her lower lip, wetting it before letting it go. His eyes flicked up to hers, and for a moment, they stared at one another. She could feel his soft exhale against her lips, smell the clean scent of mint and wine on his breath. He murmured something, but her heartbeat was too loud in her ears.

She leaned forward, trapping her arms and the book between them, waiting for the touch of his lips to hers. Then, her mind made sense of what he'd whispered in a sneering tone: "And did you enjoy Ronan's kiss, *Princess?*"

As if slapped, she fell quickly away from him, unbelieving that he could mock her so cruelly.

• • •

Warin didn't know why he felt compelled to ask it, and he attributed the reason to keeping her safe from the likes of Ronan. Hell, from the likes of himself. "I'm sorry," he said, seeing the look of betrayal in her eyes. "But you see now, don't you, how vulnerable you are to seduction?"

Her mouth opened as if she were going to say something, then she closed it in a grim line. She pressed the book she'd been clinging to into his hands with practiced care, then started to walk past him. He reached out, taking her arm, and she stopped and turned to face him. "Yes."

"Good." Warin breathed a sigh of relief. "You must take more care—"

She shook her head at him and smiled. "Not that, you silly man. Yes, I very much enjoyed Ronan's kiss. His skillful technique would thrill any woman. Now, release my arm."

"Anwyl..."

"Anwyl?" she asked, waiting. She lifted his hand away and strode across the room. "It's *Princess* Anwyl. Do try to remember that in the future." She opened the door, gliding like a queen past Madyan and leaving Warin to stare after her.

"Now what have you gone and done?" Madyan complained.

"I know of no other way to protect her from herself, Madyan," he maintained.

"Oh, you foolish man. And who will protect you?" She disappeared after her princess.

Warin looked down at the title of the book he held clenched in his hands. "Shit!" he cursed and flung the book across the library. The binding broke, and he glared at it like he wanted it to burst into flames. In the end, he scooped up the loose pages, trying to salvage what he could. It was no use, and he abandoned the pile on an end table, then slumped into a chair, his head low in defeat.

Someone entered the library, closed the door, and strode to the corner. The sound of liquid splashing into goblets trickled over the sound of the crackling of the fire in the hearth. Warin kept his head down, not caring. A pair of finely cobbled boots appeared in front of him, and he felt a goblet being nudged against his hand. He took it, and by the time he looked up, Ronan had taken the other chair in front of the hearth.

"Don't," Warin cautioned, then swallowed the contents of the goblet.

"I'm not here to lecture you," Ronan replied, holding out the bottle and pouring another round. "You already know how badly you bungled that opportunity."

"Opportunity?" He hated the way Ronan looked on him with pity. "Never mind. Just keep the brandy flowing." He held out his goblet again to Ronan, but this time, when he drank, he took time to savor the beverage, rolling the warm nuances of apple and pear over his tongue before swallowing. "I haven't decided if I should pound you with my fists or just run you through with my sword," he finally admitted.

"Why would you do either?" Ronan asked, unconcerned by his threats.

"For Anwyl. You should not have taken advantage of her."

Ronan chuckled. "Is that what you think happened?"

"Do you deny kissing her?"

"Now you're just being rude. I like to think that I comport myself with higher standards than kissing and telling."

"She's an innocent in the ways of men of our ilk."

Ronan's laughter filled the library. "Poor Warin, you are so blind. Allow me educate you on Princess Anwyl—she is not so naïve as you believe. How could she be, living at court in Sophiana her entire life? Hell, you of all people must have heard the rumors. The people of Sophiana are the most progressive group in the known realms, more so even than in your lovely Pheldhain."

"What do you know about it?"

"Enough to assure you that Princess Anwyl knew exactly what would happen when she agreed to come with me to this library. She even asked Madyan to give us a few minutes alone. She's a woman, Warin, and not some simple ingénue. A full-grown, beautiful, intelligent, and sensuous woman. Open your eyes and look at her, man. What did you think was going to happen when you chastised her like you were an old auntie?"

"I was trying to teach her—"

"A lesson?"

"No, no," he refuted, beginning to see how it had gone wrong. "She needs to know that she can't trust men to be honorable."

"Well, you proved your point there, didn't you?" Ronan stood up. "There's half a bottle left, but I would go to bed if I were you. This brandy will leave you senseless if you're not careful, and we're sailing to Acerto tomorrow."

"Why? There's nothing on that island but goats, gorse, and your infernal apple trees."

"That's not quite true," Ronan corrected as he walked to the door of the library.

"You shouldn't have kissed her."

Ronan stood in the doorway for a moment, studying him. "Perhaps you're right, my friend. But then, *you* should have." And with that parting comment, he was gone.

Warin reached for the bottle, then set it back down. He would need to be sober if he was going to fix what he had broken.

• • •

Ronan promised her a surprise, and Anwyl waited impatiently on the bow of his ship. It was a vessel from Marach, the Cathmaran state known for its shipwrights, but there were slight differences in its construction, especially compared to Warin's Marachan-built smuggling vessel that had brought her to Aurelia. This ship was leaner and with only two masts, and the sails were of a different cut. She watched as Ronan expertly steered the vessel through the treacherous waters south of Acerto Island and then turned away when he offered the wheel to Warin, wanting more than anything to keep him below her notice.

Ronan had been especially solicitous to her when they had broken their fast. She had expected him to ask how she was, but he'd only offered to show her the two pijala trees planted in his orchard. It said much that he didn't offer any platitudes.

His trees were doing well, as expected, but there were no saplings to be seen. Ronan explained that he had tried everything to get the seeds to sprout in his orchard, even consulting the book about the best choices of animal excrement for fertilization. All to no avail.

Afterward, he'd taken her on a thorough tour of his ship, explaining that he'd asked the Marachan builders to make adjustments to their designs based on his own calculations. The modifications, while hindering any long-range sailing between Aurelia and Nifolhad, greatly increased the maneuverability of his ships when navigating the coastal smallholds and eastern Aurelia. He showed her his drawings, and she immediately discerned where he had veered from the traditional designs. Being from Sophiana, a region steeped in the traditions of sailing, Anwyl had wanted to make a suggestion that had the potential to increase the speed of his ships. She held her tongue and was immediately angry with herself for doing so.

Ronan, an especially observant man, noticed that she'd been about to say something and insisted that she share her thoughts. She did. Rather than being irritated, he sketched the changes over one of his designs. And now, here she was, standing at the bow of his ship, the hood of her thick cloak whipped back by the wind. She'd given up trying to keep her head covered; besides, they were sailing southeast toward the sun and a blue sky unblemished by a single cloud.

Her anger at Warin had metamorphosed into something quite different— not sadness exactly, but a resignation of sorts. And as she attempted to sort out her feelings, Ronan joined her. She turned her head to greet him, and the wind whipped several tendrils of her dark hair from its braid. He smiled at her, tucking the wayward strands behind her ear. It was done so tenderly that unwanted tears sprang to her eyes. She turned back to face the wind. If only she felt something more than friendship for him.

"You remind—" she started.

"I was thinking—" he began at the same time. "Princesses first," he said, when they both laughed.

"I was going to say that you remind me of my brother," she said. He grimaced, and she jumped to explain. "You're very kind. And generous. Rani never discounted my ideas just because I was younger than he. He listened. And he respected my opinions and... What were you going to say?"

"I was just wondering if there was more to your mission than simply checking on the health of the pijala trees." He regarded her steadily. "If there is, I want you to know that, well, should you not find what you are looking for, perhaps you would consider returning to Meramont. We've much in common."

Anwyl pulled up her hood before turning her back to the wind. Thus positioned, she could face Ronan. Just over his shoulder and across the main deck, Warin continued to pilot the ship. "Yes," she replied, "I would consider it."

"Good. Well, I'd best go wrest control of *Dulcia's Delight* from Warin."

"Dulcia?" Anwyl asked.

"My grandmother's name. She loved sailing the Calilo Sea. It was she who planted the apple trees on Acerto Island and populated it with goats."

"So, what is this surprise you wanted to show me?" she asked, taking his arm and walking with him to the quarterdeck.

"You'll have to wait and see," he replied. "First, we must berth at the island. After that, it'll be an hour's ride."

"You've horses there?" she asked.

He chuckled. "Contrary to what Warin believes, there is more to the island than gorse and fruit trees. There's a fishing village, a small harbor, a cidery, and even a distillery for making brandy. And The Lookout is quite habitable. I stay on the island at least one week every month. The caretaker and housekeeper—she's also the cook—are married. They bring additional help from the village when it's warranted."

"And there are goats," Anwyl reminded. "Don't forget the goats."

"I would never!" he said and laughed again.

. . .

Ronan's ship flew across the waves. She responded to the slightest touch of the wheel like no other ship Warin had ever sailed. He should be enjoying this time, but he was too busy watching the too-comfortable interaction between Princess Anwyl and Ronan.

"Good morning, Warin," she greeted politely before he could say anything.

"Good morning, An—Princess," he replied, relinquishing the helm to Ronan. The situation was far worse than he'd expected. He'd hoped she'd be angry with him, but her cool greeting left him in no doubt that their newly established friendship was over. He had to at least make an attempt to apologize. He turned to her and—

"As invigorating as it was to stand at the bow," she said suddenly, addressing Ronan, "the view from your quarterdeck is exhilarating. You have a well-trained crew."

"We ran drills for days before *Dulcia's* maiden voyage. Her maneuverability is only as good as the reactions of her crew."

Acerto Island loomed, and Warin held his apology for later. The wind here was especially strong, and Ronan expertly tacked back and forth to angle the ship toward the southern tip of land. "Will we weigh anchor south of the spit?" he asked, aware that the ship had not decelerated. "Or on the western side of Acerto before rowing in?"

"Neither," Ronan called. "I've made improvements over the years." The bosun's whistle sounded, and the crew reduced the sails with practiced precision to just one. "We have to enter the new harbor at an angle and, once in, reduce the last sheet to glide the remaining distance."

Another signal from the bosun had four men with long pikes running to either side of the ship. The final sail was furled, and Warin held his breath as they coasted into a small but well-sheltered harbor. Ahead, mooring buoys waited. Ronan's men skillfully caught each of the four buoys, letting the ropes run out, slowing the feed to decrease the ship's speed. A smoother catch, Warin had never experienced, and he congratulated Ronan on his crew.

Princess Anwyl clapped with joy. "I must write to my brother about this."

The pikers winched their ropes on the port side while simultaneously lengthening those to starboard. A floating dock was extended to the ship from the pier, and a long plank was readied to drop once it was close enough. Two dock workers rolled out a raised platform. They locked it in place, and as the gangplank was lowered, Ronan held out his hand to help the princess. She politely declined.

"Princess Anwyl was raised around ships," Warin explained. "She's as nimble as your best rigger and was extraordinarily helpful to my captain, especially when we sailed north of the Crags when we fled Nifolhad with Lady Claire."

"Considering your knowledge of ship design," Ronan commented to the princess, "I'm not surprised. I would enjoy hearing about your adventures sailing the Crags."

Ship design? Warin was about to ask, but he looked up and whistled. Spread before them was a quaint fishing village, complete with an inn and tavern. The docks themselves were loaded with barrels and crates, and Ronan paused for a moment to consult with a man carrying a ledger. "Twenty barrels of cider, m'lord, are ready to be loaded. Plus, two brandy kegs and three crates of cheese."

"Cheese?" Anwyl asked.

"From the goats," Ronan supplied. "Come, let's head up to the fortress and take some refreshment before our excursion. The crew will see to your belongings."

"How far of a ride is this surprise?" Warin asked, feeling like the odd man out.

"An hour at the most," Ronan answered. When they reached the fortress, a thick wooden door swung open, and a round-faced, rosy-cheeked woman greeted her lord. He picked her up and swung her in a circle, causing her to slap ineffectually at his broad chest.

"This is Rose," Ronan introduced, setting the woman on her feet. "She runs the fortress; don't let anyone tell you otherwise. Rose, this is Princess Anwyl of Nifolhad and Warin of Pheldhain."

"Lovely to meet you, Princess." She turned her smile on Warin. "Och, I remember you. A wee gangly thing you were when you last visited Acerto. I seem to recall you chasing after that brother of yours."

"I was always chasing after Marten," he admitted, "because he was always stealing my belongings and hiding them on me. Books, quills, even my clothes once."

Ronan threw his head back to laugh. "I remember that day. We were on the beach, and he challenged us to see who could swim the farthest. By the time we realized he'd absconded with our clothes, he was long gone." He held out his arm to Anwyl. "Warin and I had to streak up to the fortress wearing nothing but our boots and some well-placed seaweed."

They were ushered into the main hall of the fortress, where they lunched on fresh fish, cider, and goat cheese with thick bread. After making quick work of the meal, they headed to the stable and the three readied horses that awaited them.

The day was pleasant, the trail smooth, and the horses were of good stock and well-trained. When the path narrowed, they rode single file, Warin bringing up the rear. As they crested the steep hill, he was able to shorten the distance between their horses. Now was as good a time as any. "Princess—"

"Are those the goats I hear?" Anwyl called out as the tinkling of bells filled the air.

"Just ahead," Ronan called back. At the summit, he waited as the valley below was revealed to them.

Row upon row of apple- and pear trees extended across the downward slope. Here and there, the bleating of the goats and the delicate chimes of their collars lent music to the day. The goatherd kept a careful watch on them so that they did not destroy the orchards.

"It's lovely," Anwyl observed.

"It's been at least fifteen years since I came here with my father," Warin reminisced. "The transformation is incredible."

"I have four varieties of apples, plus a new stand of pomerois—thanks to Lady Anna and Lord Larkin. Ah, here's my orchard master now." A wiry man approached with a basket of fruit. He handed a small apple to Anwyl, his hands looking as gnarled as the trees. "It's the king's apple," he explained.

"Thank you. What a lovely surprise, Ronan," Princess Anwyl declared.

"Dear princess, that little pomeroi is not your surprise!" He dismounted, throwing Warin a knowing look and positioning himself on the other side of his horse.

It was a generous act, especially from a rival, and Warin dismounted and move to assist her before Anwyl had a chance to throw her leg over her saddle. She steadied herself by placing her hands on his shoulders, and he held her waist as he gently lowered her to the ground. "I thought perhaps your ankle..." Warin started, wondering if she'd only accepted his aid out of habit.

"Thank you, but it's nearly better now. And I can manage with my cane." She joined Ronan where he was conferring with his pomologist, and together they walked through the vast orchard, coming to a halt before a tall, stockade fence.

"We had to build it high enough to control the goats," he explained, stopping to open the gate and allowing Anwyl to enter first.

"Pijala saplings!" Anwyl exclaimed, throwing her arms unreservedly around Ronan's shoulders and giving him a kiss on the cheek. "Look at them.

Oh, this is wonderful!" She ran to one of the three-foot-tall saplings and fell to her knees to examine its trunk, branches, and leaves.

She was so joyful that Warin didn't even mind that she had kissed Ronan, and he stepped up behind her to examine the tree.

"Thank you, Ronan. I've never been given a better surprise," she called out without turning her head. "It almost makes up for having to share this moment with Warin," she muttered under her breath. Warin stared down at her for a moment, then eased away, ignoring Ronan's wondering look.

• • •

They'd tarried two additional days in Meramont before taking to the road again. The tension between Warin and the princess grew each day. Weeks later, thanks to a cracked axel on the wagon, they found themselves in a modest establishment in Ganley. They'd all retired to their separate rooms, each seemingly tired of the other's company. Warin picked up the book he'd been reading, marking the page to finish later. He drew the most recent letter he'd received from *F.H.* and read the note. Again. Perhaps penning a reply to her would ease his growing anxiety that he and the princess would remain estranged.

He picked up his quill and paused. *Her?* When had he decided that his pen-friend was a woman? He thought about the previous letters as he studied the decisive script before him. There were none of the extra flourishes he normally attributed to a woman's hand. No, hers was the penmanship of a person who spent hours in the occupation of study and notation, a scholar with little time for embellishments and ornamentation. So why now did he assume *F.H.* was of the fairer sex? He supposed it was the quality of the letters' content. Men would not waste time writing about difficulties with other men, unless there was some political or financial loss or gain involved. Or perhaps he was entirely wrong to think that way. Perhaps the queen was correct in stating that he knew nothing of women.

He looked again at the post scriptum, more revealing now that he was cognizant of the writer's gender. "Whoever she is, she already holds my esteem for her shrewd deductions and thoughtful inquiries. I would not have entrusted one of my journals to her otherwise. But to which lady at court would the queen have granted access to the library?" For the first time since their exchange began, Warin wanted to meet this correspondent. He drew a fresh piece of paper from his writing kit, inked his quill, and began. He started with the usual pleasantries and commiserations regarding her predicament in not having the luxury of time when it came to penning a lengthier letter. Halfway through, he realized that there was not much more to write about—she had not posed any queries regarding her studies, nor had she offered any comments to his, having not yet read his journal—other than wishing her well and stating his relief that her previously mentioned dilemma was well on its way to a resolution. His quill hovered over the paper as he stared at the wall, thinking about the princess and her pijala trees. He set quill to page once more:

> *...I currently find myself in a quandary. I, too, am on a quest of sorts, one that I have no personal experience or training upon which I can draw. I find myself consulting books that I have never in my life thought to read. The subject is well outside of my purview, but I am endeavoring to find a solution, not for myself, but for another.*
>
> *I realize that this has nothing to do with our shared love of history. I can only say that I am writing to you of this as you had once confided in me yourself. In doing so, I find some small relief.*
>
> *Awaiting with eager anticipation your next letter,*
>
> *A.S.*

He folded and sealed the letter, placed it in the royal message pouch, then put away his writing instruments. After brushing off his tunic, he went in search of the messenger.

CHAPTER TWENTY

On the Efficacy of Manure

Between the clapping of thunder, the whipping of rain and wind against the shutters of the room he'd been assigned, and Warin's preoccupation with making amends to Princess Anwyl, attempting to focus on the still damaged book before him was an exercise in futility. At least Princess Anwyl was safely ensconced in her quarters. They had departed Meramont over two months ago, by way of Ganley, then Monesta, and had finally made it to Salto, where they had sojourned for two nights at the castle.

There, Princess Anwyl had met and dined with Galerin, the future lord of the smallhold. Galerin of Salto was out of the running of marriageable lords. It readily became clear that the man was besotted with his father's ward, a distant cousin, and the potential groom was soon behind them. So, they resumed their trek, riding west. The fort-like inn where they now sojourned was a day's ride from the border of Banta, and Princess Anwyl's room was at the end of the corridor and easily defendable. She remained cordial, but distant, and he was relieved that she wasn't fighting his increasingly stringent precautions.

Rumors and reports of raiding parties and missing ships abounded in the coastal smallholds. Add to that the letter from Ronan detailing a first-hand account of an attack on one of his fishing boats—the entire crew was lost save the son of the pilot—and Warin was being extra cautious. He was anticipating their eventual arrival in Pheldhain, where they would wait out the worst of the winter in the warm clime of his parents' coastal castle.

Except for the loss of his brother's ship—a mystery still not fully explained—Pheldhain seemed to be exempt from the attacks. Warin considered how closely linked his family was to the peoples of the Isles. It had been decades since the captains of the Southron Isles had shown any aggression against Aurelia—their days of pirating were long gone. Could it be possible that a new leader had emerged, one not invested in peaceful relations with the realm? Warin's own captain, for years loyal to Warin and his family, would no doubt be able to provide insight. The only problem was that Warin's family had not seen Captain Grieg in months.

His parents wanted Warin home. And as much as he was eager to see his current task for the queen finished, Waring was in knots over the final outcome. There had been a connection between Ronan and the princess, one that was reinforced when Ronan had revealed that he'd managed to propagate the pijala trees. When pressed, Ronan could not say how his orchard master had managed it. Acerto Island's climate was vastly different from that of Sophiana. It truly was a mystery, one that Warin was resolved to unravel.

Outside, lightning splintered in staccato bursts. Warin waited for the coming boom. The crack was so ear-splitting that even the thick stone walls of the inn seemed to shiver. Another flash, and he heard, not too far off, the explosion of the white bolt hitting what he hoped was only a tree. The smell of ozone hung heavy in the night air, seeping through the gaps in the windows and permeating his room. The heart of the storm was above them, and there was no calm at its center.

They'd been lucky, having made it to the inn just before the deluge broke. He turned his attention back to the book he'd been struggling to read: *On the Efficacy of Animal Manure*. Warin knew the answer to propagating the pijala trees lay somewhere in the sense-dulling tome. He had received, only days before, a letter from his father, informing him of the discovery of five new seedlings. And like Ronan, he could not explain how the growths had finally come to sprout. The orchard master had transplanted them in a secret location, and now they were thriving.

Warin had wanted to share this news with the princess, had even entertained the notion of surprising her once they reached Pheldhain, but Ronan had beaten him to the punch. There were now four places in Aurelia, all with disparate climes, where the pijala trees managed to self-propagate: the wind scourged spit of land that made up Ragallach; a mountain slope in Cathmara, the temperate vale on Acerto Island, and in a secluded orchard hidden within the borders of Pheldhain. His father had not risked specifying the location in his letter.

When an exceptionally loud clap of thunder boomed above the inn, and even his lantern flickered at the percussive force, he gave up all thoughts of reading and set the book aside. That was when he realized that he hadn't heard the persistent knocking on his chamber door. "Enter," he called, as he stood to stretch. His door opened, and Madyan slipped in.

"Is the princess safe?"

She waved away his concern with an impatient hand. "I've convinced her to take her meal in the common room this evening," she explained, then waited expectantly. When he remained silent, she scowled. "It might behoove you to join."

"I don't think that's a good idea."

"You're half-right: you don't think. You both need to deal with this problem. Hiding in your rooms behind your books and letters is solving nothing. You do realize that I'm leaving soon after we reach Pheldhain. It is time you started acting sensible and make—"

"Yield! I yield!"

She narrowed her eyes. "Good. We'll head down in a quarter hour. Be polite."

"I'm always..." His Umbren friend didn't wait for him to finish; she was already out the door, the slamming of it coinciding with another flash of lightning. He nearly jumped out of his skin as the cracking thunder reverberated through the inn, setting his teeth to rattle.

• • •

Why had she permitted Madyan to inveigle her to dine in the common room?

"There'll be singing, Princess," Lucilla chattered excitedly. Then she jumped at an especially vicious boom of thunder. "My grandmother always said 'tis better to spend such nights as this among others."

"I doubt many will venture from their homes," Anwyl replied, smoothing her hands down her skirt. She had changed from her Umbren clothing and into one of her plainer gowns. Still, the garment seemed too fancy.

Lucilla drew her to a chair and began plaiting her hair. "Oh, but the inn is full, my princess."

Though they traveled together, Anwyl had managed to successfully avoid interacting with Warin since Meramont, exchanging only the most superficial pleasantries with him. But lately, fortune seemed intent on throwing him in her path at every opportunity. From a damaged girth strap on her saddle to a misplaced traveling case, inconsequential mishaps had plagued this leg of their journey. The last incident—a sharp stone in her mare's hoof—was the oddest, for the area where she'd picked it up had been a verdant field of sheep-mown grass.

Taken independently, these minor hiccups caused no more than a few moments' delay. Irksome accidents that seemed only to affect her. But unlike before, Warin set himself to the task of remedying each occurrence with nary a scowl or roll of eye.

Anwyl regarded her coiffure in the hand mirror that Lucilla provided her. "It's perfect. I haven't worn my hair this way in some time, and your skill is admirable."

Lucilla beamed. "I'll just go dump this water and then return to tidy your things."

Anwyl nodded, not really paying attention. She was thinking about *A.S.*'s last correspondence. Madyan entered the room. "Ready, Princess?"

She nodded, and with Madyan, Anwyl made her way to the stairs that would lead to the common room. She'd spent the afternoon tying knots and mats to settle her thoughts and hoped it had been enough to maintain an air of cordialness toward Warin.

• • •

"Here she is," Madyan spoke, indicating with a nod the arrival of Lucilla. The girl smiled tentatively, and Warin slid over to make room on the bench. Doing so put him directly across from Madyan. From his vantage, he had a nearly unobstructed view of the room. His only blind spot was directly behind him, but Madyan would keep watch in that direction. His instincts had been screaming that there was some deliberate effort aimed at delaying them on their journey, and Warin never disregarded his gut feelings.

There was also the issue of Daisy—that young woman who had assisted Anwyl when she had first arrived in Aurelia. Tomas had written to say that the girl had never returned to Ragallach, so he and Ailwen tracked down the family that had visited the castle. Her parents, while confirming that they had a daughter named Daisy, also stated that she fell ill two days after their departure and died before they returned home. No one in the family could recall meeting another girl during their travels. No one except a seven-year-old boy who insisted that Daisy's friend had traveled with them for at least a day and a night. Who was this girl? Where had she gone? And why could no one except the boy recall meeting her?

Warin had been on alert ever since the princess had been abducted by Herlewin and Eunice's men, but even more so now. Each day, tiny calamities seemed to afflict the princess, two, three, four times—enough occurrences to considerably slow their progress. Warin doubted that even Lady Eunice would be brave enough to try to hamper their journey, not after Madyan's foray into Dinhyll. Yet one never knew, especially with Lady Eunice. His thoughts were interrupted when four crusty loaves of steaming hot bread were set before them.

Madyan and Anwyl looked at each other. "This is too much for us," the princess whispered. Lucilla rapped on the extraordinarily hard crust with her spoon.

"It's a custom here in Salto," Warin explained. "Here, let me." He took his loaf and cut off the top portion, swapping it with the princess's, then repeated the process with Madyan's loaf and Lucilla's, until all four boules had been cut. "You only eat the soft bread in the center." No sooner had they finished than the serving girls returned. One carried a tureen, the other a deep ladle, and they spooned a healthy portion of goose stew, one laced with carrots, turnips and cabbage, into the hollowed-out loaves.

"It smells wonderful," Anwyl exclaimed.

"It tastes even better," he promised, and showed them how to eat the stew Salto-style by breaking apart the cut off tops of their loaves and dipping the chunks into the trenchers. "It's considered rude if you eat everything, leaving naught but the crust."

"Seems a waste," Madyan pointed out.

"Not at all," Warin explained. "You see, the boules are given to those less fortunate. Your bowl could end up feeding a small family this evening."

"But I've seen no one who seems as if they're in need in this smallhold," the princess observed. "King Godwin keeps his people well-fed and cared for."

"True," Warin agreed. "His laws do require the lords and ladies of his realm to care for all of the tenants, from the youngest babe to the oldest grandmother." He frowned. "But not all territories take the same care. Of late, there has been an influx of new families into Salto, Banta, and Pheldhain. Our seasons are more temperate, our lords more generous than in—"

"—Dinhyll," Lucilla meekly stated.

"Quite so." He finished eating the top portion of his loaf, leaving the remaining stew in the trencher untouched. "It's cyclical. Every few years, there is an exodus from some ill-managed smallhold. With fewer mouths to feed, the smallhold recovers, and people move back. If the smallhold is run properly, the cycle stops. There are always families moving from one region to the next, with a few exceptions.”

“Meramont,” Madyan put in.

“And here, in Salto.” Anwyl was frowning, and he followed her gaze. At a nearby table, two portly men sat, devouring every scrap of food set before them. “Not everyone here is from Salto, Princess Anwyl. And not everyone cares to understand the customs and traditions of others.”

“But you do,” she noted, almost as if paying him a compliment. It was, perhaps, a peace offering on her part. The serving girls had returned with more wine. They ran out before replenishing Lucilla’s cup, but a kitchen boy materialized and filled it. One of the serving girls chided him for straying into their domain, and he slipped away. Warin set his napkin on the table next to his trencher, and the others followed his lead.

The serving girls smiled and thanked them, whisking away the remains of their meal. The innkeeper, a stout woman with rosy cheeks and a harried look, came to the table. Before she could ask if they’d enjoyed their supper, Anwyl complimented her on the delicious stew. And so began an exchange of recipes between the two. Warin watched her as she captured the heart of yet another stranger.

“...apple tart with fresh cream,” the innkeeper was saying, and Anwyl nodded enthusiastically. The woman sashayed back to the kitchen, her wide hips keeping time to the music of the clattering utensils, cups, and plates. Moments later, a large pie was set before them, and Anwyl did the honors of serving each a generous slice. Warin grinned when he saw that his three companions had each left a small portion behind. He stabbed at his last piece and dragged it through the remaining cream on his plate, then ate it with gusto.

“Thank goodness,” Lucilla exclaimed, finishing her dessert. Madyan and Anwyl laughed and followed suit.

“To Salto,” Warin toasted, “and their generous traditions and delicious food.” The others lifted their cups to his, and they all drank. Madyan pushed the last slice of tart toward him. “You’d best not let it go to waste, Warin, seeing as it won’t be given to anyone.”

Warin happily dug in while the others sipped their wine.

“When we reach Pheldhain, how—Lucilla, are you all right?” Madyan asked suddenly.

The girl’s face contorted, and she doubled over in pain.

"Lucilla!" the princess cried.

The girl had gone pale, and sweat beaded across her features. "My stomach," she managed.

"I'll get her upstairs," Madyan offered, giving Warin a look and silently communicating to him to guard the princess. "Come on, Lucilla," she coaxed.

The innkeeper returned, distressed that someone had fallen ill. "We all ate the same food, and the rest of us are fine," Warin assured her. "It must be something else."

Princess Anwyl had picked up Lucilla's cup and was sniffing it. She stuck her finger in and tasted a drop. A look of shocked anger swept her features, and she held out the cup. "One thing was different."

The innkeeper smelled the remains, then dipped her finger in for a sample. "This tastes like blackthorn berry wine," she said. "But we have none of that here. An' if we did, it wouldn't do to serve it until it's aged. Can make a person downright sick if…"

"Perhaps we should discuss this in the kitchen," Warin suggested, noticing the number of people taking an interest in their conversation. The innkeeper led them away, her earlier sashay replaced by a march that would put a general to shame. The serving girls confirmed that it had been the kitchen boy who had refilled Lucilla's cup.

"Tweak!" the innkeeper yelled, and they all turned to the sound of feet running up the steps from the cellar. "My grandson," she explained. The lad appeared, a lock of hair sticking out at an odd angle above his ear.

Warin guessed him to be around nine years old. A gentle interrogation ensued, revealing that the wine merchant and his wife had given the boy the bottle during his regular delivery. He'd issued instructions that it should only be opened for special guests. "His wife knew the princess was staying here," Tweak announced. "And when Molly here yelled for me to bring another bottle for your table, I remembered this one and brought it up. Here, I'll show you." He took them to a wood crate where various jugs and bottles had been placed. "It was right there, I swear."

"Check the room, girls," his grandmother ordered. "Quick like, lest someone else falls ill!" They rushed out.

"It's all right, Tweak," Warin assured. He turned to the innkeeper. "Where can we find this wine merchant?"

"On his way to Monesta," she supplied. "We're on his regular route.

"It wasn't Bert who came today," Tweak interjected. "'Tis my fault; I didn't think to question him. He said that he was Bert's cousin, and that Bert was sick. He was in Bert's wagon, and it was Bert's team hitched to it, straw bonnets on their heads like always."

"Tweak," the princess asked, "can you describe the wife?"

"I think so," he said, then frowned and scrunched up his face trying to remember. "She was...she...I think she was his wife. She looked like a wife."

His grandmother cuffed the back of his head, gently, and rolled her eyes.

"I hope your friend will be all right. I'm really sorry, Princess. I didn't know."

"You're not to blame, Tweak," Princess Anwyl insisted, then turned to his grandmother. "I'm sure it's just a misunderstanding. Could you make up a tonic of vinegar, mint, sweet onion juice, fennel, and a pinch of snakeroot?"

"Yes, of course. But what's snakeroot? I've never heard of that."

"It's a common herb in Nifolhad that is used to induce vomiting," the princess explained.

"I might have some sweet myrtle or soapwort; it should have the same effect."

"I'll have to give her a dose immediately and make sure she expels everything in her stomach."

"I'm sorry, Princess," Warin said, "but you must return to the safety of your chamber." After ensuring that the innkeeper would go to Madyan herself, Warin pushed at the door to the common room, wedging it open a bit and peering through the gap. He would ponder the issue of the princess's knowledge of the exact remedy to blackthorn berry poisoning later.

"You can take the back stairs," Tweak suggested. "Course, it'll be a bit tight for you. Only me an' the maids use 'em."

Warin followed the boy through the kitchen to a narrow door hidden from view by a large cupboard. Anwyl slipped past them and entered first. The farther up they climbed, the darker it became, and the more Warin was forced to stoop. Upon reaching the door, she pushed at it, only to find that it was locked.

"It'll be locked, m'lord," Tweak called up from below, and Warin gave a beleaguered sigh.

"Stay here," he ordered, knocking his head on the ceiling when he turned.

Tweak raced up before he could descend and handed the key to him. "Gran'mum says to keep it until tomorrow. She'll tell the maids to use the main stairs." He started to race back down the steps, heedless of the confining space, but then stopped and turned. "The wife, Princess, I think her hair was blond." He frowned again as if concentrating hurt his head. "Yes, blond. And she was young."

Warin turned and remembered too late to duck, bashing his head against the ceiling again. His eyes had grown accustomed to the dim lighting filtering up from the bright kitchen, and he could just make out the princess's worried expression where she stood on the landing.

"Tell me that you've noticed too," she whispered. "Tell me that I'm not imagining things. That this is more than just a run of bad luck." He stopped one step below her. "More like little acts of sabotage."

"You're not imagining things," he assured her. "Someone is deliberately trying to delay us." He moved to one side of the stairwell. "Good thing you knew the exact recipe to counteract the bad wine." He waited for her to respond, watching closely.

"It wasn't just bad wine," she divulged. "Blackthorn poisoning causes pain, but the symptoms will pass quickly if given the proper remedy. That wine was laced with something else...imp berry, crab's-eye, I'm not sure what."

"Crab's-eye! But that's deadly if ingested! So that's why you want Lucilla to vomit. Princess, are you Fenrhi?"

"What? No! Warin, no. I'm not Fenrhi." She stared at him. "I was tutored by a Sylvan woman. I thought you knew that." She looked away, and he knew in his gut that she wasn't telling him everything. "I need to check on Lucilla," she insisted, but he continued to regard her, waiting. "My tutor was a master, all right? Is that what you wanted to hear? I may be trained, but I'm not Fenrhi. I just happen to have extensive knowledge of Fenrhi poisons and antidotes. It was necessary for our survival, Warin. Diarmait's favorite method of murder is poison. If you only knew the things that I have seen, then you might understand."

"Oh, I think I know a little, Princess," he said, recalling his disjointed memories.

"What does that mean?" she demanded.

This wasn't the time to hash out the vague recollections that had been plaguing him, and he held up his hands in surrender. "Nothing. Never mind. Here, let me get you to your chamber." He tried to squeeze by her to unlock the door. It was no good; there wasn't enough room on the landing for them both. The way he was hunched over, he felt like a buzzard. When he tried to fit the key to the lock, he fumbled it. The sound as it clattered down the steps echoed in the stairwell.

"I see it," she said and sidled past him, not realizing that Warin was standing on the hem of her gown. He caught her mid-fall and hauled her back up to the landing and into his chest, straightening as he did so and cracking his head yet again. "Oh dear," she breathed. "That'll be your third goose egg."

He couldn't think of a coherent reply, standing so close to her, noticing the way her breasts pushed up against his chest, and how perfect his hand felt supporting her at the small of her back. And when she reached up to gently probe his bashed skull, he forgot all about wanting answers about that day in Sophiana. Her face was so close to his, both of her hands in his hair, her fingers searching his scalp. She must have realized that he had stopped breathing, for she stilled and stared straight into his eyes.

"Oh, hell," Warin cursed, giving in to his desire. He closed the gap until his lips settled upon hers. And when she didn't immediately give him another cosh on his head, he kissed her in earnest. Though she kissed him in return, he sensed her hesitation. He pulled back to regard her and saw both sadness and longing warring in her gaze. Wanting more than anything to erase the pain in her eyes, he leaned forward again.

• • •

He kissed her! And if she didn't do something, he was going to kiss her again. Her heart could not bear it, not when she had so successfully warded her emotions. Quickly, Anwyl pulled her hand from where her fingers had tangled in his dark locks and pressed them against his lips just as he leaned in. She looked everywhere but at him as she tried to take an impossible step back in the confining stairwell. He took her fingers in his large, warm hands. She felt the cold ache where he had held the small of her back, now abandoned.

"Anwyl?"

"I'll get the key." She turned, her shoulder brushing against his chest.

"Anwyl, please."

She unlocked the door and pushed it open, startling a maid who had been stocking the closet shelves with fresh linens. Anwyl stepped regally into the upstairs corridor, trying to outpace Warin. She needed a moment to assemble her wits before he began with his apologies for having kissed her. She was almost to her chamber, but he caught up with her and pulled her into his room, shutting the door behind them. She crossed her arms and put as much distance as she could between them.

"Anwyl, I—"

"It was a mistake, Warin. Don't worry, I'm not angry. Such a tight space, you must have thought when I touched your hair—"

"Mistake? Princess, that kiss was no mistake. The only mistake was not realizing that it was you at the masquerade."

"What masquerade?"

"Don't try to insist that it was Lady Beth and not you. I never forget a kiss."

"How wonderful for you," she said dryly, and narrowed her eyes at him. He had found her out. She took a steadying breath, lifted her chin, and stared straight at him. She was a princess of Nifolhad; she had faced worse trials than this. She wouldn't excuse what she had done that night, concealing the truth from him, but she would—

He crossed the room to her. "I wanted to kiss you, Anwyl. I've wanted to since you made me wash my hair with vinegar."

"You don't have to say that, Warin. I appreciate you trying to spare my feelings, but I know kissing me is the last thing you wished to do. I know what you truly think of me."

"The stable," he said, making her recall that horrible moment again. "Anwyl, I knew you were—"

"Please just stop. Moments ago, you kissed me against your better judgment. 'Oh, hell,' you swore. I know you think me foolish, but I am not. You do not need to teach me any more of your lessons."

"I..." he began. "I wish I had never..."

"I know. It's all right, Warin."

"No, no." He raked his fingers through his locks, and she almost smiled at the gesture. "I'm making a mess of this. Look, I wanted to kiss you. I *want* to kiss you. Please, trust me when I say this."

"I do trust you, Warin. I trust you with my safety, but it's not enough, is it?" She stopped, opened her mouth to say more, then searched his room as if it held the answer to what was bothering her. And then it came to her, and she stared straight at him. "How could I ever trust my heart to a man who doesn't trust me in return?" She left him staring after her as she stepped from his room. But he followed her, not allowing her to make her way to her chamber alone. Always the dutiful guard.

"We still have to discuss our run of misfortunes," he reminded.

"Tomorrow," Anwyl stated, brooking no argument. He opened her door but did not allow her passage within. With the weight of his gaze upon her, lifting her eyes to his was the hardest thing she'd ever done.

"I've been a fool, Princess. I will make it up to you, and one day, you will trust me in every way that counts."

She swept past him and shut the door, throwing the bolt in place, loud enough so that he could hear it. Four, she thought, taking a deep breath through her nose; three, another breath, exhaling through clenched teeth; two, relaxing her jaw, and one. She wanted to throw something. Not even her ropes would be able to tease the tumult from her mind. For the first time, Anwyl wished she had a confidant. Lucilla was in her own room, being tended to by Madyan. But even if they were standing in front of her, she could not imagine spilling her heart. Nor could she to any of the ladies at court, not even Queen Juliana. Especially Queen Juliana. She would do nothing to tarnish the trust the king and queen had in Warin, especially over something as trivial as a brokenhearted princess.

If only Rani were not so far away. By the time he received her letter, her problems would be resolved with her marriage to another man. Best not to worry her brother. On the table in her chamber sat her writing box. "Should I?"

She sat at her table and pulled out a clean sheet of paper and her carved quill.

Dear A.S.,

I pray this letter finds you well. I myself am looking forward to the day when my current journey is over and done. Indeed, it is the thought of making your acquaintance that keeps me going. With you, I am able to express more than my love of history. Perhaps it is because you and I have kept our correspondence anonymous that I feel so unencumbered. After reading your personal journal and musings, I recognize the traits of a man who does not judge or condemn a person without knowing the facts.

I mentioned in my last letter a bettering of relations with a certain difficult person. Alas, what I thought was a growing respect and understanding turned out to be nothing but smoke. The more I revealed of myself, the more I was misunderstood. Verily, it was my openness and willingness to prove myself, and on more than one occasion, that has caused this state of blindness in my acquaintance.

But all is not so dreary as I make out. I will acquit myself with better judgment in all things. To that end, I am returning your treasured journal. Your writings allowed me to see the beauty of the region, with its balmy climes and seafaring people, and it means much that you trusted me with your personal history. For the latter part, I thank you more than you can know.

Your friend,
F.H.

Post Scriptum: I read your journal several times and wrote about one of the more enlightened courtship rites with which I'm familiar (separately enclosed).

Post Post Scriptum: Please excuse my lapse—caused certainly by my current predicament—in not asking after the mystery that is troubling you. If I may be of assistance, you need only write.

Anwyl folded the letter and then reached for the wax to seal the paper. This was one letter she would not send; she had been much too forthcoming about her emotions in it. She would simply write another in the morning. As she held the wick to flame, she frowned. It wasn't trimmed from the last use; she always trimmed her waxes. To do otherwise invited soot and ash into your writing box. Had her troubles so distracted her?

While she pondered this, she dropped a glob of heated wax onto the letter, then pressed her thumb into it. She wrapped the journal and placed both items into the pouch. There was a rap at her door.

"Anwyl?" Warin called. "Can we talk, please?"

She remained silent.

"All right. I understand. But I wanted to let you know, Lucilla is resting. She'll be fine." There was another soft rap on her door. "Anwyl?"

She ignored him and climbed into her bed, eventually falling asleep to the steady fall of wind-driven rain on her window.

$$\cdots$$

Kings Glen

"My heart revolts against such a conclusion," Juliana swore.

"Mine, too," Godwin replied. "There is more to this, no matter what the council says. I will not believe that Pheldhain is involved in the attacks."

THE NAKED MOON   201

"The very lack of evidence is disturbing. Just because the Pheldhainian coast has not been raided does not mean Lord Marin has suddenly reverted to the ways of his ancestors. He and his sons have been staunch allies of our house. No, some other scheme is afoot. Tell me, which council member spoke out against House Pheldhain?"

"More than one, unfortunately. Iter, Monesta, and Prato have all had their goods, those transported by ships from Meramont, taken."

"All on Meramont ships..." She thrummed her fingers. "I've had news that one of Meramont's fishing boats was attacked, its crew murdered, all save one boy."

"Ronan's representative was Pheldhain's strongest defender in the council meeting. So was Lord Baldric of Whitmarsh. Then word came from Sterland about a raid on a small fishing village there. The survivors claimed they saw two ships. One of Southron Isles design. The other, Pheldhainian."

Queen Juliana rose from her chair, unable to contain her impatience. Before she could speak, her husband continued. "Dinhyll's agent at council also expressed his disbelief that Pheldhain was involved."

"Now, that *is* interesting."

"I thought you might find it so," her husband said. "Especially after reading Warin's account of the abduction in Redavel."

"It's doubtful that Lady Eunice is behind these raids. She doesn't have the resources, nor the access to ships. But she might take advantage and, from the corners of the room, have someone whisper in the ears of their smallhold neighbors."

"Spreading rumors is her forte, is it not?"

Juliana took a seat, leaning back against her husband. "It's odd that we suddenly have unrest among the territories and trouble with the Southron Isles, even as the civil war in Nifolhad comes to its end."

There was a knock on the door, and his valet entered the study and bowed. "An urgent message from Floresta, sire." Godwin read the letter and then handed it to Juliana.

"Both of their pijala trees have been stolen?"

"So it seems," her husband worried aloud. "They are not the first either. I was just about to tell you, the trees in Meramont are missing. Fortunately, the saplings Ronan propagated are in a secure location and thriving."

"Husband, Lady Ingrid received word last week from Monesta that her trees were destroyed in a fire. She wants to petition you for replacements. I'm starting to think that the mishaps plaguing Princess Anwyl's journey are something more. The loss of pijala trees occurred immediately following her departures from those areas affected."

Juliana and her husband sat in quiet contemplation. Finally, Godwin stood and paced. "I will send word ordering increased protection for the pijalas, especially in Ragallach. As for the shipping of goods, for now, I'll recommend overland transport. This will hurt Meramont."

"I wonder..." the queen started. "No one family profits if the shipping lanes are disrupted, for most of the territories and smallholds use them. But if someone was set against damaging both the houses of Pheldhain and Meramont by these attacks..."

"You think the incidents related?"

"I'm not sure. From what Anwyl has written, Lord Ronan is a strong candidate for marriage. His ships transport most of the smallhold goods, while Pheldhain handles the larger territories and imports from Nifolhad and the Isles. And if Ronan is trying to remove another from contention..."

"But why try to implicate Pheldhain?" he wondered, and the queen smiled. "Dear wife, what do you know?"

"Only that there is a connection between our princess and Warin, though both are too stubborn to allow nature to take its course."

"Two rivals for her hand. One impacted by attacks on his ships; the other implicated."

"I dislike pointing this out, but we only have Ronan's word that his smallhold was attacked. No. It's not possible. Not from Meramont."

He took Juliana's hands. "I know that you count Warin a friend, my love. He has been one of the most loyal of the royal guards. I cannot write to his family directly, not if the council insists on investigating the rumors. However—"

"I can speak with Lady Murel. Lady Caroline can join us as well. We three should be able to come up with a plan that circumvents the council. And I will write to the princess immediately."

• • •

Weeks later in Castle Pheldhain

Lord Marin paced while his wife studied what charts they had of the Southron Isles. Those maps that did exist were woefully lacking in detail. "Grieg's been gone too long. He and *Lita's Pearl* have disappeared just as Marten and his crew have."

"We will solve this mystery, my love. Give it time."

He strode to the broad window overlooking Pheldhain's largest port. "There's more. Murel has written from Kings Glen; there seems to be a concerted effort to bring our house's loyalty into question."

"But who would do such a thing? And why?" Lady Téana asked. "We still have friends at court and in the territories—Sterland, Morland, Chevlain, Stolweg, and Cathmara."

"I noticed you did not mention Baldric from Whitmarsh?"

"My cousin will stand in support of us, but being King Godwin's right-hand man, he must appear neutral. Especially if we are called before the council."

"Warin could answer a great number of questions if he were here. He should have arrived weeks ago." Lord Marin stared at the map before him. "I'll send some men to meet him in Banta. If anything were to happen to Princess Anwyl under his watch..."

"I think we'd best prepare for any eventuality."

CHAPTER TWENTY-ONE

Fair Fight

Market Day, Salto

Anwyl took a deep breath, relishing the scouring scent of saltwater on the breeze coming up from the docks. Warin walked beside her, on guard, his hand resting comfortably on the pommel of his sword. Anwyl carried her cane, though she no longer needed it. It had been Madyan's idea, after Anwyl had refused to carry her quarterstaff through the busy market stalls. Madyan held no such reservations, and trailed somewhere behind them, watching their backs.

They'd been five days delayed due to Lucilla's illness. But the promise of a sunny day and her newly returning strength, plus Warin acquiescing to visiting the market, had the young woman up and dressed and out of doors. Lucilla was in the next stall, admiring the local crafts made by Salto's famed tatters. She held up a piece of intricately worked lace, and Anwyl nodded to her to purchase as much as she needed. She and Madyan had been teaching Lucilla some rudimentary defense skills, but her incapacitation had put her training on hold.

Across the aisle, Anwyl stopped to admire a beautiful watered silk from one of the better fabric purveyors while Warin waited patiently beside her.

"That color suits you, Princess," he said. Hearing him, the vendor agreed and draped the fabric over his arm, demonstrating how the hue transformed as the sunlight hit the cloth. It reminded her of the colors of the sea, and Anwyl began the process of bargaining for a good price.

"Remind me to bring you along the next time I set sail for a trade run."

Anwyl smiled politely at the compliment and then crossed the lane to see what Lucilla was purchasing. Only...Lucilla was nowhere to be found. "Warin!" she called out in alarm, but he was already searching over the heads of the market-day crowd. Without his advantage of height, Anwyl couldn't see through the throng of people.

"There!" he said, pointing to a narrow opening between two of the buildings. She turned to see if Madyan was around. "Stay close to me, Princess." He grabbed her hand and wove his way through the crowd. When it thinned enough, he drew his sword with one hand and tucked Anwyl behind him with the other.

In the alleyway, a man was dragging Lucilla away. She kicked and fought against him, slowing his progress. When she saw Warin, she cried out for help. They were maybe twenty paces away.

"Warin!" Anwyl called out as two armed men came up behind them.

Warin turned, keeping her behind him, and began to defend them against the two swordsmen. Anwyl raced to Lucilla, her cane raised to attack the man who had grabbed the girl. He pulled a knife and came at her, but she used her cane to deflect the blade and then followed through with another hard *thwack* to his wrist. The dagger went flying, and she advanced on him, raining blows to his arms and shoulders, pushing him farther away from Lucilla. He dove for her, and she pivoted on her good foot, spinning out of his reach, and then grabbed the back of his tunic and used his momentum to throw him forward into the building. He wouldn't be getting up for a good while.

Anwyl helped Lucilla from the ground. Though she was trembling, she'd kept her wits and picked up the discarded dagger. Anwyl kept her close behind her and turned to see how Warin was faring.

It was clear that the attackers had some training, but they were no match for Warin's prowess with the sword. The two men couldn't see it, though. They must've believed that since they were still fighting, they had a chance. The way in which Warin worked his sword, it was as though he wanted them alive for questioning. He risked a glance at her and, reassured that she and Lucilla were safe, redoubled his attack on the two cutthroats, disarming one in a flurry of clashing steel, and then wounding the other. She'd never seen Warin in action before, and he was quite magnificent to behold.

"Princess!" Lucilla cried out in warning. Two additional men were racing up the alley from the opposite direction, each with a sword. A shadow flew over her, and she looked up as her instincts made her duck, but it was Madyan using her quarterstaff to vault over their heads. She landed and ran forward to confront the new players. Seeing her, the smarter of the two men turned tail and ran, taking the one who had grabbed Lucilla with him. The other was not so fortunate. He was set on doing harm, screaming his war cry and running straight for Madyan. At the last possible second, Madyan changed course and charged to the side. She leapt and, scaling the wall and racing up the side of the building and above him, brought her staff down on his head. He fell in a great tangle of limbs, his sword sliding down the alley toward Anwyl. Madyan hadn't wasted her time with incapacitating the attacker; her strike to his skull was a crushing one.

Anwyl scooped up the fallen sword. "I've got Lucilla," Madyan yelled. "Help Warin."

She nodded, taking the dagger from Lucilla and running toward the entrance to the alleyway. The disarmed attacker had pulled out a hidden blade and was lifting it to throw at Warin. Anwyl threw first, and her blade landed in his shoulder—he fled the alley and disappeared into the throng.

"Damn!" Warin swore, looking at the three dead men. "Anwyl, are you hurt?"

"I'm fine. You?"

"Good. Lucilla?" he asked the trembling girl.

"I didn't know them," she cried, her eyes wide.

"She's unhurt," Anwyl answered for the surprisingly resilient girl.

"Madyan?" Warin asked next.

"I'm sorry I was late," she said, looking quite vexed. "Someone tossed a bag of coins into the street, and the crowd started fighting. I had to run over them to get here, literally." She gazed at the dead man. "The others got away," she complained.

"I scratched his face," Lucilla said, holding up her bloodied fingernails. She should have been shocked by the brutality of the attack—Madyan had killed a man not five paces from where Lucilla had stood. Unless, Anwyl considered, she'd been witness to violence before. The very idea warranted some digging.

"Let's get back to the inn," Warin ordered. "Madyan?"

"I have her," she said of Lucilla. "You did a good job of defending yourself," she told the girl, and Lucilla nodded, her spirits bolstered.

Warin took Anwyl's arm, then looked outside the alleyway. The crowd seemed much the same to Anwyl. In the frenzy to collect the coins, no one had noticed the attack. Her mind reeled at the overt and planned out assault. "Lucilla was only bait," she whispered as Warin nodded to Madyan to take the girl back to the safety of the inn.

"They knew you would go after her," he said.

She put her hand on his arm and stared up into the turbulent blue of his eyes. "I wasn't the target, Warin. You were. Madyan recognized it too."

He looked taken aback for a moment, then determination settled over his features. "Not here," he whispered, and they hurried back the way they'd come.

...

The Islet

"He finally broke, Captain. I thought I'd met my match," Rowly confided, draping his arm over Vala's shoulder. "But once Vala and I combined our efforts, we were able to push him over the edge. She made him believe that she was his cousin and—"

Dorn held up his hand. The captain of the Pheldhainian ship had been amazingly resilient. A challenge such as that could not go unmet. "Did you discover his identity?" he asked Vala as she extricated herself from Rowly.

"Oh, aye," Rowly answered in her stead, looking positively giddy. "No less than the heir to all of Pheldhain!"

"Lord Marten! This news almost makes it worth the wait." He leaned back to appreciate how this would hurt House Pheldhain. "Imagine, never knowing what happened to your son." He smiled at the thought. "You've earned your keep today, Rowly."

"And Lord Marten?"

"Is there anything else to be learned from him?" Rowly shook his head. "Then consider him part of your wages."

"Perhaps he still has value, if you'll allow me..." Vala said, speaking for the first time since entering his hut. She looked ill, but that was to be expected. Very few people could appreciate the genius of Rowly's talent.

"Go on."

"He would make a powerful weapon, if properly used."

"Can you control him?"

"I won't know until I try. And if I'm unsuccessful, you can still give him to Rowly."

She was right, of course. It would also be a chance to see just how strong Vala's Kena abilities were and if he should consider her a threat. "Do it," he ordered. "And don't look so crestfallen, Rowly. I've given you enough playthings already."

Dorn sat at the crude table that served as his desk. His original plan of destroying the truce between the Southron Isles and Aurelia—leaving both prime for his picking—seemed so shortsighted now. He never dreamed that fortune would hand him this opportunity to land a crushing blow against Aurelia by turning one of their noble sons against them. Vala had an astute mind, one that could see multiple outcomes and possibilities. He would have to reward her, and soon. Perhaps it was time to appoint her as his advisor. Odo and Rowly had their uses, but what Dorn wanted would take subtle planning, not brute force.

CHAPTER TWENTY-TWO

Meeting the Parents

Castle Pheldhain

Lucilla ran her fingertips over the silky fabric of the gown she was modeling. "I've never owned anything this beautiful."

"After what happened in Salto, I thought you deserved something as lovely as you, so I wrote to Lady Téana with your measurements." Lucilla had been melancholy since their adventure in the alley, and Anwyl hoped, now that they would be staying in one place for a couple of months, her spirits would lighten. This new gown was in the elegant Pheldhainian style, and the young maiden looked lovely in the pale-blue fabric that offset her loose blond curls. Anwyl gazed down at her own gown, wishing she could have worn a more comfortable Fenrhi garment, but hadn't wanted to dampen Lucilla's happiness. Besides, she was meeting Warin's family—Lord Marin and Lady Téana, and their extended family—for the first time.

She smiled at Lucilla, then rose from the dressing table and stared down at her trim figure. The violet gossamer silk from Sophiana wafted in the gentle breeze coming from the balcony. The wide band of her Fenrhi sash had been wound 'round her slim waist—the bottom edge following the contours of her hips' flare and then up, to just below the deep V of the gown's neckline. She plucked at one of the edges of her sash, pulling it so that more of the seed pearls were visible. Her dark hair, plaited at the back of her head, hung in a long braid over her shoulder. She'd not worn this dress before in Kings Glen. The revealing cut and delicate silk cloth might have caused a scandal. Not so, here in Pheldhain.

Though the castle housing Warin's family was in a different style than that in Kings Glen, the appointments and quality of workmanship rivaled that of the Royal Palace. From all appearances, Pheldhain was an extremely wealthy territory, and she wondered how much of it had to do with smuggling.

Certainly, some of the décor in her current accommodations could have been crafted in Naca'an, or even Sophiana, for that matter. She wished she could ask Warin directly, but she was still trying to keep a respectable distance between them. For his part, he hadn't sought her out, either, making himself scarce. She wondered if his absences had to do with the devastating reports coming in about the pijala trees.

Five of the eight orchards they'd visited had been plagued with either destruction or theft. The two trees that had been thriving in Meramont had disappeared, roots and all. At least, the seedlings on Acerto Island were safe. Even more damning, the only places affected were those orchards that they had visited. In Ganley, the orchard master had led them through an extensive hedge maze—even he had become lost—before coming upon the pijala trees. Perhaps he had the right of it, for Ganley's young trees were still safe.

That which bothered Anwyl most was that, for the first time since coming to Aurelia, she had not felt welcomed. She noticed the growing rancor after the attack in Salto, an animosity that followed them into and through Banta. Granted, no one there had been openly rude to her, but nor were they as friendly as they had been in the other smallholds and territories she had visited. Warin fared much worse—the Bantans were overtly hostile.

Perhaps that was what was bothering him. They had planned on resting two nights in the southwest corner of the smallholds. Though the innkeeper was—Warin assured their party—as hospitable as usual, there were other guests in the common room whose dark stares bordered on threatening. Madyan suggested they retire to their rooms to dine in private. Warin had ventured back out with the intent of conversing with the innkeeper. He returned an hour later, looking both angry and perplexed. Of the conversation, he only related that he needed some time to ponder the situation and would seek his father's counsel when they reached Pheldhain.

What Warin didn't know was that Madyan, too, had slipped out to reconnoiter. She could pass unseen under the noonday sun, if she was so inclined, and after her rounds, came back with some of the story she'd overheard.

The pijala trees they had just visited in Salto had been destroyed hours after they'd departed. Someone had taken a blade and cut a neat circle, girding the slender trunks of the two trees. Thus amputated, water would be unable to wick its way to the branches and leaves; the trees perished. She was heartbroken that someone would intentionally destroy that which she had pledged to protect. Now, a rumor was being maliciously spread throughout the smallholds that Warin was culpable. It was outrageous.

To compound the situation, there were more reports that several ships and a few southern coastal villages had been attacked and pillaged, and that the only territory unaffected was Pheldhain. Anwyl looked around at the luxurious appointments in her chamber. No, she refused to entertain the notion.

For all their differences, Anwyl believed Warin to be steadfastly loyal to King Godwin. The way he had spoken of his parents likewise credited his entire family. And Warin took his charge—her very well-being—as seriously as she dedicated herself to the welfare of the pijala trees. The destruction of so many of them was the same as an assault on her very person.

"Oh!" It suddenly occurred to her that Warin would see these attacks as failing in his duty. No wonder he had insisted on leaving Banta at first light the next morning, most likely determining that, in Pheldhain, he would be better capable of protecting her. His parents must have thought the same, for they sent a sortie to meet and escort them over the border.

"Is everything all right, Princess?" Lucilla asked, putting away Anwyl's hairbrush, pins, and other accoutrements.

"I was just thinking about Banta. Nothing to worry over, I'm sure." Lucilla cast her eyes away. If Anwyl didn't know the young woman any better, she would almost say she'd done so guiltily. Come to think of it, ever since she had consumed the tainted wine meant for Anwyl, the girl had been a storm of nerves. "Are you still feeling poorly, Lucilla?" She nodded but would not meet Anwyl's eyes. "You're safe here; Warin won't allow any harm to come to you. *I* won't allow it." Her reassurance seemed to have the opposite effect on the young woman.

"Oh, Princess, I have to tell you—"

Someone tapped on the door, then Madyan slipped in, followed by two others. "Murel!" Anwyl greeted, sweeping forward to hug her friend. "And Caroline!"

"Princess!" they returned with equal exuberance. It was only after they all hugged and kissed and asked after one another and the goings on at court did Anwyl remember to introduce the young Lady Lucilla, explaining how she came to be her lady-in-waiting.

"Lucilla, you were about to say something," Anwyl remembered. "Can it wait until later?" Her somber nod had Anwyl rethinking the delay, but then

Lady Caroline pulled the girl away, regaling her with a story about when she was young and had met some of Lucilla's relatives.

"She seems very sad," Murel noted as they walked down the corridor.

They were steps behind Lucilla and Caroline when a servant arrived, carrying a courier's pouch from Kings Glen.

"I'll take it to your chamber, Princess," Lucilla insisted, accepting the satchel from the man.

"All right, but just set it on my desk and then catch up with us."

"My aunt would like you to meet the family in my uncle's study first," Murel stated. "Take your time, Lucilla. I'll send one of my cousins to escort you to the great hall."

Anwyl steeled herself to face Warin and, with Madyan by her side, joined Murel and Caroline as they wended their way through the sprawling castle.

• • •

My ship? Warin demanded again, not believing his ears. His face was grim. "You're sure?"

"With my own eyes did I see it, flying over the waves toward the Southron Isles," his cousin Tanfiel said, putting his hand on Warin's shoulder. "I don't think Grieg would betray our family, not in a million years. But why hasn't he returned, at least to refit?"

"He must be onto something. If Marten's trail was truly cold, Grieg would be here. I trust the man," Warin swore, putting any argument to rest. His father nodded, knowing how close Warin had grown to the old salt. Grieg was family—hell, the man was more like an uncle than some of Warin's own relatives. "Grieg and my ship have naught to do with the raids, or the destruction and theft of the pijala trees, for that matter. Some plot is afoot here; some other house is trying to weaken our relationship with the royal family."

"But who?" Lady Téana asked. "We've no enemies at court."

Warin grimaced.

"Oh, goodness. Who have you insulted?"

"Not just me," Warin protested. "He's been a canker sore on the ar—"—Lord Marin gave him a stern look—"on the posterior of almost every Royal Guard. I speak of none other than Lord Herlewin of Dinhyll."

His father snorted. "That milksop? He has no power. It's Lady Eunice who controls the smallhold—wait, you didn't happen to offend Lady Eunice, did you?"

"*Any* insult or injury to her son would be considered an insult on her own person," Lady Téana pointed out.

"I was protecting Princess Anwyl's honor," Warin defended. "They thought to trap her into marriage, and—"

"The way I remember it," Princess Anwyl interjected, sweeping into the room ahead of his cousin Murel, Lady Caroline, and Madyan, "I had already managed the brute before you arrived. Or was it not I who struck him the blows to his head?" Her voice was light, almost teasing, and she stepped forward to greet Warin's family.

Warin's mother rose from her seat, took the princess's hands, then kissed her cheeks in the Pheldhainian fashion. "I thought it would be nice to get acquainted with the princess before the banquet begins," his mother explained.

Released from his mother, Princess Anwyl stepped forward and exchanged greetings with Tanfiel, Lord Marin, and finally Warin. "In all truth, your son *did* save me from an awful predicament. But I'm afraid we both made an enemy of Lady Eunice that day."

Was this another peace offering, Warin wondered? Though the princess smiled, her eyes were unreadable.

"She's a horrible woman," Lord Marin put forth. "Always has been."

"Then there is a strong possibility that Lady Eunice and her son are responsible for the sabotage of the pijala trees," Warin pronounced. "It would be a superlative way to strike at the princess, implicating our house along the way."

"At least in regard to the pijala trees," Lord Marin agreed. "But they have no ships with which to harry Aurelia's coasts."

"Someone could be helping them," Princess Anwyl put in.

"It's possible," Warin acknowledged, launching into a new discussion with his father about possible candidates.

"Gentlemen, ladies, Princess, we should head to the great hall," Lady Téana reminded. All the men but Warin followed the women into the hallway. Lady Caroline was telling his mother about Lady Lucilla, and he heard her remind herself to ask after Lucilla's brother. Princess Anwyl lingered behind, perusing the titles in his family's extensive collection of books.

"You're welcome to read anything here, but I'm afraid you'll find that most of the offerings will bore you. They are mainly histories."

"But why should that bore me? Someone wise once pointed out to me that it is to the past that we should look for inspiration—I myself believe that the past can assist one in avoiding mistakes in the present."

Behind her, Warin threw up his chin. He had written nearly those same words months ago to *F.H.*

"Perhaps I'll return here tomorrow, for if I am truly welcome..." She turned around when he did not answer immediately. "Oh, you were just being polite. I understand. Libraries are very personal. I—"

"You are very welcome here. I would not have offered if I didn't mean it, Princess Anwyl." He leaned against the doorjamb.

"If you're sure," she said, staring wistfully at the packed shelves and nooks.

"I promise that I am," he said, crossing his fingers over his heart. "Now, why don't you tell me why you are loitering here with me instead of heading to the great hall?"

"Princesses do not loiter. Perhaps it is you who is straggling behind."

He cocked an eyebrow at her and waited.

"Oh, all right. The theft and destruction of the pijala trees cannot go unchallenged, nor can it continue unchecked! An attack on the pijala trees is an attack on me, and an attack on me—"

"Is an attack on Nifolhad."

"Just so!" she enthused. "We must flush out the culprits. Show the realm their deceit."

How had he ever thought to mistrust her? Her loyalty to her family, to her friends, to him...he could never believe that she would be involved in the loss of his cousin. But there was still the question of what had made him lose his memory of that day in Sophiana.

"So," she continued, drawing out the word, "I've been thinking about what's been happening to the trees, and I have a theory. And a plan."

"And?"

"If I tell you, you must promise to let me help." She ran her fingers over the spines of the books on the shelf before her, as if anxious about his response.

"You want to set a trap."

"Yes!" She spun to face him. "I didn't know if I could ask you, you see, because of our differences. But then, I came to see the folly in that line of thought. You, Warin, are the only person that I *can* ask."

"Then you don't think I'm responsible?"

"Warin!"—her finger jabbed him in the chest—"How could you think that? The very idea is ridiculous. You persist in believing me to be some silly little princess who has no sense of the world."

Something *had* happened to his memories in Sophiana, he was sure of it. But if the princess had been a part of it, he no longer cared. She would have had a good reason. He stared at her, seeing her in this new light, and it was as if a grindstone had been lifted from his shoulders.

"I do not think that you are a silly princess. I only said what I said that day in the stable because I thought you were beginning to have feelings for me. But"—he held up a hand to stop her when she looked ready to interrupt— "please, let me finish. I can admit now that it was me. I was attracted to you. I have...had...I had a certain reputation at court, and I was worried that you would be hurt. I was wrong to say those things, and I'm trying very hard to earn back your trust."

Taking a step closer to him, she set her hand on his chest, covering the spot that she had poked. "I trust you already, Warin. I trust you to keep me safe. I trust that you will do your duty." She removed her hand and retreated—the spot where her fingers had lingered still warmed his skin. "I just won't trust you with my heart. We should go to the banquet," she said, effectively changing the subject. "But first, we will work together on my plan, yes?"

"Was there any doubt?"

She studied him for a moment. "No. Let's work out the details tomorrow."

He held out his arm to her, and she took it. At least she was talking to him again, and that was a good start. "Am I permitted to pay you a compliment, Princess?" The corner of her lip twitched. "I have never seen you look as exquisite as you do this evening."

Her half smile transformed before his eyes into a wide grin. "Thank you."

"Our Pheldhainian style suits you."

She laughed. "Warin, this gown is from Sophiana." They launched into a discussion on the similarities and differences between Pheldhain and Sophiana, and the conversation carried over into dinner and on into the evening. The entire time, Warin parsed out her every statement, trying to gauge the veracity of his suspicion that she was the anonymous woman with whom he'd been corresponding.

Later that night, in the privacy of his rooms, he flipped the latest letter from *F.H.* over in his hands, even holding it up to the light as if willing the paper and ink to divulge its author.

Dear A.S.,
I pray this letter finds you well...

He read the letter for a third time, imbuing each word with her lyrical Nifolhadian cadence, like a song, tapping out a gentle rhythm. He sank into the deep chair set before his hearth, one hand holding her letter, the other raking fingers through his hair. Her other letters were strewn across the table next to him. He stared at the paper, wishing it could speak, knowing the voice would belong to Anwyl.

Was he an even bigger fool than he imagined? He compared the first and last letters. The writing was the same, though the ink of the latter flowed across the page with nary a snag or blot. Anwyl had shown him the writing implement her brother had gifted to her. The one with a smooth gold nib rather than a rough quill. He ran his finger over the line *"...it is the thought of making your acquaintance that keeps me going"* and imagined her whispering the words into his ear. An incredibly bold statement, considering who had written it. He lifted the paper to his nose and breathed in, willing it to give up the spicy citrus scent that lingered about the princess.

All along. She had been there all along. A woman of deep thoughts and dedication to the same subjects he held so dear. A woman who could dig a hole one day, then launch into an adventure the next. Beautiful. Passionate about things that were important to her. Able to parry flirtations one moment, then delve into the most complicated topics the next. He'd been blind. Intentionally blind. He saw now, finally, how deeply he must have wounded her.

He set the letter with the others, then buried his aching head in his hands. She'd claimed she would never trust her heart to him. "More the fool am I." There was a soft rapping at his door, and he bade his visitor enter. The swishing of skirts had him rising more out of instinct than civility.

"Do sit back down, Warin," Lady Caroline ordered, pouring herself some of the wine he had been drinking and gazing at the letters scattered about. "Ah." She sat in the chair across from him, taking a moment to artfully arrange her skirts before pinning him with her gaze. "Queen Juliana was worried that your eyes would remain shut forever, so she asked me to join Murel. But now I see that you may not need my assistance after all."

"Queen Juliana? Of course." Warin thought about how well she had orchestrated the anonymous exchange of correspondence. "Why didn't she just tell me?"

Lady Caroline took a sip of wine and continued to silently regard him.

Warin closed his eyes, imagining the queen's reasons. Knowing how much she cared for the princess. "Even the list," he said, more to himself, admiring his queen with a new level of awareness. "Does Anwyl know?"

"No. She must come to the realization on her own that it is you to whom she writes. For her to do so before she is sure of your regard would be disastrous. I assume that confidences were shared; imagine how foolish she would feel."

Warin thought about what she'd written to him regarding the strange courting rituals she'd heard about...how the higher one's station in the region, the more detailed the training. *F.H.* had never told him how she came by the knowledge she'd described. But now he knew that she must've been writing about Sophiana. Anwyl's station was the highest of any woman there. He swallowed, not sure if he could think about her that way. And the moment he thought it, images of her naked, with tousled hair, and lying spent on scattered silk cushions... Oh, he could definitely think of her that way.

"Never mind. I can see from your face that some of your correspondence has been of an intimate nature."

"Not in the way that you think," he replied. "Caroline, she will never trust me. She has said as much already."

"The very fact that she said so means that she's still thinking about it. Take heart, Warin."

"Can you help me?"

"Most assuredly," she scoffed, as if offended that he would think otherwise. "Let's begin with a new letter."

• • •

Princess Anwyl crept along the dark hallway, her footsteps as silent as any Umbren-trained princess could be. If light spilled from under his door, she would know that he was awake. Surely, Warin would want to talk about their plan now instead of in the morning. It was an excuse to see him, she admitted, and she couldn't believe she was giving him another chance. But his willingness to collaborate had given her hope.

She turned the corner and stepped into the corridor leading to his chamber, only to immediately pull back. Taking care to remain in the shadows, she waited and watched. Warin's door was open, the soft wavering light of his hearth washed across the tiled floor. A shadow swayed across the threshold, and Warin danced out of his chamber and into the hall with a smiling Lady Caroline in his arms. Anwyl did not wait to see more.

• • •

The Palace in Sophiana

"I only discovered the connection by accident," Radha explained, trying to keep up with her cousin, King Ranulf. "Ni'mala had made a list of the Fenrhi who'd borne children by relations to Diarmait. Mirra was listed."

Ranulf stopped before a thick wood door. Outside, four guards waited, along with a woman wearing the same Kena blue as Radha.

"This is Sandrine. She is one of our strongest truthseers." Sandrine bowed, and he gave her a quick nod.

The door was opened for them, and he, Sandrine, and Radha stepped in, followed by two guards. The cell where they were holding Prince Bowen was richly appointed. He sat near the hearth, sipping wine and reading a book. He held up his finger to them and continued reading. Just as Ranulf took a menacing step toward him, Bowen snapped the book closed and rose from his chair.

"Are you here to tell me that my incarceration is finally at an end?"

"Sit back down," Ranulf ordered.

Bowen sneered but did as bade.

Ranulf nodded to the guards, and they advanced on Bowen, tying him to the chair. The prince was strangely relaxed.

Radha walked over to where the bottle of wine sat with several goblets. She poured herself a glass, then held one up to her cousin, who nodded.

"An excellent bouquet on that batch. You must tell your vintner that I'm impressed," Bowen observed.

Ranulf signaled to one of the guards, and he clouted Bowen on the head, knocking him sideways. Sandrine gasped, but Radha caught her arm before she could intercede. Over the next half hour, the guards took turns hitting him. When they finished, Bowen's face was bruised and bloodied. His former insouciance beaten out of him, he stared at Ranulf with unadulterated hatred.

"Still not talking?" Ranulf asked. "I'm pleased to hear it. You might not know this, but I like to invent things. Some of my inventions help people, while others...well, you of all people can imagine, can't you?" He nodded to the guards. They went to either side of Bowen, but just stood there doing nothing.

"You were supposed to bring it!" one of them whispered.

"I thought you had it."

. . .

Despite his rattled head, he laughed, wincing at the pain in his jaw. *King* Ranulf had come here to intimidate him, then botched it.

"Shut him up," King Ranulf demanded, and one of the guards punched him in the gut. He doubled over, bloody spittle dripping onto his breeches. "Go get it. Now!" Through the hair hanging in his face, he watched Ranulf walk over to where the wine had been poured. Radha joined him. They seemed to be disagreeing over what should happen next, but he couldn't make out the words. The Kena woman who had screamed looked familiar, and she quietly made her way to his side.

"Are you all right?" she whispered, pretending to tend to him in case they looked over. "Prince Bowen, can you understand me?"

"Where's Mirra, the other seer?"

"They know she's your cousin. They took her, but not before she found me. I made sure it was me who was brought here to read you." She pulled a wafer from her sleeve and placed it in his hand. "This will give you strength, my prince."

"Sandrine!" Radha shouted.

"Why would you help me?"

"Mirra is, was, my half-sister. They took her, my prince. I think they killed her. The Fenrhi have—"

"Sandrine, what are you doing?" Ranulf demanded, crossing the room.

"Eat it! Quickly!" she whispered.

Ranulf closed the gap, yanked Sandrine away, and threw her against the wall. She fell to the floor, moaning.

"Rani!" Radha yelled, stopping the king from striking the woman.

"I was only seeing to his injuries," Sandrine cried.

And while Radha calmed her cousin and Sandrine cowered on the floor, he slipped the wafer into his mouth and swallowed. The guards returned with a small wooden box, studded with pegs and notched metal wheels. He could well-imagine the pain it would cause. Then, a strange feeling began to fill him. It was invigorating, and he drew himself up in the chair and smiled at their foolishness. They would never break him. Radha and King Ranulf turned to him.

He stared at Sandrine. She held out her hand, and the king drew her up from the floor. "I didn't hurt you, did I?" he asked gently.

"No, my king."

"How does your daughter like her toy?" Ranulf asked one of the guards.

"She loves it, my liege. She still hasn't been able to solve the puzzle, but she gets closer every day. Thank you for remembering her birthday, sire." He picked up the wood contraption from where he'd set it, and he and the other guard departed.

Three chairs were brought in, and the two women and Ranulf sat down before him. "It is a very efficient poison, my king," Sandrine explained. "You may begin your questions any time."

"Will there be pain?" Ranulf asked.

"Only if he lies."

"Excellent. First question—what is your name?"

"It's Bowen," he spat at them, then screamed at the searing pain burning inside his skull.

Sandrine *tsk*'d and shook her head. "We will not move past this question until you answer honestly," she explained. "And refusing to do so will only make it worse. Again, what is your name?"

"Bowen," he seethed, then threw his head back and screamed again when it felt as if he were being scalped.

"Third time's the charm," the king said.

He gnashed his teeth together at the building pressure in his skull while they sat across from him, benign smiles on their faces.

"What. Is. Your. Name?"

"Danold," he ground out, and instantly, the pain subsided. He'd nearly bitten through his tongue trying to resist. He slouched in his chair, breathing hard. It felt so good now that the pain was gone.

"You're admitting that you are not Prince Bowen?"

"Yes," he breathed, and his body was infused with the most pleasurable feelings. He wanted to laugh at how wonderful it felt to tell the truth, almost the same as bedding a woman. But he had to protect Bowen, so he steeled himself against the next question.

Sandrine had risen and returned with a damp cloth. She gently dabbed at his face, wiping away the blood. "I told you the wafer would make you strong, and it did," she said in a sing-song voice. "Just tell the truth and you'll go on feeling like this—strong and happy."

She sat back across from him and nodded to the king. Even before Ranulf uttered a word, the pain in his head started building again. This time behind his eyes. Just before he screamed, he heard the king say, "Next question."

CHAPTER TWENTY-THREE

Trust

Spending her night trying to reconcile what she had witnessed between Warin and Lady Caroline had left Anwyl exhausted. Saddest of all, she wasn't even angry with him; he was simply being true to his nature. She was only relieved that her presence had gone unnoticed.

And what about Lady Caroline? When last she saw her friend, she was well on her way to securing a husband in Cordhin. Had the relationship soured? Or was it simply that she and Warin would always be intimates?

Taking a deep breath, she reexamined her feelings. This time, honestly. She was disappointed. In Warin, a man who had promised to prove to her that she could trust him with her heart; in Lady Caroline, for her capriciousness. And most of all, in herself, for giving Warin another chance. Again.

She gazed out her window at the pre-dawn sky. Perhaps in an hour, she could try to find the kitchens and something to eat. Anwyl leaned back on the banquette and let go a long, drawn out, lung-emptying sigh.

Her current mission would solve everything. Once she decided on a husband, she could move on with her life. She loved Queen Juliana, but, honestly, assigning Warin to be her guide was torture. Unable to rid her heart of her feelings for him had made it impossible to find someone new. She wished she could speak to her brother.

Something stirred her memories, and it had naught to do with Ranulf. *Brother.* It was there, just out of reach. She could almost grasp it.

The rap at her door sent the threads of her memory scattering. "Brother! I mean, bother!" Setting aside her rope, she marched to the door, pulling it open and expecting to see Lucilla. It wasn't.

"Princess," Lady Caroline crooned, taking a covered tray from the hands of the scullery maid behind her and sweeping into Anwyl's chamber. "I wasn't sure if you would be awake, so I only tapped lightly. I rose early, you see, despite keeping a late hour, and I thought that we could break our fast together."

"A late hour?" If she could've, Anwyl would've kicked herself.

"Yes. I was visiting with Warin. As you know, we are old friends. I once thought that we"—she waved her hand in the air as if erasing the thought that had occurred to her—"never mind. I needed his advice about Cordhin. He knows all about Cathmaran betrothal customs, and I want to be sure to outsmart those northern women. He was very helpful; I quite literally danced my way back to my chamber."

Anwyl realized too late that her mouth was hanging open.

"I'm not *that* old. Really, Princess," Caroline chirped happily. "I am young enough to remarry, perhaps even start a family."

"That's not...I wasn't..."

"I'm only teasing you, my dear. Here, have some tea, and I'll make up a plate for you. If you haven't tried Pheldhainian palm pastries, you haven't truly lived. They're made with honey and sprinkled with salt crystals from the Southron Waters." She handed a plate to Anwyl, then made one for herself. After sipping at her tea, Caroline sat up straight. "I nearly forgot! The queen asked me to give this to you. It arrived after the last messenger departed from court."

It was a letter from *A.S.*! He had written to her, after all. She wasted no time breaking the seal. "Oh, Caroline, I'm being rude..."

"Nonsense. I'll meet you in the courtyard later. I believe we are all going to see the pijala trees together." Anwyl smiled and, as soon as her friend departed, tore open the letter.

Dear F.H.,

I must begin this letter with a confession. For some time now, I have realized that I have been corresponding with a woman, just as you, with your keen intellect, have most likely deduced that I am a man. When I made the discovery, I was surprised only in that it did not matter to me. We are two like-minded souls who share an affinity for history. It was natural that, with our mutual respect for one another, our correspondence would turn to topics of a more personal nature.

It's important that I correct your high opinion of me. I am not exempt from the trait that afflicts your traveling companion. I, too, am judgmental. While I have determined you to have a mind worthy enough for me to share my writings, theories, even my thoughts, I rarely hold others in such regard.

It is my belief that all men present false fronts. Outward appearances we show to the world and by which we are measured. Our words and our actions project the impression we wish to make. In truth, we pretend to be what we believe the world wants us to be. It is a necessary façade, one that can only be shed when one finds another whose soul closely matches their own. I wonder, do women not do the same? I suspect that both sexes project their ideals onto others rather than seeing people for who they are. Alas, these issues are better left to philosophers and not historians.

Perhaps in meeting, you would have discovered other traits in my character that you could not abide. It is even possible that we were already introduced and formed no attachment, simply passing by one another. Which brings me to that which I am loath to write—this must be my last letter to you.

It pains me more than I can say, but there are matters of great importance to which I must attend. Issues of family honor, loss of trusted friends, and yes, even love itself. Worse, our correspondence has distracted me from applying myself to securing my future happiness. And here, I must thank you. For it was your insight that showed me how blind I was to the full depth of character of another.

My mother once passed on some wisdom to me. She told me that first impressions are merely scratches. Only after one polishes the surface can they see the beauty of what lies beneath. We fool ourselves every day in believing that finding love does not take hard work. And though I do not believe in love at first sight, I do trust in love forever.

Perhaps this is why my mother loves my father so deeply. She's the first to admit that he was not her hoped-for prince but now gives thanks that she took the time he needed for him to see her as his queen. I hope that when the day comes for me to find my very own princess, she will see past my veneer and celebrate that which I am underneath.

Always your friend,
A.S.

Struck mute, Anwyl slumped un-princess-like against the back of the banquette and stared at the hearth. She choked out a noise that was halfway between a gut-wrenching sob and a hiccup of laughter, and then slapped her hand over her mouth as if to smother any more reactions. In less than a half day, her emotions had run the gamut—hope, anger, jealousy, elation, and now a miasma of feelings she could not name. How could A.S. take away her only lifeline? She rose and strode to her writing desk, compelled to reply to him. What could she say?

Don't leave me.

I need you.

I don't want to be alone.

She sat back down, defeated, then jumped up again. She picked up the letter, crumpled it into a ball, and immediately smoothed it out to reread. She pondered *A.S.'s* professed crime. Had she committed the same?

When Warin did not fit her idealistic views, had she unknowingly transferred her regard to an unknown stranger? No, not a stranger. *A.S.* would never be a stranger to her, not after reading his journal. She looked at the last sentence for a third time. The irony of it all.

A *knock* interrupted her warring thoughts, and she opened her door to find Warin at the threshold, hand poised to knock again.

"Good morning, Princess," he greeted. "I saw Madyan headed this way and told her that I would fetch you. It will give us a chance to go over our plan before heading to the orchard with the others." He espied her escritoire. "Oh. I've interrupted you. I can—"

"I was just putting my things away. Come in." She picked up her various implements, placing them securely in the writing box. "Who is joining us today?"

"Lady Caroline, Murel, Madyan. And my father, of course, as he knows where the pijala trees have been planted."

"And Lucilla?" she asked, recalling how her writing box had been in disarray.

"*Yes*," he said carefully, and she met his gaze.

"You believe her to be involved?" Anwyl frowned. "It fits, doesn't it?"

"I'm afraid so."

"She's been using my paper and old quills, even my sealing wax. But I don't know to what end. I never take off my ring, so she has no way of forging my seal."

"Where do you keep your old signet?"

"Of course," Anwyl realized resignedly, pointing to the pouch in her writing box. The evidence against Lucilla was damning.

"Hardly anyone would know that you have a new seal and so would not question a decree supposedly written by you. I'm sorry." He looked around her room, noticing the tray of pastries. "I see that you've already eaten. Do you mind if I grab one of these?"

"Go ahead. Lady Caroline dropped them off earlier," Anwyl said carefully.

"I'm surprised she woke so early; she kept me up until the late hours," he explained, taking another bite. "I'm sorry to say that she will soon be married."

"But why would you be sorry?" She poured tea for them both. They sat before the hearth, and she picked at her food.

"She will visit the altar before you. I must tell you, Princess, that my feelings for you haven't changed." He held up his hand when she started to protest. "No, it's true. But I understand that you need time to come to trust me, and that time is one commodity that you do not possess. You must marry, and soon."

She waited.

"Don't think that I didn't realize how delaying our departure from Pheldhain has affected your plans. A five-week sojourn before sailing to Sterland will now probably stretch into two months. It means much to my family that you are helping us to protect the honor of our house. It means even more to me."

The intensity of his regard had her looking away. She brushed at some imaginary crumbs, then met his eyes again, determined to change the subject. "I like Lucilla, Warin. I think she is someone's pawn, forced to participate in some scheme. The way she reacted in the alley when we were attacked...she's been witness to violence before, I'm sure of it. Someone is threatening her into working for them. It would make sense, especially if Lady Eunice is involved."

"You may be onto something. Think about all the little obstacles that have been set in our path. They did not begin until she joined us."

"Yes, but they were meant to delay us, not do harm."

"And the poisoned wine?" Warin reminded her, standing up and pacing. "The attack?"

"I'm not entirely convinced that they are related. Something she said that day, about not knowing the attackers."

He spun around to face her. "She said that?" he demanded. "I wish you had told me. Why would Lucilla expect to know who was attacking us? Princess, this looks very bad for the girl."

Anwyl gestured for him to sit. "There's something else, Warin. Something I haven't told even the king and queen."

"You said you trusted me..."

"Yes, trust. An important little word." She took a deep breath. "I was sent here to do more than just tend to the pijala orchards," she started. "I was sent to determine if more of the Kena than just Rhiannon have infiltrated Aurelia."

"Ah," he said. "So, the poison at the inn..."

"If you recall, even though it was Lucilla who drank it, the boy said it was meant for me. I might have been incapacitated and unable to tell you what needed to be done to counteract the poison. In the alley in Salto, I was exposed and could have easily been taken or killed, but those men were after you, Warin."

"Threats from every direction, including Rhiannon's followers."

She nodded. "Yes. From the very beginning. From when we first traveled from Ragallach to Whitmarsh."

"The missing girl...Daisy."

"Yes, Daisy. I hate to think that she was responsible for that family's daughter's death, but it's possible. It is what Aghna and Ranulf feared, which is why the destruction of the pijala trees must be stopped. These rogue Kena may not be responsible for the loss of the saplings, but they are taking advantage of the fact that you have been implicated and public opinion is against you. It would've been simple for a Kena to plant a kernel of hate in the minds of the men who attacked us in the alley."

"They fanned the flames against me," Warin surmised. "But why should the Kena care about me, a Royal Guard in Aurelia?"

"Not the Kena, but the person behind them. Bowen. Rhiannon was his half-sister, one of many. And he has a grudge against the Royal Guards. For the death of his brother. Against you for taking Claire from under his nose. And for bringing me here to the safety of Aurelia."

"You?"

"I was once betrothed to him. After my parents died, Rani broke the pact."

"Your brother sent you here to be protected; you might've died from that poison. No one would have known what to do." They both stared into the dying flames in the hearth. Warin looked bleak.

"Fortunately, no lasting harm was done," Anwyl soothed. "Lucilla has recovered. Besides, I'm sure you and Madyan would have figured out what to do." Anwyl sipped her tea.

"Lucilla might not have had a hand in that incident, but the pijala trees are another matter. She was with us when we visited the orchards and in a position to communicate the locations of the saplings. Remember, she didn't travel with us to Acerto Island, and the seedlings there are safe. Could she be Kena?"

"No. It doesn't fit. She could not have faked that level of fear when she was taken. And remember, she said she didn't know the men who attacked us, reinforcing the supposition that there are two separate threats to you and your family. Also, the trees in Redavel and Prato were destroyed or taken," Anwyl reminded him. "She joined us after we had visited those two smallholds."

Warin rubbed his knuckle and thumb along his jaw in contemplation. "If it is Lady Eunice who is behind this, and I believe it to be, it would have been an easy task to discover the whereabouts of the saplings belonging to her two closest neighbors."

Anwyl gazed out the window of her room. "Lady Eunice is a conniving woman, but I still can't imagine how Lucilla could be coerced into betraying me, or even you, for the likes of House Dinhyll. They must have some hold over her, something that would betray her very nature."

"For once, I wish Marten were here; my brother was always good at solving a mystery." Warin rose from his seat. "We should go. You might want to wear your cape. It's—"

Anwyl grabbed his arm. "That's it! When I first met your parents, Lady Caroline said that she meant to ask after Lucilla's brother."

"But didn't Lucilla say that she was an only child?"

"Not exactly. She only said that she was alone and that her grandmother and parents were dead. Warin, they must be holding her brother. It would explain everything. Why, if someone were threatening Rani, I would do anything to save him. I'm so happy right now."

"Happy?" Warin chuckled.

"Yes. She is protecting someone she loves. Reason enough to forgive her the betrayal. At least for me." She was still holding Warin's arm, she realized, and when she began to pull away, he covered her hand with his.

"I promise that no harm will come to her. After we capture the true perpetrators, I'll see to rescuing her brother. I swear it to you."

"You would do that—rescue her brother—simply to make me happy?"

"No, Princess. I'll do it because it is the right thing to do. Just like promising to help you to root out the Kena once this current mystery is unraveled."

"And in the stable, when you said those things about me to Tomas, you thought you were doing the right thing?"

"At the time, yes." They continued walking and had almost reached the others when he added, "I've been known to be wrong."

Anwyl smiled. Perhaps *A.S.* had given her a gift in his last letter, for this was the first time she was seeing Warin for who he truly was, not the dark-haired romanticized stranger that Ni'Mala had promised.

CHAPTER TWENTY-FOUR

Trappings

"And just what do you think will happen if you tell her?" Lady Caroline demanded; Warin didn't reply. "Just as I suspected, you have no idea. Look, there will come a time when you can tell the princess that you are F.H."

"A.S." he corrected, and she rolled her eyes.

"You said it yourself—she doesn't trust you with her heart. Imagine that she discovers that you are Ass—"

"A.S.," he repeated stubbornly.

She waved his reminder away with a flutter of her hand. "How will that help your cause?"

He had no answer, and she patted his arm. "Just so. Think, my friend. She has asked for your help. In my experience, you either trust someone completely or not at all, despite our princess's need to categorize everything. Telling her now will only make her more entrenched in her own reasoning. Heed me in this, Warin," she finished, then left him alone to ruminate over her recommendation.

He had about an hour before his assignation with Anwyl to sneak out to guard the pijala trees. If they were fortunate, they would discover who was behind the mayhem and clear his family's name, all in one fell swoop.

He'd enjoyed collaborating with Anwyl, formulating their plan and smoothing out the myriad details, even setting their priorities: protect Lucilla and her brother; secure the trees; and obtain irrevocable proof of Warin's family's innocence. He had agreed with her assessment but secretly inserted another priority to the top of the list—protect the princess, even if that meant permitting the culprits to escape.

He strode into his chamber and found it already occupied. "What gave us away, Madyan?"

"You've been too nice to each other. Normally, you are sparring with words, ignoring that the other exists, or staring longingly at one another when you believe the other person isn't looking. You're up to something."

While Warin filled her in, Madyan quietly listened. "As you now know our plan, can you help me to keep her safe?"

"She'll never know I'm there. What time are you heading out?"

"I'm collecting her in a quarter hour." Her face was unreadable. "What is it, Madyan?"

She paced. "I can count my good friends on one hand, Warin, and you are numbered among them."

"But?"

"If you hurt her, you'll find out exactly what it means to be on the wrong side of an Umbren-trained Fyrjian. Promise me you'll be careful."

"Princess Anwyl is better equipped to hurt me than I could ever hurt her."

"I'm relieved to hear that you've finally figured that out," she said, satisfied with his reply. "I'll go now. If I hear or see anything, I'll signal you."

After she left, Warin pulled out the nefarious list from the queen. Anwyl was supposed to choose a husband from these prospects; his name was not among them. Yet Lady Caroline had assured him that the queen encouraged such a union. He stared at the names on the list, then stepped to his hearth with the intention of burning it. There was a soft rap on his door, so he stuffed the paper into his tunic as the princess slipped in.

"I couldn't wait," she said, throwing back her hood.

"I was just coming to get you," he said at the same time. He stared at her. She was beautiful. Excitement glinted in her eyes in a way he'd never before noticed.

She'd slung a bag across her chest and was adjusting it over the dark wool cloak from Ragallach. But even taking the layers into consideration, she appeared bulkier than her slim self. She shrugged when she saw him looking her over. "In case it's a long wait." She stepped closer and peered up at him. "Is there something wrong?"

"Not at all. I am looking forward to catching these cretins."

"Then let's go," she said eagerly.

"Stay close to me; I know how to get us there without notice." He led her through the maze of the castle, through the gardens, and then on to the orchards. She kept apace and was nearly as silent as he.

The tiny glen where the pijala trees held center stage was surrounded by a high boxwood-wall. "Where shall we hide?" she whispered.

Warin pointed to one dark corner. "There's a hidden recess. It should be large enough for us both." He ushered her to the hiding place, and she pulled a small rug from under her cloak and handed it to him. He spread it out as she wriggled the strap off her shoulder and down her torso until she could step free of it. "What else did you bring?"

"A blanket," she answered, sitting on the rug. "Some bread and cheese and warm mulled wine in case it turns cold."

"I'll be right back," he told her, and stepped to the center of the garden square, peering into the shadowed alcove. The princess's dark clothing hid her completely, and satisfied, he slipped back in and sat beside her.

The breeze coming in off the sea was steady, and the leaves still clinging to the branches rustled. He loved the smell—a combination of salt air and dry, crisp foliage.

"What are you thinking about?" the princess whispered, low enough that the susurration of leaves would be enough to mask her words.

"If you listen closely, you can just hear the waves breaking on the beach. This time of night, under the moon and stars, it's beautiful down there." She remained quiet, so he continued. "The night air smells of home."

Her reply was a nearly silent sigh expelled in a tiny puff of air.

Warin felt the same. "I've been away so long that my home seems to be everywhere but in Pheldhain."

"Once in a while," she whispered longingly, "I'll smell something that reminds me of Sophiana. Or hear a noise, like the tinkling bells the goats wore in Meramont."

"You must miss your home."

"Sometimes. But like you, it doesn't feel like my home anymore."

"I believe home is in a person's heart, never a place." Warin waited for her to respond, but she only nodded in the dark.

"In Sophiana, I could hear the waves breaking on the beach from my chambers. It was my lullaby when I was a child; later, a song that lured me away from the summer palace. I would sneak out at night, sometimes to swim, sometimes just to watch the tide."

Warin sensed rather than saw her smile. "I'll bet your brother had something to say about you sneaking out at night."

"How did you know?"

"If I were an older brother..." He stopped, not wanting to compare himself to Ranulf. "He would have wanted to protect someone as beautiful as you."

For a while, they remained silent as the night hours marched by in the garden and the sea played its siren song in the distance. "Rani knew he could not keep me locked away," she eventually whispered. "He assigned me an escort wherever I went, even during the day. When the urge came to chase the tides, I went and was followed. It wasn't the same, knowing that I wasn't alone on the edge of the Virin Sea. I went less and less."

"Was it difficult?" he wondered aloud, not really meaning to ask.

Beside him, she sighed and laid her head against his shoulder. "It was necessary."

Warin tried imagining being followed everywhere he went, even within his own home. "I miss it, though," she continued. "And Rani understood, which is why he encouraged me to learn everything I could about sailing. You see, swinging on a line or standing at the bow under full sail...it's the only time I feel free." She turned to him, her eyes wide, the green replaced by the glassy black of her pupils. "I was very much looking forward to sailing on your ship again. And I hope that Grieg is safe. He understood me a little, I think, allowing me to help when we sailed from Nifolhad to Aurelia."

"I'm sorry that I didn't." In the dark of the alcove, he could barely make out the glisten of a tear as it rolled down her cheek. She probably thought he couldn't see it, or he was sure she would have wiped it away or turned her face from him. "I think I do now. Understand."

She quietly moved away from him, and then stood to stretch her limbs. "It's nearly dawn. I don't think tonight will be the night."

Warin got to his feet. "They may not come at all. What better way to implicate House Pheldhain, leaving our trees unmolested?"

"But we'll try again, won't we? We have to protect your family's honor."

He wanted to pull her tight against him and hold her in the circle of his arms for her loyalty, but he forced himself to only nod. Then she did the most unexpected thing—she stood on her toes and kissed his cheek. He took her by both arms, needing more than anything to press his lips to hers, but not daring to. Under the unfurling dawn, her expression betrayed nothing of what she was thinking, and that alone made him let her go. She turned, reaching for the untouched bag of food while he picked up the rug and folded it.

"Try to get some sleep," she advised, and then she was a shadow, slipping away along with the last vestiges of the night.

. . .

Anwyl waited until Lucilla retired to her room before changing into her Umbren garb. When she had returned in the morning, she'd been able to snatch a few hours of rest. Her hopes for an uneventful day had been thwarted. Warin's family had received a letter from the king—a group of Royal Council members would be visiting Pheldhain to determine who was responsible for the coastal raids as well as the destruction of Anwyl's trees. That they chose to begin in Pheldhain spoke volumes.

For nearly two weeks, she and Warin had surveilled the pijala trees; no attempts were made to disturb them. She was beginning to think that Warin was right—whosoever was behind the theft and destruction of the young trees had done so expressly to implicate his family. Leaving Pheldhain's trees untouched and unthreatened would only direct more suspicion their way. And they were running out of time; the Royal Council would arrive on the morrow. Would suspicion be enough for the council to decide against House Pheldhain, or would they need tangible proof? She was betting on the council needing more, and if her supposition was true, whoever was acting against Warin's family would have to strike before their arrival. That meant tonight. *Of course!* Waiting until the last minute would not give House Pheldhain time to remedy the attempt to implicate them in what amounted to treason.

Anwyl would have been more worried, save for the letter from Queen Juliana expressing her trust in Warin and his family, and then asking that Anwyl project Nifolhadian support for the Pheldhainian nobles. She didn't need to be asked; she would support them, no matter what. Drawing the hood of her cloak over her head, she peered down the dimly lit hall. Anwyl had walked the route enough times with Warin to know the way, and they had agreed that she should meet him just outside the castle. She wondered if Warin knew that Madyan was aware of their late-night watch. Anwyl had no doubt that her Fenrhi friend would be hidden somewhere near the orchards, readily available to lend a hand if needed.

As she slipped down a set of back stairs, Anwyl felt a prickle of anticipation building in her breast. She felt sure something would happen this night and soon found Warin waiting in the shadows. His expression had grown more and more worried, and he and Anwyl had conversed less and less in the late hours.

They settled in to wait for possible saboteurs, neither speaking. Hour after hour passed by, and Anwyl yawned.

"Go ahead and try to sleep," Warin offered, putting his arm around her and drawing her closer so that she could rest her head against his shoulder. There had not been any contact between them since she had kissed his cheek that first night. Even now, she didn't question her motives for the small act, for she just knew that he had needed a friend. She closed her eyes.

Eventually, Warin's breathing grew steady and deeper. Had he fallen asleep? For her own part, though she had stilled, she remained alert. When his fingertips brushed her wrist as it lay across her lap, she controlled her breathing, lest he know she was awake. Back and forth, gently, barely touching, he stroked a small area of her skin, and she felt the slightest lift of his chest as he pulled his hand away and sighed. And she realized then that she could trust him with her heart, but it would be her choice *if* she would give it to him, and when. He would wait.

As he drew his hand away, she reached for it and entwined her fingers with his. He grew very still, almost rigid, and she lifted her head. Even in the dark, heat sparked from his brilliant blue eyes. Her gaze flicked to his lips, and she watched them firm into a tense line. She tracked the contours of his stubble-covered cheek, and he clenched his jaw at her examination. His hand, still held by hers, twitched a little tighter, and she understood that these tiny fissures in his practiced composure had been caused by her. Her lips softened in a gentle smile, knowing he was watching her as closely as she regarded him, and she was rewarded when his breath sieved through clenched teeth.

He'd given her control, over everything, and she saw how it cost him. "All right," she whispered, flicking her eyes up. He remained close but unmoving—perhaps he hadn't understood. But then his head slanted lower, and his lips, a moment ago so tight, seared a path across her own. This was not a heated kiss like the one in the stairwell. This was incendiary, igniting her very blood. Try as she might to hold on to a string of sanity in order to assess her reaction, she couldn't. She lost herself. Willingly. Finally.

Their lips parted, and their tongues danced. She'd let go of his hand to wrap her arms around his broad shoulders, holding him to her as he held her to him. His hands splayed across her back as he lowered her to the rug. And then he was above her, his legs cradled between hers. She felt him there, pressing hard and heated against the juncture of her thighs, and her hands grew wild. This was what she had always dreamed could be between them. Better than their masquerade embrace; better even than her own imagination, which had painted this moment over and over in her mind since she had first met him in Sophiana.

A nip to her lower lip brought her back to bear, and she gasped with pleasure. Teeth. She'd read about that once, about how lovers could nip and tease, but she'd forgotten. She gave herself up to his searching lips, arching her neck to give him access to those sensitive spots she knew existed, but that had yet to be awakened. And when he licked and sucked his way down her jaw and behind her ear, she purred into the night. Slowly, he nipped his way back to her kiss-swollen lips, then lifted his head to peer down at her. His eyes were wild, and Anwyl exalted in feeling his heaving chest against her bosom. He seemed to be searching her face for some clue, and she touched his cheek, her expression an open book, giving him the answers he so desperately sought. He opened his mouth to say something, but remained silent, for in the night, a clicking noise sounded, softer than the tapping of a beetle. A signal.

"Madyan," she whispered, and he pushed himself up.

"She's been here—"

"Every night," she finished as he rose from the ground and held out his hand for her to do the same.

"You knew?" he whispered.

"Yes, but please don't tell her. It would only make her mad that she's not completely undetectable."

He tensed and then placed himself between her and the opening of their alcove. She was closer to where his unsheathed sword leaned against the boxwood, and she handed it to him before grasping her quarterstaff. In the shadows, his blue eyes blazed out at her, and he drew in a slow, controlled breath through his nostrils. She did the same and, at first, noticed nothing. Then, on the soft breeze that gusted past their dark alcove, came the scent of freshly turned soil. Soon after came the crush of muffled cart wheels as they rolled over the verge. Two men, one pulling a handcart while the second pushed from behind, entered the clearing. When they stopped and removed their shovels from the cart, Warin tensed to move.

Anwyl stayed him with her hand, and he gazed down at her. She cast her eyes near the entrance to the enclosure, and Warin understood. As the men began their work, another, larger man, one with a sword at his hip, entered. Warin and Anwyl waited until he came closer, heedless of the fact that he had put the cart between himself and his only path to escape. And so, Warin moved to spring the trap they had so meticulously planned, capturing the man. His servants, too, were waylaid—one by Anwyl and the other by Madyan when he tried to flee.

Now, the only thing remaining was to secure them, wait until the morrow, and take down the instigator.

Everything in Its Proper Place

My pardon, Princess Anwyl," Lord Herlewin conspired as if he had Pheldhain's best interests at heart. "But I believe the council's representatives are simply eager to put behind them these ridiculous suspicions that House Pheldhain is colluding with certain groups in Nifolhad." He took a step closer, crowding her, and smiling down his greasy nose. He was using that ingratiating tone that only practiced sycophants could. She resisted the urge to draw back from his foul breath, noting that Madyan was stalking the man. Herlewin hadn't noticed that she'd come up behind him.

"What is this about Pheldhain and Nifolhad?" Madyan murmured into his ear.

He startled sideways and into the wall, and Anwyl gave him a satisfied grin. The disgusting man had thought to intimidate her. Even though he was a head taller and twice as broad, Madyan's presence had him shrinking.

"I see you for what you are," Anwyl accused, her voice low and even. "A bully and a coward. And I am not interested in any of your false platitudes."

His eyes darted to where the others had begun to move off, and, finding no quarter, he blustered through his response. "I am only repeating what I've heard, mind you, but it's not escaped the notice of the council that the attacks on the pijala trees and on the coastal villages and cargo ships coincide with this newfound *union* between Pheldhain and Nifolhad."

"Union?" Anwyl prompted.

"Between you and Lord Marin's son. I have tried to—"

"Allay these rumors?" she finished. Her friend touched her arm. "I'm almost done, Madyan." She pinned Herlewin with her glare. "Any union between Warin and me is not open to speculation. You would be wise to remember that, Lordling, else suffer the consequences."

"Are you threatening me, Princess?"

"Of course I am."

"I've been nothing but a contrary voice against those who see your relationship with House Pheldhain as circumspect. It would be best to remember that."

"The princess remembers everything," Madyan warned. "So does Nifolhad." Herlewin broke away, nearly stumbling in his haste. "Was that wise, Princess? Antagonizing him like that?"

"Perhaps; perhaps not. But it was fun, wasn't it?" Anwyl took her friend's arm and led her toward the others.

The council members sent to investigate the allegations made against House Pheldhain included Herlewin; King Godwin's younger son, Prince Reynald; Lady Serna from the Island of Taon; Lord Hanar from Crevalo; and Lord Wymark from Sterland. Anwyl inwardly grimaced—Wymark was on her list of possible husbands.

Ahead, Warin's mother was trying to convince the entire group that a half hour of refreshment after their long journey would not be amiss; she looked bewildered that the council representatives were so insistent on immediately viewing the pijala trees.

Anwyl felt a stirring in her core and knew, without turning, that Warin had come to stand behind her. His knuckles coursed unseen from her hip to her shoulder and back again. "Are you ready?" he murmured to her, and if not for the assembled group, she would not have been sure he wasn't talking about something far more intimate. Finally, the timing of their affection for one another was in harmony, and the experience was both unnerving and seductive. "Watch Herlewin, the way his words assuage on the surface yet are riddled with innuendo. Like his mother, he's a master manipulator."

"He could be of the Kena. He's that adept," Madyan agreed, reminding Anwyl and Warin that they were not so nearly unnoticed as they believed. Warin's hand, gently settled on Anwyl's hip, withdrew, but she reached back and took his fingers in hers for the briefest of clasps.

"Come on. It's time to finish this." He stepped forward, drawing Anwyl with him; the council members averted their eyes. They were uncomfortable, and she realized that they didn't want to believe Pheldhain was complicit in the destruction of the pijala trees and coastal raids.

Prince Reynald offered his arm to Anwyl, and they trailed behind as the group walked to the glen where the saplings were growing. "I'm sorry for this," he said. "But Father said my presence was necessary to quash these veiled aspersions on Pheldhain's honor."

"I'm sure King Godwin has the right of it."

"So, you're going to keep me in the dark?" he accused with a chuckle, and Anwyl rewarded him with a smile.

"How is your wife?" she asked innocently. "This will be your second child, yes?"

"Yes, and she's doing quite well. I'll have a new son or daughter before winter's end." They carried on with their niceties just before Warin drew the group to a halt at the entrance of the clearing. "Anwyl," Reynald whispered, "you must promise to let me know if I can help in any way."

"Only if you give my thanks to your father for sending you. It means the world to Warin."

"My older brother and I almost came to blows fighting over which one of us would get to travel here: a few weeks in balmy Pheldhain instead of braving the early winter winds sweeping down from the Kaldemer. Besides, I owe Warin. He taught me everything I know about, er, never mind."

At that, Anwyl laughed gaily, drawing the attention of all. She smiled at each member of the council in turn, even though most were only able to meet her eye for the briefest of moments, as if they were embarrassed by the unfolding events. But there was no mistaking the expression on Herlewin's face when he noted that Prince Reynald was escorting her. She let the lordling wrest control of the party once more, and he hastened through the hedged entrance to the glade. He drew to an abrupt halt. The others behind him, eager to put the matter to rest, continued, herding Herlewin forward.

Two perfectly tended pijala saplings, planted five paces apart, awaited. Herlewin sputtered, then tried to regain his composure.

"It seems that Herlewin was expecting more," Reynald whispered.

Anwyl winked at him. "You asked if you could help…"

"Anything."

"When Madyan offers to show you an interesting section of the garden, please go with her and take the council with you."

He nodded, then stepped away.

"At least Pheldhain's trees remain safe," Prince Reynald announced. "Lady Téana, you mentioned something about refreshments after our long journey." He took her arm, making sure to position them near Madyan as they exited the clearing. The rest of the council filed out behind them, walking at a leisurely pace.

Only Herlewin remained, alone with Anwyl and Warin. "This isn't over," he seethed, striding back and forth next to the pijala trees. When Lucilla slipped in, throwing a fretful glance in Lord Herlewin's direction, he glared at the girl.

"A letter," Lucilla stated meekly, then bobbed a curtsy and made a hasty retreat. Herlewin moved to stop her, but Warin stepped in his path.

"You harm one hair on that girl's head and, this time, it won't be a garden stake hitting you on the head."

Herlewin shoved past him. "It's not the girl who'll need protection."

Anwyl turned to Warin. "We should join Madyan and the others." Remembering that she had forgotten her pack in the alcove in the excitement from the previous night, she skipped over to retrieve it. Something on the ground caught her eye: a tightly folded piece of paper. She slipped it into the pocket of her cape, then rejoined Warin. He wound his arm around her waist, drawing her up against his lean frame, then bent his head to kiss her.

"For luck," he said.

"You think we'll need it?"

He shook his head. "Not really, just an excuse to kiss you."

"Warin, you need no excuse," she managed, her breath having been stolen. He crushed his lips to hers again and then ended the embrace too soon for her liking.

"Come on," he urged, "or we'll miss the excitement." Taking her pack from her, he led her through the maze-like gardens. They entered a walled parterre, and all eyes expectantly turned to them. Warin placed his fingers to his lips, nodding to Prince Reynald. He walked to Lord Hanar, who stood beside a cart with six pijala saplings, root balls wrapped in burlap. On the ground next to the cart sat three bound-and-gagged men. Next to them stood a rail-thin boy, one who kicked at the men when he thought the others were not looking. A panicked voice rose above one of the ivy-covered garden walls, and the council members silently drew closer to the barrier.

"Please, Lord Herlewin, it wasn't my fault. I gave them directions, just as you ordered. It must've been Lord Harsk who betrayed you."

"Harsk! My cousin would never betray me. Now what do you know? Tell me, girl, or it will be more than a broken arm for your brother."

"I don't know anything!" Lucilla, already having been gently interrogated by Anwyl and Warin, was now playing her part perfectly. "Please, don't hurt Winn anymore. I've done everything that you've demanded. Haven't I provided you with a copy of Princess Anwyl's seal so that you could forge your letters?"

"How did you know I forged letters?"

"I guessed, m'lord. And didn't I give you instructions on finding where the pijala trees were hidden?"

"Yes, but you failed your most important task. The stolen trees were supposed to be here!" Herlewin's voice rose an octave. "These gardens go on forever. You're positive you gave Harsk the right location? Tell me!"

"Yes! I did everything you commanded!"

"Then where are the trees?"

"I want my brother!"

"Shut up, you stupid chit! It was all perfectly planned, and you've ruined everything! When did you last see him?"

"Before I left Nocanyella."

"Not your brother! Harsk!" Herlewin bellowed.

"Three nights ago, m'lord. What about Winn? I did everything you ordered, Lord Herlewin. You promised to let us go."

Anwyl regarded the council members; to a one, they were appalled.

"You'll be done when House Pheldhain is declared treasonous and that princess bitch from Nifolhad is sent back to her country in chains!"—*Slap!*—"You little bitch! How dare you strike me?"

"Don't you talk about Princess Anwyl like that," Lucilla yelled. "She's kind and beautiful and—*Ow!*"

Warin reacted faster than Anwyl thought possible, swiping at some hanging ivy to reveal a hidden gate. He burst through, with Anwyl and the rest of the council on his heels, to discover Lord Herlewin fending off a kicking and scratching Lucilla. The boy ran around the group and joined his sister in pummeling Herlewin. Herlewin shoved the boy to the ground, then viciously turned on Lucilla. But two strides later, and Warin was on him, drawing back and delivering such a blow with his fist that Herlewin flew backward through the air.

"Are you hurt, Lucilla?" he asked.

"No. But Winn?"

Winn jumped to his feet, ready to defend his sister again. "Lou!" he cried, running to her arms.

Lord Marin appeared with several of his soldiers and ordered Lord Herlewin, Lord Harsk, and the other conspirators to be secured until the king's men could retrieve them. Lady Eunice's complicity would be determined later.

Lady Téana clapped her hands to bring some much-needed calm to the shocked council members. "Come, even in Pheldhain, the days grow cool as the shadows lengthen. Let us all to the banquet hall for food and drink."

Prince Reynald walked beside Princess Anwyl and Warin. "This is a story that will inspire songs: the foreign princess helping the dashing guard to save the honor of his family's name and discover the truth behind the destruction and theft of the mysterious pijala trees. But how did you know what they were up to?"

"It was the princess who divined their plan," Warin admitted. "What better way to implicate my family than by transplanting into our orchard the very trees which were stolen, then facilitate the council's arrival to bear witness to our alleged theft? We knew they were behind the plot, and thanks to Lucilla, were made aware of Harsk's presence in the area—the young lady was much forthcoming, once assured that her brother would be safe. She'll give a statement to the council about Lord Herlewin and his cousin, Lord Harsk."

"But how is it that her brother is already here?" Anwyl asked.

Warin grinned.

"You liberated him!"

He nodded. "I sent Tanfiel to retrieve him from Nocanyella the day we discovered she was not an only child."

"Was it this Lucilla who caused the delays during your journey?" Prince Reynald asked.

"Yes, but she was coerced," Anwyl defended, placing a hand on the prince's arm. "She and her brother have suffered enough; I would not see her punished."

"Nor would my parents, I believe. It was an oversight on my grandfather's part that brought her family under the control of Dinhyll. And after this day, I'm sure the council will correct the error, placing Nocanyella Keep where it belongs, with Crevalo. We'll make sure Lucilla and Winn inherit what is rightfully theirs."

"Thank you, Reynald. She has a good heart, and they both deserve better."

"We miss you at court, by the way. Especially Mother."

"I had thought to journey to Sterland and then Nifolhad after this, but now that..." Anwyl trailed off. She wasn't sure how much Prince Reynald knew of her ulterior quest. Wymark was here, and she could, in good faith, say that she had done her duty in considering him.

"Warin," the prince said, coming to a halt. "Could you give us a moment?" Warin looked as if that was the last thing he wanted to do, but he nodded and caught up with the others. "How goes your search for a husband, Anwyl?"

His question was so direct that Anwyl laughed. "Forgive me," she begged. "I was reminded of Lady Claire's observation that Nifolhadijans tend to dance around the point while Aurelians get right to it."

"I was informed that there was a list, and that your schedule would be expedited if Lord Wymark were to arrive in Pheldhain. You'll pardon me for saying so, but I don't think he would suit. Now, Ronan of Meramont perhaps."

"Perhaps." They continued to walk toward the castle. She sighed. "I'm afraid matters are more complicated than I had thought."

"Anwyl, my mother wanted me to remind you that the list is only a piece of paper with a few eligible names penned across it. The final decision rests completely in your hands." They entered the hall, and all eyes turned their way, but Anwyl's gaze instantly fell upon Warin. "And in your heart, I think."

She turned from the blue eyes that had captured her attention from across the room and focused on Reynald. "But will it—"

The prince's lips lifted at the corners when he saw Warin striding toward them. "'Tis rare that one of our station can choose a partner for love, Anwyl. Do not waste this gift." He nodded to Warin and handed Anwyl into his care.

CHAPTER TWENTY-SIX

Loose Ends

Warin stared at the ceiling of his chamber, unable to fall asleep. A week had passed since the council had decamped. Anwyl had deemed it wiser to winter the stolen trees in Pheldhain, then return them to their rightful orchards once the weather warmed. She and Pheldhain's orchard master had crowded the saplings together, covering them with mulch and heeling them in for the winter. It was the best they could do to give the temperamental saplings a fighting chance. Prince Reynald had written royal missives to the affected smallholds, outlining the plan.

Lord Brontson of Crevalo had also come and gone, escorting young Lord Winn back to Nocanyella Keep. He would assess the keep's needs and that of Winn's people, banishing those loyal to Dinhyll back whence they came. Brontson would eventually assign a guardian to assist the young lord with running the keep. Prince Reynald journeyed with them, lending royal gravitas to the newly drawn borders. Nocanyella had been finally incorporated into Crevalo. Madyan and the princess had decided that Madyan should accompany Prince Reynald, offering him an extra layer of protection—there still were Kena women roaming the land. Lady Caroline had gone along, but not before telling Warin that when the time came to reveal to Anwyl that he was *A.S.*, he would know.

Lord Wymark had returned home. During his time in Pheldhain, Warin had given the princess space to meet with him, though it nearly killed him to do so. He should've burned the cursed *list* to ashes months ago. The trouble was, he couldn't find it.

The hour was late, or early, depending on how one looked at it, and Warin flung the blankets from his bed. He swung his legs over the side, slipped into his breeches, and shrugged into his shirt. Activity was what he needed. To that end, he left his chamber, climbing the stairs that would take him to the roof of the tower. The fresh air would help him clear his mind and focus on the happenings of the past few weeks.

When the council had finally departed, they had taken Lord Herlewin and Lord Harsk with them. The two men would eventually have a chance to argue their actions before the king and queen. Warin did not envy them. As for Lady Eunice, word had come that she had suffered some great malaise upon hearing of her son's activities and was unable to travel. It made no difference; the king and queen would send their representatives to her and see that justice was leveled against House Dinhyll; its fate as a smallhold would be determined with the new year.

That left the attempts on his and Anwyl's lives and the attacks on the coastal settlements. Before Prince Reynald had departed, Warin and his parents, along with Anwyl and Madyan, had apprised him of the threat of the rogue Kena women. Madyan would help him to brief the queen and king once they arrived in Kings Glen.

Warin made it to the top of the broad round tower, and continued to pace in a circuitous route, nodding to the posted watchmen. His thoughts drifted naturally to Anwyl—always to Anwyl. Whenever he tried to speak of their embrace that night in the orchard, she put him off or changed the subject. Anwyl had given all her time to training with Madyan and to mentoring Lucilla.

He gazed out over the orchards and farther, to where the rising moon lifted over the Southron Waters. Nearly full, it was enormous, and its glow swathed the distant breaking waves, turning the sea froth luminescent.

He could not press Anwyl, he knew, so he forced himself to not seek her out. Once, he had seen her in the orchard, but her head had been bent in concentration over some correspondence, and so he did not intrude. Perhaps she was reading a letter from Ronan, or Wymark, or even Tomas.

But the kiss. Their kiss.

He relived the moment in his mind's eye, wondering if she hadn't placed as much import on the embrace as he. The thought nearly made him stumble, and he stared out into the night, questioning his interpretation of the moment. Low clouds scudded across the southwest, bringing with them warmer temperatures. Their weak shadows resembled giant ghostly animals migrating over the beach, their progress uninhibited as onward they marched over the outer curtain of the castle.

If Warin hadn't been watching the phantom shadow-beasts, he wouldn't have seen the furtive movements of someone climbing the wall. The person stilled, as if sensing detection, and waited in the shadows, long enough that Warin believed it'd been a trick of the night. But when a larger cloud doused the moon's light, he saw, just barely, someone pull up and over the wall. The guards on the tower had missed it.

The drop to the ground on the other side was a good ten feet. If he left now and gave chase, he would miss the intruder's destination. He waited, peering more intently when the clouds covered the moon, for that was when he knew the trespasser would move. There he was! Just along the inside edge of the orchard, a dark figure headed for the beach, where there was sure to be a waiting skiff.

Warin took the fastest route he knew, his path cutting a nearly straight line to the shore, but when he reached its edge, he found the beach empty. The sand was undisturbed. He veered to the right and came across a bundle of dark clothing hidden in the dune grass, and a blanket. It made no sense.

A soft breeze wafted, bringing the aroma of spice and citrus to his nose: Anwyl. He knew exactly where she would be and turned to gaze out at the sea. Finally, he saw her, much farther out than he'd expected, her skin glistening in the moonlight. An arm, a foot, another arm, the curve of her hip as she took long, steady strokes, swimming parallel to the beach just past where the waves were breaking.

On and on, she swam, and so he sat and watched until, finally, she dove under the surface and flipped back around, her feet kicking like the tail of a dolphin. She was a beautiful swimmer. How many times had she escaped the palace to brave the waves? Several, if she knew enough to time her excursion so that the guards would not cross her path.

Months ago, his instinct would have been to chastise her for being so reckless. What if the raiders had decided suddenly to attack Pheldhain? What a nice catch she would make. She swam by, continuing on a westerly course. Despite the fullness of the naked moon, the waves were low and even. Not a single ship could be seen on the horizon, nor any smaller boats near the shore.

There hadn't been a report of a raid in over two weeks, not since Lord Herlewin's and his lady-mother's plot had been exposed. Warin's parents held out hope that a connection would be made between House Dinhyll and the raids, but Warin thought it unlikely. His ship and Captain Grieg were, as yet, unaccounted for. And the landlocked Dinhyll had no experience with sailing, nor—

A rustling of palm fronds to his left interrupted his train of thought. Anwyl approached, her silhouette darker against the shadowed trees that reached nearly to the water's edge. It occurred to him suddenly that she would be naked and—no, he should keep that image out of his head. She was paces away from stepping from the screen of the trees. He should turn away before the moonlight could expose her. He couldn't make himself do it.

The scrub palms hid most of her body, and she hesitated, only moving forward in perfect time with the cloaking of the moon by a passing cloud. Still, he could make out the lush curve of her hip, the nip of her waist, and—he imagined this last—the round fullness of her breasts. How bold she was as she walked to where her clothing lay hidden in the tall grass. She was watching him, and, when she reached down to pick up her garments, he turned his head back to gaze at the sea, knowing he would go to her if he continued to stare in her direction.

Warin sat in the sand and swallowed—hard—and began counting the waves while the rustling of fabric whispered and teased his imagination. Finally, she stood before him, and when he reached up, she took his hand and settled down in front of him. He shifted, so that he too was on his knees. She'd donned her chemise and leggings, but her tunic and sash were neatly folded and sitting atop her boots. The moonlight glinted off the grains of shell on her cheek, brow, and hair, and Warin reached out, wiping away a few specks.

Her chest rose and fell, as if she'd been holding her breath until his touch. He gently speared his fingers into her saltwater-dampened locks and pulled her closer. She leaned toward him, meeting his lips as he slanted his to her mouth. The initial taste of salt gave way to the sweetness he knew to be Anwyl. It was a deep kiss, one that promised infinitely more, and when they finished, he rested his forehead against hers.

"Are you cold?" She shook her head, staring at the sea, and he remembered how she had told him about her childhood escapes that had ended with an ever-present escort. "I saw you go over the wall. Had I known it was you, I would have given you your privacy. I know what this means to you, this stolen moment." It confounded him—her need to be independent and his desire to keep her safe. "I'll leave if you want me to."

"My entire life, I've been protected," she finally said, her smile bittersweet. "All I've ever wanted was to have a few moments alone like I've had here. Four nights ago, when I snuck out for a swim, it was so fine. But there was something missing. Three nights ago, I knew that what was missing was you.

Last night, I came here again, hoping that you had found me out. But you remained absent. I almost didn't venture out tonight. But the moon, the waves..." She took his face in her delicate hands. "I saw you watching me as I swam by, I usually go much farther, but I couldn't. I had to turn around. And then I thought I was being foolish. I thought you would scold me"—he opened his mouth to deny her words, but she placed her fingers on his lips—"so I continued swimming."

Her emerald eyes burned into his, and he held helplessly still as she gracefully settled herself on his lap, facing him. "So, no, I am not cold. How could I be, knowing you were here, waiting?"

"I'm so in awe of you, Anwyl," he whispered. Her dark tresses clumped together as they dried, falling away from her face and down her back like thick ropes of seaweed. He set his hands on her hips, exerted the slightest pressure, and drew her a fraction closer. She smiled and shook her head, then took matters into her own hands, giving him no quarter as she wrapped her arms around his shoulders and pressed herself fully against him. He thought about the letter she had written, describing the tutelage of a faraway place, the intense instruction in pleasures of the mind and body, and knowing now she had been writing about her own history. Had she kissed another man as she had kissed him? He should tell her, now, that he was *A.S.* "Anwyl, wait—"

"I've waited over two years for you, Warin. Longer. My entire life. No more." Her gaze held a challenge he could not refuse, and true to her words, she wasted no time taking his lips in a breath-stealing kiss.

He lost himself then, his will, and their kiss deepened. He dragged his mouth from hers to nip along her jaw. Her head tilted back, sacrificing the long column of her neck to his marauding lips. She moaned when he tasted her collarbone, doing so again as he brought his hand up to cup her breast. She was exactly as he imagined, and he massaged her with skilled fingers until her chest heaved. Gently, teasingly, his thumb brushed against her nipple, and she gasped, arching her back for him. For more.

He supported her, her hips sliding forward, her center pressing against him. She must be able to feel him there, hard against the juncture of her thighs. In all the years that he had dallied with the ladies from court, the barmaids, the serving wenches, he'd never once lost control. But this? It had never been like this. This was something different, and he was not entirely sure he could survive her. His need to bury himself in her heat was overwhelming. She deserved so much more, and he wrested control over himself.

He dragged his mouth from her neck, kissing and nipping at her exposed skin. Under his thumb, her nipple hardened, inviting him to taste her there. He accepted, sucking her through the fine linen of her shirt until she moaned and writhed in his arms. Did she know how her motions affected him? She must. How could she not? And that she knew and did not draw away incited him further. He drew at the loose ties of her collar, one by one, until he pulled the ribbon free and nudged the damp fabric away, exposing her breast.

She gasped when his mouth touched her bare skin, blessedly sitting straighter and relieving the heated pressure on his groin. Her fingers stabbed through his hair, holding his head to her breast, and her kisses rained down on his head. Upright as she was, both of his hands were free to roam. Whilst he nudged her collar and shirt away from her other breast, he sought her engorged nipple, gently rolling it betwixt thumb and forefinger. He skimmed a hand down her back, hooking his fingers in the waistband of her leggings, teasing, swirling, then stretching his long fingers lower, following the clothed cleft between her buttocks.

Her breathing turned harsh, and she growled, releasing his head and pushing him away. Warin wasn't finished with her breast, and fought to remain, but she was persistent. Breathing as hard as she, he slanted his gaze to hers. This was a version of the princess he'd never imagined existed, wild and ravenous. Her pupils were wide, nearly erasing the emerald green of her irises. She descended on him, surprising him with a fierce kiss, before pulling away again.

She crossed her arms, and he wondered if he'd pushed too far, then watched, stunned as she lifted the hem of her chemise, pulling it off and over her head. She gave him a *what-are-you-waiting-for?* expression, and Warin wasted no time acquainting himself with her glorious body, losing himself in his worship of her.

She took advantage of his distraction and slid her hands down his chest and stomach to where he was excruciatingly hard. She held him, gently at first, then with more confidence when he moaned his appreciation. He broke away just long enough to remove his shirt, because he needed her naked body against his like he needed air to live.

She gasped again when her breasts touched his bare chest, and he plundered her mouth with his lips and tongue. He was determined to give her pleasure, and when he reached down to touch her between her legs, she moaned into his mouth and lifted her arms around his neck to support herself.

Thank heavens, too, for if she had continued stroking him, he would not have lasted.

He drew away the tie that cinched her Umbren leggings around her waist. Loosened, the fabric slipped, riding seductively low on her hips. He played with her, expertly driving her passion, sliding down, cupping her mons, his fingers dancing over where she would be most sensitive. He continued kissing her, nipping at her lips when she seemed unable to breathe, slowing only long enough to let her catch it, all the while rubbing and caressing her. If she'd ever experienced this before, he didn't care. And when that telltale tightening of her features screamed that she was close, he pressed his other hand against her, forcing her forward against his knuckles. Her body ratcheted, and he clamped his mouth over hers to swallow her scream.

Only when she was reduced to muffled whimpering did he ease back from her. The taut rod of her spine loosened, and she sank against him, cheek to chest, her breasts heaving. Her shoulders shook, and he realized she was laughing. "Anwyl?"

She lifted her face to him, and he pushed her wild locks from her forehead. "That was... I had no idea. I mean, I'd been taught, through books and lectures and diagrams, but that was—"

"There's more," he told her, ridiculously happy that he had been the first to give her that pleasure. "Next time—"

"Tonight. Now."

In that moment, Warin knew he'd found his equal. A woman he could love and who could love him in return, blending her life with his, sharing in whatever adventure was thrown their way. "Yes, but on one condition."

"Anything."

"Agree to be my wife."

"Well, of course." She swatted him as though it were a foregone conclusion. She jumped up and stripped off her breeches, standing before him in all her glory. He laughed at her outrageousness, then could do naught but stare at what she offered. Her body, toned from the rigorous workouts she'd done with Madyan, glowed in the moonlight. And then he saw them, the markings on her thigh. He reached out his finger to touch the green and soot-colored tendrils inked into her flesh.

"You told me that you were not a Fenrhi."

"Does it matter?"

"Nothing matters but us, Anwyl," he said, taking her hand and kissing her fingers. "But I would like to hear the story one day."

She knelt back down. "Take off your clothes first; it's only fair." He reached for the ties of his breeches, then paused, aware that he was still hard. "I won't be shocked. I may have never... Look, I've seen naked men before. Let's just leave it at that."

She ogled him as he leaned back to pull off his breeches, her eyebrow lifting and her lips twitching in appreciation. She scooted closer to him, then sat, her bum perched on her heels. He rolled to his side to face her, his erection heavy against her thigh, and touched the green designs marked there, reminding her that she had a story to tell.

"First, I am not Fenrhi. I told you that I was trained by a Sylvan master. It was necessary. There were attempts made on us. Poisonings, mostly. Rani more than me. Then we discovered that our parents had been murdered by Diarmait. He poisoned hundreds just to make it appear that they'd died of a sickness sweeping through Sophiana. Radha was adamant that I be trained as a Sylvan.

"When the Sylvan master said that she could teach me no more, I asked to be marked. My friend Hedra, the Sylvan artist, arrived weeks later. She did this for me." She was watching him as he traced the patterns.

"I guess you could say I'm a healer, at least when it comes to knowing the antidote for poisons. The Fenrhi...they don't lie when they say they are neutral. They'll sell death to the highest bidder, then turn around and sell the cure to the victim." He studied the markings as she continued, standing to give him an engaging glimpse of her other thigh. "Venna was my Umbren trainer—it was she who sent the Umbren artist to Sophiana when my training was complete."

The dark, sooty tendrils were nearly black. "Exactly how much Umbren training do you have?" Warin asked, rising to face her.

She grinned, and before he could react, she hooked her leg around his, pulling his foot out from under him while slamming the heel of her hand against his opposite shoulder. She toppled him to the ground, then followed after to pin him there, her forearm at his throat, one knee wedged dangerously between his legs. Warin chuckled and wrapped his arms around her waist, then rolled her onto her back and rested on his side next to her. "All this time, thinking that you were so fragile and in need of my protection. That must have irked you to no end."

"At times. But it was also endearing."

"You really did have things in hand when Herlewin accosted you, didn't you?"

She rolled to face him, her expression suddenly serious. "It was instinct. Pure reaction. It's one of the ways the Umbren train. But if you hadn't found us before Lady Eunice..." She shuddered, and he pulled her closer. "He was on the ground, and still, I went into a state of shock. That he thought it was his right..."

"I know, sweetheart." He tucked his knuckle under her chin. "I'm sorry. It's one thing to know that you can protect yourself, and quite another to find that you have to." He kissed her forehead, her nose, then her lips.

"In Nifolhad, I was taught to always be wary; still, my brother kept me safe. Then I came here. I hated how Herlewin made me feel afraid and ashamed. I've only felt that once before."

"At the Breakneck Tavern," Warin confessed, leaning back as she set her cheek on his chest and draped her arm and leg over him. "I was there."

"Of course, you were." She was silent for a few minutes. "I was so angry at you for what you had said about me in the stable, then embarrassed. It's part of the reason I avoided you at court."

He traced his fingers over her bare arm, enjoying the softness of her skin. "Only part?"

She nodded. "I could always tell that you didn't trust me."

Warin couldn't deny it.

"Why?"

"My cousin. His ship had been sighted in your harbor. That was the last trace of him," he admitted. "I know you could never have had any hand in his disappearance."

"One of the missing emissaries was your cousin? I didn't know, Warin. I could have—"

"It's all right. But I think Murel's brother is gone forever."

"Murel! She never said anything either."

"You'll get used to that. For all our bravado, Pheldhainians tend to keep to ourselves when it comes to our family."

She nodded. "I've a confession to make to you."

"Is this about what happened to me in Sophiana?" he asked, and she nodded. "I keep thinking that I've forgotten something. I have, haven't I?"

"Radha was talking to Aghna about me; it was very personal. Something Ni'Mala told me before she became the Fenrhi Mother. Something so embarrassing that, had I been there, I would not have allowed her to tell Aghna. You accidently overheard." She looked around, not meeting his eye, then lifted her chin. "I didn't know until it was too late. Radha begged Claire to help her. Together, they *suggested* that you forget."

"I remember drinking something."

"A tonic to counteract the pihaberries you'd already consumed." She sat up and stared at the sea. "I'm so sorry. I would have borne the embarrassment rather than allow you to be manipulated. And you mustn't be angry with Claire. Radha convinced her that it was important to protect me. I think Claire *saw* something between us."

He pulled her back down to him and kissed her nose. "I'm glad you told me. I always wondered. I wanted to trust you, but something held me back."

"You're not angry?"

"No, not at all." He stroked her hair. "To think, every misadventure we had, I always blamed you for your recklessness. But you were always in control. Swinging on the lines of my ship, slipping into the Stolweg River to save the cart, everything." He cupped her cheek. "I'm sorry, Anwyl. I never understood you. I didn't try. I was too unhappy."

"Why?" She had grown serious again, and she traced her fingers around the hard planes of his chest, seesawing back and forth over the muscles of his abdomen, then back up again.

"Honestly? I think I was jealous. Of Trian and Claire, and of Lark and Anna. My two closest friends were settling down. I realized that my dream—a family, a wife to love—would never satisfy me, though I denied the truth of it. I need someone with whom to share life's adventures."

She snorted prettily. "You certainly get enough of that with me." She stretched closer and kissed him. Her hair was a mass of tangles from the drying saltwater, but she'd never looked more beautiful. She was the least self-conscious woman he'd ever met; she knew exactly who she was and was confident to her core. "Why are you smiling at me like that?"

"There are very few maidens in Aurelia who would be as comfortable as you...lying next to me...naked."

"Once I'm sure about something, I don't believe in holding back. Or waiting. I saw how devastated Rani was when he heard that Aghna had been killed. He wore his sorrow like armor. It worked out in the end, but he was lost for three years. It's been difficult for me, adhering to all the unwritten rules you Aurelians so love."

Warin chuckled. "I'm not complaining."

She gave him a censorious stare. "Warin, I'm serious when I say this—we've wasted too much time already."

"Is that a command, my princess?"

"Say that again."

"My princess?" he asked, then kissed her shoulder.

"Mmm'hmm."

"Shall I kiss you here, my princess?" He pushed her shoulder back and moved his mouth toward her dark nub. She answered with a moan, and he descended on her breast, kissing and licking, then pulling at her nipple with his lips and teeth. "Shall I touch you lower, my princess?" She growled, and he ran his fingers, tracing circles around and around, down her stomach, and lingering in the crisp curls between her legs.

Ever-so-lightly, he teased, lower and lower, until he reached her heat, then pressed with his finger. She was already wet when he penetrated, just a little, her hot sheath. He wanted her so badly, but this was her first time, and it had to be perfect. He mouthed his way over her ribs, noticing with a smile the spot that caused her to jerk.

"I love that my princess is ticklish." He would take the time later to discover just how much, but for now, he continued kissing her stomach, pausing at her navel, loving the heated scent of her mixed with the aroma of clean seawater. The route that he followed with his lips meandered, giving his fingers time to properly tease her where she burned. Touching her lightly, he skimmed over the surface of her passion, pressing gently until she moaned and opened her thighs for him. He continued tantalizing her, never giving her more than a taste, as his mouth explored the surface of her hip. He moved lower, and she drew up her knee. She would be ticklish in that crease where her thigh met her torso, and so he avoided it, not wanting to break the spell he was weaving with his fingers and tongue.

He shifted so that he was kneeling between her legs, never stopping his stroking. She had thrown her head to the side, but his new position won over her curiosity, and she opened her eyes to stare at him. He fluttered his fingers over her in a new rhythm, and she gasped. "Do you like this, my princess?"

She stared at his hand, and he saw her eyes shift to his erection. "Yessss."

He inserted the tip of his finger into her heat again, amazed at her wetness. "I'm not wasting too much time?"

"It's perfect. You're perfect," she managed, then moaned when he withdrew his fingertip and pushed it back in, giving her just enough to tantalize. He added a gentle swipe of his thumb over her hidden bud, and she crooned. On and on he went until she lifted her hips in an attempt to get more. But he refused her, wanting her pleasure to be drawn out until there was nothing left of her.

When she squeezed her eyes shut again, he lowered himself down, wrapping his arm under her thigh and hip so as to splay his long fingers over her stomach, holding her, pressing her down into the blanket-covered sand. And still he teased her until, gradually, he replaced the motion of his thumb with his tongue. She didn't notice at first, at least not until he used his lips to pull and suck at that tiny button of pleasure. She cried out, and he gazed up at the rapturous expression on her face. He drew his fingertip up, and dragged his tongue down, reversing their positions, and she gave a strangled moan. She tried to lift her hips, but he held her down, using his tongue to give her what his finger refused. For a long time, he supped, feeling her every intimate quiver, withdrawing just enough to keep her from tipping over the precipice, then pushing her back to its edge.

When he deemed it time, he slipped his fingertip in, but this time pushing deeper and caressing her inside before withdrawing. She'd flung her arms wide and was thrashing her head back and forth. The muscles of her inner thighs shivered as she moaned unintelligibly. He pushed his finger deep, again and again. Then added another, stretching her. She was near to bucking free of his arm, and this time when she began to tense, he didn't withdraw, but worked his hand, dipping back down to take her in his mouth. Hers was an ambrosia that he'd never imagined, and he sucked there until her sheath clamped down on his fingers, and she found her release. Wave after wave of it.

Her body was still pulsing as he kissed his way up her stomach, pausing to appreciate her breasts, before propping himself on one elbow to stare down at her rapturous face. She lifted her arms, slowly, as if lead weights had been tied to them and wrapped them around his shoulders. Her emerald eyes, when she finally opened them, leveled him with a look of satisfaction that could only be described as bestial in its intensity. And when her lips curled in appreciation of his efforts, he felt her shift her hips so that his shaft was at her entrance. "I thought I knew, but I didn't. I was taught that coupling with a man was the ultimate pleasure. But how could anything be more perfect than what you just gave me? Warin, please, show me." She hooked her leg over his hip, drawing him closer.

"You astonish me, my princess." And he pressed into her, slowly, so as to allow her to gradually accommodate his size.

"Remember what I said," she ordered, her hunger for him drawn out in each syllable. "No more wasting time." She thrust her hips to take him all the way, giving a small gasp when her maidenhood was pierced.

She held herself to him, gasping, and he reached for her hip to support her. "Easy." Her hips and back were arched and stiff. "Let go, my princess. Just a little. That's it." And he followed her, still buried deep, as she eased herself back down.

"That wasn't too bad," she admitted, her voice shaky. "I read that I should move, but this is good too."

"Such praise," Warin teased, pleased to see her blush. She was clamped tightly around him, so he held himself still. Her gaze flitted over his face, questioning. "There's a little more to it, my princess. You just need to ease your muscles."

She looked bewildered for the first time since he'd met her. And then understanding came to her face. "Oh. Oh!" She closed her eyes, and he could see her concentration.

"Anwyl," he coaxed. "Open your eyes. There's no hurry." She did, and he kissed her cheek, nuzzled her neck, and nibbled her earlobe. Little by little, her thighs released their vice-like hold until the rest of her muscles followed suit. "I'm going to move now, all right?"

She nodded, and he lifted away from her, just a fraction, then pressed forward again. Each withdrawal a little farther, each thrust a little deeper, until she began moving with him. He kissed her deeply, thrusting his tongue against hers, urging her to follow his rhythm. Her knees lifted, and she pressed her heels into the blanket as he worked to reawaken her senses in a manner completely different from before. "This is so much more logical," she observed, panting each word.

Warin reached down, slipping his long fingers between them so that he could heighten her pleasure. She responded immediately, screaming out his name, then throwing her hips hard against his downstroke. He felt her pleasure well where he was cradled inside her, and then erupt in waves. The force of it took him with her in a combined release.

It was sometime later when he realized his back had stopped heaving and Anwyl was drawing lazy circles over his shoulders. "Finally, a chance to put my studies to practical use," she whispered, and he chuckled.

"Yes, love, but not tonight." He rolled them so that he was on his back and she on her side.

"You're in the sand," she noted. "Come on. Come swimming with me." She sat up and pulled at his arm. Her energy was infectious, and so he went with her. They didn't swim but took turns rinsing each other off before walking hand in hand to the half-buried blanket.

Warin shook it out, taking care that the breeze didn't blow the grit back on their wet skin. Anwyl had pulled on her chemise, then held out his shirt to help him into it. They steadied each other, putting on their breeches, laughing at the awkwardness. She was about to say something, but she looked past him to where the eastern sky would be lightening. "Time to head back, my princess." He took her hand, directing her to the path that led through his favorite spot in all Pheldhain.

"Warin, what are they called?" she asked, staring at the bushy trees ranging along both sides of the path, creating a tunnel with their milky white blossoms.

"Lunastra trees. The blooms brighten the world only when the stars and moon light up the heavens." He plucked one of the white five-petaled flowers and tucked it behind her ear. "The flowers are delicate, but the tree's thorns protect them."

"Thank you." She stood on her toes and kissed him.

They reached the quiet castle, the posted guards nodding discreetly before resuming their rounds. Warin delivered her to the door of her chamber, gave her a kiss rife with promise, and then turned to find his own bed.

"Warin," she whispered after him, and he stopped. "The poison in Salto, we should talk to your parents. I don't think our troubles are over."

"No, they're not. But get some rest. We'll see my parents later today." She nodded and then slipped into her chamber. Warin grinned all the way to his rooms; Anwyl had agreed to marry him.

CHAPTER TWENTY-SEVEN

Ass

By the time Anwyl woke, it was very late in the morning. She sat up in her bed and stretched, luxuriating in the delicious aches that had settled in her muscles. She grinned, remembering the how and the why. On the table next to her bed was the lunastra flower, already showing its wilt. She heard a tap on the door and, guessing that it was Lucilla with the water porters, slid back under her blankets.

"Good morning, Princess," Lucilla chirped with a sweet smile, directing the porters to fill the tub while she arranged the drying rugs on a stool.

"Good morning, Lucilla. What do you have there?" Lucilla had placed a tray with various crystal dishes and vials next to the bath water.

"Bath oils and salts"—she paused, waiting until the last of the porters left the chamber—"from Lord Warin."

"You saw him this morning?" Anwyl asked, then *oohed* when she saw the lunastra flowers floating in the bath water.

Lucilla giggled as she pulled the privacy screens in place around the basin, then tidied up Anwyl's things from the night before. "It's a shame that this flower wasn't put in water. Would you like me to press it for you?"

"Oh yes, that would be lovely." She finished bathing while Lucilla busied herself with laying out her garments. "That'll be your breakfast, my princess," Lucilla announced when there was another tap on the door.

Anwyl dried herself, wrapped her wet hair in a towel, then slipped into her clothes. She came around to find Lucilla frowning down at the tray of food. "It's almost double what you normally eat. Are you expecting anyone?"

"I don't think so." She looked at the tray of food and noticed the vase of milky white blossoms. Warin must have realized that, after their night together, she would be ravenous. By the time she had finished eating her breakfast, Lucilla had rubbed her hair dry and pulled it back in a loose braid.

"It's cooler today, so I'll set out your cloak." She shook it out before draping it over the back of a chair, and a folded bit of parchment fell out. Anwyl plucked it from the floor, trying to recall how she came by it. She nodded absently as Lucilla departed, staring at the paper and taking another bite of honeyed pastry. It was dense and moist, almost a cake, though Warin insisted the palm-shaped delicacy was a bread. He claimed it was better the next day when it was slightly stale, and one could moisten it with milk and eat it out of a bowl.

She stared at the paper, studying it with a sense of unease. It was free of both address and seal and folded into a tight square. The outer creases were soft, as if the note had been read many times. Then she remembered—she had found it in the orchard where she and Warin had set their trap for Herlewin. It must belong to him or someone in his family. She took another bite of her breakfast, finished her tea, and then donned her cloak. She glanced hungrily at the bread, buttered another slice, and pocketed a couple of apples before going in search of Warin to ask him about the note.

He was waiting right outside her door and when he saw her, he pushed away from the wall he'd been leaning against. "Lucilla said you were almost ready, so I waited."

She gave him a wide smile, running to his arms. He swung her about, her cloak flaring around them, banging them both in the legs. "Apples," she explained, brushing at something on his shoulder. "Sorry, I got some butter on you."

"Hungry this morning?"

"Yes, as a matter of fact." She ate the rest of her bread as they walked down the corridor. "I fown a wetter," she mumbled, covering her mouth while she chewed. It was most un-princess-like of her, and she stopped to swallow. "Oh, excuse me!"

Warin chuckled, and he touched his fingertip to her lip. "More butter," he explained. "It's a general rule in Pheldhain that etiquette must be broken when eating palm bread. Go ahead and finish, and I'll fill you in while we walk to my father's study." He steered her down the corridor. "I think we must first discuss our surety that there are Kena spies here." Anwyl nodded. "And then I would like to tell them our news." He stopped walking and turned to face her. She was swallowing her last bite, her eyes wide. "Why do you look so stricken?"

"Please tell me there aren't any challenges in Pheldhain such as they have in Cathmara. Poor Claire and Trian. I mean, if there are, I'll fight for you, of course I will. I'll do battle for you, if that's what it takes. But it would be so much simpler to—"

Warin stopped her with a kiss. "If you're sure, you need only say yes, my princess."

"Yes!"

The door to his father's council chamber opened, and Murel came out. When she saw them standing together, their arms wrapped around each other, she quickly shut the door. "Just a warning—your mother is in there. If you two enter looking at each other like that, she's going to insist you get married immediately."

Anwyl giggled.

"And what would you know about how we are looking at each other?" Warin demanded.

Murel rolled her eyes and ignored his question. "Come on, everyone else is ready. I've briefed them on what you've told me about the different poisons. And news came in about"—she opened the chamber door, and they filed in—"your ship."

No sooner did they enter, wishing everyone present a good morning, than Lady Téana took one look at them and started clapping. She rushed across the room and embraced Anwyl. "Oh, finally! I'm so pleased for you both!" And just like that, the discussions about poison and ships were tabled. His mother pulled her into a fierce hug. "I suppose you'll want to have the ceremony in Sophiana."

"I was thinking that it might be better to get married in Kings Glen, or here. Your gardens are beautiful, and a smaller celebration would be lovely."

"Yes, I know just the place," Lady Téana exclaimed. Warin came to her side, slipping his arm around her waist. They talked for a few minutes about wedding plans before Anwyl and Warin brought them back to the topic they'd come to discuss. Together, they explained how the Fenrhi were organized, and how a faction had split from the temple.

"You see, I came to Aurelia as Nifolhad's ambassador, and to plant the pijala trees, giving you a chance against these rogue Kena, if they chose to infiltrate your realm. But, also to determine if they already have."

"And you think they have," Lady Téana stated.

"We know it," Anwyl replied.

"It's why Madyan went with Prince Reynald," Warin added. "To protect him."

"But Murel told us about this Rhiannon woman from the Kena," Lord Marin reminded. "And she's dead."

Anwyl nodded to Warin, and he told his parents about the maid from Ragallach named Daisy, and then the incident with the wine. "Anwyl recognized the poison as being similar to what a Sylvan might concoct."

Warin's father leaned back in his chair, scrubbing his hands over his face just like Warin was wont to do. "Best we are prepared for anything. Do you know how to counteract these poisons?" Anwyl nodded. "Then we should start by making a list of the herbs you'll need."

Warin pulled a sheet of paper from the credenza behind them, and a fresh quill and ink. "We can have Cook and the master gardener check our stores," he said, hand poised to take notation from her.

"Golden root. And periwinkle," Anwyl began. "Oh, this would be so much easier if we were in Sophiana. I don't suppose you have corpse root here?" From their looks, she could tell they didn't know to what she was referring. "The root is bulbous; some people think it resembles a man's body...No? All right, you can scratch that one off the list," she said to Warin, studying what he'd written. She gasped, then she pushed away from the table. She pulled the folded piece of paper from her pocket and held it with shaking hands.

"Anwyl," Warin said, his voice sounding as if he were far away. He reached to take the paper from her hand, surely knowing what it was, but she moved it out of his reach. "Please, you don't need to—"

She unfolded the paper, her eyes scanning the writing. It was *The List*. And it was written in the same elegant script as the names of the herbs that Warin had just penned. The same handwriting belonging to *A.S.*

Warin took a step closer, reaching for her as she wadded the list up into a ball. She looked up at him, hoping beyond hope that there would be confusion in his gaze, but his eyes betrayed him.

"Anwyl, I can explain. Please."

"You're...You...You...*A.S.*!" She threw the paper at him and stormed from the room.

. . .

"Ass?" Lady Téana demanded, frowning at him. "Warin, what have you done now?"

"Not ass, Mother, *A.S.*," he explained. "It's short for *Aurelian Scho*—it doesn't matter." He stared at the paper she'd thrown at him: *The List.* "Oh, hell. Father, we'll finish this later. Right now, I need to—"

"Go!" he ordered, but Warin was already running out the door. He didn't bother asking if anyone had seen her, for he knew exactly where she would go—the beach. As he had the previous night, he took the shortest route, hoping to arrive there before her.

• • •

Warin would be on her heels. So Anwyl flew down the corridor, needing some time to think...alone. The last place he would look for her would be in his own chamber. She had to know for sure; had to see it with her own eyes. Her letters, the ones she'd signed *F.H.*; his journal. She found them easily enough, bundled and tied up neatly with silk ribbons. She sat on his bed, and read everything she'd written to him, trying to determine what had given her away. There was nothing. About to leave, she saw his journal. She opened it up, finding the page she had inserted—her intimate experiences in Sophiana. Did he know even then that it was she who wrote to him? A folded slip of paper fell to the floor, and she picked it up. Her name was written on the outside, and she opened it.

> *Dear ~~F.H.,~~ Anwyl,*
>
> *I promised not to write you again. You, my Fellow Historian. But I can do nothing but stare at the paper, begging me to pick up my quill and scratch some ink upon it. I can no longer resist, for writing to you has been one of my greatest joys.*
>
> *Looking back, I think that I must have always known it was to you I wrote. And yet, I never did, not until the night when you quoted my own words back to me.*
>
> *I remember my shock that evening, and returning here to reread your letters, searching for clues. I wanted to tell you right away, but a mutual friend suggested otherwise, telling me that I would know when the time was right.*
>
> *It was never right.*
>
> *And then you gave me your heart.*
>
> *I hope that when you discover that A.S. and I are the same, you will understand, and hopefully, as I did, see how obvious it was all along. And I pray that you will forgive me. If you do, I promise that we will share and collaborate*

with not only our minds, but our hearts as well, for you hold mine in your hands already.

With all my love,
Warin

She stared at the paper for what seemed like an eternity. And when someone entered the room behind her, she folded it and slipped it back into his journal. She stood, smoothed her tunic, and turned around to face him.

"One of the maids saw you enter," Lady Téana said softly.

"Where is he?"

"Looking for you, I imagine." She held out her hand. "Come, Princess, let's take a walk. We can talk, if that is what you need."

As they journeyed through the palace and out to the grounds, they passed through the most beautiful gardens upon which Anwyl had ever laid eyes. Flowers and lush plants grew in wild abandon, but viewed as a whole, the design was an extraordinary construction meant to delight the senses. Too soon they left the tropical paths and climbed the steady grade that took them to the uppermost terraces.

She'd been so caught up in her feelings for Warin, she'd neglected to really look at his home. The palace was a type of architecture that she knew not existed. Domes abounded, like those in Kantahla, and filigreed spires, too, but rather than appearing heavy and forbidding, the collection of towers and buildings was elegant and airy. She stopped a for moment, and Lady Téana regarded her with a soft smile. "It's so beautiful," Anwyl breathed, as they continued walking through one courtyard after another, each filled with fountains and ponds. Elegant birds, on long, stilted legs and plumed in blue- and green feathers strutted lazily as a soft breeze brought the delicious, spiced scents from the gardens below.

"Would you like a tour?"

"Yes, but not yet. I'm sure you would rather I speak with your son."

"There will be time enough for that. Why don't I show you my favorite spot?" Anwyl nodded, and they turned away from their current path.

They walked through several...rooms? Anwyl didn't know what to call the open spaces made of delicately carved stone screens and climbing trellises. Finally, they came upon a spacious courtyard. There was a small pond in one corner, fed by a spring gurgling from a fissure in the rock face. In the water, a pair of fisher minks cavorted. Lady Téana took some dried fish from an ornate box and fed them.

"They're beautiful," Anwyl exclaimed, smiling and laughing at their antics.

"They come and go as they please," Lady Téana explained. "But they spend more time here when the winter sets in. It never freezes in Pheldhain, but the evenings do grow cold."

Anwyl looked over the low wall to the southeast—the whole of the port, and the strait, and then to Barb Island resting in the hazy distance. Pristine beaches bracketed by lush palms stretched like an open invitation to the southwest. A lone figure paced the shore. Warin.

"I believe he'll be returning to the palace soon, Princess. You'll have to decide if his crime is worth losing him."

"Please, call me Anwyl," she begged. "There was no crime. Just...miscommunication." Below her, Warin turned, and she lost sight of him as he strode from the beach and into the cover of the palms. Anwyl turned and stared up at the towers of the castle. Where had the day gone? The sun was setting, washing the creamy stone pink, and setting thousands of glistening specks alight as the waning rays hit the bits of mica embedded within.

"My favorite place at my favorite time of day, nearly. In another hour, it will seem as if the entire face of the palace glows as if lit from within," Lady Téana stated. "Come, let's sit; I've already sent for refreshments. I won't press you for details concerning my rashest and wisest son. He's always been a man of contradictions. Don't think that I haven't heard that he is the biggest rake in all of Aurelia. But he wasn't like that as a young man. He was shy and studious." She continued to tell Anwyl stories from Warin's childhood; and Anwyl thought about his journal, and the woman from the Southron Isles and how she had helped shape Warin into the man he became.

"He let me read his journal," Anwyl admitted. "Though he didn't know at the time to whom he lent it."

"Did he now? Never once has he shared his private writings. Why you? Especially as he did not know to whom he gave it."

Anwyl sipped at the wine that had been brought to them. She, too, had written to Warin about her personal experiences, things she'd told no one. "He must have known it was me—not in his head, but in his heart. If I'm honest, it was the same for me."

"So, you'll forgive him."

"I can't," Anwyl said with a soft smile. "There is nothing to forgive."

"I am so pleased to hear you say that. I'll find him and let him know you are here."

"Thank you for helping me to see the truth."

"No thanks are necessary. When I found you, I could tell you were already on your way there."

. . .

Warin had searched the beach, the library, the orchard. Hell, he even checked to make sure her mare was still in the stable. He went to her chamber, nearly frightening Lucilla out of her wits. He'd been just as shaken. The girl had Anwyl's traveling trunks open, her garments folded in different piles on her bed. She was packing to leave.

Warin stalked to his parents' study, determined to enlist their aid in salvaging his relationship. He barged in, only to find his father sitting at his desk, reading a letter. "How can you be so calm? Anwyl has gone missing!"

"Nonsense," his father denied. "I have had no such reports from the guards. Besides, she's much more sensible than that. I can see why you're so taken with her."

"I have to find her. I have to explain."

"I'm sure she'll want to see you when she's ready, Warin. Give her some time."

"There is no time! Lucilla was packing to leave. I have to make sure that she's safe...even if she no longer wishes to—"

"Warin," his mother softly interrupted. "She's waiting for you on my private terrace."

His father set his hand on Warin's shoulder. "Go to her. And this time, try not to make more of a mess of it." Warin's mother swatted at her husband, but he didn't wait to hear if anything more was said. He was already racing down the corridor to his parents' apartments and his mother's secluded terrace.

He ran the entire way, and when he reached the terrace, he didn't see her, not at first. She was sitting off to the side, in his mother's favorite spot, watching the sunset light up the palace. Her back was to him, and he didn't know how he managed it, but he stood still, willing his breath to even. Her head lifted slightly, and she seemed to relax.

"Come sit down next to me, Warin," she said calmly before he could utter a single word. "I've poured you some wine."

He was by her side in four strides, and she continued watching the changing color of the sun reflected off the palace. "Anwyl, I—"

"Shh. Not yet," she murmured. "Your mother said this was the best part." She handed him his glass.

He stared at her, at the goblet, then at her again.

"It's so lovely and peaceful," she whispered, as he lowered himself to the stone bench.

And finally, he followed her gaze. "I'd forgotten this."

"You never wrote about this in your journal. Why?"

"Maybe I didn't have the words to do it justice." And then the princess did the most amazing thing. She took his hand in hers and leaned against him. "Anwyl, you must forgive me. I—"

"I can't, Warin," she said simply enough, and his heart was crushed. "You didn't do anything wrong. No more than I."

"But the letters..." he said, not yet willing to believe his ears.

"What about them?"

"I discovered your identity. I didn't tell you."

"When? Three weeks ago? You wrote to me as *A.S.*, told me you could no longer keep up our correspondence. Had the roles been reversed, I probably would have done the same. I did do the same, at the masquerade. I let you go on thinking you had kissed Lady Beth."

"But..."

"You sent me your journal, my love. Your writing cried out your name with every turn of the page. I didn't see it because I wasn't ready to accept what Ni'Mala had foretold."

"What does the Fenrhi Mother have to do with all of this?"

"It has to do with what Radha made you forget." She continued to gaze at the view—the palace, the gardens below, the sea, and the burnished orb melting and losing its shape on the horizon. "Before she became the Mother, I met her. She told me to study, to prepare myself to be Rani's most trusted counsel because he would need me. She had foreseen my parents' death but didn't tell me, thinking to spare me the pain. Instead, she asked me if I wanted to know what fate had decided for me when it came to love."

Then Anwyl laughed softly, as if the memory pained her. "I didn't care about love; I was still too young. But I said yes."

"What did she foretell?"

This time, she laughed outright. "Only that I would fall in love with a dark-haired, blue-eyed stranger. There were years when I hated her for that. You can't imagine the embarrassing situations I fell into because of her prediction."

"I don't think I want to," he said but smiled at her when she arched an eyebrow at him. "I haven't been exactly chaste, Anwyl, as I'm sure you have heard from our friends at court. I would be a hypocrite if I judged you by a different set of rules."

"Will you do something for me, Warin, for us? Right now, right here?"

"Anything for you," he murmured, then kissed her, finally. He pulled back and watched as she drew one of her hairpins from the coiled braids on her head. Instead of a blunted point, the tip was needle sharp. He gazed into her eyes, trying to understand what she was asking of him. "Anwyl, is that a weapon?"

CHAPTER TWENTY-EIGHT

Warnings

The Islet, somewhere in the Southron Isles

"And you're sure he was spotted?" Dorn demanded. Captain Juna nodded, but it was to Vala that he looked for confirmation.

"It was the same ship that has been scouring the uninhabited isles. The one that nearly tracked Odo back to our location."

Odo grunted, not liking it when Vala pointed out his incompetence. "They were never close enough to distinguish my ship as *The Sea Hare*, so stop dredging it up."

"I only meant to point out that Captain Juna did a remarkable job of keeping out of sight of their barrelman, even sheltering in an inlet while they sailed right past. So close, Juna recognized the ship as *Lita's Pearl*." Vala smiled triumphantly as she presented that last bit of intelligence.

"No one cares," Odo complained.

"What else?" Dorn asked, for in Vala's eyes was a look of great satisfaction. She nodded to Juna.

"*Lita's Pearl* is more oft than not commanded by Captain Grieg," Juna supplied. "He's the only captain from the Southron Isles whose been given leave to work for one of the Aurelian noble houses."

Vala gave Juna an encouraging nod.

"*Lita's Pearl* belongs to none other than Lord Warin and is merely captained by Grieg while Pheldhain's second-born son carries out his duties as a Royal Guard."

Odo sneered. "So what? This changes nothing."

"Quiet, Odo," Dorn hissed, for by Vala's gleeful expression, he knew there was more.

"As soon as we confirmed that they found our castaway, we sailed to one of the smaller isles and made port. It was a risk, I know, but we didn't even have to ask about Grieg," Juna stated. "The patrons at the inn were eager to share their gossip."

"It seems that Grieg has been searching for Lord Marten since he was taken. And he's been looking for us as well. But what was most interesting is that which they told us of Lord Warin." Vala paused for effect. "It seems, my prince, that none other than Lord Warin has been assigned to protect and escort a certain Nifolhadian Princess throughout Aurelia."

"Anwyl of Sophiana," Dorn whispered, uncaring that Vala had slipped and spoken his title. It no longer mattered. His plans were now in motion, and nothing could stop what was to come. It would be months before word of his whereabouts would reach Aghna and Ranulf.

"And they are, right at this moment, sojourning in Pheldhain," Juna provided. Odo sat down, somehow knowing for once that he should keep his remarks to himself.

"My prince, is it not now time to reveal yourself?" Vala asked. He gave her a shrewd look, trying to determine if she had some other motive, but she only stared at him with her big eyes. It was true—he hated pretending to be a simple captain. Hell, anyone who met him knew he was more, even Juna, on some level, deferred to him as if he were noble. Prince Bowen rose from the table with a new plan. A better plan.

"You're sure that Marten was rescued by his younger brother's ship and is on his way home?"

"They may have already made port."

"And he's still susceptible to your influence, Vala?"

"Yes, my prince. He will do as instructed and, should he survive long enough, will insist on traveling to Kings Glen to meet with the Royal Family. He'll tell the king and queen that he has uncovered information about a pact between Queen Aghna and the Southron Isles. And when they least expect it, he will draw his blade and kill his king."

"And if I wanted to amend his instructions?" Bowen held up his hand, not wanting to hear an excuse before he told her what she must accomplish, even at the risk of her own life. "Close the door, Odo. Juna, Vala, take a seat. We've some alterations to make. And if we are successful, I'll be able to return to Nifolhad and much sooner than expected."

• • •

The King and Queen's Royal Bedchamber, Kings Glen

The king watched as his wife paced after reading the letter sent by Queen Aghna. The report contained both good and upsetting news. Months after the liberation of Brynmara, the Fenrhi were still tending to the sickest and most injured of the prisoners held in the tower. One man in particular clung to life, a man they believed to be one of the envoys sent to Nifolhad nearly four years past. He was in Sophiana now, and Ranulf had written that he grew stronger each day—they hoped he would soon be able to tell them his identity.

"If I had to go by the description alone, I would have to say that it's Lord Jesper from Pheldhain," Juliana stated. "But the age of the man...Jesper was only twenty-three when we sent him, not in his forties, as Ranulf wrote."

"Torture can age a man," he said grimly. "We must instruct Murel to be cautious in her hope. This man may not even be Aurelian, let alone her lost brother." His wife nodded but continued to pace. Godwin knew it was the second half of the letter that had her agitated, the part about Princess Anwyl.

"I know you care for her," he started, "and have come to love her like a daughter. You mustn't be too angry with the princess for not divulging all of her mission to us."

"I am not angry with Anwyl. Aghna should never have put her in such a position." His wife sat on the edge of their bed and stared at the hearth. "She must have felt terrible, forbidden to discuss her objective with us. No wonder she never truly opened up to me or my ladies."

"But she did befriend Ladies Caroline and Murel."

"More like they befriended her. I know from Caroline that she divulged very little personal information. It is why it took me so long to recognize the connection between her and Warin."

The king regarded his wife with new appreciation and chuckled. "I wondered that you threw them together again after they appeared to have no interest in one another at court. Have you had any news?"

"It is why I sent Lady Caroline to Pheldhain. Warin is past due for some queenly advice. I hope he took it to heart." She slid under the blankets he'd lifted for her and settled next to him.

"You are deliciously cruel, my love, sending Warin with the princess and making him assist her in finding a groom. Too bad there really wasn't a list. That would have made the journey even more interesting."

"Ah, that. I crafted a list, then had Warin transpose the updated names." Godwin laughed when she explained how she had ruthlessly slashed through his name. "It wasn't truly necessary to have one, but I wanted to make Warin squirm for once."

"I wish I had been there to see his face. The biggest rake in the realm deemed not quite up to snuff by his queen."

"Did you know, my dear, that Anwyl and Warin have been writing to each other for almost a year now without ever suspecting to whom they corresponded?" He shook his head. "The unrequited attraction between them was dragging on far too long. I sent Caroline to give Warin a good kick in the...quill. We'll soon hear more on the subject—Lady Caroline is due to arrive any day."

Godwin kissed the top of his wife's head, and they fell silent for a moment. "What about the other issues?"

"The Kena women? I think the princess tried telling me that she suspected more than one had come to our shores. She told me that Rhiannon, the woman defeated by Claire on her wedding day, was the most powerful of their kind."

"Except for our Lady Claire," he reminded.

"It seemed as if the princess had been trying to reassure me that the attack on House Cathmara was a unique situation, one that could not happen again. But then there was the strange disappearance of her maid from Ragallach, a girl named Daisy. And most recently, she wrote about how her new maid, a young noblewoman named Lucilla, was poisoned. She believed the poison to have been of Fenrhi origin."

"Have you and Kathryn made any progress with your latest translations?"

"A little. I've told you about how Ladies Anna and Claire were foretold of by the shared prophesy on the dagger that has been passed down through the women in their line. We know that 'With night, do stars find strength' refers to Anna, but too much was lost regarding what we believe was written for Claire. Kathryn translated something about a dance and the number six—if you recall, Claire was marked for the six Fenrhi castes. And the word dance may not be accurate. Anwyl showed Kathryn different ways to read the old runes, so the symbol could also mean organization or even leader."

"Leader?"

"Yes. And there was something that Warin once told me about when he first visited the Southron Isles. How the people there pray to a female deity. He saw an altar with a multi-armed goddess, carved from wood and gilded with gold and enamel and encrusted with jewels. There were symbols.”

“Let me guess. Six?”

“Of course.”

“I don’t suppose Warin drew the symbols?”

“At the time, I didn’t think to ask. It only ever came up one other time. He mentioned that some of the symbols on the Stolweg henge looked similar.”

“And Claire remarked that those same symbols were carved in places around the Fenrhi temple, didn’t she?” Godwin asked.

Juliana shook her head. “No, not in the Fenrhi Temple, but in the ruins of the Fyrost Desert. When last Kathryn visited Lark and Anna, she brought up the old dagger, the one that Claire now holds. And she revealed to Anna what she and I imagined the words to mean. But Anna had a different, fresh view. *With night do stars find strength.* We always thought that her ‘night’ referred to those tortuous years spent being married to Lord Roger. But she posited that her ‘night’ is Lark. He holds my grandfather’s dagger after all—the one set with onyx, and her own armor inlaid with silver stars.”

“And Claire and Trian?”

“Before she left, Anwyl mentioned studying Claire’s dagger. In addition to the two other symbols, there is a third, partial rune. It’s similar to the old Fenrhi symbol for the queen bee, also the royal symbol of Nifolhad.”

“Trian, according to his father, dreamt of a queen honeybee when he and Claire were separated. A tenuous connection, but the old wolf insisted that there was some fantastical quality to Trian’s dreams. What do you and Kathryn think? Will there be six women, all matched with six men?”

Juliana nodded.

“Three realms linked by six runes. And six Fenrhi castes.”

“It’s possible. Kathryn’s latest research found a reference to another prophesy, this one of Nifolhadian origin. One about a man whose loyalty crosses borders and seas.”

“Warin,” he guessed, and his wife nodded. “Then why do you look so worried?”

“Because this man is fated to die unless another life is sacrificed.” She pulled a letter from her robe. “Ranulf wrote to me separately. The Fenrhi Mother foretold that Anwyl would lose her heart to a stranger from foreign lands, one with hair as dark as her own, but with blue eyes. Later, she insinuated that the princess was marked for something greater, but that she would have to risk everything, even her life."

"Have you written to the princess yet? To Warin? We must warn them to be careful."

"The messenger rode out an hour ago. I only pray that he is not too late."

CHAPTER TWENTY-NINE

Homecoming

Castle Pheldhain

"We'll have to tell my parents," Warin said, staring at the twin bandages wrapped around their palms. After he helped her into her gown, Anwyl turned in his arms and smoothed her uncut hand over his broad and deliciously naked chest, stopping for a moment at the spot above his heart that always seemed to draw her touch.

"Are you worried about my reputation?" she murmured, trailing fingers down his sides and lower, then grasped him gently and caressed him until his arousal grew and pressed into her palm. She flashed her eyes up at him in surprise. "You are...I read that some men could..." She ran her fingernail down to the base of his shaft and back up, and he sucked in a breath through his teeth. She smiled at him and arched an eyebrow in invitation.

"But we've just gotten you back into your gown," he teased, and she pouted. "You know we'll be late if we do," he warned but was already maneuvering them to the sturdy table that was set before the broad window overlooking the sea. "It's too bad there's not enough time to get you naked again."

He pulled up the hem of her gown, letting the silk slither up her legs, then placing the loose folds in her hands. "Careful, you don't want to crease the fabric," he warned when he saw her gripping the cloth. Then, he knelt before her and set his wicked lips to her navel. A spike of pleasure shot from her core straight down to where she was already swollen from their earlier play, and Anwyl gasped. He murmured something, but before she could ask him what he meant, he lifted her so that she balanced on the very edge of the table. He spread her knees wide, looked up at her with a devilish grin, then took her in his mouth. Anwyl's hands fluttered at the onslaught of his lips and tongue, and she let go of the silk, the folds puddling in her lap, impeding his exploration. With deliberate slowness, he bunched up her gown into loose pleats, and placed the fabric back into her care before pressing his face to her center once more.

"Warin!" She didn't know if she called out his name because she was no longer capable of balancing on the table's edge or because she was pleading to him for more. She didn't care. When his hands cupped her under her buttocks to support her, she threw back her head and focused on the exquisite feel of his lips and tongue. Her panting grew rapid and even more vocal, and he eased back, teasing her with barely perceptible flicks, until she calmed enough so that he could devour her again. Over and over, he brought her to the pinnacle, only to let her back down. And when she could not take any more, for she had taken to a strange sort of soft keening, he rose up before her, letting her slip from the sturdy table.

He kissed her then, holding her close to his body, her skirts forgotten as gravity drew them to the floor, creating a silken barrier to what she wanted most. What she needed most. And as his hand slid down between her legs and touched her through the silk, and she thought, finally, he will let me go, she discovered that it was not nearly enough. She rolled her hips forward, grinding against his arousal, marveling at his strength and patience. "Having had you twice already allows me the control I require to push you further than before," he growled in her ear, his fingers walking the silk of her skirts up her thighs.

She tried to lift a knee to hook her thigh around his hip, but Warin shook his head. "Not like that, my princess." He spun her around so that she was facing the window and pressed her against the hard, unsatisfying edge of the table.

"Lean forward and place your hands on the wood." She obeyed him and felt the silky slide of her skirt on her legs as he drew it up, gathering it and pushing it over her buttocks so that her posterior was bared to him. He pressed the cloth into her hands again—she would have to hold her garment if she wanted him to take her. She turned her head to the side, and saw him admiring her behind, then felt his hand run down her lower back, lingering and tracing ticklish swirls on her backside. His long fingers dipped between the two globes, lightly, teasing her with a sensation she had not thought possible.

"Too bad we don't have more time." He took her by the hips, held her steady, and she felt him, his arousal, thick and hard, nudging against her. She cried for more, and he gave her what she coveted, thrusting and withdrawing again and again, driving her to a new brink.

She tried to twist to see him, wanting the image fixed in her mind: she, bent over the table taking him into her body; he, plunging and thrusting, the muscles of his thighs and buttocks clenching. The very image had her near to toppling over the edge. But she wanted to take him with her or be taken with him. That's when she noticed them, one terrace down, a group of three walking by. "Warin!" she whispered in alarm, and he leaned over her to peer out into the dusk. She turned her head, and he kissed her and smiled, never once slowing the pumping of his hips.

"Shh," he whispered, nibbling her earlobe and swirling his tongue in and around her ear, his eyes fixed on the group as they paused to take in the view of the sparkling sea. "They can't see us here in the shadows, but they'll certainly hear you if you keep crying out my name." And as if to incite her to that very restriction, he reached under her and between her legs and caressed her, circling gently, then plucking at her nub.

"Not fair," she hissed, then was unable to stop herself from crying out as her climax crashed through her body. And Warin, after straightening behind her and grasping her hips again, rocked into her with slamming thrusts until he, too, joined her. If the guests below heard him shout, she didn't care. She was finally sated, riding out the waves of her coming as Warin held himself sealed deep within her. He fell forward, breathing as harshly as she, one forearm taking his weight, his other arm and hand still cupping her, tracing lazy circles and drawing out her orgasm until she was completely spent.

"I suppose I'll need to change my gown," she finally managed, as he drew her up, allowing the now wrinkled and creased fabric to fall to the floor.

"Only if you don't want the others to know why we're late," he said with a chuckle. "Lift your arms, I'll help you."

"At least with this style, I don't have to worry about stays."

"I wouldn't be so quick to dismiss all of those restricting clothes if I were you. One can be quite inventive when dealing with laces and ties." She widened her eyes, trying and succeeding to imagine what his talented hands could do to her when she was trussed up in shifts and corsets and laces. He waggled his eyebrows and gave her a lascivious grin as he pulled on his breeches and she selected another garment.

"I love you, my princess," he declared. "And I'm the most fortunate man in the world that you love me back."

"I feel the same…"

"But?" When she didn't continue, he lifted her chin with his finger and waited.

"There's a saying in Sophiana," she started. "Adding fuel to an already robust fire invites ill flame."

"I see. We shouldn't risk our good luck by wallowing in it. All right then, I am the most ill-fated man in the world, for I must sit through a celebration in honor of our engagement instead of bedding my new wife in as many ways as I can imagine."

Anwyl laughed. "You are incorrigible, Warin. Promise me that you'll never, ever change."

"I promise," he said and took her arm. "Now, let's get to the banquet hall before my family sends everyone out to search for us."

"Everyone? I thought tonight was just close family."

"Yes, well, it is by Pheldhainian standards."

Later that evening, Anwyl learned what it meant to have a small family dinner in Pheldhain. There were at least three dozen family members: men, women, and children of all ages—even a newborn babe. She must have looked a little lost, for Lord Marin came to her rescue and escorted her to a seat between Warin and Lady Téana.

"I bet my wife said this would be a small family gathering, didn't she? You should know that anything involving family in Pheldhain is never a small affair. Believe it or not, we are a third our normal size." He patted her hand reassuringly as she looked around. "It's our custom to dine with the entire family, children"—a little boy ran past them chasing a dog that had absconded with his toy—"and pets included."

"Warin tried to warn me," Anwyl said, smiling at the ensuing tug-o-war.

"Do you have large family events in Sophiana?" Lady Téana asked brightly.

"No, not really. It was always Rani and me. And Lord Etain. Our cousin Radha was there for a while, but then she went to the Fenrhi temple. We lost our parents when we were young."

"Oh, you poor dear," Warin's mother consoled.

"My brother and I had each other; it was always enough." Anwyl gazed longingly at the closeness of this group. She could immediately identify the people who had married into the family, for Warin's relatives all had similar features. Dark hair; smooth, olive-toned complexions; many faces dotted with eyes in varying shades of blue. There was japing, smiling, and even bickering, but it was as plain as day that these people loved and supported one another.

"This must seem rather informal for you," Lady Téana said, having heard her wistful sigh. A hush fell upon the room, and all eyes turned toward her. Even the dog seemed to be cocking his head as if waiting for her reply.

"I think it's rather wonderful." And just like that, everything in the room reverted to its former organized chaos. Warin's mother patted her hand and beamed at her. She met family member after family member as they came to offer well-wishes to the engaged couple. And after the last dish was taken away, Warin stood, holding up his glass in one hand and drawing Anwyl from her seat with the other.

Conversation ceased as he cleared his throat to speak. He smiled at her, and she nodded. "The princess and I wish to—"

The doors to the banquet hall crashed open, and Grieg and his first mate entered, a skeleton of a bruised and broken man hung between them, his toes scraping the floor as they dragged him into the room.

"Marten!" Lady Téana cried, knocking over her chair as she ran to help her eldest son. Lord Marin was right behind her.

"Go!" Anwyl urged Warin. "I'll see to it that his room is readied." He nodded, then ran to join his parents. "Murel," Anwyl called before Warin's cousin had a chance to join them. "I need your help. Show me to Marten's room. We must have bandages and any herbs or salves that have been stored in the palace."

"Follow me," she said, and they sprinted from the hall, sending servants running with orders for hot water and blankets and anything else they might need. By the time Warin's parents had Marten settled onto a pallet and transported to his chamber, Murel and Anwyl had fresh linens covering his bed, hot water steaming in the hearth, and a string of servants entering and leaving with every imaginable medicament.

Lady Téana was shaking as Warin, Grieg, and Lord Marin carefully laid Marten on the bed. Murel looked horror-struck at what had been done to her cousin but turned to Anwyl for guidance. "Something strong to drink for Lady Téana," Anwyl said. She caught Warin's eye, and he nodded.

Anwyl was swift in her examination of Marten. He was breathing but unconscious. Her fingers detected no cracked skull, but his shoulder was dislocated and, by the puce-colored bruising, had been out of its socket for some time. Two fingers of one hand appeared to have been flayed, another— dare she think it—bitten off.

Lady Téana, having recovered herself, drew closer. "Can you help him, Princess?"

"I'll try," she answered, unsure if even her skill would be enough.

Lord Marin came to stand beside her. "If this is too much for you to bear, I can—"

"This is not the first time I've helped a victim of torture. I'll not waver."

Warin's father nodded.

"Strip him, please. I need to assess his injuries if I am to know where to begin." Warin blinked, then nodded to Grieg. As gently as they could, they cut away Marten's clothes. His body was a patchwork of burns and cuts and lash marks.

"Heavens preserve us...he was bitten," Lady Téana choked, and her husband drew her away.

"I need to check his back," she said, and Warin helped her to roll Marten partially to his side. As she suspected, the damage to his person was negligible there.

"They must have tied him down," Murel said.

"No," Anwyl said flatly. "His torturer didn't bother with his back; you can't gauge a man's agony if you can't see his face."

"Then you know who did this?" Lord Marin demanded.

"Yes, I've seen his work before." She surveyed the damage. "It's a blessing that Marten is unconscious. Resetting his shoulder will take all of us; it's been locked out of place for some time. I can pop his fingers back into place on my own, but his other hand..."

"What's left of the damage will have to be removed," Warin finished for her, and she nodded. "Tell us what to do." And she did, starting with the dislocation. When she paused above Marten's fingers—three were wrecked completely, his thumb and little finger strangely spared—Lord Marin took the knife from her.

"I'll do it," he said calmly, and they went to work. Murel opened the shutters when the smell of cauterized flesh grew too powerful. Then they bathed him, cleaning and debriding each and every wound.

Anwyl applied herbs, honey, salve, and bandages, and they rolled Marten to his side to change the soiled linens from their toil. She showed Murel how to remake the bed, then had Grieg stoke the fire in the hearth to a roaring blaze. "Cover him only with a sheet," she instructed. "And keep the shutters open for fresh air. We'll have to check his hand every few hours. If even the tiniest amount of rot occurs..." She didn't need to tell Lord Marin that his son would lose his arm next. That, or his life.

"Take her to her room, Warin," he ordered. "See to it that she is bathed and rested." And Anwyl would have smiled that he was issuing orders to her, but she was too exhausted. It had to be very late, she realized, and looked out the window, surprised that the dawn had already come.

"I'll be back soon," she told him. "He won't wake, at least not today. But if he comes to, try drizzling some honeyed water between his lips." She was still giving Lord Marin instructions when Warin scooped her into his arms and carried her from the room.

Lucilla was waiting, a hot bath already drawn for Anwyl, and Warin bade her leave. She curtsied and departed without a word, closing the door behind her. Then, he set Anwyl on a chair and proceeded to remove her gown. It was ruined, of course, covered in blood and gore. When she was naked, Warin lifted her and then lowered her into the steaming bathwater. She sank below the surface, bubbles trickling up from her lips and nostrils. When she resurfaced, Warin scrubbed her from tip to toes. He towel-dried her hair, pulled a sleeping rail over her head, and tucked her into bed. She watched as he stripped out of his own clothes, washed himself, and climbed in after her. He snuggled up behind her, spooning her until she fell into a deep sleep.

Anwyl woke several hours later. Alone. But he had left a note. She ran her fingertip over the elegant script, the writing she had grown to love and anticipate, marveling still that Warin and *A.S.* were one and the same.

My Sweet Princess,

I have gone to my father's study where we will meet with Grieg and hear all he has to relate of the many months that he has been searching for Marten. You did so much for my brother last night; please stay in bed to rest. I will return as soon as I am able.

Your Love

Anwyl held the note to her chest, then stretched. She could rest later. She dressed, pulled her hair into a braid, then left her room with the special satchel that had been gifted to her by the Sylvan. She met Lucilla in the corridor.

"I knew you would be awake, my princess, so I brought you something to eat," she said, handing her a pastry still warm from the kitchen. "Lord Warin showed me where to find his brother's quarters so that I could direct you there. He also said that most of the herbs you requested have been delivered."

Anwyl nodded, following the girl through the maze of palace corridors, terraces, and gardens. When they reached Marten's room, she paused. "Lucilla, I've been meaning to ask you...would you like to learn something of the healing arts? I could train you on some of what I know, and I could use your help."

"Oh, yes, Princess. I would like to be useful."

Anwyl lowered her voice. "Warin's brother is...he's not a sight for the faint-hearted, Lucilla. If you think that you won't be able to—"

"Pardon me for interrupting, Princess," she said shyly. "But I helped my brother whenever he was hurt by Harsk. I'm not weak-stomached."

Anwyl smiled softly at her young charge. "Of course you aren't. But what was done to Marten goes beyond anything you can imagine. His mother is probably in there, and I want to make sure you are prepared. I don't want her more upset than she already is."

Lucilla nodded solemnly.

Anwyl tapped gently on the door, then entered. They had followed her instructions perfectly. The room had been kept warm, even allowing for the open shutters. Lady Téana sat in a chair next to the bed. She was staring at her son. Upon realizing that they were no longer alone, she blinked several times and focused on Anwyl. "Princess," she started, then rose from her vigil. "You must be exhausted. Let me get you some tea."

"Nay, Lady," Anwyl said in a soothing voice. "Please don't get up. Lucilla," she added, "will you see to tea for all of us?" The young woman nodded and went to the hearth.

"He hasn't woken. Not once."

"It's much too soon. Besides, it's better that he wasn't conscious last night." Anwyl lifted his eyelids, studying his irises and pupils, looking for a reaction that would tell her that he had not lost all function. She opened her satchel, pulled out a round piece of polished silver and angled it to catch the light streaming in from the window and redirecting it to the eye she held open. Marten's pupil immediately contracted. She repeated the process with his other eye; there was no reaction. Then she held the mirrored surface below his nostrils. A faint, but steady steaming on the silver told her that his breathing had evened.

"What does it mean, Princess?" Lucilla asked softly, handing Lady Téana a cup of warm tea.

"Well, if his pupil changes in size when hit with light, it's a good sign that his head is sound." She put her hand on Lady Téana's arm. "His other eye might be too swollen right now to react, or it might be too damaged. His breathing is improved. You raised a strong man, Lady Téana."

"Please, Anwyl, I think you can call me mother. If you would like to, that is." She stared at the bandage wrapped around Anwyl's hand.

"We were going to tell you about our handfasting last night," Anwyl said, plucking at the gauze that covered the cut across her palm. "But..."

Lady Téana drew Anwyl into her arms and hugged her. "Thank you. I think that you have managed to save both of my sons."

Anwyl swallowed and nodded. She gazed at the array of items on the table. "I have Lucilla to help me. Why don't you get some rest while I check his wounds and dressings? I'll send Lucilla immediately if there is any change."

Lady Téana nodded, but before she left, Anwyl called to her. "Does Marten have a favorite flower? I know it is a strange question, but sometimes a scent can make a person feel safe. If he—"

"Eucalyptus," she replied. "He always loved the smell of eucalyptus leaves. I'll have some brought here immediately"— She paused before closing the door, looking uncertain.

"I promise you that I won't leave him."

Lady Téana nodded and then was gone.

"Lucilla," Anwyl said, "let's get started."

She showed the girl how to prepare everything that they would need before beginning their labors. It turned out that Lucilla had a strong stomach and deft hands. She only gasped once, and that was when she saw the bite marks on Marten's torso. "How could a person do that?" Without waiting for an answer, she changed the dressing. The worst wounds, the amputated fingers, Anwyl tended to herself. Marten was a lucky man: there was no odor to indicate infection, nor reddening beyond what was already injured.

His dislocated shoulder, too, had stayed in place, but they would have to monitor him closely. Any thrashing about as he healed might cause a recurrence. She explained all of this to Lucilla, then showed her how to bundle certain herbs to burn as incense.

"Sage, lavender, and sweet grass," Lucilla pointed out. "But what were the crystals that you placed down the center?"

"Dried sap from the pijala tree. The Sylvan believe that sage helps to cleanse the spirit, lavender brings peace, and the sweet grass replaces the negative with positive thoughts. But the pijala resin clears the mind and expands its ability to heal. Now that you know how, make at least a dozen bundles." Anwyl set her tightly bound herbs in a ceramic bowl and lit the end with a piece of kindling from the hearth. She ground out the flame but made sure the herbs were left to slowly smolder, giving off a pleasant, clean-smelling smoke. She placed it on the table next to where Marten lay supine.

Lucilla was already working on a third bundle. The girl was a natural, using the exact portions of herbs and wrapping them expertly so that the crystals would be heated and burn one at a time as the dried plants smoldered. Anwyl next drew out a small crystal vial. The door to the chamber opened, and Warin and his father entered. "Extract of pihaberry," she explained to Lucilla as they looked on in interest. "Very concentrated."

She placed a single drop into a cup of fresh water, stirred it with a glass rod, then used it to place a few drops between Marten's lips. She set the rest next to the incense.

"I remember my grandmother burning cedar chips when I was young and ill," Lord Marin said. "Your incense reminds me of those days."

"Cedar is very purifying," Anwyl agreed softly, then took the cloth sack Warin held out to her. She could smell the eucalyptus through the fabric, and she handed it to Lucilla. "Put a few of these in water, Lucilla, near the window; the breeze will diffuse it."

"How are you?" Warin asked, coming up behind her and wrapping his arms around her in a protective circle.

"Me?"

"Yes, you."

"I'm all right. Lucilla has been a great help. How is your mother?"

"Resting. But she won't be able to stay away for long."

Lord Marin had taken a seat next to the bed, setting his hand gently on Marten's forearm. Anwyl sat next to him, then explained everything she was doing and how she hoped it would help his son. And when Lord Marin asked her about her experience with other people who had been tortured as Marten had, she begged off answering, saying that it was important that all negative thoughts be purged from the room whilst Marten's life hung in the balance. He nodded, seeming to understand. When a tired Lady Téana returned, Anwyl asked Lucilla to show her how to use the herb bundles and administer the tincture of pihaberries and water. Warin's father had questions that needed answers, and she followed him and Warin to his study.

"His name is Rowly," Anwyl started before he could ask. "Or that is what the very few who have survived his torture were able to tell us. And when I say very few, I mean exactly three people, two of them Fenrhi women. Their survival was deliberate, as was Marten's, and serves to give us a message."

"Why would a torturer from Nifolhad need to send us a message?" Lord Marin demanded, shouting, though Anwyl knew it was not at her.

"The message is not from Rowly but from his master," Anwyl revealed, not wanting to believe it. "Rowly serves Prince Bowen." Warin sat down next to her and took her hand. "We have to assume that he knows that it was your ship that carried me to the safety of Aurelia. He's a vengeful man, much like his father, only more dedicated to hurting others. And he has reason to especially hate me."

"You?" Lord Marin stated. "What makes you think that?"

"When Anwyl was young, she and Bowen were promised to one another," Warin answered for her.

"He wants revenge against us because you broke your engagement with him?" Lord Marin asked. "But that had to have been years ago."

"It wasn't the only thing I broke," she explained. "I also broke his nose. And with it, his pride."

CHAPTER THIRTY

Secrets

Warin was amazed at how quickly his brother was recovering. With Anwyl or Lucilla constantly at his side, he was awake and lucid within a week of his return. His body was growing stronger, what with steady food and water, not to mention the various tonics that Anwyl prescribed, and it was only another week before he was shuffling around the grounds of the castle.

Warin pulled his eyes away from the horizon and looked over to where his brother was standing next to Anwyl at the prow of *Lita's Pearl*. Entire months had disappeared from his memory, but that which he could recall was that an illness had swept through the crew, followed by a fire. From there, his recollections gave out. He couldn't remember if he'd abandoned his ship or if it had sunk, and he couldn't recall anything about his crew. At first, the memories of his torture were lost, until he'd insisted on seeing the damage. When the eyes fell upon the bite marks, he spoke not a single word for three days. He admitted, finally, that he remembered a man and a woman. The name Rowly meant nothing to him. When pressed, Marten could only remember the pain—trying to bring back the images caused his body to break into violent tremors. Warin's entire family owed Anwyl for Marten's life. He doubted his brother would have survived without her Sylvan-learned care.

Warin stared at the waves. Hundreds of miles away in Sophiana, another victim of torture was being tended to by other Sylvan women. A man who very well might be his cousin, Jesper. And Anwyl had been engaged to the man responsible. Warin shuddered, imagining his bride in Bowen's clutches.

Grieg came to stand next to him at the wheel. They would make Barb Island in the next hour. "You've been too long from your ship, Warin. She's missed you." Grieg nodded toward Anwyl. "I suspect that you've been occupied elsewhere of late. It's good to see that you've finally opened your eyes to the princess's many charms. But I need to tell you something. I need to..." Grieg trailed off.

"This is a first," Warin stated, and laughed. "Captain Grieg, at a loss for words." Only Grieg did not appear amused. "What's troubling you?"

"I don't want either of you to be hurt," he said. "There's something you need to know. Something I should have told you years ago—Marlita urged me to do so—but there never seemed to be a good time. And you were always content to woo your ladies at court. But now...I fear I am too late."

"Damn, Grieg. What is it? Am I cursed or something?" His mentor and friend stared hopelessly at him. "Grieg?"

"Marlita has certain gifts. In you, she saw an early death. She...well, she intervened on your behalf."

"Intervened? With whom? That six-armed goddess I saw painted on her wall?" Grieg looked surprised. "She had an altar in her home; I saw her praying to it. A fearsome-looking creature, that goddess of yours. Tell me, what does a Southron Island deity have to do with me?"

"You made an impression on Marlita, Warin. She read you...in a similar way that Lady Claire can. Except, for Marlita, the Goddess"—Grieg lowered his voice to a whisper whenever he said *goddess*—"gifted her with the ability to see a person's final days. And knowing your life would be shorter than most, she asked that the Goddess fill it with adventure, and, well, pleasure. And you've had that, your entire life. It's why you have such wanderlust; why you could never settle down."

"She placed her hands on me. Here and here," Warin said, touching his face and chest. "It was like she wasn't there; I couldn't make out her words. Grieg, I never wanted adventure. You know me better than anyone; you should have stopped her. Hell, I don't think I even believe what you are saying." His denial rang false to his ears.

"It was done before she consulted with me. The women of the Southron Isles... Look, for every gift the Goddess gives, there is a price. And Marlita paid a great one so that you could have some happiness in your life."

Warin stared at the princess. "How long did Marlita's goddess give me?"

His rancor drew a sharp look from his friend. "It doesn't work that way. Marlita thought she was helping you. You might not be here today if not for her interventions."

"Interventions? Exactly what else did she do for me?" Warin realized he had raised his voice and looked over at Anwyl. He waved to her and smiled, and she turned back to her discussion with Marten.

"She made a bargain with our fanm—our queen. To extend your years. As long as you don't marry for love, you are safe." Warin squeezed his left hand into a fist and stared at Anwyl's back. She sensed his regard and gave him a tentative wave. Her left palm, like his, was no longer wrapped in a bandage.

"And what happens if I marry for love?" Warin asked, giving his princess a reassuring smile when she frowned at him. Grieg remained silent. Warin handed the wheel to him, no longer interested in seeing his ship into port by his own hand. "Grieg?"

"I'm sorry, Warin. Fanm Larenne punished Marlita for her meddling in your fate. But I love you like a son, and I took up your cause and asked that your life be spared. I begged the fanm to petition the Goddess."

"And how did your goddess reply?"

"The Goddess granted my request."

"At what cost?"

Grieg stared at Anwyl. "A life for a life."

"Damn it, Grieg!"

"Princess Anwyl is safe, Warin. As long as you don't marry, no harm will come to her."

Warin's palm burned. He flexed his fingers at the imaginary pain. Only a thin, red line remained as proof of their handfasting. "Don't worry, Grieg. I don't believe in your goddess's curse. And don't say anything to the princess. I'll tell her later when we're alone. For now, I don't want anything to ruin the surprise that awaits her." He left Grieg at the wheel and went to stand next to his bride, laying his hand over hers where it rested on the rail.

• • •

Warin had promised her a wedding gift, and when he mentioned a trip to Barb Island, she was never so happy. It had been her idea to bring Marten along, hoping the trip on *Lita's Pearl*, a ship very much like his lost *Sea Hare*, would somehow shake loose something in his memory. His inability to recall that which transpired was unnatural, and Anwyl had used every herb in her arsenal to try to help him, all to no avail. She had already written to her brother and Aghna that Prince Bowen was somehow involved in the raids along the

Aurelian coast. The day after she sent the messenger with the same information to King Godwin and Queen Juliana, she received a royal post with a letter from her cousin Radha, stating that the man they held as prisoner in Sophiana was not Prince Bowen. Queen Juliana had written separately, urging her and Warin's family to take every conceivable measure to remain safe. Barb Island's fortress was well-fortified and manned with some of the best soldiers in the realm.

The trip to the island took a mere two hours. Out of habit, Anwyl took Marten's measure, noticing he looked a little paler than the day before. He had been looking forward to the jaunt and promised to not overexert himself. "Are you sure you are up to this, Marten?" she asked.

"Warin told me about what he has in store for you. I would not miss your reaction for all the pearls in Pheldhain."

They mounted their horses, and Warin led the way; an escort of five soldiers followed the trio at a discreet distance. Soon, they were out of the island's port town and climbing the steep but fertile hills of Barb Island. When they made the first rise, Warin pointed southwest. "That's where we will be staying this evening."

The fortress seemed to grow out of the lush forest surrounding it; its stone was the same mica-infused granite of the palace. That's where the similarities ended—no airy terraces or filigreed spires and domes here. This fortress had been built with only defense against invaders in mind.

Warin clucked his tongue, and his horse started down a path that led in the general direction of the fortress. As they rode up another rise, he pointed out the various trees and plants growing on the island. The sound of tinkling bells drifted in and out over the shuffle of hooves on the loamy path and the calling of birds in the trees.

"Are we on Acerto Island?" Marten quipped, and Anwyl giggled. "Seriously, Warin, since when did we start raising goats in Pheldhain?"

He grinned. "The nannies were a gift from Ronan," Warin explained to Anwyl. "That, and a very interesting book from his library."

Her ears perked up at that. "Which book? I never really had a chance to peruse his titles."

"You did pick up at least one—*On the Efficacy of Animal Manure*."

Marten burst out laughing. "What a romantic surprise!"

Anwyl remembered the book, and how she'd shielded herself from Warin with it. "You were lucky I didn't throw it at you," she teased, then gave Marten the abbreviated version of his younger brother's attempt to teach her a lesson.

"It sounds, brother, as if you were the one who was schooled that night."

"Indeed," Warin allowed and grinned. He pulled up his horse just before they cleared the rise. The tinkling of bells and the bleating of goats drifted over from the other side. "Did you know, dear princess, that even though goats, deer, and sheep have multi-chambered stomachs, goats process what they eat much faster? When they eat certain seeds, those seeds are not digested as they are with sheep. They are expelled from a goat's body, looking exactly the same as when they were ingested, save for a slight thinning of the outer shell. And these undigested seeds—"

"That's really disgusting, Warin," Marten said.

But Anwyl was watching Warin closely, grasping what he was telling her. "Goats! Of course!" She kicked her horse into a canter and made the rise ahead of the two brothers. Spread on the slope below was a high-fenced paddock. Perhaps a half dozen nanny goats, their ram, and their kids wandered around the perimeter of the enclosure. A goatherd sat nearby with his dog, tending to the small herd.

Warin dismounted, then helped her down. "Go ahead, my princess." She lifted up on her toes to kiss him in full view of all and sundry, then ran to the enclosure. She heard his astonished laughter as she pulled open the gate and stared in wonder. Four tiny pijala trees, no higher than her knees, were happily growing in the mowed space.

"Goats!" she exclaimed again when Warin and Marten reached her. Warin nodded, but Marten looked puzzled. "Goats, Marten. Or rather, goat excrement. Oh, Warin, you're a genius!"

"I took a chance," he said. "The goats on Acerto Island...you mentioning the goats intermingling with the sheep in Ragallach were similar to those in Sophiana. And then the book. You shoved it at me, and then I threw it across the room."

Anwyl gasped. "You surely didn't."

"I promised Ronan that I would repair it myself and send it back." He regarded his brother. "You would be amazed at the many qualities and uses of animal waste. Just wait until I talk to mother about pullet—"

"Stop already," Marten surrendered.

Anwyl laughed and knelt next to the closest sapling. Warin got down next to her. "Thank you, my love," she told him. "I could not have asked for a better wedding gift." A strange look flashed through his eyes, and when he leaned in to kiss her, she pulled back. "Oh, no you don't. What was that? What's wrong?"

Behind them, one of the guards shouted a warning. She turned to see Marten, on all fours, his body wracked with violent coughing. She and Warin raced to his side, and though Marten tried to hide it from them, they saw blood-specked spittle on his hand as another shudder coursed through him. One of the soldiers had the forethought to grab his waterskin. Anwyl poured some onto a kerchief, dabbing at Marten's lips as he struggled to breathe.

"I'm all right now," he managed to wheeze. "It may be that I'm allergic to goats."

"Right. How long has this been happening?" She handed him the water as he sat back and leaned against the fence, then studied his coloring. The red blotching on his face from coughing so hard had given way to a bluish pallor. But as his breathing settled, his color returned to normal.

"The attacks started when I was in the hut on that islet," he said, then looked sharply at Warin. "I remembered something!"

"Don't worry about that right now," Anwyl ordered, but gently. "Let's get you to the fortress, and then we'll talk about this islet."

Warin held out the water to him again, and Marten took a sip and leaned into his younger brother. "The fits always pass after a few minutes. Do you mind fetching the horses, Princess?"

Anwyl touched the back of her hand to his forehead, then rested her fingers on his neck to evaluate his pulse. It was steady again. "Promise to tell me if you feel another fit coming on."

Marten nodded.

"I'll be right back."

• • •

"Are you going to tell me what's wrong?" Marten demanded, and Warin pretended ignorance. "We've had our history, little brother, but I know when something is bothering you. Confess."

"Marlita," he said, and before Marten could ask what a woman Warin had been with over a decade past could have to do with him now, Warin told him about her circumventing of some fateful sentence placed upon his head by a goddess he knew nothing about. He looked up to see if Anwyl was on her way back, but she was talking to one of the soldiers. She glanced his way and nodded to him, then turned her attention back to the soldier. She was describing something to him with her hands, pointing back along the trail.

"I'm so damn lucky to have found her, Marten," he said. "And now Grieg says it may come down to either my life or hers? Where's the justice in that?"

"Since when did you start believing the predictions of some unknown goddess?" Marten asked, chuckling. "Of any god or goddess, for that matter? Look, Grieg and Marlita, they could be wrong. We really don't know anything about the Southron Islers."

"I know Grieg, and he's worried. Both for me and the princess. In all the years we've known him, he's never once told us an untruth." Marten nodded at this. "And the things I've seen in the last few years. The Kena women who can control a person's thoughts and actions. The Sylvan can create poisons that kill a person by slowly eating away at them—it can take years—or another type that takes a person's life in seconds. Truthseers, pihaberries, the return of the fabled rímara falcons in Cathmara, and Lady Anna of Stolweg, not to mention her sister Lady Claire and her gifts. You don't know, Marten. I've been studying history my entire life, and now we're living it, right smack in the middle of some great change. Nifolhad, Aurelia, the Southron Isles. Something is about to break, an event that will shake the foundations of the known realms."

Marten grabbed his arm. "If what you say is true, then shouldn't you speak to the king? In fact, I'll go with you!"

His brother's grasp on his arm was strong, considering how his fingers had been dislocated. There was a strange gleam in Marten's eyes, like a zealot. He patted his brother's hand, easing his death grip. "I think he knows," Warin soothed. "I've seen the books and scrolls that Queen Juliana has been working on—not the content, just the bindings and parchments—and they are old, dating back generations. Hell, some of the texts are runic." He and Marten glanced over to where Anwyl was still talking with the guards.

"So yes, Marten, I am worried about some foreign goddess forcing a fate upon me that I do not wish. And I'll tell you this—I will not allow Anwyl to sacrifice herself for me."

"Does she know?" his brother asked, starting to push himself up from the ground, making it to his feet with Warin's support.

"No. But she's smarter than any other person I know. It's only a matter of time before she figures it out. Grieg is putty in her hands. If she senses even the slightest misgiving, she'll have it out of him. If you were not so ill, she would be pouncing on me for answers. For now, she's probably chalking up my unease to being worried about you."

Anwyl brought their horses closer to the gate. "I sent one of the guards ahead to make sure your room is prepared," she explained.

Warin gave Marten a boost into his saddle, and his brother started toward the fortress, one of the soldiers riding by his side. He turned to Anwyl, but before he could kiss her, she stood on her toes and kissed him.

"Thank you for bringing me here. And for solving the mystery of growing pijala saplings. Goats! Wait until Rani hears." She placed her foot in his laced fingers, and he boosted her up before mounting his own horse.

. . .

When they reached the fortress, Warin saw to the horses, and Anwyl went in search of Marten's room. She rounded a corner and saw him talking to a maid. He was nodding to her, and before Anwyl could reach them, the woman continued on her way, walking in the opposite direction.

"Marten, is this your room?" Anwyl asked, for he looked a bit dazed. "Why didn't she help you to bed? You look pale."

He stared helplessly at her, but then allowed her to lead him to his room. A fire was burning in the hearth, and eucalyptus cuttings had been set on a worktable. This was a fortress, not a castle or palace, and the room was small and utilitarian. Still, the space smelled clean and fresh and had been swept and dusted, and someone had brought in a comfortable chair and footrest and set it near the hearth. Marten made for it, and once comfortable, Anwyl spread a throw over his lap. She stood in front of him, and he shifted his legs, giving her room to sit near his feet. It was time for Warin's brother to face the truth.

"I already know," he said. "I'm dying."

"Yes."

"I thought I would have more time with my brother," he said. "And my mother, she won't—"

"She's a strong woman, Marten. And you know that Warin and your father will help her. I will as well." He frowned, then stared into the flames. "I might be able to—" Her voice broke.

"You won't be able to save me, Princess. I think they poisoned us on the ship. It drove us mad. I don't know how I survived it...the woman helped me, I think, before Rowly. Whatever they gave us has been eating away at me."

Anwyl started to shake her head, to tell him that she had written to the Sylvan, that she would be able to help him, but they both knew her letter would take too long to reach Naca'an. If she had been able to tend to him when he was first dosed, she might've been able to save him. It had been almost a year already, and who knew what else he'd been given?

"It's all right. You gave me the greatest gift already—time. Time to be with my family, to talk with my mother and father, to see my brother happily in love."

Anwyl swallowed back her tears.

"How long do you think I have?" he asked her.

"A few months. Time enough to be with your parents. But it won't be an easy passing, Marten. I can give you herbs to take away the pain."

"Months...I thought it only days," he said. "I left them letters. Not for Warin, though. I believed that I would die here, on Barb Island, and that I could talk to him instead. In this room. I wanted to apologize for how I treated him when we were younger. For what I did, sending him with Grieg to the Southron Isles when..." he trailed off, and his head nodded back against the chair.

"Marten," Anwyl said softly, touching his hand. "Warin let me read his journal. I promise you, he holds no ill-will for what happened then."

"'s good," he whispered, then closed his eyes.

Anwyl stood, lifted his legs onto the footrest, and pulled the blanket up over his chest. She was stepping away when he opened his eyes. "Don't tell him," he begged. "I want to make it up to him; I still have time."

"I don't think he—"

"Just don't tell him. Swear it. Swear that you will let me do it."

"All right, I swear," she promised, not wanting him to get more worked up and trigger another attack. "Get some rest, Marten." He was asleep before she made it to the worktable to prepare the herbs and eucalyptus.

CHAPTER THIRTY-ONE

Catch of the Day

"**P**ardon me, Princess Anwyl," a soft voice called. The thick walls of the fortress let little light into the corridors. Oil lamps hung at intervals, providing scant illumination, and Anwyl could just make out that it was Senia, the shy daughter of one of the permanent soldiers serving on Barb Island.

"Good day, Senia," she said, smiling at the girl. Anwyl had been on her way to what served as the main hall to meet with Warin and his brother. As far as she knew, Marten had yet to speak to Warin about the gravity of his condition, and it broke her heart knowing how hard Warin would take the news.

Senia curtsied to her. "Lord Marten asked me to tell you that he was feeling more energetic this afternoon and that he and Lord Warin would meet you on the beach. I can take you to the steps, if you like."

She followed Senia out of the fortress, and when Anwyl saw the archway that led to the steep, secluded steps to the beach, she thanked the young girl for her help and then continued by herself.

The timeworn steps were rounded with age, but Anwyl walked confidently to where she guessed the brothers would be waiting. The fresh air on the beach would do a world of good for Marten's health. Unlike the beach below Pheldhain Castle, Barb Island's shore was only a tiny strip of sand surrounded on both sides by steep rock formations. To reach it, one had to brave the treacherous steps that had been carved out of the cliff wall—a wrong turn could send a person plummeting down to the rocks below. The trek was well worth the effort, for the dangerous path led to a secret grotto where it seemed the rest of the world ceased to exist. Perhaps Marten wanted a private spot in which to tell Warin about his condition.

The path was lovely, with the tree branches arching over the steps; strange, lanky bunches of moss hung in delicate clumps, shifting silently with the breeze and muting all other noise. She didn't remember the steps being this numerous and half-expected to come upon the sand with every turn of the path. Finally, the stairs ended, and she walked along the outcroppings of scrub palm growing from the tall boulders on her right. She saw Marten first and waved. He waved back, but hesitantly, and Anwyl slowed, not wanting to interrupt the moment when he told Warin the truth. But he smiled awkwardly and beckoned her forward. As she walked toward him, rounding the largest of the boulders, Warin's back came into view. Marten's face looked pained, and she wondered if the steep trek had been too much for him. There was a skiff farther down the beach, so perhaps they could row to a place where the return trip to the fortress would not be so taxing. Warin still hadn't turned to greet her, and suddenly, Anwyl felt the disharmony of what was before her.

Even though he stood upright, Warin's body was sagging, as if he was being propped up by something. Or someone. Marten started toward her, his face a mask of confusion and fear. There was a cosh in his hand, and Anwyl stumbled backward.

"Warin," she called anxiously. She could see blood on his collar. Marten took another step, and Anwyl retreated. Warin's body was pushed to the side, and she saw the woman—though she wore the garb of a Sylvan, Anwyl immediately knew she was Kena. She had to get help. For Warin and Marten.

"Get her. Now," the woman commanded.

"I don't want to hurt her, Vala," Marten begged. Anwyl turned and fled, racing to the boulders and the steps that would take her back to the fortress.

"Get her, or *he* will!" she yelled, and Marten gave chase. Anwyl rounded the boulders, glancing over her shoulder to see how far back he was. He was ill; surely, she could outrun him. She slammed into another body, falling back, and scrambling away like a crab. Behind her, Marten and the woman named Vala arrived.

A man with pig-like eyes and a wicked grin towered over her. She kicked out at him with her booted feet, striking his shins.

"She's feisty, this princess. Our prince will have his hands full, breaking her in."

Anwyl struck out again with her feet and connected with his kneecap.

He grunted in pain, then fell on top of her, pinning her with his mass. "Hold her arms, damn you," he shouted at Vala and Marten.

"Do as Odo says, Marten," Vala ordered, and Marten grasped one arm while she took the other. Anwyl bucked her body, trying to get free.

"That's nice, Princess," he said with a leer.

She immediately froze and then threw her head toward him, aiming her forehead at his nose. He anticipated her, pulling back far enough that his nose wasn't crushed. Still, he winced when her forehead connected. Then she gnashed her teeth, trying to take a bite out of him. But he was too quick.

"Enough!" He levered himself up, grabbed her legs, and flipped her over. Her arms, still held above her head by Marten and Vala, twisted painfully. But it was nothing compared to the agony of being hoisted to her feet by her neck and held suspended, her toes dangling uselessly above the sand. She kicked back, finally landing her heel between his legs. He roared in pain and flung her away, throwing her against one of the boulders. She had just enough time to cradle her head, or her skull would have cracked. Even so, she was rattled and slid down into the sand.

Odo came at her again, but Marten stepped in his path. "Get out of my way!" He ripped the cosh from Marten's hand and then shoved him aside.

Anwyl tried to crawl away, but it was too late. Pain cracked through her skull as Odo brought the weapon down against her temple. She felt the sand under her cheek, tasted the salty grit in her mouth, and knew that she had fallen. Sparkles of light winked in and out before her like tiny twinkling stars. But even with the throbbing pain in her head, her instincts screamed at her to move. She crawled, clawing her hands into the sand and pulling herself away.

A shadow fell over her, and she turned to see what was blocking the sun. Something swung toward her head, and Anwyl watched it, transfixed. Her body refused to obey her and move out of its path. When it connected with her skull, a bright light blinded her, and then everything in her world went dark.

• • •

She woke up, shivering, on a rough-hewn wood floor. The room seemed to lift up, then down, again and again, each time leaving her stomach and head behind. Everything was dark, and her only sense that seemed to be working was smell. Rotted wood, salt air, and the acrid odor of vomit assaulted her nose, making her retch. She fell back into unconsciousness.

Hours later, Anwyl blinked in the gray stillness of pre-dawn. She could just make out the outline of her room, and as it shifted, Anwyl realized that she was on a ship. A terrible pressure built in her gut, and she wondered if—Odo, she finally remembered—had kicked her there. Then she realized she had to relieve herself or she was going to wet her clothes. She stilled her breath as she listened for a sign that she was not alone. Nothing. She crawled on hands and knees away from where a dim sliver of light indicated a possible door, following the wall of the room.

There was a scraping sound behind her, and her bladder nearly released in her fear. But it was only the leg irons they'd put her in. She inched forward another foot, and her hand knocked into the far wall. There was nothing she could use except the corner. When she finished, she crawled back the way she had come, collapsing with exhaustion. Strange voices wove in and out of her dreams and nightmares.

The next time Anwyl opened her eyes, the room, though it had no windows and only one door, was diffused with a sullen gray light. On her back, she stared at a large, open grid that had been cut into the ceiling, and it took a moment for her to realize that it was an oiled tarp that had been suspended from the ceiling to cover a grill or hatch. She was in the hold of a ship. The tarp sagged in the center, weighted down by the puddle of water that had accumulated. It had rained.

When she rolled over to her hands and knees and pushed herself to a sitting position, she scanned the room. A bucket had been set next to her, with a dented metal cup hanging from its handle. She dragged it closer—water. And something else. Better to stick with the rainwater. Using the wall, she pulled herself to her feet. The room had a low ceiling, and she was able to tug the tarp and sluice a thin drizzle of rainwater into her mouth. Not knowing how long she would be on the ship, she only drank a little. It was time to investigate the space. She started with the area she'd used as a privy, and saw another, but much filthier, bucket. So she took a cup of water from the bucket that was next to her to dump in the privy pail. It was when she was hobbling back that she saw a large shape in the other corner. Her stomach sank.

"Warin," she whispered, getting down on her hands and knees and stretching out to reach him—she only made it halfway across the empty hold. "Warin," she said a little louder. "Warin, can you hear me? Please, my love. Tell me you're all right." She quieted and listened. Finally, she heard him breathe, steady and strong. There was a bucket next to him, and the cup was under his arm. Drugged, then. She went back to her side of the room, grabbed her cup with the intent of filling it with rainwater when he woke, but a noise outside the door had her dipping her cup in the bucket, taking just a bit, then lying on the floor and feigning sleep. Fresher air filled the space as the door was opened, and she heard the footsteps of several people enter.

"Looks like she finally woke up," a man's voice said quietly. "She drank some water, at least."

She sensed someone kneeling before her, and through her closed eyes, saw the light from a lantern being held near her face. "I think she's half-awake," a familiar voice spoke—Vala, from the beach.

Anwyl groaned and swatted ineffectually at the air as if she were in a stupor. She twisted around, facing the wall, and curled into a ball. Not knowing what talents this Kena woman had, she cleared her mind of thought and evened her breathing until she sounded as if she slumbered.

"Leave the bucket of water; there's enough for another day. And change the privy pails. They'll be fine on their own until tomorrow."

Anwyl heard the footsteps of someone crossing the space, first to the corner where Warin was asleep, then to where she had relieved herself.

"Post three guards on watch tonight, Juna. I don't want Odo getting in here again. He almost killed them both."

"I want him off my ship, Vala."

"Shh. Be careful. The prince has spies everywhere and..." Her voice trailed off at the end, and Anwyl heard the door being pulled shut and a lock being set. She rolled over and, lifting the chain attached to her leg to keep it from making too much noise, she stood. At the suspended tarp, she filled her cup with rainwater and drank. She filled it again, and then stretched out on her stomach as far as she could, trying to reach the place where Warin slept.

She heard a groan. "Warin!" she whispered. He rolled over, and she gasped. His face was a swollen mass of bruises and cuts. "Oh, Warin, what did they do to you?"

He didn't seem to hear her as he dragged the bucket closer, trying to dunk his cup. She had to stop him. "Warin! Don't drink that; it's been poisoned. I have water for you right here. Warin, you must listen to me."

He moaned something, and Anwyl stretched, pushing her cup as close to him as she could. "It's right here, my love. Just come a little closer." He at least stopped trying to drink the water in his bucket, pushing it aside before falling back asleep. It was another hour before he moved again, this time slightly more alert.

"Warin, it's Anwyl. You must come closer to me. I have water for you over here. Please."

"Anh'l," was all that he could manage, but he pulled himself up to crawl toward her.

"Yes, my love. I'm right here. Come, I have water." He reached for it and barely caught the lip before pulling the cup closer and drinking. He pushed it back toward her, then collapsed where he had crawled. "Just rest, my love. You'll feel better soon. I promise."

She lay down, extended her arm as far as she could to reach him, and prayed that he would wake long enough for her to tell him that he would have to feign sleep when the others returned. Then, she rested her head on her outstretched arm and felt the tears stinging her eyes. She was about to wipe them when she felt a touch. Warin had reached out his hand to her. He held her fingers, and when she squeezed his, she felt him tighten his grip. And though he fell back asleep, he did not let go.

Cargo

They were ready the next day when the door to the hold was unlocked, and they feigned a mixture of sleep and restlessness. It was Vala and the man from before. Anwyl cleared her mind, hoping Warin was able to do the same.

"Give them fresh water so they can rouse themselves enough to eat," Vala whispered.

When they departed, Anwyl and Warin discussed whether it was a trick. They decided they would continue pretending to be drugged, but only one of them would eat while the other would wait to make sure that Vala had not tampered with the food.

When alone, they sat as close to each other as possible. Warin couldn't reach the tarp where the rainwater had collected, and thanks to another cloudburst, had been replenished, so Anwyl refilled his cup, pushing it toward him whenever he needed more.

"How are you holding up?" he asked her, and his voice in the near-pitch black hold caressed her soul and soothed her mind. He was a darker shape reclined before her in the inky space, and she longed for the daylight hours to arrive so that she could see him more clearly.

"I'm all right. Hungry. My head finally stopped throbbing. You?"

"The same," he replied, though Anwyl knew it to be only a part-truth. When she let the silence stretch, he added, "I can breathe through my nose again, and I can see from both eyes now."

"That's a good sign. What else?" He didn't answer right away, and she realized he was trying to spare her the more gruesome details. "Please, Warin. Even though I can't reach you, I might be able to help."

"I thought my ribs were broken."

"But you don't now?"

"When I draw in a deep breath, I only ache."

"It's not a sharp pain?"

"No. Anwyl, Odo kicked me. It's difficult to stand up...to relieve myself." He grew silent.

She knew the only way forward was for her to diagnose him matter-of-factly. Perhaps it was better that they could not see one another. "Undo your breeches, Warin, you need to tell me what you feel. If he kicked you and caused a tear, there will be blood. If one or both of your—"

"I understand," he interrupted. She heard him shift, and after a moment, he asked, "What next?"

"Do you feel any stickiness from dried blood...or a rip in your skin?"

"No. And before you ask, I didn't have any blood in my urine."

"Good. I need you to palpate your, uh...testes. Are they in their usual position?" She heard him hiss. "Does the pain go up into your stomach?"

"Yes, still, they're where they're supposed to be," he said, sounding relieved. "And the pain is only between my legs, though I think my pride is wounded more. This is not how I expected to converse with my new bride," he whispered and chuckled, making her smile.

"Nor I with you. Nausea?" she asked.

"No."

"Give me your hand." He did, and she ran her fingers over his wrist. "Your pulse is steady, and I don't think you have a fever. I think, like your ribs, that you've been badly bruised. With no access to herbs, I can't prepare a poultice, so the only thing you can do is rest. Good news, considering our current predicament, for there is nothing else we can do."

"Anwyl," he said softly, "I promise that I will protect you when the time comes."

"As I will protect you," she replied and loved him all the more that he didn't contradict her. Then her stomach growled. "I could use a piece of palm bread right about—Warin, I forgot!" She pulled out the handkerchief she'd wrapped the bread in and carefully pulled it open. "I grabbed these from my room, the morning we were taken. They're completely crushed, but the crumbs are better than nothing. Here, give me your hand."

"You eat it," he told her, then his stomach grumbled loud enough for her to hear.

"If we are going to protect each other, we'll both need our strength. You can give me your hand right now," she ordered. He did, and she directed him to where she had divided the crumbled pastries, setting the piles on the kerchief on the floor between them.

"We haven't talked about Marten yet," he said after they finished eating.

"I was waiting until you were ready."

"They were controlling him." He sounded unsure.

"Don't you dare think that he has committed treason or that he had any choice in this, Warin. He didn't."

"But he eats pihaberries."

"He was gone for almost a year. I doubt they gave him any. Add to that the torture and the effects of the poison, and it would have been impossible to resist Vala and Rowly."

"Poison?"

Anwyl was silent, but she reached across the dark space, and her hand found his. "Marten wanted to tell you himself, Warin. He only has two or three months. I'm sorry."

"I should have figured it out. On the beach, he wasn't himself. He kept telling me not to worry. That he had a plan. I heard a noise and turned away from him. There was a woman, and she nodded. Marten struck me from behind. Before I passed out, he said he had to do what they commanded, that it was the only way to save me. They haven't killed us yet."

Anwyl didn't say anything.

"What are you thinking?"

"Even if we were free of these chains," she said, "it wouldn't do us any good while we're in the middle of the sea. Not with Odo on board and an entire crew under Kena control. Do you have a weapon?"

"No, they searched me and confiscated my knives. What about you?"

"Just my hairpins. I want you to take one. Weave it into the seam of your breeches, where you can reach it whether your hands be tied in front or back."

"You should keep them."

"Warin, if you love me, you will let me share one with you. I already concealed mine in the lapel of my tunic. Please, Warin." She pushed the needle-sharp hairpin across the floor to him, placing his hand on the blunt end. "Careful, one side has tiny, serrated teeth, so make sure you don't slice your breeches open." She could see his silhouette shifting as he hid the slim weapon and realized that the darkness was receding. When he was done, he looked up at her, and she could just make out his features.

"You are so lovely with your hair down," he said and smiled. And when she looked down to hide the glistening in her eyes, he took her hand. "We'll escape, Anwyl," he whispered. "We just have to wait for the right moment."

"They'll be back to check on us," she said, cleaning up the stray crumbs and stuffing her kerchief in her pocket.

"Anwyl."

She met his eyes.

"We'll be all right."

She nodded, and they separated, going back to their opposite walls. It wasn't too long after that the door was unlocked.

"Check them," Vala ordered. "They should be awake by now."

She felt her hair being brushed away from her face, and she made a sleepy grumbling noise, batting at the hand disturbing her. Across the room, she heard Warin grunt as if someone had nudged him.

"Almost, Vala," a man whispered.

"Good. Leave enough food for two days and fresh buckets of water. I want them awake and aware when we rendezvous with Prince Bowen."

• • •

Her scalp burned, and coming awake, Anwyl clawed at the hand that held her by her hair. She tried to scream but gagged instead on the piece of cloth that had been stuffed in her mouth. "Not a word, little bird," the man who held her murmured. "Just a bit of fun before you meet your prince."

Anwyl scissor-kicked her legs, catching the man in the gut with one boot and his chin with the other as he doubled over. He backed away only long enough to return the favor by kicking her repeatedly in the stomach.

Across the hold, Warin roared in anger. "Let her go! I'll kill you for touching her!"

Anwyl struggled to move away from the continued onslaught, curling up to protect her head and ribs. The filthy wad of fabric had slipped too far down her throat, cutting off her air.

Vala raced in, three men pouring in behind her. They pulled the man away, but he came back at her. "You fool, Odo," she hissed. "Pull that gag out at once! She's choking to death!"

But Odo seemed content to watch her do just that, waiting until her bile came up out of her nose, scorching the inside of her nostrils. Tears of pain streamed unchecked from the corners of her eyes—she was about to die. Odo lurched toward her, and she shrank back, but he only reached into her mouth to rip the suffocating cloth from her throat. In her waking-panic, she had swallowed half of it, and the removal had her retching all over again. Spittle, bile, and specks of half-digested food sprayed all over Odo's booted foot. When he pulled his foot back to kick her again, he was tackled by two sailors and sent sprawling to the far side of the hold.

"Tie her hands," Vala ordered. "And be quick about it."

The third man grabbed her hands and tied them in front of her. The knot was a simple one, and as the hemp cut into her wrists, Anwyl held her tongue. When the time came, she could easily escape her bonds.

Odo, calmer now, squatted next to her, his porcine leer leaving no doubt in her mind what he was thinking. She had heard enough stories of what his victims had endured to know to leave well enough alone. This was the man responsible for most of Prince Bowen's handiwork. Odo's cruelty was only second to two men: Bowen and Rowly. He reached down and grabbed at her breasts, twisting one hard enough that a cry escaped her lips. There was a muffled yell from across the room.

"Enough!" Vala shouted, and Odo lurched toward Warin. He aimed a vicious kick at Warin's groin, but before his boot connected, Warin log-rolled into him, sending Odo sprawling forward. Before anyone could stop him, Warin swung a loop of his chain around Odo's neck and pulled it tighter and tighter, as if trying to remove the man's head. Odo struggled to his feet, taking Warin with him. The monster heaved himself back against the wall, trying to dislodge Warin. But Warin had angled them so that he was in the corner of the room, and Odo's bulk ended up protecting him from the other men.

Odo's eyes swelled in their sockets, and his tongue grew enormous. Anwyl couldn't find it in herself to pity him. Her brother had tried to protect her from the worst of the atrocities committed by this monster, but her Sylvan instincts had her seeking out the few survivors, if only to help them by easing their inevitable passing.

"Let him go, or the princess dies," Vala's called out. It was the calmness of her voice, more than anything else, that captured everyone's attention. Upon seeing the blade Vala held to Anwyl's neck, Warin swung the chain out and over Odo's neck and shoved him to the middle of the room with a booted foot. The other men stepped back, wary of his makeshift weapon.

"Get out, Odo!" Vala ordered. "Your prince said that he wanted Lord Warin alive and the princess untouched. Look at her face. What do you think he's going to do to you when he sees what you've done?"

For the first time since Anwyl had come awake, Odo looked uncertain. Vala had the upper hand, and he stalked from the room.

"Are you all right?" Warin called to her.

"Secure him to the wall," Vala ordered. "And take care that he doesn't get you with that chain!" Warin had been poised to attack again when Vala tightened her grip in Anwyl's hair and pressed the knife closer to her neck. "In case you were wondering, this blade has been treated with poison, so if you want her to live, I suggest you relax."

Warin glared at her, but conceded, dropping the loop of chain. Vala released Anwyl, shoving her back against the wall. "I told him the chains were too long. Fool." She crossed the room; one of the sailors pulled a chair in from outside the door, and she sat. "You three may leave." The sailors scrambled out of the room, but not before she yelled after them, "I want to know who was supposed to be on duty when Odo got in."

She turned to Anwyl. "You may answer him now."

Anwyl slid down the wall, remaining stubbornly silent.

"Look, I'm not heartless. If it weren't for me, his brother would have been dead a long time ago. I did everything I could to purge the poison from him, but Odo used too much on the crew." A man entered the hold and shut the door behind him. "Juna," she greeted. "How is Odo?"

"Breathing," he replied, sounding not at all pleased by that fact.

"A shame," Vala said, and Anwyl and Warin exchanged looks. "Help the princess to her feet so that she can get closer to Lord Warin."

"Are you all right?" Warin asked her again, quietly.

She nodded. "My hair has seen better days."

Across the room, Vala snorted.

"You look beautiful," he assured her, but there was something he wasn't telling her. "Just remember that no matter what happens, I love you."

"What do you—"

"Pull her away. Quickly!" Vala ordered, and the sailor dragged Anwyl back to the wall. She had just settled back down to the floor when the door swung open and Odo entered again. Two men followed behind—Prince Bowen and Rowly.

Bowen *tsk*'d when he saw Anwyl's condition. "Odo, this is no way to treat my future bride." He squatted in front of her and smiled, pushing a stray lock of her bedraggled hair behind her ear. His perfectly white teeth glistened, and not a single blond hair was out of place. Even his unshaved whiskers looked orderly. Bowen was as devilishly handsome as the first time she met him. He was a perfectly made man, all except for one slight imperfection. She studied him—his icy blue-gray eyes, his lips, his sculpted jaw—and asked him the only thing she could.

"How's the nose?"

CHAPTER THIRTY-THREE

Lines

"What did..." Bowen started to ask, and Anwyl laughed at him as his perfect face bloomed red. He backhanded her across the mouth, but she was ready for it. She did what her Umbren trainer had taught her—minimize the impact while making it appear that a mighty blow had been dealt. She flew sideways, purposely banging her hand against the wood planking at the same time that it appeared that she cracked her head. Across the room, Warin pulled against the chain holding him to draw attention away from her, and she sent him a signal that she was all right. She saw the pain behind his anger and knew how much it was killing him to remain upright. The prince walked over to him.

"You're taller than your brother," Bowen said, his calm demeanor and banal statement as he assessed Warin terrifying. There was a certain madness to Bowen—Anwyl had felt it all those years ago when he'd taunted her. She worried that Warin's superior wit would only cause him more injury.

"You had a brother once, and just as evil as you, I recall. It's a good thing he's dead. You really should join him," Anwyl goaded, wanting his focus away from Warin. "What a family you have." She spat as Vala listened with interest. "Abandoned by your mother as an infant. That must have been difficult for Diarmait to explain when you were so young. How you must have disgusted her, being the child of rape. Why, she even hid the fact that you had a younger brother. Bowen and Roger, both begot by violence—no wonder you are the way you are."

Bowen strode toward her, swung back his leg to kick her, then stopped, suddenly regaining his composure and narrowing his eyes. "My bride must be able to stand when we make our vows." He knelt and murmured to her. "I've been looking forward to our wedding night for some time, Anwyl."

She recoiled when he caressed her cheek.

"Don't touch her!" Warin shouted, and Bowen looked at him with an amused expression.

"Oh, this is wonderful. You've fallen for the princess." He walked back to Warin, stopping just out of his reach. "Let me tell you something about the intimate education given to the princes and princesses of Sophiana. When it comes to the royal line, the training is extensive, especially in certain pleasurable subjects. I daresay that my cousin Aghna is enjoying herself with Anwyl's brother."

He returned to Anwyl and then squatted, running his fingers down her throat and between her breasts, lower, and then, as if realizing others were still present, drew away. "But the princesses, their education is...elevated. I've even heard that the mistresses who run the Fenrhi Blood Caste are called upon to provide instruction." He turned to Warin. "You do know about Blood Caste, don't you? Ah yes, I can see by your expression that you do. The things those women can do." He turned back to Anwyl. "Well, I'm looking forward to finding out just how much—"

Anwyl spat in his face. Blood and saliva dripped down his cheek, and rage burned in the frozen ice of his eyes as he tried to maintain his control. In that moment, she realized something about herself, something that her Umbren trainer had said would take time to determine—she was capable of killing.

He stood, towering over her. "Transfer the Pheldhainian to *Reacher*, then tie him to the rail. I have something special in mind for him." Bowen stared down at Anwyl as Warin was dragged, kicking and struggling, from the cabin. "You, Princess, will be mine, *willingly*."

"I will never agree to marry you, Bowen. I would rather die first."

He laughed at her. "I don't think so. You see, my sweet, after Vala is done with you, you won't be able to resist."

"Let Warin go, and I'll do whatever you want."

"You care about him, don't you? Love him, perhaps?"

Anwyl shook her head, and Bowen laughed at her.

"I'm not so blind as you think. I saw through your feeble attempts to distract me. But even if you don't care for him, he most certainly loves you. Don't worry...I have plans for Lord Warin, now that his brother has been used up. He'll survive this day, but he won't like it. And you, you will do what I want, whether or not I set Warin free." He leered. "Though...if I enjoy your performance later, perhaps I'll rein in Rowly, just a little."

At the door, he turned to Vala. "See that she is cleaned up and amenable to marriage before you bring her up on deck. And make sure Juna's men secure her before swinging her over to *Reacher*."

"I don't know if I can—" Vala started. She stopped when Bowen crowded her. "As you wish, my prince." He smiled on his way out, slamming the hold's door behind him.

"He's going to torture Warin," Anwyl cried, as Vala approached her with a clean rag.

"Of course he will." She gently dabbed at Anwyl's lip. "But there may be a way that you can stop him from giving the Pheldhainian to Rowly." Captain Juna entered. "Don't mind him; he's loyal to me. Is all ready, Juna?"

"It is, m'lady. The prince and his men are crossing over. The Pheldhainian made it, as well, though Bowen's men gave him a dunking. He's still breathing, though."

"Good," Vala said. "We'll be done soon."

When Juna left the hold, Anwyl gave the Kena woman an appraising look. "He's loyal to you, not Bowen. What about you, Vala...do you blindly follow your prince?"

"I'm loyal to myself," Vala said. "Now stop talking and listen to what I have to say."

"Why should I?"

"Because I'm trying to help you. And before you ask, I'm doing this because by helping you, I'm helping myself." She held up a thin silver band with a dark gem set upon it and then slipped it onto Anwyl's little finger. "The gem is sharp and has been treated with poison. One scratch and you have the means to kill Rowly. Of course, you could opt to use it on yourself to escape being Bowen's bride, but you should know that he will torture Lord Warin. He'll give him to the brute as a plaything. Rowly's been known to keep some of his victims alive for years. It's your decision."

"I could use it on you right now," Anwyl threatened.

"And then what will you do?" Vala asked scornfully. "Now listen, we haven't much time. Bowen expects me to give you a tonic that will dampen your innate ability to ward off Kena interference. He expects me to manipulate you into following my instructions."

"But you're not going to? Why?"

"Part distraction; part revenge against that foul man."

"Odo?"

"He should not be allowed to go on living while my sisters... Never mind. Just listen."

Anwyl made a fist with the hand wearing the ring and nodded.

"If you want a chance at Rowly, you will act docile when you are taken above deck. Pretend to be in a daze—I already know that you're quite capable in that regard. Do not cause any trouble when we are hoisted across to *Reacher*. And when we get there, nod and acquiesce when the prince questions you or asks you to do things. You want him to accept that you believe the lies that he will tell you."

"Perhaps I should just kill Bowen."

"You're a smart woman, Princess. What will you do afterward? Even if you manage to defeat Rowly and Odo, you'll be on a ship surrounded by two dozen men, all loyal to their Prince. Enough. We must go. Now."

"But you could help, Vala," Anwyl whispered. "You could deal with Rowly, or Odo, or even Bowen."

"I won't cross that line; I can't betray Bowen to such an extent. I only want to survive him. Once he marries you, he will no longer need me."

"Then help Warin. Please!"

"It's too late for the Pheldhainian brothers. Bowen has plans," she said. "It's time to go. Remember, you are supposed to be under my influence."

The door to the cabin opened, and three sailors waited to escort her. As they led her onto the deck, Anwyl thought that it would be brighter, but the sky was an ominous blanket of low, gray clouds. She would play the part ascribed to her by Vala but only after she ascertained Warin's well-being. When she was delivered to *Reacher*'s deck, she found him, gagged and tied to the starboard rail, a rope tied around his leg with a string of sea caltrops attached to its end. She kept her head lowered and peered at her surroundings through the strands of her hair.

"Is she prepared?" Bowen demanded.

"Of course, my prince," Vala insisted. "She will recognize him, but I have dulled her senses and her recent memories. Her royal blood makes it impossible for me to control her completely, but the poison should last long enough that she will be susceptible to suggestions."

"For how long?" Bowen demanded.

"Long enough to bed her if you marry today. I could have given her more of the poison, but then she would be as she is now for weeks, possibly permanently."

"As long as she is able to breed, I don't care if she is as dull as a turnip."

As he walked around her, placing his hands on her hips as if measuring her ability to reproduce, Anwyl focused inward, finding her balance. It was easy once she imagined that she was creating a knot of spectacular intricacy. He completed his circuit, his hands never leaving her middle, and then splayed his long fingers over her stomach when he stopped before her.

"Unfortunately, many of the ingredients needed to create her current state interfere with the getting of a babe. But if you wish, I could…"

"No. My seed taking root is our priority" He flexed his fingers, pressing against and squeezing her abdomen. "Just how compliant is she?"

"Extremely impressionable. If I may, my Prince?" Bowen nodded, and Vala whispered something to him. "Take her to the Pheldhainian," Vala ordered. One of Juna's sailors took Anwyl's arm and led her to Warin, then let her go. She stared at him, allowed a tiny frown to crease her brow, and ignored the confusion in his eyes.

"Not too close, my princess," Bowen murmured in her ear.

"Why is he tied up?" she asked quietly, as if afraid to speak.

"We discovered a plot involving this man and an attempt to do your brother harm. He was using you to get near the royal family of Nifolhad."

Anwyl blinked and stepped back, hoping that her performance was believable. "Rani," she whispered.

"Yes. This man wants to murder Rani. And you."

"But why? I don't understand."

"He's an enemy of Nifolhad, Princess."

Warin gave a muffled yell, and one of the sailors clouted him with a belaying pin. He strained against his bindings, trying to reach her. It was the hardest thing Anwyl had ever had to do, but she cowered from him, tucking herself behind Bowen as if needing his protection. Warin cried out against the gag tied around his mouth again, this time in defeat. He fell back against the railing just as *Reacher* pitched in the sea's growing swells. To the south, darker clouds were building in the forbidding gray sky. Anwyl had never seen anything like it—the mass appeared to be boiling. She turned her attention away from the tumultuous sky just as a hot wind gusted across the ship's deck. Bowen was watching her again, and he lifted her chin with his finger. She blinked up at him as if trying to focus.

"Do you remember who I am, Anwyl?" he asked.

"You're Prince Bowen."

"No, my dear," he said. "Who I am to you?" She stared at him, waiting. "I'm your betrothed. Don't you remember? When we were very young? You were promised to me."

"Did I hit you?"

"Yes. But only because I tried to kiss you," he lied. She bobbed her head as if remembering it how he described it. "Would you like me to kiss you now?"

"I..." She gazed about them, as if embarrassed that there were so many people there to witness the embrace.

"It's all right, my dear, for we are to be married today."

She stared helplessly into his cold eyes, presenting an outward calm while her mind struggled to maintain her composure and not retch. Bowen smiled, shot a triumphant glance at Warin, then tilted his head to hers. Surprisingly, his kiss was gentle, and he drew away to gauge her reaction. "Tell me, Princess, did you like that?"

She nodded.

This was a test of some sort, and she saw the growing suspicion in his eyes. With her bound hands, she reached up and took hold of his collar. Standing on her toes, she pressed a kiss to his lips. He froze at the contact, but she allowed her lips to linger, willing his to soften and kiss her back. When he didn't, she drew away, not at all concerned that her features betrayed her distress. But Bowen gazed at her, and then pulled her roughly to him, slanted his mouth over hers, and plundered her mouth. And heaven help her, Anwyl pretended to respond, kissing him back with equal ardor. It was a brutal kiss, his lips bruising, his teeth nipping just a little too hard. He ran his hands all over her while the crew around them jeered. Anwyl played along, panting and moaning at all the right moments, as he molested her with his mouth and hands.

When he finally stopped, he turned his face toward Warin and deliberately ground his hips against hers. Anwyl gasped, then tried to draw him in for another kiss. She wanted his attention off the encroaching storm and anywhere but on Warin.

Bowen set her away from him, turning her so that she faced Warin, then pushed her closer to him. Anwyl resisted, leaning back into him as if fearful. "He can't hurt you, Anwyl," Bowen soothed, standing just out of reach of Warin. "I won't let him. Do you trust me?"

She nodded dumbly. "With my heart," she answered softly, quickly pinning her gaze on Warin and hoping that he knew that she was speaking to him.

"Good," Bowen said. "I bet you want to see your brother again?"

"Rani," she said, sighing wistfully.

Bowen smiled.

"Yes, Rani." He led her away. "He'll be so happy once we're married, my dear princess. I promise."

Rowly was edging toward Warin, and Anwyl pretended to stumble into his path. He caught her and set her straight. "I'm getting married today," she said wonderingly. "Are you here to give me away?"

Vala made a show of pulling her away. "I don't think that is wise, Princess. I'll do it," she said, making the offer to Bowen.

But Bowen chuckled. "Oh no. I think Rowly is better suited."

Odo stepped forward. "My prince, until you are wed, I do not think she should be left untied."

"Do you not believe in her sincerity, Odo?"

"I only meant to say that she might endanger herself. What if she were to fall overboard?"

Bowen gave a curt nod. "Can't have that, can we?" He gazed up at the sky. "Not with this weather coming upon us."

"The storm will hold off, my prince," Vala said softly, but with the full authority of a master Kena. Anwyl shivered.

"The storm will hold off," Bowen repeated.

"I should board *The Salt Wife*," she suggested.

"Odo, secure the princess," Bowen ordered. "Vala, get back to Juno's ship." Odo dragged Anwyl away. "It's for your own safety, my dear," Bowen crooned as Odo hauled up her hands by their bindings and secured them to the mast.

"You are very mean," she said to Odo, knowing Bowen was still watching. "I don't like you."

"And you are a spoiled bitch," he said, grabbing her chin and forcing her to stare into his eyes.

"Odo! Enough!" Bowen yelled, and Odo squeezed her face just a little tighter, then whipped his hand away. It was meanly done, almost as if he had slapped her.

When he finally stepped away, she gazed about her as if amazed by the ship's rigging, all the while taking stock of the crew, the lines, and the ship anchored nearby. It was of a Southron Isles design and, as she peered at it from under the strands of hair that had come loose, seemed to be ready to set sail. Why had no one on *Reacher* notified Bowen? Her crew stood at position, the captain at the wheel. Vala was moving toward the cast lines which had brought them over—one of Juna's men waited for her at the rail. Bowen, Rowly and Odo were deep in discussion on the other side of the ship, and Odo kicked out his foot at a pile of rags at their feet. Only, the pile moved, pulling itself into a tighter ball.

Marten.

The wind kicked up again, whipping her hair around her head, teasing her tendrils from her scalp and sending the tips lashing against her cheeks and neck. Stranger still was that the windsocks hung limply from their mounts. Warin was staring at her, his loose hair blowing wildly about his head as well.

The ship, rising and falling in the increasingly larger swells, creaked, and finally, a real gust of wind strafed the deck, bringing with it not the humid moisture of the sea, but a warm, dry scent. If she were not on a ship in the middle of the Southron Waters, she would've sworn it smelled of the Fyrost Desert.

"Where's Vala?" Bowen called.

Vala stopped halfway to the rail where Juna's man waited. "Why are you still here? Get back to *The Salt Wife* and have Juna make for the islet." She nodded, then hurried over the rail to the waiting skiff below.

"Cast off those lines as soon as she's aboard," Bowen yelled. He still didn't seem to notice that the other ship was already prepped to sail, and Anwyl wondered at his mistake.

Odo called out in a mock-sermonizing voice, "Who among us will give away the bride?" When Rowly stepped forward, he tossed him a piece of cloth. "She'll need a veil, won't she?"

"Go on," Bowen agreed. "Put it on her. You can give her a fatherly kiss on the cheek if you promise not to bite her." Rowly flinched but then lumbered over to where Anwyl remained secured to the mast.

She lowered her chin, allowing him to brush back her hair and secure the cloth to her head, tying it with a piece of rust-stained twine he had pulled from his pocket. "I've never been a father," Rowly said, sounding as proud as if she truly were his daughter. "My prince said I could kiss your cheek, but I won't if you're afraid. I promise I won't bite you. You are too lovely." He clenched and unclenched his hands as if he couldn't control them. "Besides, I would never bite a face. Prince Bowen knows this, and I—"

"Hurry it along, Rowly," Odo shouted.

"That man scares me," Anwyl whispered, softer than a feather, and Rowly leaned closer.

"Don't worry, Princess. I won't let him hurt you."

She nodded, managing to keep her head lowered. "Thank you, Rowly. You're a nice man." She gave him a tremulous smile. "I guess it's all right if you kiss my cheek," she whispered and slowly lifted her chin.

Rowly closed his eyes, pursed his hideous lips, and leaned forward. Faster than a hornet, Anwyl swiped across, then darted in, and Rowly drew back in surprise. She held his gaze as her deadly work dawned on him. She'd used her hairpin to slice his neck, just below his collar. The tilt of his head from when he had leaned forward to kiss her cheek kept the blood flow to a minimum, and what there was of it trickled down his chest only to be hidden by his tunic.

He blinked at her, unable to speak, and a look of respect settled over his features. Keeping his head cocked to the side, the notorious torturer bowed to her, then walked away, his life surrendering to death with each beat of his heart.

He came to a stop next to Warin. No one seemed to notice anything odd in his behavior, at least not until a fit of coughing wracked his body. Bowen and Odo approached him, leaving Marten alone in a pile.

Vala had made it to the other ship. Juna's crew was already hopping to set sail. Anwyl turned to check on Warin, her gaze sweeping west just as a beam of sunlight pierced the darkening skies. It winked out a moment later, as if the clouds demanded total dominance over their realm. But it had been enough time for Anwyl to espy that which the unnaturally sullen day had hidden— another ship was drawing near, and Anwyl was almost positive it was *Lita's Pearl*. It seemed everyone, save her, was blind to its arrival.

Bowen was staring at Rowly, as was Odo, still unsure as to what was wrong. Then, they watched as he drew a long pin from his throat, stretching his neck and bleeding his life's blood on the deck. He lurched toward Bowen, the pin held out as if to stab his master, and Anwyl understood—Rowly was what Bowen had made him. He missed and landed with a resounding thud on the deck. Odo howled his rage and turned toward Anwyl while Bowen stared down at Rowly as he crawled toward Warin. The prince could not seem to drag his eyes away as Rowly held out the pin against Warin's legs, and so didn't note Odo's imminent attack on Anwyl. She couldn't help Warin if she were dead, and so she focused on setting herself free.

Gripping the rope above her, she turned and used the pegs on the mast to shimmy her way up, releasing the tension on her bindings. Odo made a grab for her as she sought to undo the simple knot, but she was soon free and knocked his hands away, pulling herself out of his reach. When he jumped for her, she deflected his strike, catching his wrist with the deadly stone on her finger, swiping it long and deep into his flesh. He pulled back from the sting, and she narrowed her eyes at him in grim satisfaction. "A gift from Vala."

Before he could react, she was up the mast and onto the main boom. Across the deck, Rowly's bloody trail disappeared over the rail. Bowen let out a howl that froze her blood as the body of Rowly sank under the swells of the water. Warin was nowhere to be seen.

Bowen shook free his frozen state and then looked up to where she hung in the rigging. An evil grin spread across his face. He had seen what she had not—Rowly must've knocked Warin overboard, but one of the caltrops was wedged in the railing. With a tremendous heave, Bowen loosed it. Anwyl heard a great splash, knowing Warin had hit the water—the heavy iron would pull him mercilessly to the bottom of the sea. On the deck, Marten struggled to stand, then tipped back over the rail and into the sea as well. Finally, someone shouted out that another ship had arrived, but it was too late.

Anwyl pivoted to run down the boom and dive in after them, but Bowen's men were nearly upon her. As *Lita's Pearl* sidled dangerously close to *Reacher*, she secured her hands in the rigging; the sailors running toward her did not. The rending of wood was deafening as the other vessel side-swiped *Reacher's* prow. Anwyl's assailants were sent flailing to the deck. Others were thrown overboard when Bowen's ship nearly keeled. Warin's ship, with Grieg at her helm, groaned, then rebounded a short distance. Bowen remained miraculously unscathed and was shouting orders to what remained of his crew. Then he saw Odo collapsed against the far rail, the poison already leaving him brutally disfigured. The prince bayed like a wounded dog as his henchman and friend died the same death that he had ordered for so many others. He stood, eerily calm, and watched as *The Salt Wife* carried Vala away.

The skies chose that moment to open up, sending a driving rain and gale force winds against the ship. Anwyl trembled in the rigging, but Bowen seemed immune to the tumult. He ignored the shouts of his men and the grappling lines hurled at *Reacher* from the other ship. Through the sheets of water streaming down from the sky, Anwyl saw several men being hauled from the water onto Warin's ship and the limp body of a man dragged up after them. Was it Warin or Marten? A flash of lightning slashed through the dark, lending brief illumination to the nightmarish scene. The unconscious man's limbs were free—Marten, then. Warin was truly gone. *Reacher* began to list as the storm raged, and Anwyl dragged her attention back to her own peril.

Below her, Bowen directed more men into the rigging. A man bore down on her, ax in hand. She was ready and disarmed him, knocking him off balance and sending him crashing to Bowen's feet. Lightning cracked again, this time hitting the bowsprit where it jutted from the ship. Wood splintered in a thousand directions, and she ignored the sting when a piece sliced her temple.

The ship rocked again as the grappling lines were cut, and Grieg ordered his crew to push off the floundering vessel. They were leaving! Another two men were upon her. Before they could reach her, Anwyl made a strategic cut to a line and let the counterweight of dropping tackle pull her up to the main gaff. Below, Bowen climbed after her.

Her only chance to survive meant reaching *Lita's Pearl* before the storm pulled the vessel too far away. Lightning struck the foremast as she grabbed another line and ran down the gaff as fast as her feet would carry her. Bowen was on her heels. He screamed, expecting her to stop when she reached the end. Instead, she threw her body out and over the water, arcing around the mast as she hung from the rope, piking both legs forward and back again to increase the momentum of her swing. A great gust of wind threw her forward even faster, scooping her up like a giant hand and flinging her in a great circle. She risked a glance at Bowen, but he was already gone. *Reacher* was aflame, the conflagration made more intense by the storm's relentless wind. She flew high, swinging on her tether past the stern. She should've been able to see *Lita's Pearl* by now. A gigantic wave surged up toward her, and Anwyl frantically searched the surface for a bit of flotsam for which she could aim.

• • •

After coughing up a lungful of seawater, Warin was up and on his feet.

"I thought we'd lost you, m'lord," the sailor named Kory, who'd pulled him from the drink, panted. "If it weren't for Lord Marten..."

"Marten?" Warin demanded. "Where is he?"

Kory shook his head. "When that devil freed the caltrop, Lord Marten went over the rail after you." Warin looked down at his ankle—the rope was still attached, but only an arm's length remained, dangling, its end cut clean through. "How did you free yourself from the rail?"

"The princess lent me a blade," he said, thinking about the hairpin now lost forever. "Then Rowly managed to take me with him when he went over." Warin grabbed Kory's shoulder. "I may have lost my brother, but I will not lose my wife!"

Grieg was at the wheel, shouting orders to the crew to reduce sail—one of the upper foresails whipped and cracked in the wind, tethered to its yard by a single line. A giant swell lifted his vessel, then dropped her back down, nearly on her side. Warin and Kory caromed down the almost-vertical deck, smashing into the railing. Warin, with a line still wrapped round his chest, made a mad grab for Kory's wrist as the impact against the rail had the man flying past it and toward the water. He caught him and hauled him back as the ship righted herself. It was a testament to Grieg's skill that *Lita's Pearl* didn't capsize. Together, he and Kory raced back across the deck.

"There's *Reacher*!" he shouted.

"But where's the princess? Was she washed over the side?"

Warin's gaze strafed the deck; she was nowhere to be seen. "Not my Anwyl!" he shouted over the clapping of thunder. "She's in the rigging!" he said, pointing to the mainsail's boom and staring helplessly as a man with an ax ran toward her.

Lightning split the sky, and Warin was blinded by white light as it exploded *Reacher's* foremast. Anwyl, holding a line, was flying up to the mainsail yard. Bowen was on her heels. *Lita's Pearl* lurched again, and Anwyl disappeared from view. But Warin knew to his core, as he watched her sail fearlessly up to her next perch, what she would attempt. He'd seen her do it before, though not in a raging tempest. Before his vessel could toss him across the deck again, he freed himself of the rope around his chest, and ignoring the pain in his ribs, he climbed the shrouds, swinging from the lines and using the momentum from springboarding off the mast to carry him faster to an upper yard. *Lita's Pearl* veered away from Bowen's ship, and Warin shouted to Grieg. "Keep her alongside!"

Grieg shouted a new set of orders, and slowly, too slowly, their course corrected and brought them closer to the sinking Nifolhadian ship. If he was to help her, he would have to time his leap, *Lita's Pearl* would have to remain level, and the heaving waters could not pitch them in another direction— everything would have to be impossibly perfect. A channel of roiling sea stretched between the ships, and as Anwyl raced down the length of the yardarm, running in the opposite direction, Warin waited for his instincts to tell him it was time to throw himself forward to catch her. His curse, a life filled with success after success, only needed to work one last time. And as Anwyl cast herself into the deluge and he lost sight of her, he imagined her, flying in a broad arc at the end of her rope, coming around the stern and closer to his arms.

To his horror, he realized that his princess had miscalculated Prince Bowen's determination to have her. He was running down the same boom she had used, only toward *Lita's Pearl*, to intercept her in her mad bid to be free of him. Once caught, Prince Bowen would drag her under the waves—of this Warin had no doubt.

She hadn't emerged from the sheets of rain—the seconds stretched into an eternity—and then the massive crest of water between the ships dropped, and he saw her. She was a thing of beauty to behold as he raced down the boom and hurtled himself into the air to meet her, a fantastic creature of myth and legend. There was no time to worry that he had miscalculated his leap. He had to trust that they would be together again.

• • •

Anwyl knew she wasn't going to make it, and she prepared herself to hit the hard surface of the water. Then she saw Bowen running up the boom, up instead of across, for his ship canted desperately in the waves. She thought she heard Bowen's scream of rage as, miraculously, she felt herself being lifted again.

A crack of thunder struck, its concussive force sucking the wind from her chest. In that split second between the bang and the bolt, she thought she glimpsed a dark shape hurtling alongside her. Then the shocking-cold whiteness of a lightning bolt struck *Reacher*'s other mast, silhouetting Bowen as the beam under his feet splintered. He clawed at the air, catching only rain and wind, and then hurtled toward the sea.

Anwyl closed her useless, blinded eyes and opened her palm, releasing the rope. She might live; she might die. If the latter, then she would be with Warin once again. It was out of her hands.

But suddenly, the hard band of an arm seized her around her middle, and the solid body of a man drew her close to his side. The course she had traveled curved in an opposite arc, telling her what her eyes could not: she was headed toward *Lita's Pearl*. Her weight added to their speed, and she felt him pull her up against him.

"...*hit...hard*," he said, and her ringing ears almost tricked her into believing the voice belonged to Warin. "...*ree, ...ooh, ...un!*" They separated upon crashing into the deck, rolling apart—how far she didn't know.

Lita's Pearl lurched forward as the mainsail caught a consistent wind, and the sea evened out under the ship. Breaking free from her stunned state, a blinded Anwyl crawled to where she thought the man who'd rescued her might have landed, sweeping her hands back and forth.

Strong arms caught her up, roaming all over her, checking for injuries. Her ears were still ringing, but she could just make out her name being called over and over. She reached up with both hands and found his battered face. "Warin?" she asked tremulously.

She couldn't make out his words, but he nodded, turning his head in her hands and kissing her palms. "It *is* you, my love. My Warin." Anwyl touched his lips, then leaned in to kiss him. He kissed her with equal ardor, and when he pulled back, she heard sounds but couldn't distinguish their meaning. "I can't hear...the thunder..." she yelled. "I can't see either. What's happening? Did Marten make it?" He picked up her hand and placed her palm on his cheek so that she could feel him shake his head. "What about *Reacher* and Bowen?" she shouted and felt his grin.

He placed his fingers to her lips, and she smiled.

"I was yelling, wasn't I?" she asked in what she hoped was a more dignified voice. He nodded.

He helped her to stand, and the tempest which had shaken them until they felt like bags of bones was gone. They must've sailed free of it. Warin led her carefully across the deck, taking her hand and setting it on the rail. He stilled, his body tense, and she turned her back on the sea and shivered. He shook free of whatever had captured his attention and scooped her up and into his arms. Anwyl held onto him as he carried her to what she hoped where dry quarters.

She let him strip off her sodden clothes, then dress her in what must've been one of his shirts before tucking her into his bed. A few minutes later, she felt the mattress dip. "You should"—she realized that she was yelling again and quieted her voice—"change into dry clothes." But even as she said it, her hand brushed his arm, and she discovered he had done just that.

"Can oo ee anying?" he asked, and touched her forehead, lifting her eyebrows. She felt his warm breath on her face. She sensed a brighter patch in the darkness and tracked the light. A lamp, perhaps.

"A little."

"...ou eard me?"

She nodded. "Enough to understand you. There's less noise to compete with in here."

"...ut appen...?"

She frowned and felt his fingers gently tap her ear and temple. "The lightning. I was staring at Bowen when it struck. The crack and the explosion. Everything is dark. And the ringing in my ears is so loud."

He pulled her closer, wrapping her in his arms, and she reached up and caressed his cheek. Her limbs felt leaden, and she sensed Warin shared her exhaustion. "Don't fall asleep yet," she begged. "There's something I must tell you."

He nodded, then kissed her temple.

"Thank you for rescuing me."

CHAPTER THIRTY-FOUR

Alliances

Juna gave the crew the new heading that Vala had ordered, one that was not the Southron Isles. She stared back at the strange storm that, now that they were a good distance away, shocked her by its concentrated intensity over one specific target: *Reacher*.

"That's unnatural, Juna," she called to him, then turned in surprise when he did not answer.

"We don't speak of the Goddess when she's angry."

"But you'll tell me," she cajoled, putting every ounce of persuasion she possessed into her request.

"It wouldn't be wise to attract her attention."

He narrowed his eyes at her, and Vala felt the oddest sensation as her control over him slipped away.

"I'll take you where you need to go, Vala, because I think I owe you my life many times over. And I would've protected you from Odo without your special persuasion. But you're going to have to stop trying to manipulate me. It won't work anymore. Not now that I've seen Her with my own eyes."

The gray clouds were giving way to patches of blue the farther east they sailed. But behind them, the dark center of the storm raged, shooting multiple lightning strikes into the sea. Vala wondered if the Pheldhainian ship had escaped. Had the princess been able to use the ring she'd given her? And if she had, who had been her victim? It no longer mattered, for if she had been on *Reacher* when the storm struck, she would be as dead as the others. Odo, Rowly, Warin and Marten of Pheldhain, and her own kin, Prince Bowen.

She thought about the power of the goddess the Southron Islers worshipped. A being that could command a storm, one who could break the control of a Kena mind, control reinforced by Sylvan poison—such an entity, if she even existed, would be a formidable foe. Or an incredible weapon. For the first time in Vala's life, she was truly afraid.

"We'll be fine, Vala. Look." The dark clouds behind them were dissipating. "We were not the lives She wanted sacrificed."

Vala shivered. The sails were full, and Juna's crew relaxed as the wind carried them east. One of the men approached, nodded to her, then waited for Juna's orders. "Every last one, save Vala," he said, and the sailor nodded, drawing his blade. He gave a shrill whistle, and Vala watched as the men from the Southron Isles attacked the Nifolhadian sailors placed on *The Salt Wife* by Prince Bowen to bolster the crew. They were efficient in their attack, giving no quarter and tossing the bodies overboard.

When the violence was over, they came, one by one. To Vala, they presented their bloodied blades, holding them out to her. She hadn't only lost control of Juna, but of every Southron Isler on the ship.

Juna took out his stained blade, then lifted her arm, pushing up her sleeve. He pricked his skin, adding more blood, then touched the flat of the dagger to her, leaving a stamp of red. "It's an offering to you." He nodded to the next man.

Vala stared at his bloodied knife, then held out her arm to him. Eleven weapons. Eleven of her countrymen dead. Each man bowed to her after completing the task, and when the strange rite was over, she used the tip of her own blade to scratch a line into her skin, marrying all their blood. "When I broke with Prince Bowen, I did so knowing that I would be unable to return to Nifolhad. He was my last link to that dark land. Even my Fenrhi sisters have declared me and my followers their enemies."

"Women of your ilk are revered," Juna supplied. "Though you manipulated us for purposes not your own, we always knew you protected us from Bowen and Odo. Had you not given us the order to sail, the Goddess would have surely destroyed this vessel along with *Reacher*."

"Who is this goddess of yours?" she asked.

"It no longer matters. She will never accept us back into her heart. She spared us, yes, but in letting us sail east, she has cast us from the Southron Isles. We're like you now—without country. As far as the crew is concerned, where you are, that is home."

Vala startled at that. "But not you?"

He set his hand on her shoulder. "I am loyal to you, Vala. And without your coercion; such a bond is much more powerful. When the men gave you the blood of their weapons, they were asking you to accept them as yours, along with the responsibility for their lives."

She stared at the meager crew. Behind them, what storm clouds remained were breaking apart. The setting sun washed them crimson and fuchsia. "A gift from your goddess."

"You are beginning to understand." He turned eastward, studying the emerging constellations as they began to light the darkening sky. "It wasn't known that women like you existed outside of the Southron Isles. Fanm Larenne would kill you if she knew. And then she would search out all the others like you and do the same. Do you really believe that we will find a safe haven in Aurelia?"

"I don't know," she said. "But I have a girl in place in Meramont, and she once sent word that Lord Ronan was a fair man. Better to start there than with his king and queen."

• • •

"You're alive," Anwyl said, still amazed by the fact.

"We both are," Warin pointed out as she stood behind him and ran her hands over the angry contusion covering his side. He winced as she examined the area, running her fingers along the curves of his ribs from sternum to side to spine. "Hmm," she said as she came around to stand in front of him. "Possibly cracked, but smooth, so perhaps only bruised. What were you thinking, flying out to catch me like that?"

"That I wanted to hold my wife again."

"I was speaking rhetorically." She gave him a little smile.

"Shouldn't you wrap my ribs in some constraining corset?"

"It'll only impede your breathing. If you hold yourself still—no twisting or lifting—you should be able to manage."

"Now for your face." Grieg came in, heard, and whistled when he saw the damage. She took the extra linens from him and a box that held the ship's medicaments. He ran a tight ship, she noted when she opened the lid—every herb was fresh, the implements sharp and clean.

"You look worse than you did before she cleaned your face." He bent down to study Warin more closely. "Another half inch, and you would be seeing half as much."

"Then I'm blessed that my princess is doubly beautiful," he quipped, and Anwyl rolled her eyes, but smiled when she saw that he meant it.

She began with the gash above his eye—his eyebrow had been split clean through. She *tsk*'d. "He didn't tell me that they had beaten him so badly," she said to Grieg, stitching up the cut and daubing salve over it. She wrapped a bandage crosswise over his forehead. "It's too deep to let it heal on its own, but the herbs should help him knit back together." She gazed at the man she loved. "You'll carry a scar. How does your nose feel?"

He drew breath through his nostrils. "The left side is still plugged." He tugged her closer, so that she stood between his knees.

"Then avoid blowing your nose, if you can. No sense dislodging the scab before it's ready." She tilted his head back to gaze up his nostril. "If it doesn't come away in a few days, I've some tweezers at the castle." She looked at Grieg.

"We'll make port in three days," he confirmed.

"Open up," Anwyl ordered, gently tugging Warin's jaw. The right side of his face was grossly swollen. She'd already ascertained that he didn't have a cracked jaw, but the inside of his cheek was badly lacerated. She touched her fingertip to his upper and lower molars. "Three loose teeth," she announced. "Soft food only for the next week."

She mashed some yarrow in a bowl with a bit of honey, then wrapped it in a piece of cheesecloth, making a tiny, flat packet. "Keep this tucked between your teeth and cheek."

"It's a good thing you were blinded by the lightning, or you would have jumped ship, seeing him like this," Grieg joked. "You should have seen his hair, standing all on end."

"Again?" Anwyl asked, laughing. "You and lightning."

"Never mind that," Warin said, trying to put an end to their sport. Anwyl asked Grieg if he had any vinegar aboard, and Warin gave his captain a signal, likely thinking Anwyl would miss the covert gesture to leave. Behind her, the door to the cabin clicked softly closed, and Warin's hands ran up her back, drawing her closer. "How are you, my princess?" he asked, mumbling just a little, due to the bundle in his cheek.

"Faring better than you, if appearances mean anything," she promised as he traced the bruises enlacing her neck—just one of the reminders left behind by Odo. "And yes, I can see quite perfectly." She reached forward and ran her hand through his locks, noticing the static crackle as some of his follicles lifted toward her fingers.

"You, too," he said. "I think it's you the lightning is attracted to—I'm just an innocent bystander."

She laughed at that. "Come on, let's get you settled." She pulled him up and then eased him back against the cushions. She started to step away to pour him some water, but he took her hand and pulled her next to him on the bed.

"I saw what Odo did to you. Are you all right?" He ran his fingers in circles over her thighs. "I'm not talking about the bruises I can see." She leaned her face into his hand when he cupped her cheek. "If he's not already dead, I *will* kill him for hurting you."

"I, uh, already took care of that." He lifted an eyebrow. "Thanks to Vala. She gave me poison to use on Rowly, but as you saw, Rowly met a different fate."

"At your hands as well."

She nodded.

"I do so love my deadly little princess." He took her hands in his, and his expression grew serious.

"I'm all right, Warin. I did what I had to do to help us survive. And the world is a safer place now that it's been rid of those two monsters. And Bowen...I'm sorry for—"

"Don't you dare apologize for what you had to do. I love you, Anwyl. Even if you hadn't told me in your own way why you had to kiss him, I would still love you. Everything you did to make him think that you were in his thrall was one more nail in what I hope will be a very waterlogged coffin." He took the packet she'd made him from his cheek.

"You need to keep that in your mouth"

"What I need to do is kiss you, my princess." He propped himself up, managing to wince only a little, but Anwyl pushed him back against the cushions.

"I've a better idea," she said, slipping from the bed and padding to the cabin door to lock it. She walked back to him, shedding her clothes along the way, then as gently as possible, straddled his thighs. She waited as he took stock of her cuts and bruises, pausing to frown at the marks on her breast where Odo had grabbed her.

"They'll fade away, along with the memory of how they happened until the only thing I will recall is how it feels to be alive, with you, right at this moment. Now, if you don't mind, I need to examine all of you." She undid his breeches and pulled them off to survey the damage he'd sustained when Odo kicked him. She noted with satisfaction that his virility was intact, had noticed it when she had stripped for him. But there was a disturbingly large contusion at the juncture of his left leg and hip. She cupped him—tenderly—feeling his testes, using his expressions as much as what she felt to diagnose the injury.

His eyebrow lifted in invitation. "I'm still in dire need of your lips."

Anwyl smiled, then crawled up him, taking care to not let her weight rest on any of his injuries, which were pretty much everywhere. She leaned down, touched her lips to his in a kiss filled with promised passion. She kissed his chin and jaw and neck, trailed her lips over his collarbones and chest, breathing in his scent. She rested her cheek above his heart, just for a moment, knowing the contact would warm her. Then she moved down his chest, paying special and lasting homage to his nipples before slinking her body lower, past his bruised ribs. At the contusion on his leg, she hovered, then kissed him gently there, and the hiss that whistled through his teeth had nothing to do with pain. She moved to his other thigh, repeating the gesture, but taking him in her hand as she did, then finally, taking him in her mouth.

Warin speared his fingers through her hair as she sucked and licked, holding her to her task until he could no longer hold his hips steady. She tongued him, long and lasting, from base to tip, and took a fraction of a moment to gauge his reaction. His eyes were shut, and he groaned in pleasure, but she noted the wince of pain each time he thrust his hips. She descended once more, drawing him deep into her mouth, and again, then thrice more before she lifted away and trailed kisses back up his body.

His hands found her breasts as he urged her up so that he could torture her nipples in return. And Anwyl hung over him, wanting to press herself against his torso to relieve the sweet torment between her thighs. But it was Warin's turn, she knew. He needed to take her as much as she needed to take him. And she allowed him to draw her up even farther until her now-tender nipples brushed against the rough-hewn planking above the bed. She pressed her hands into the wall, unable to find purchase, but his strong hands held her, supporting her in the impossible position.

She dropped her gaze to him, and he smiled up at her before pulling her closer. And then he took her, much in the same way she had taken him, with his lips and tongue and teeth. It was a glorious assault, the sucking of his mouth and plunging of his tongue, the drawing of her sensitive nub between his lips. And when she cried out his name, begged him to not stop, he lifted her just a fraction away, teasing her.

"Please," she entreated, and he obliged, taking her in his mouth again until she climaxed above him, collapsing against the wall. Finally, she carefully slid to his side to stretch out along his length. And when he hissed in pain as he rolled toward her, she pushed him gently back and smiled, cat-like.

"I have an idea," she said, touching his still hard shaft. She got on her knees next to him and gently pulled him up. Arranging the cushions behind him, she assisted him so that he could sit, leaning back against the cushions and the wall. Then she posed his legs, pulling them slightly apart and bending his knees. Finally, she climbed over him, straddled his hips, and took him in her hand. Centered above him, she lowered herself, inch by wonderful inch, until he was seated deep inside her. She searched his face for any traces of pain and, finding none, lifted away from him to lower herself once more.

"All right?" she murmured. He took her hips in his hands and helped her to lift back up by way of an answer.

Anwyl rode him then, completely, utterly, triumphantly. She took him into her heated core over and over, watching his face as his control began to shatter. Except for his hands on her hips helping her up and down, she did all the work, wanting to be in complete control. And then she undulated her hips as she rose up and slid down, and he groaned. She reveled in the power she held over him as she tensed and pulsed. His muscles tightened in that telltale way, and she allowed him to set the pace for his release. All she wanted in this moment was to give him what he had given her—heart, body, soul.

She drew back so that she could watch his face as he had watched hers. But he looked far from being out of control, and his eyes smoldered back at her. And when he shifted his hands from her hips to cup her buttocks, Anwyl shivered in pleasure. "Not yet, my princess," he said, continuing to work her until her thighs trembled with the efforts of her exertions. And in giving herself over to him again, she felt that brilliant, pinpoint pressure growing again. Warin smiled devilishly up at her.

When she didn't think she could lift again, when she thought the exquisite sensation of having him hard inside her would never end, he stretched his fingertips to tickle her in a way that she'd only read about. Anwyl shuddered as the new sensation drove her over the edge, fracturing her apart in an orgasm the likes of which she had never felt before. In the shattering of her climax, her muscles spasmed uncontrollably, taking Warin along with her. She could feel him high inside her, his seed pumping from his body into hers, until finally, Anwyl slumped forward against his shoulder.

Warin held her close to his chest as their breaths and heartbeats calmed. "All better?" he asked her, seeming to know that she had needed the lovemaking as much as he did.

"Mm-hmm." She nuzzled his neck and sighed contentedly. "You just wheezed, though. Are you in pain?"

He chuckled against her ear, causing goose bumps all over her. "It was worth it." She eased herself off him and then helped him back down the bed. When he was good and settled, she snuggled up close to his body. And in one another's arms, they fell back asleep.

CHAPTER THIRTY-FIVE

Marten

Warin was the first to wake. Judging by the light streaming through the multipaned windows that made up a small rectangular section of the stern, it was still morning. His cabin took up two-thirds of the width of *Lita's Pearl*—the other third of the stern was comprised of Grieg's quarters. The space boasted a large chart table that served multiple purposes, from dining to devising, and Warin thought with a smile, gazing upon his beautiful wife, perhaps some other entertainment as well.

He eased himself from the bed, sore and with a noticeable ache in his thigh. Anwyl had been right—Odo had missed his target completely, but the bruising on the joint had caused the pain and swelling to migrate. His ribs, when he stretched, were subject to a different agony altogether.

He slipped on his breeches and shirt, then gingerly picked up the clothes Anwyl had shed the evening before. That was when he noticed a folded piece of paper near the door. Recognizing Grieg's tight script on the outside, he stooped to pick it up. Behind him, Anwyl whistled at the view, and he turned in time to watch her stretch like a cat, the early morning sun bathing her limbs in light. He whistled admiringly back at her, then tossed her clothes onto the bed.

"Best guess is that we have about ten minutes before Grieg comes a'knocking with breakfast and news."

"How disappointing," she said, taking an eyeful of him again and stretching languorously. She sat up to don her chemise, and then pointed to the paper in his hand, her usual curiosity getting the best of her.

"A note from Grieg." Warin scanned the writing on the outside, then flipped it over to read, holding a second folded note in his other hand.

This letter was delivered to me the day you and the princess were taken from Barb Island. I could tell you what it says but reading it will better bring Marten's voice to the words.

"It's a note from Marten to Grieg."

Anwyl sat up. "Warin, I saw Bowen free the caltrops that sent you into the sea. And I thought that you had drowned, especially when I saw Marten being hauled from the water. At least, I thought it was Marten at the time. Your arms and legs had been bound. The man I saw pulled onto this ship had free limbs."

"I used your hairpin to saw through most of the rope binding my wrists...had almost finished when Rowly came at me. In the struggle, I dropped your pin in the water. But Rowly had knives on him; I don't know how I managed it, but I grabbed one as he took me with him when he fell. I was able to cut through the rest of the rope while I was hanging upside down from the rail. I didn't have time to cut myself free from the caltrops."

"When Bowen started to free the one that was wedged in the railing, your brother saw. He must've known that he couldn't stop him in time, so he slipped over the rail on purpose. I watched him."

"When they pulled me aboard, there was a length of rope still attached to my ankles, but it had been cut through. The caltrops were gone. Anwyl, I never had a chance to do it myself. Marten must've..."

Anwyl took the letter from him, and he nodded.

"His handwriting is so like yours," she marveled, and then read aloud.

"Grieg,

Warin told me of the curse that was laid upon his head, and I must wonder if it would not have happened had I not made you take him to the Isles when he was younger. When he first told me, I scoffed. But as he went on to explain the wondrous things that he has witnessed in recent years, my incredulousness wavered. And when I, helpless to stop myself, betrayed my brother, I realized that my view of the world outside of Pheldhain was shuttered."

"Curse?" Anwyl asked.

"Keep reading, and I'll explain when you're done."

"Perhaps this goddess of the Southron Isles, who is fabled to curse and gift in the same breath, is real. And if she exists, then Warin's days are truly numbered. From what I understand, her sufferance of his blessed life is dependent on him not falling in love and marrying. My friend, his bachelorhood ended when he and the princess were handfasted.

Your goddess is a terrible creature to require a life as payment for love, and I will not allow my brother to offer up his own for Princess Anwyl. Because that is what he will do; I saw it in his face and heard it in his words. Just as she would sacrifice herself for him.

Though Warin does not yet know, I am dying. I wish to give my final hours meaning.

When you see my brother, tell him I am sorry for my part in their abduction. Tell him I love him, and I wish him every happiness with Anwyl. And tell him that I hope to redeem myself by saving them both.

Make sail for the Isles, Grieg, spare not a minute to refit. Bowen and his men will likely take Warin back to an islet where they have made their base. I overheard one of the men call it Misery Cay. But I only know it as a place where evil thrives.

Sincerely,
Marten"

She set the letter aside and laid her head on his shoulder.

"Marten," Warin whispered and closed his eyes.

A knock on the door interrupted his mourning, and Anwyl slipped her legs into her breeches as she hopped across the cabin to unlock the door. Warin leaned back against the wall, the pain in his jaw and face rebounding with a viciousness that made his skull ache.

Grieg poked his head in when Anwyl swung open the door, then nodded to someone behind him. Kory followed him in, carrying a tray laden with food, including a rather large bowl filled with gruel.

"It's good to see you breathing, m'lord," Kory whispered, "an' Princess Anwyl too." Grieg sat while Anwyl took the tray from Kory and set it near the bed. He got the sense that she was examining him again. She stared at the contents on the tray, then picked up the pot of tea and sniffed. "Meadwort?" she asked, and Kory nodded to her.

"I reckoned he'd ache more today than yesterday. The swelling appears to be lessening, but he looks worse for it."

Warin growled, not liking the way Grieg was examining his face. But Kory was right; his head ached more and more with each passing moment. He reached for a piece of bread from the tray.

Anwyl lifted her eyebrow at him in challenge. "I wouldn't, if I were you." She closed her eyes and shook her head when he bit off a large chunk.

It was as if his teeth had exploded and were ricocheting in his skull.

She relieved him of what remained and handed him a cup of tea. "Do you have any feverfew, Kory?"

"I'll check. Might be that we have some lavender in the galley."

"Beer?"

"Now *that* we have."

"Good. Add some cowslip to it, if you have any. The combination with the hops will knock him out like nothing else."

"And if *he* doesn't want to be knocked out..." Warin stated, regretting gritting his teeth as he said it when a fresh wave of pain cracked through his head.

"Drink your tea, dear," she murmured with a smile, nodding her thanks to Kory as he backed out of the cabin. "If you're a good patient, I promise to watch over you whilst you rest."

Warin took another obligatory sip.

Anwyl nodded, then held out a new purse of herbs for his cheek, waiting expectantly for him to open his mouth, which he did willingly. She sat next to him with gruel and spoon in hand, blowing on the first bite to cool it. "Other side of your mouth," she warned. "Don't worry about the pouch; I'll replace it with another when you're done eating."

Grieg cleared his throat. "You read the letter, I see. I'm sorry your brother had to die, Warin, but at least his death counted for something, and he simply didn't waste away. You and the princess are alive today because of him."

Grieg grew contemplative, and Warin knew there was more.

"What's on your mind, Captain?" Anwyl asked softly, echoing his thoughts.

"After we make port, I'll need *Lita's Pearl* again."

"You're going to get Marlita," Warin guessed between bites.

"Aye."

"What's wrong?" Anwyl asked, sensing the unease between the two.

"The Fenrhi women you call the Kena," Grieg began, "those with gifts like Marlita and her sister...such women are revered in the Isles. Fanm Larenne is the most powerful, and it is her interpretations of the Goddess's will that we follow. But the Fanm was wrong about you and the princess. And when she finds out, she will suspect Marlita of interfering again. There will be consequences."

"But how could she find out?" Warin asked.

"You're forgetting *The Salt Wife*," Anwyl said.

Grieg nodded. "I saw the ship that sailed off before the storm hit. Captain Juna was her master once."

"He still is," Warin added.

"He and his crew have been missing a long while. I'm glad to hear he survived Prince Bowen. But I don't understand how he could be in league with him."

"He was beholden to Vala," Warin explained. "She's Kena, and if I'm not mistaken, related to Bowen."

"She could control an entire crew?" Grieg asked, astounded.

"With the help of certain herbs and minerals," Anwyl interjected, "she could and did. But her loyalty isn't to Bowen; it's to herself. Do you think they'll sail for the Isles?"

"If they do, it'll be death for all of them. Word will get to the Fanm; it always does. Right now, I'm more concerned that she knows there are women as gifted as she. She's bound to take measures to remain the most powerful. She will use the Goddess for her own purposes, and you saw what the storm did to *Reacher*."

"But how could she know about the Kena?" Warin asked. Grieg stared out the mullioned window. "Ah. You told her."

"I had to. There is a prophecy concerning the Known Realms," he began, "and a reckoning. It has made her afraid. And when she's afraid, she's dangerous. Marlita knows more about it than I do, possibly more than even the Fanm."

Anwyl slanted a look at Warin, and he remembered the translations she'd been working on with the queen.

Grieg noticed. "You've heard of it?"

"Perhaps it is not the same..."

"Do not tell me," he said. "If I am captured trying to free Marlita, it's best I do not know."

"Is Marlita imprisoned?" Warin asked.

"She serves the Fanm—she must obey the Fanm's commands."

"But she's wealthy," Warin argued. "Her home was beautiful. She walked freely among you. I saw nothing to indicate that she was bound to service."

"She lives her life at the whim of the Goddess, so of course, she should have comfort and wealth. She bears the mark."

"Mark?" Anwyl asked, and Warin took her hand. "What kind of mark?"

"Like the one on Warin's chest."

"On my chest!"

"Surely, you've noticed it. Or someone who has seen you naked has remarked upon it—er, no offense, Princess."

Anwyl laughed. "None taken. We have no more secrets from each other." She turned to Warin, placing her hand above his heart. "It's here. I was never quite sure, because the light has to be just right to see it."

"Not the light," Grieg corrected, "the beholder. You can only see it if your eyes are open to the possibility. All those years ago, the Goddess touched you through Marlita. When she escorted you back to the ship that morning, your collar was open, and we all saw the mark. Did you not wonder that the crew did not harass you after your night with her?"

"I thought it was out of respect for Marlita." He drew open his collar, looking at his chest. "I've never noticed."

"Because you did not know to look for it."

Anwyl, knowing it wasn't a figment of her imagination, saw it clearly now, like five fingertips and the heel of a hand at its base. She touched her fingers and hand upon it, and again had that sensation that she was not at sea, but in the desert, and it seemed to her that his heated skin glowed. "Blue, like the summer sky," she said, and Grieg nodded.

Warin looked down, his eyes wide, perhaps from truly being open for the first time. "This goddess of yours...she can mark people and control the weather. What else?"

"No one knows for sure, except perhaps the fanms who have held power over the generations. There are some of us who believe that the Goddess is as much a captive to the fanms as are the women like Marlita. I must go back for her. And if I'm successful, you'll see me again. If not, Kory will see that *Lita's Pearl* returns home. Either way, the crew will never be able to return to the Isles again."

"Their families?" Anwyl worried.

"They have none to speak of, except each other," Grieg said. "I made sure of it when I picked them. Sailing with a Pheldhainian was always a risk, and I'm the only captain allowed such license. The Goddess has been interested in you for a very long time, Warin."

"From this day forward, *Lita's Pearl* is yours, my friend."

"But you love this ship."

"I always will. But I'm looking forward to designing a new one with my wife. Take her, your ship, I mean, and rescue Marlita."

Grieg wiped away a tear. "Thank you, my friend." He turned when Kory reentered the cabin, carrying a pitcher of beer. "Now listen to the princess and get some rest."

He was almost out the door when Anwyl called to him. "Did anyone see what happened to Bowen when *Reacher* was—and I realize how odd this will sound—*attacked* by the storm?"

Warin took Anwyl's hand. "I promise, you're safe. It's not possible that anyone on that ship could have survived."

"But Bowen wasn't on the ship!" she declared. "I thought you knew, or I would have said something sooner. He jumped from the yardarm, after me, but with no rope. Didn't anyone see?"

Grieg shook his head. "I'll ask the crew. But Princess, if he went into the sea near *Reacher*, it would have been impossible for him to survive."

Anwyl sighed. "Bowen has an ugly way of escaping his fate."

CHAPTER THIRTY-SIX

The Goddess Revealed

Kings Glen

So much had happened in the last few months. When she and Warin had returned to Pheldhain and related the sad news about Marten, it had been Lady Téana who had been the pillar of strength for her husband and Warin. Rather than a big wedding, they all agreed that a small family gathering would be the best way to celebrate their nuptials. By then, Anwyl knew exactly what a small family event in Pheldhain meant, and she enjoyed every minute of the celebration. What had surprised her and Warin was when his mother had insisted that a priest be called in to wed them properly. Not for propriety's sake, for in Pheldhain and Sophiana both, handfasting was the preferred way to marry. Lady Téana, upon hearing that Bowen was not on his ship when it was reduced to soggy kindling, wanted no chance that the marriage could be called into question. And now, newly returned to Kings Glen, there was no impediment to Warin sharing her chamber in the royal apartments.

The king and queen had given them the afternoon to wash the road's dust away and rest before they would meet in the library. There was much to discuss about all that had transpired, things she and Warin's family thought best to not put in letters. Anwyl wished, and not for the last time, that Madyan had not sailed for Naca'an, for she could have relayed the recent events to Rani and Aghna better than any letter. As it stood now, Murel had been entrusted with the details and, with Tomas as her escort, was already in Sophiana. There, she was reunited with her brother, for word had come that it was indeed Jesper who had been rescued.

Anwyl stood before the tall looking glass in the bathing room and tied off the end of her long braid. She could hear Warin in the main chamber, and she called to him that she was almost ready. He poked his head in and smiled at her as she wound her braid into a bun.

"Here, let me," he said, taking the hairpins back out of her hair and handing her a box. He let her braid fall down her back as he watched her expectantly.

"Another wedding gift?" she asked, touching the thick rope of Pheldhainian pearls that hung around her neck. She opened her present and grinned.

"May I do the honors?" he asked, pointing to the eight needle-sharp hairpins in the box.

"As long as you don't accidentally cut my braid off," she laughed. "They are exquisite, but why so many?" she asked, noting that the ends perfectly matched the seven gems in her signet ring, plus one more.

"So that you can coordinate your hidden arsenal with your garments." He reached for the pin tipped with a fat emerald, and she stayed his hand.

"The one with the conkle pearl, please," she said, wanting to honor his home, and he smiled and finished securing her braid. "You're almost as good at setting hair as Lucilla."

"I may have asked her for a few tips before she left to visit her brother. I never want you unarmed again, Anwyl. The royal jeweler finally came around to my pressure and made these, complaining the entire time that he was not a blacksmith, and it was beneath him to make weapons." He turned her around so that he could examine her hair from the front. "Of course, Pheldhainian pearls are hard to come by, and a gift of a couple of smaller ones made him see things my way."

Anwyl stood on her toes and kissed her husband. Regretfully, it was only a brief embrace, as they were already running behind. "You should have heard him when I went to retrieve these," Warin continued.

"Still complaining?"

"On the contrary," Warin laughed. "He wanted to know if I needed anything else—corset chains that could be used to bind one's arms, armbands hiding garrotes, bracelets for shackles, brooches that—"

"He did not," Anwyl argued, and laughed.

"You caught me. The corset chain and bracelet shackles were my idea," he teased, then kissed a trail down her neck. "But weaponry was the last thing on my mind when I suggested them."

"Very thoughtful of you," she replied playfully. "I would welcome the chance to tie you up." She slipped past him upon seeing that seductively dark light spark in his blue eyes. "I have a present for you, as well, though it's not exactly from me." She handed him a pouch, one bearing the royal seal of Nifolhad.

He unbuckled the straps and pulled out a wood box and then read the letter tucked within.

Dear Warin,

When Aghna and I determined that Anwyl should wed, we both hoped that she would choose a man who could love and respect her. A man whose joy for life and learning was matched only by her own. We thought of you, Warin, though we did not say it. And now, after hearing stories about you from your cousin Murel, we can only say that your match is a perfect one.

Your cousin is a rare jewel, and she and Tomas have been regaling us with stories of your adventures with my sister. Lightning? Please convey to Anwyl my relief that she now has someone else on whom to practice her many cures and concoctions. I, too, have been made to submit to her vinegar treatment. As your brother-in-law, if I can offer you one bit of advice regarding Anwyl, heed these words: keep her away from bloodworms and briars, especially if you have the sniffles.

I understand that you are fond of writing letters and keeping journals, so I have enclosed a wedding gift for you.

Sincerely,
Your brother-in-law, King Ranulf
Post Scriptum: Aghna was insistent that I inform you that you are now a Prince of the Realm. We expect you and Anwyl to visit us in Nifolhad to celebrate your nuptials and to formerly bestow the title upon you. Welcome to the family!

He opened the box. "It's a writing instrument like yours." He pulled her into his arms, kissing her senseless.

"As we're already late, what trouble could another ten minutes cause?" She didn't wait for an answer and recaptured his lips with hers, pulling him down into the deep cushions.

• • •

It was a week of celebrations at Kings Glen, and Warin was happy that the festivities honoring his marriage to Princess Anwyl were finally winding down. There had been little time for them to be alone, and after the royal audiences, feasts, and dances, he yearned to spirit Anwyl back to Pheldhain.

King Godwin had only asked for a short briefing on what had transpired in the Southron Waters—if one could call a nine-hour council meeting brief. He and the queen commanded that all the widely flung facts be organized in a cohesive manner before deciding what was to be done next. This meant sending for Lady Kathryn, Claire and Trian, and Anna and Lark. Warin had sent word to his parents that if Grieg returned to Pheldhain with Marlita, they were to sail to Glenport immediately, then journey upriver with all possible haste to Kings Glen.

Warin and Anwyl had spent hours in the Royal Library with the queen. To a one, they immersed themselves in what writings they had of the Southron Isles and worked to discover any possible link between the women there and the Fenrhi. A broad banquet table had been brought in so that they could spread out their findings to better organize them before the reinforcements arrived.

Each day, seemingly unconnected pieces of information were added to a pile that had yet to be sorted until they had gleaned what they could from the tomes and scrolls and ancient parchments housed in the vast library. It had been Warin's idea to create a giant diagram to show the links between not only the known realms, but the Fenrhi and the women of the Isles, as well as the several henges littered throughout Aurelia.

Seeing the multitude of facts take shape on paper, King Godwin ordered the royal carpenter to construct a panel to which the diagrams could be pinned and linked with thin ribbons. Most recently, Warin worked on transposing his drawing of the goddess from Marlita's home onto a swath of canvas. And when Anwyl asked if the many-armed goddess he'd seen on the wall had been colored, paints and brushes were brought in, and soon he was adding symbols to his reproduction, details he had thought forgotten.

If not for Queen Juliana, Warin and his bride would have camped out in the library day and night. He knew Anwyl to be an excellent historian, but both were shocked by how easily the details fell together when they combined their efforts. Warin had never before felt as close to any person, and it made him love Anwyl all the more. She stood next to him now, with a sketchbook in one hand and a charcoal drawing stick in the other. "The darkest symbol," she said, pointing to the upper left arm in his depiction. "It's similar to one that I saw once in the Umbren texts that Venna had me study, except that it curved more toward the bottom half." She sketched it out to show him, perfectly reproducing his work and giving them a side-by-side comparison.

"You're very artistic," he said, drawing her close and setting down his brush.

"Mmm. So are you." She kissed him, then pulled back to study his face. "I would love to draw you, especially now that you look like you again."

"Except for the scar."

"I like the scar. It reminds me that you can be dangerous."

"Ahem." They both turned to see Queen Juliana, who was tapping her foot imperiously. "You both realize that it is almost dawn, don't you?" He and Anwyl looked at each other guiltily, for she had already forbade them from staying up too late. "Must I remind you that you are newly wed?" Then she saw how much progress Warin had made, and she approached the canvas. "She's beautiful," she said in a hushed voice. "The colors...I would not have thought there would be so many. Princess, these almost match the colors of the Fenrhi castes. Except for the Umbren black."

"But Umbren isn't black," Anwyl corrected. "The garments they wear are woven of many dark colors, especially deep violet. Just as Warin painted."

"This Southron goddess...she looks as if she is giving the symbols as gifts," Queen Juliana noted.

"Except for the green rune," Warin pointed out. "In fact, the way she has it lowered, near her hip, and the others raised up, it's almost as if she is hiding it. Now, the Blood Caste has no symbol that we have found, but if you look over here at the exiflos..." He stepped forward to show the queen but stopped when she narrowed her eyes. He moved back to stand next to Anwyl, who was looking fetchingly sheepish.

"I will not be distracted by this," Queen Juliana intoned. "You are to return to your apartments and get some rest. A guard will be posted outside the library, so do not even attempt to return until well after noontime." She pointed toward the door, but, as Warin passed, he saw amusement glint in her eyes.

Thus banished, they returned to their rooms in the pre-dawn hours. Instead of falling exhausted into bed, they spent the early morning making love and discussing their recent discoveries. Warin's ribs had healed, and their bruises had long faded, so there was nothing to impede their adventurous lovemaking. And when they did eventually fall asleep, they did so soundly.

It was hours later when Warin woke to the most pleasant dream of the princess, and he rolled to encircle her in his arms. Only, he found himself unable to move. His panic was short-lived when he discovered that his captor was none other than his wife. She sat cross-legged, staring down at him. She had banked the fire in the hearth so that the room was toasty, then pulled the blankets down to display his nakedness for her perusal.

"Anwyl, what are you doing?" He tried to move his legs, but his ankles were tied as well.

"I woke before you and was bored, so I decided to make some knots." She crawled down the bed, then stretched out, also naked, with her face near his feet.

"Do you think you might want to untie me now?"

"Oh no. That would be contrary to my desires."

"If you untie me, I'll be better equipped to see those desires satisfied."

"Tempting," she drawled, staring at his legs. "I'm more inclined to finish my research. Especially now that you are fully recovered..." She ran her fingertips, as light as a feather, from the crease of his hip, down his thigh and shin, all the way to his toes. "It's time I found out where your sensitive spots are. It's only fair, as you seem to know all of mine and—"

"Anwyl, I only—"

"—seem to take great delight in finding those places where I am acutely ticklish." She propped herself up on her forearm and smiled innocently at him. Her gaze traveled back, took in his growing arousal, and her face split into a grin. "Yes, well, I already know you're sensitive there."

Her fingers hovered over the soles of his feet, then she withdrew, and Warin let out the breath he'd been holding. He was terribly ticklish there, something he'd managed to hide his entire life. She sat up on her knees, swung a leg over his torso, and fluttered her fingertips over his chest and collarbones. "Your neck and ears never seemed to mind my lips and tongue. Sensitive, yes. Ticklish, no."

She leaned down to bathe his nipples with broad laps of her tongue, then darted at them with its tip before sucking them. Warin's hips lifted in response, nudging her; she held herself aloft and out of reach. "Not here either," she said, scooting back and sitting just above his knees. She had tied his ankles apart, so her own thighs were spread, offering him a tantalizing view.

"Now most men cannot help but to be sensitive here," she said, teasing and knuckling the crease where his thigh met his hip. "However, I already know you to be immune."

"Most men?"

"So I've read..." She slid farther down, kneeling between his ankles. "I wonder...behind the knees?" She brushed her fingertips there, and he pretended that she'd found a ticklish spot by gritting his teeth together and tensing his leg. "It's not fair." She pouted, sitting up, then backing up to the end of their bed. "A man should have at least one weakness. One thing he is unable to control."

"But I do!" he countered. "I have you!"

She beamed at him. "That's so sweet. Thank you, my love. But you do know that this was your fault?" She reached for his ankle to untie him. "You gave me the idea when you told me what you had commissioned the Royal Jeweler to make."

He laughed. "I'm just glad that you are as good at making knots as you are at untying them."

"What makes you think I'm letting you go?"

"You found my weakness: the back of my knee!"

She shook her head at him. "You know better than to try to fool me, Warin." He was in for it now. He watched helplessly as, crawling backward and smirking at him, she disappeared over the end of the high bed. Her head came up dangerously close to his foot, and then he felt her fingertip on his heel. She pressed gently and held it there, not moving, and stared at him. And just when he thought she would have mercy on him, she scratched her nail up the bottom of his foot.

It was like getting struck by lightning, and he should know. His eyes were squeezed shut, and it took him a moment to realize that she had only done it once and had stopped. When he lifted his head to gaze at her, she ran a nail up the arch of his other foot. Warin twisted violently against the silken cords that she had used, but they held, as he knew they would. He waited, and when nothing happened, opened one eye. She was staring between his legs. He had forgotten how aroused he'd been and was shocked to see that he had grown even more so. His wife looked back and forth, then poised her fingernail near the bottom of his foot. Warin groaned, knowing what was coming, and when she scratched his sole, his entire body tensed, and his hips lifted.

"Now *that* is interesting," Anwyl said, then repeated her torture until his toes were curled tight and his erection was ramrod straight.

Warin was breathing hard, and it took him a few moments to notice that she had paused. He looked for her, but she had disappeared again at the foot of the bed. He heard trickling water and wondered what she was doing. She came up again with a damp rag and proceeded to wash his feet. The cloth was warm, and her hands deft, and she massaged his heels, arches, and the balls of his feet. Amazingly, it felt wonderful, and Warin felt the tension slip from his muscles. There was a tenuous moment when she washed between his toes, but then she started on his other foot, working her way to his heel, even kneading his ankle and calf. She finished with his other leg, then ran her hands up his thighs as she crawled back up the bed.

"There was more that I wanted to do," she said, staring at his arousal. "But I am finding this too distracting."

"More? How else could you possibly torture me?"

"Never torture...experimentation." She bit her lower lip suggestively. "You'll just have to wait and find out another day." And when she reached under his knees and tickled him there, Warin didn't even try to fake a reaction. "Especially, as you fibbed. Are you comfortable?" she asked.

"I would be more so if you were under me and I was untied." He circled his hips in invitation.

"Why do you keep asking me to untie you?" Anwyl laughed. "Surely you know me enough by now that I am extremely thorough with my research."

She turned around, straddling his abdomen but facing away from him. He could see how wet she was, as she took him in her hand to stroke him so that he, too, would be ready. But he was already so aroused by how she'd stripped him of control, it wasn't necessary. Leaning back, she positioned him at her entrance, and then slid her hips forward as he plunged up and into her. She supported herself with one arm behind her while her other hand touched them where they were joined. She wasted no time bringing herself to a gentle climax, and when done, slowly lowered herself so that she lay atop his chest—her back to his front, his shaft still buried inside her as she undulated against his gentle thrusts.

"We've never really discussed the training I received in Sophiana," she said, her words soft and rhythmic. "You've heard the rumors, though, haven't you?" Warin groaned. He couldn't get deep enough in this position, and she turned her head and smiled at him. "Well, they're mostly true. For example, did you know that there are different erotic regions on the body? Not just the breasts or the other expected areas."

He watched as she teased her nipples into hard points, then ran one of her hands down her body to touch him where he was still thrusting inside her. "Other, very delightful, unexpected places." Her knees were still bent, and she pulled herself upright to kneel above him again. Sliding her hands to his thighs, she gave him what he so desperately sought, and he thrust up, again and again, and deeper than before. She rode him, rolling her hips in a seductive dance, then sat up straight, taking her time, easing him forward so that he was nearly vertical inside her.

Her hands slid down his thighs as she curled her body over his knees, stretching her arms out to scratch her nails on the bottoms of his feet.

The combination of thrusting inside her, the unusual angle, the intensely pleasurable shock of her nails, all had him yelling out her name. His hips lifted completely from the bed, pumping up and out and down until he had no idea which direction to go. But Anwyl stayed with him, anticipating his thrusts as she repeatedly raked her nails up and down his feet.

"Anwyl," he gasped at the excruciating pressure, "you're killing me. Please." She pulsed down around him as his hips lifted again and touched his feet lightly, teasingly, before scratching her nails. And when she traced those eight tiny weapons over the tops of his feet, from his toes to his ankles, Warin speared up into her, so high that she could no longer reach his feet. She pulled her curled body up and held on to his thighs as he climaxed. When he was finally able to see straight, he saw that she, too, was out of breath. He slipped out of her, and she fell forward onto his thighs.

"Hell, Anwyl. What else did you learn?"

Her body shook as she silently laughed.

"Promise me that you'll experiment on me again, and soon." He stared up at the ceiling, still bound, and wanting to hold her in his arms. "I hate to disturb you, especially seeing as you're so relaxed, but do you think that you could untie me now?" Her foot glided up his arm, and she snagged the end of the cord tied to his wrist with her toes and tugged. The knot easily came loose. Warin reached over and undid the other wrist as she released his ankles and slipped to one side of him. He reversed his position so that he hovered over her, nudging her knees apart. He pressed down against her buttocks, still so aroused by what she had done, and found himself growing hard again. Lifting one of her knees higher, he positioned her slightly onto her side, pushing a cushion under her stomach to support her. Then, he entered her where she was still wet and hot and dripping. She sighed his name, and it was the sexiest sound he'd ever heard.

"Lift your arms, Princess," he ordered, his voice but a whisper in her ear, and nibbled at the lobe as his hips pumped into her. She managed to raise one, the arm that was safely pressed against the bed. He pulled the other up, and she instinctively brought it down again. "No, it's only fair. Keep your arm raised, or I'll stop what I'm going to do next."

She moaned as he thrust deeply into her, nudging her farther down the bed, and she wound her wrist around the same cord she had used for his ankle. Satisfied, he let go of her arm, and turned her so that he could fondle and tweak her breast as he licked and nibbled her ear. Then, sliding his hand lower, he brought her higher, his fingers expertly dancing at the juncture of her thighs as his hips drove into her heat. She whimpered, and he knew she was close, so he levered himself over her, pumping hard into her body, and when he felt that telltale tightening, he dipped his head down and licked and nipped her under her arm where she was intensely sensitive. She screamed as a stronger, longer orgasm racked her body, taking him with her over the edge for a second time that morning.

Epilogue

We must listen to the queen more often when she orders us to take a break," Anwyl whispered with a giggle as Warin escorted her to the private dining room. They'd been caught in the library again well after midnight and so had retired to their room to rest and make love. Exhausted, they had slept through the morning and into the afternoon. When they did not appear back in the library, a note had been slipped under their door, asking them to join the king and queen for a casual meal, and only at their leisure. They bathed and dressed—and kissed—and then made their way through the palace. They skirted most of the common areas, still too wrapped up in each other to be able to bandy courtesies and flirtations, and found themselves standing outside the private dining room. The door was ajar, and voices could be heard from within, one raised above the others.

"Is she all right? Perhaps I should go check? You sent the note over an hour ago." The questions were answered with more murmurings, and Anwyl grinned at Warin.

"I know that voice," she said excitedly, and pulled open the door and rushed in, pulling Warin behind her. "Radha! You're here! In Aurelia!"

Her cousin's anxious face was replaced by a look filled with relief and pleasure. And Anwyl realized that perhaps she and her cousin would no longer be at such odds. Warin was busy greeting others, as well, and when Anwyl turned around, she saw both Claire and Anna, with their husbands, Trian and Lark. Lady Kathryn, too, had arrived, as well as Lord Baldric and his wife, Lady Noura. The king and queen rounded out the party. It took an hour for her to greet everyone properly, and to catch up on who was having a baby, which horses had been bred at Stolweg and Chevlain, including the Fyrjian Desert breed, and how Warin and Anwyl were handfasted, then wed. Radha shared the well-wishes from Aghna and Rani, and even gave a report on how well

Murel and Tomas were faring in Naca'an. Princes Reynald and Erwin appeared and immediately cut through the small talk by suggesting they grab something to eat before everything grew too cold to enjoy.

It was a happy occasion, but Anwyl knew that it would end with a longer, more serious discussion in the library. Warin, seated beside her, leaned in and whispered, "We'll have time for a little dessert later."

She nodded, and then fell back into conversation with Radha. "I'm surprised Ni'Mala let you travel here. Won't the Fenrhi need a Kena artist?"

"I've been training my replacement," Radha explained. "As my duties on the new Fenrhi council grew more demanding and my dual fealty to the Fenrhi and Queen Aghna and Rani caused me to have to travel more, it was clear that my days as an artist were waning."

"You do not lead the Kena?" Warin asked.

"Oh, no. And I wouldn't wish it either. My opinions are much too strong for Kena leadership. I suppose that was part of the problem when Rhiannon took over. No, a steadier, calmer, and more seasoned hand is now in charge." She looked around the table and, satisfied that no one would hear, she whispered to Anwyl, "You were right not to tell me that you were being marked. I would have tried to stop it. But now, I understand that it was a necessary rite for you. One that you chose. I'm proud of you, Anwyl."

"And I'm proud of you as well."

"Me?"

"Yes, you. You've grown. You are finally seeing past your preconceptions of me—for that, I'm eternally grateful." Her cousin stared at her, not sure if she was the brunt of some jest. But then she saw the truth of it, and she leaned back and laughed.

"A family joke," Warin explained when all eyes turned to their small group. He understood, Anwyl knew. They had oft-discussed the similarities between growing up with Radha and with Marten.

Radha stood suddenly and then bowed to the queen and king. "With your permission," she asked, and they nodded. A servant appeared with a box, and Radha opened it. She lifted out a thin circlet of gold and set it on Anwyl's head. "You are a Princess of Nifolhad now, as well as Sophiana." She reached into the box again, and brought forth another, slightly larger, band. "And you, Warin, are now a Prince of Nifolhad." She winked at him. "And don't think that this little presentation will get you out of the ceremony when you visit our realm again. Aghna and Rani need these happy occasions to give the people a sense of stability."

Warin looked a little lost, and Anwyl took pity on him. "Don't worry. I'll teach you some of my knots to help you work through your nerves." Reynald and Erwin slapped him on the back, and Trian and Lark bowed deferentially to him, earning them a scowl from Warin. But they were smiling, and Warin chuckled at their gesture.

King Godwin cleared his throat. "I think it's time to move our party to the library. Anwyl and Warin have spent many hours organizing the information that you're all here to discuss and provide additional insight."

In twos and threes, they made their way to the library. Radha took Warin's arm and, with Trian and Larkin listening in, began telling them about the ceremony and how Warin was expected to bring witnesses to the event. Anna joined Reynald and Erwin to discuss their horses, and Claire fell in with Anwyl. Her friend was walking slower than the others, and soon they were out of hearing of everyone else.

"Did you know?" Anwyl asked.

"About you and Warin? Yes, but not only because of my sight. There were others who knew you both who could also see it."

"Queen Juliana," Anwyl admitted. "And Tomas. Madyan too." At the mention of their Umbren friend's name, Claire's expression changed. "What is it? Radha didn't mention Madyan in her news, and I was going to ask her later."

"I only know what your cousin told me," Claire said. "And it's not much. Madyan returned to Nifolhad, and then to the Fyrost Desert. Her people required her return, they claimed. No one has heard from her since."

"Did Aghna send someone into the Fyrost to find her?"

"She did. As did Ni'Mala. Their messengers were met and treated graciously. And after being reassured that their Malikáfyr was thriving and tending to the needs of her people, they were escorted back out of the desert."

"So, Madyan is what we expected—greater than a desert warrior and Umbren master. She is the rightful leader of the Fyrjians." Anwyl paused mid-step. "They said she was thriving? What exactly does that mean?"

"I wondered the same." They continued on in silence for a moment, and then Claire took Anwyl's arm. "Tell me, Anwyl, are you enjoying married life?"

"It is better than I ever imagined. Only..."

"What would you like to know?"

"Will Warin and I have children?" she whispered worriedly.

"Is there some reason you shouldn't?" Claire asked.

"Oh no. It's just that we don't want them yet. Not for a while."

Claire stopped, and seeming to look inward, she smiled. "You'll have a large family, but not until you want one." Warin had stopped and was waiting for them with an expectant expression, and Anwyl nodded to him with a grin. Claire laughed upon seeing the exchange. "I knew you would be good for one another; I just didn't realize how—" She stopped midsentence, her jaw dropping as she stood before the open door to the library. "You both did this? Together?"

"Queen Juliana, too," Anwyl averred as they entered.

"Nonsense," the queen interjected. "I retrieved books, ordered food and drink, and kicked them out every few days."

Warin stood next to her, and they looked at each other, as everyone else spun in circles to view their efforts. Anwyl hadn't really looked at what they had accomplished as a whole—the size of it was astounding. After they had filled one great board with connected information, several others had been brought in. These, too, were covered with lists and notations and strings and ribbons. In the center of it all was the depiction of the goddess that Warin had painted.

Radha stepped before her, eyes wide. "You saw this? In the Southron Isles?"

"Yes. Why?" Warin asked.

"Because I have seen this, too, in the Mother's archives. Only slightly different."

"I've seen her as well," Claire said. "In a dream I had when we slept in the Fyrost Desert. The night spent at the oasis when Aghna, Madyan, and I fled the Fenrhi Temple."

Radha stared at the seated goddess. "I remember her differently. Something here isn't right."

"She's not finished," Warin admitted. "I can't remember the sixth rune." They all stared at the one arm without a colored symbol.

"No," came a soft voice from the door, and they all turned to see an exotically garbed woman standing there. Behind her, a sailor from the Southron Isles. "You are not missing a symbol. You have simply remembered the Goddess wrong—a natural mistake caused by your mind's insistence on symmetry. The Goddess only has five arms."

The woman speaking walked over to Warin and smiled at him. "I am pleased to see that you survived," she said. "And you as well, Princess."

"You must be Marlita," Anwyl said, taking her hands and smiling at her. Her skin was cold to the touch. "But you are unwell!"

Captain Grieg came in and stood next to the woman, supporting her by her elbow. "Please, can someone bring a chair? She's extremely weak."

"Of course," the queen said. "Bring her closer to the fire where it's warm." Anwyl and Grieg helped her to sit, and Anwyl held a cup of sweet wine to her lips.

"Can you bring me some parchment and paint?" Marlita asked, and Warin handed her the palette and brushes he'd been using; Lady Kathryn set a blank sheet before her. Marlita painted her fingertips, each one a different color. Then she swiped the brush loaded with red paint over the heel of her hand. She pressed her four fingers and thumb to the paper, then let the base of her palm touch. When she pulled it away, everyone standing around her looked at the symbol, then at Warin's painting.

"We've seen that mark!" Anna stated. "Remember, Lark? On the henge."

"There's a cave near the sea in Morland," Lady Kathryn said, "with drawings and runes. It's there too."

"And in Sophiana, and Naca'an," Radha added.

While everyone in the room discussed the symbol, Anwyl gently wiped the paint from Marlita's chilled fingers. She placed the woman's hand in Grieg's. Warin tried to give her another sip of wine, but she shook her head and placed a weak hand just above his heart. Then she reached for Anwyl and touched her in the same place. A faint blue aura faded as she pulled away. She motioned to Anna and Lark and Trian, repeating the gesture upon them. Claire was last, and she leaned forward and took Claire's hands, pressing one to her own heart and head, then touched Claire in the same places. Claire gasped, then nodded to Marlita, some silent message having passed between them.

She then turned to Princess Anwyl. "You've seen, as have you, Warin. Now, the others will as well." She lifted her gaze, and the room grew silent to hear her words.

"Three have been made whole so far," Marlita whispered. "But the fourth must save the fifth. It is the only chance for the five to triumph over the sixth."

Her hand slipped from Warin's chest, and her chin dropped. Anwyl checked her pulse, then nodded to Claire. "It's there, but she needs rest. I don't know how much longer she has."

Grieg shook his head. "The farther she is from the Isles and the Goddess, the weaker she becomes. She was holding on for this moment," he said. "She finished what she set out to do."

"And what was that?" Radha asked.

"Give you fair warning," he said. "The Goddess is restless, and a storm is coming, faster than we thought." Grieg wavered on his feet, then collapsed to the floor. Anwyl, Claire, and Anna dropped to help him.

"They must have exhausted themselves getting here. Is there somewhere they can rest?" Trian carried Grieg from the library whilst Lark scooped Marlita up in his arms. They followed Prince Reynald as he directed them to suitable chambers.

Anwyl walked over to the painting, dipped a brush in the white paint, and blotted out the arm without a rune. She carefully repainted the symbols to match Marlita's design, then stood back. The others returned, and Warin stood behind her when she turned to her friends. They nodded to each other, silently communicating that which they all had seen.

Later that night, while the queen, Lady Kathryn, and Radha oversaw the transfer of their research to a larger room, Anwyl and Warin waited in their apartments. It wasn't long before there was a rap on the door, and they opened it to allow their friends entrance.

"Can you see them, Claire?" Anwyl asked. "The auras?"

She nodded. "Trian observed them first," she answered.

"Yours are amber," Anna said, looking at her sister and Trian.

"I always wondered about your birthmark, Warin," Lark said. "But now you and the princess both seem to have a blue glow about you."

"Ours are white," Anna remarked, taking her husband's hand.

"Almost," Claire said. "It's pale gray."

"Earth, Kena, Mother," Warin noted. "We're missing the warrior and the healer. I wonder who will represent Umbren and Sylvan? And what about the heel of the hand?"

"So, my friends, where do we start our search?" Trian asked.

Anwyl looked at each of her friends, then at her husband. He nodded to her. "Everything begins and ends with Blood."

The End.

ACKNOWLEDGEMENTS

It took a good four years for me to bring book three of the Heart & Hand Series to light. So much happened in that time—some things were rough, like the pandemic and certain politics which I won't discuss, but other things were wonderful, like watching my twins become adults.

With everything that went into bringing *The Naked Moon* to life, I want to make sure to thank Nat at KaNaXa for her amazing cover art, including redesigning both *Wild Lavender* and *The Queen's Dance*. She did a fantastic job finding the perfect characters, setting the moods for each book, and connecting the series in a visual way I didn't think was possible. I also would like to thank both Kay Copeland and Cindy Ray Hale for helping me to catch my typos and punctuation issues.

It goes without saying, but I'll say it anyway, that I appreciate the support from my friends and family over the years. Your constancy of interest in my writing has helped me in more ways than you can imagine.

And finally, I'm so very grateful to the many readers who have picked up copies of my books, some of which who have even left reviews! I promise that book four, featuring Lady Murel and Lord Tomas, won't take nearly so long to publish.

THE HEART & HAND SERIES

Wild Lavender
The Queen's Dance
The Naked Moon
The Shadow Healer
Book Five, Coming Soon

ABOUT THE AUTHOR

From San Diego, where I met my Montanan husband, to San Francisco, where I married him, to Chicago, where the twins were born, this Michigander wanderer-at-heart settled once and for all in Northern Virginia. Here, I continue to write, work, and play. Oh, and tweet gratuitous pics of #TullyTheDog, our vizsla.

Follow me on social media and more:

- Twitter & Instagram at /nkelleherauthor
- Facebook at /nicoleelizabethkelleher
- Newsletter: For exclusive content such as deleted chapters—"Strawberries" and "Belly Button" to name two—subscribe to my newsletter at http://eepurl.com/cA1mBH
- Website: nekelleher.com